EVIDENCE

In a half-built mansion in one of LA's glamorous neighbourhoods, the bodies of a young couple are found, murdered in flagrante and left in a gruesome post-mortem embrace. A grisly crime for veteran homicide cop Milo Sturgis and psychologist Alex Delaware to solve. The male victim was eco-friendly architect Desmond Backer, who disdained the sort of grandiose superstructure he's found dead in. Mr Backer was notorious for his seductive powers — the exception being his ex-boss, Helga Gemein. Milo and Alex's list of suspects grows ever longer, as the homicidal mix includes conspiracy, and a vendetta that runs deep. But the investigation veers in a startling direction — Alex and Milo end up on the wrong end of a cornered predator's final fury.

Jonathan Kellerman is one of the world's most popular authors. He has brought his expertise as a clinical psychologist to more than two dozen bestselling crime novels. He is the author of numerous essays, short stories, scientific articles, two children's books and three volumes of psychology. He has won the Goldwyn, Edgar and Anthony awards, and has been nominated for a Shamus Award. Jonathan Kellerman lives in California and New Mexico, with his wife, writer Faye Kellerman, and their four children, one of whom is the novelist Jesse Kellerman.

JONATHAN KELLERMAN

EVIDENCE

Complete and Unabridged

CHARNWOOD
Leicester

First published in Great Britain in 2009 by
Headline Publishing Group
London

First Charnwood Edition   ΟΙ/Ι⸜
published 2010
by arrangement with
Headline Publishing Group
An Hachette UK Company
London

British Library CIP Data

Kellerman, Jonathan.
  Evidence.
  1. Delaware, Alex (Fictitious character)– –Fiction.
  2. Sturgis, Milo (Fictitious character)- -Fiction.
  3. Child psychologists- -California- -Los Angeles
  - -Fiction. 4. Police- -California- -Los Angeles- -
  Fiction. 5. Suspense fiction. 6. Large type books.
  I. Title
  813.5′4–dc22

  ISBN 978–1–44480–312–9

Published by
F. A. Thorpe (Publishing)
Anstey, Leicestershire

Set by Words & Graphics Ltd.
Anstey, Leicestershire
Printed and bound in Great Britain by
T. J. International Ltd., Padstow, Cornwall

This book is printed on acid-free paper

To Faye

1

I tell the truth. They lie.
I'm strong. They're weak.
I'm good.
They're bad.

This was a zero job but Doyle was getting paid.

Why anyone would shell out fifteen bucks an hour, three hours a day, five times a week, to check out the empty shell of a rich-idiot monster-house was something he'd never get.

The look-see took fifteen minutes. *If* he walked slow. Rest of the time, Doyle sat around, ate his lunch, listened to Cheap Trick on his Walkman.

Thinking about being a real cop if his knee hadn't screwed up.

The company said go there, he went.

Disability all run out, he swallowed part-time, no benefits. Paying to launder his own uniform.

One time he heard a couple of the other guys talking behind his back.

Gimp's lucky to get anything.

Like it was his fault. His blood level had been .05, which wasn't even close to illegal. That tree had jumped out of nowhere.

Gimp made Doyle go all hot in the face and the chest but he kept his mouth shut like he always did. One day . . .

He parked the Taurus on the patch of dirt just

1

outside the chain-link, tucked his shirt tighter.

Seven A.M., quiet except for the stupid crows squawking.

Rich-idiot neighborhood but the sky was a crappy milky gray just like in Burbank where Doyle's apartment was.

Nothing moving on Borodi Lane. As usual. The few times Doyle saw anyone it was maids and gardeners. Rich idiots paying to live here but never *living* here, one monster-mansion after another, blocked by big trees and high gates. No sidewalks, either. What was that all about?

Every once in a while, some tucked-tight blonde in Rodeo Drive sweats would come jogging down the middle of the road looking miserable. Never before ten, that type slept late, had breakfast in bed, massages, whatever. Laying around in satin sheets, getting waited on by maids and butlers before building up the energy to shake those skinny butts and long legs.

Bouncing along in the middle of the road, some Rolls-Royce comes speeding down and kaboom. Wouldn't that be something?

Doyle collected his camouflage-patterned lunch box from the trunk, made his way toward the three-story plywood shell. The third being that idiot castle thing — the turret. Unfinished skeleton of a house that would've been as big as a . . . as a . . . Disneyland castle.

Fantasyland. Doyle had done some pacing, figured twenty thousand square feet, minimum. Two-acre lot, maybe two and a half.

Framed up and skinned with plywood, for some reason, he could never find out why,

2

everything stopped and now the heap was all gray, warping, striped with rusty nail-drips.

Crappy gray sky leaking in through rotting rafters. On hot days, Doyle tucked himself into a corner for shade.

Out behind in the bulldozed brown dirt was an old Andy Gump accidentally left behind, chemicals still in the john. The door didn't close good and sometimes Doyle found coyote scat inside, sometimes mouse droppings.

When he felt like it, he just whizzed into the dirt.

Someone paying all that money to build Fantasyland, then just *stopping*. Go figure.

He'd brought a good lunch today, roast beef sandwich from Arby's, too bad there was nothing to heat the gravy with. Opening the box, he sniffed. Not bad. He moved toward the chain-link swing gate . . . what the —

Stupid thing was pulled as wide as the chain allowed, which was about two, two and a half feet. Easy for anyone but a fat idiot to squeeze through.

The chain had always been too long to really draw the gate tight, making the lock useless, but Doyle was careful to twist it up, make it look secure when he left each day.

Some idiot had monkeyed with it.

He'd told the company about the chain, got ignored. What was the point of hiring a professional when you didn't listen to his advice?

Sidling through the gap, he rearranged the chain nice and tight. Leaving his lunch box atop raw-concrete steps, he began his routine.

3

Standing in the middle of the first floor, saying, '*Hel*-lo,' and listening to his voice echo. He'd done that first day on the job, liked the echo, kinda like honking in a tunnel. Now it was a habit.

Didn't take long to see everything was OK on the first floor. Space was huge, big as a . . . as a . . . some rooms framed up but mostly pretty open so you had clear views everywhere. Like peeking through the skeleton bones of some dinosaur. In the middle of what would've been the entry hall was a humongous, swooping, double staircase. Just plywood, no railings, Doyle had to be careful, all he needed was a fall, screw up some other body part.

Here we go, pain with every step. Stairs creaked like a mother but felt structurally OK. You could just imagine what it would be like with marble on it. Like a . . . big castle staircase.

Nineteen steps, each one killed.

The second floor was just as empty as the first, big surprise. Stopping to rub his knee and take in the western treetop view, he continued toward the rear, stopped again, kneaded some more but it didn't do much good. Continuing to the back, he reached the smaller staircase, thirteen steps but real curvy, a killer, tucked behind a narrow wall, you had to know where to find it.

Whoever had paid for all this was some rich idiot who didn't appreciate what he had. If Doyle had a hundredth — a two-hundredth of something like this, he'd thank God every day.

He'd asked the company who the owner was. They said, 'Don't pry.'

4

Climbing the curvy staircase, every step crunching his knee, the pain riding up to his hip, he began counting out the thirteen stairs like he always did, trying to take his mind off the burning in his leg.

When he called out 'Nine,' he saw it.

Oh Jesus.

Heart thumping, mouth suddenly dry as tissue paper, he backed down two steps, reached along the right side of his gear belt.

Touching air.

Now *he* was the idiot, there'd been no gun for a long time, not since he stopped guarding jewelry stores downtown.

Company gave him a flashlight, period, and it was in the trunk of the Taurus.

He forced himself to look.

Two of them.

No one else, one good thing about the turret, it was round, mostly open to the sky, nowhere to hide.

Doyle kept looking, felt his guts heave.

The way they were lying, him on top of her, her legs up, one hooked around his back, it was pretty clear what they'd been doing.

Before . . .

Doyle felt short of breath, like someone was choking him. Struggling to regain his air, he finally succeeded. Reached for his phone.

Right in his pocket. At least something was going OK.

2

Milo calls me in when the murder's 'interesting.'

Sometimes by the time I get involved, the body's gone. If the crime scene photos are thorough, that helps. If not, it can get even more interesting.

This scene was a three-minute drive from my house and intact.

Two bodies, wrapped around each other in a sick parody of passion. Milo stood to the side as a coroner's investigator clicked off shots.

We exchanged quiet 'Heys.' Milo's black hair was slicked down haphazardly and his green eyes were sharp. His clothes looked slept-in, his pallid, pitted complexion matched the smog-gray sky.

June gloom in LA. Sometimes we pretend it's ocean mist.

I studied the bodies from a distance, stepping as far back as I could, careful not to touch the curving plywood wall. 'How long have you been here?'

'An hour.'

'You don't get to this zip code too often, Big Guy.'

'Location, location, location.'

The coroner's investigator heard that and glanced back. A tall, pretty, square-shouldered young woman in an olive-green pantsuit, she took a long time with the camera, kneeling, leaning, crouching, standing on tiptoe to capture every angle.

'Just a few more minutes, Lieutenant.'

Milo said, 'Take your time.'

The kill-spot was the third floor of a construction project on Borodi Lane in Holmby Hills. Massive frame-up of an intended mansion, the entry big enough to seat a symphony orchestra. The kill-spot looked like some sort of observation room. Or the turret of a castle.

Massive was the rule in Holmby. A whole different universe than my white box above Beverly Glen, but walking distance. I'd driven because sometimes Milo likes to think and make calls while I take the wheel.

A few rafters topped the turret, but most of the intended roof was open space. Breeze blew in. Balmy, but not enough air movement to mask the smell of wet wood and rust, mold and blood and excreta.

Male victim on top, female victim pinned beneath him, very little of her showing.

His black designer jeans were rolled to midcalf. One of her smooth, tan legs hooked around his waist. Brown pumps in place on both her feet.

Final embrace, or someone wanting it to look that way. What I could see of the woman's hands were splayed, limp. Flaccidity of death, that made sense.

But the leg propped up didn't fit; how had it stayed in place postmortem?

The man's legs were well muscled, coated with curls of fine blond hair. Black cashmere sweater for him, blue dress for her. I craned to see more of her, couldn't catch anything but dress fabric. Some kind of shiny jersey. Hiked above her hips.

The man's hair was longish, light brown, wavy. A neat ruby hole stippled by black powder punctuated the mastoid bulge behind his right ear. Blood ran down his neck, slanted toward the right, continued onto the plywood floor. Long dark strands of her hair fanned wide on the floor. Not much blood around her.

I said, 'Wouldn't her legs have relaxed?'

The CI, still photographing, said, 'If rigor's come and gone, I'd think so.'

She worked at the crypt on Mission Road, in East LA, had managed to maintain the rosy-cheeked glow of a habitual hiker. Lots of outdoor death scenes? Late twenties to early thirties, rusty hair tied in a high ponytail, clear blue eyes; a farm girl working the dark side.

Putting the camera aside, she got down low, she used two hands to lift the man's midsection gingerly, peered through the resulting two-inch space. The wraparound leg collapsed like a folding chair improperly set. 'Yup, looks like she was propped, Lieutenant.'

Looking back at Milo for confirmation, her hands still wedged between the bodies.

He said, 'Could be.'

The CI raised the male victim a bit higher, studied, lowered him with tenderness. The investigators I've seen are generally like that: respectful, swimming in more horror than most people encounter in a lifetime, never growing jaded.

She stood, brushed dust off her trousers.

'She's not wearing panties and his penis is out. Obviously, there's no erection so there's no way they'd stay . . . connected. But there is a crusty whitish stain on her thigh, so even if they were posed, looks like they consummated.'

Kneeling again, she pulled the man's crumpled jeans high enough to search his pockets. 'OK, here we go.'

Hefting a blue vinyl wallet secured by a snap button.

Milo gloved up. 'No car keys?'

'Nope, just this. Let me tag and then you can go through it. I didn't see any civilian cars parked on the street, maybe it started as a jacking?'

'And everyone ran up here and these two started getting it on?'

'I was thinking an intended jacking, the bad guy changed his mind?'

Milo shrugged.

'Sorry, Lieutenant. For shooting my mouth.'

'At this point,' said Milo, 'I'll take anything I can get.'

'I'm new on the job,' she said. 'I'm sure there's nothing I can teach you — guess it's time to flip them. I'll do a liver temp and see if we can close in on TOD.'

★ ★ ★

Moments later, she was cleaning off the meat thermometer.

Milo said, 'And?'

'Probably somewhere during the last twelve hours, I'm sure the docs will be able to tell you more.'

9

The male victim's face was a husk of the handsome, smiling visage on the driver's license in the blue vinyl wallet. Desmond Erik Backer, thirty-two years old last February, five eleven, one seventy, brown and brown, apartment on California Avenue in Santa Monica, an address that put it three blocks from the beach.

The wallet held two hundred dollars in fifties and twenties, two gold credit cards, a couple of wheat-colored business cards, a photo of a little blonde girl around two wearing a lace-trimmed, red-velvet dress. TAG Heuer sport watch around left wrist, no other jewelry. No pale stripe of skin suggesting a wedding band, removed discreetly or otherwise.

Milo showed me the handwritten inscription on the back of the child's portrait. *Samantha, 22 mo.* No one else would've caught the twitch in his eyelid.

He flipped to a business card. Desmond E. Backer, AIA, *Gemein, Holman, and Cohen, Architects.* Main Street in Venice.

'Nice watch,' he said, checking the back of the TAG for an inscription. Blank. Checking the leather label on the jeans. 'Zegna.'

The CI said, 'But her dress looks a little low-rent, don't you think?'

She inspected the label. 'Made in China, polyester . . . short and snug. Could she be a working girl?'

'Anything's possible.' Milo returned the wallet. As he bagged, took notes, he continued to study the bodies.

No sign of the female victim's purse. Generic

gold hoops in her ears, three similarly non-descript silver bangles around one slender wrist. Light makeup.

He got down close to her right ear, as if wanting to impart some secret. 'She shampooed recently, I can still smell it.'

The CI said, 'I also smelled it. *Suave*. I use it myself.'

'Expensive?'

She chuckled. 'With my pay scale?' Growing solemn as she took in the dead woman's pale face.

Even degraded, an extremely nice-looking woman with a taut, full-breasted, somewhat low-waisted body, a smooth, oval countenance, and huge eyes, slightly down-slanted. Brown in life, filmed the color of dirty pavement by death.

Pink gloss on slack lips. Clean nails, no polish. The CI's probing had revealed no bullet holes anywhere on her body, but the sclera of the woman's eyes were marbled and speckled by hemorrhage and her long neck was swollen and bruised and bisected by an angry magenta line.

The CI pointed out the crusty, milky blotch on her thigh. Checked fingernails. 'Doesn't look like anything under there. Poor thing. Is it OK if I pull her dress down?'

'Do that,' said Milo. 'Soon as our techies get here and print them and the room, you can transport.'

'Any idea how long that'll take?'

'You in a hurry?'

'We do have another call, but no problem, Lieutenant.'

11

'Your drivers are paid by the hour.'

'Yes, sir. Anything else?'

'Nothing comes to mind, Ms . . . ' Squinting to make out her ID badge. 'Rieffen.'

'Lara. You're sure there's nothing else I can do for you, Lieutenant?'

'I'm open to suggestions, Lara.'

'Well . . . I'm just feeling my way around, don't want to miss anything.'

'You're doing fine.'

'OK, then.' To me: 'Nice to meet you, Detective.'

Milo said, 'This is Dr Delaware. He's a consulting psychologist.'

'Psychologist,' she said. 'For a profile?'

Milo knows I rate profiling just below reading tea leaves and political polling. 'Something like that.' Glancing at the rickety spiral framework that led down to the second floor, he said, 'We're OK here, Lara, go take your next call.'

CI Rieffen gathered up her stuff and hurried down.

When her footsteps had stopped echoing, he pulled a panatela from a pocket of his forlorn, lint-colored windbreaker, jammed it in his mouth but didn't light up. As his jaw bunched, the cigar tilted upward.

He stared at the bodies some more. Got on the phone and searched for Desmond Backer's registered vehicle.

Five-year-old BMW 320i. He put a BOLO on it, with instructions to transport but not search until processed forensically.

Pocketing his cell, he said, 'Caught in the act but maybe staged to reconstruct.' Half smile.

'The little death followed by the big one.'

He studied the sky. 'No casings says our boy was careful, unless he's nostalgic and likes revolvers. No bullet holes anywhere but the one in Mr Backer's head, and the diameter says probably small caliber. With her purse gone and no vehicle in sight, I'd say a jacking might indeed be part of it. Except Backer's wallet is full of cash and that watch is serious money.'

I said, 'Maybe this was about her and the purse has nothing to do with robbery.'

'Such as?'

'This early I'm better with questions than answers.'

'Join the club. Now all I need to do is find out who the hell she is. Any insights? Won't hold you to them.'

'No sign of struggle and a contact wound says the bad guy achieved control early on. That could be the result of good planning. My bet is they were staged — there's almost a theatrical quality to the position.'

'Something personal.'

'Strangling's about as up close and personal as it gets,' I said.

'Control with a small-caliber gun? Shoot him first, she's too freaked out to resist, just lays there and gets choked out?'

'Maybe there were two killers.'

'Repositioning them,' he said. 'That could be a statement — jealous rage. Ex-boyfriend follows them here, watches them do it, goes bananas.'

'If this was a tryst-spot, it's pretty unromantic. No wine, no weed, no chocolate, not even a blanket.'

'Maybe the bad guy took all that with him. Getting rid of the evidence. Or wanting a trophy. Or both.'

'Leaving them this way could also be a way of demeaning them further. Which could mean jealousy.'

'Or a sadistic psychopath.'

'Maybe,' I said, 'but what doesn't fit that is the lack of overkill, her not being posed with her legs spread. There's something subtle here. Possibly victim-specific. Taking her purse points to her being the main target. Wanting to hold on to a part of her.'

He circled the turret, took in the view to the west, lit up and blew out a blue stream that ribboned up through the rafters. 'Hot date under the stars. Why here, specifically?'

'Backer was an architect, maybe he'd worked the site. Maybe he had a key, brought her up here to impress her.'

'I designed the Taj Mahal, baby, so do me? If so, Backer's involvement was at least two years ago because that's when the job went on ice. And he wouldn't need a key, the chain's long enough to swing the gate wide. That from the rent-a-cop who discovered the bodies. According to him, he reported it to his bosses but they shined him on. Which is consistent with security being a joke: one guy, seven to ten A.M., nothing on weekends, and the most lethal weapon they let him use is a flashlight.'

'Why'd construction stop?'

'Guard asked about that, too, was told to mind his own business.'

I said, 'An abandoned site would suit Backer if he liked to party here. With this woman, or others. Given the discrepancy between his clothing budget and hers, I'd start with lower-paid employees of his firm.'

'Office romance with the receptionist, unfortunately she's got a possessive significant other. One thing: The guard says he's never seen evidence of other trysts.'

'We're talking the nervous-looking, skinny fellow with the limp.'

'Doyle Bryczinski. Applied to the department, got into a serious TA, messed up his leg.'

'Milo made a new friend?' I said. 'What's his favorite food?'

'Begrudging me the occasional helpful citizen?'

'God forbid.'

'Bryczinski came across nervous to you?'

'When I drove up, he watched me. When I made eye contact, he pretended he hadn't been watching. I'd also be remiss if I didn't point out that you just described Bryczinski as a wannabe cop who sounds extremely frustrated about the lack of control in his life. Guy like that, girlfriend throws him over for someone cuter, smoother, richer? In the exact spot you brought her, yourself?'

'The guy tries to help, all of a sudden he's a prime suspect?'

'Like the song goes,' I said, 'suspect the one you're with.'

He took a long sour look at the bodies, made his way toward the rickety spiral staircase. 'Let's get to know ol' Doyle a little better.'

3

Doyle Bryczinski said, 'Oh, man, they look . . . worse.'

'Worse than when you found them?' said Milo.

Bryczinski turned away. 'They're more like . . . people.'

'And less like . . . '

'I dunno, it was like . . . unreal. When I found them, I mean.'

'Helluva way to start your day, Doyle.'

'My day starts at four thirty,' said Bryczinski. 'Take care of my mother before her attendant shows up at six, then I got to drive straight out here.' Head shake. 'Then I find *this*.'

'Mom's sick?'

'She's all kinds of sick. Used to live with my brother then he moved to Nome. That's Alaska.'

He licked his lips. Small, fragile-looking man, nervous as a rabbit. Without a gun, he'd have trouble controlling anything.

Before bringing him up here, Milo ran background. Bryczinski had accumulated several unpaid traffic tickets. The disabling traffic accident was a one-car, which usually means DUI, but Bryczinski's blood alcohol had fallen short of the criterion.

When asked to come up for a second viewing, he said, 'Sure.' Then: 'How come?'

'We could use your help, Doyle.'

The guard's limp turned the three-story climb

16

into a plodding ordeal.

Milo let him stand there for a while, getting an eyeful of the bodies. Sweat beaded Bryczinski's hairline. His back curved in an unhealthy way. Forty but he looked fifty, with wispy sandy hair gone mostly gray and a narrow face sunken in all the wrong places. Five seven, one thirty soaking wet. Small, cheap flashlight hanging from a belt drawn to the last hole. No one was serious about keeping this site secure.

'Anyway,' he said.

'You're sure you don't know them.'

Bryczinski's eyes narrowed. 'Why would I?'

'Now that you can see their faces, I mean.'

'I see 'em but I sure don't *know* 'em.' Backing away toward the wall. Just before he made contact, Milo took hold of his arm.

Bryczinski tensed. 'Hey.'

'Sorry, Doyle. We need to print everything. I'm sure you know the drill.'

'Oh, yeah. Sure.'

Milo said, 'This kind of situation, I have to ask all kinds of questions. You're up here more than anyone. Meaning if anyone comes by, messes the place up, you'd be in the best position to know.'

'I'm here but I ain't up *here* much.' The guard stamped his foot lightly. Plywood thrummed. 'Once I check up here, I don't come back.'

'Don't like the view.'

'I'm working, got no time for views.'

'So no one ever messes around up here.'

'Like who?'

'Anyone,' said Milo.

'Like some homeless guy? You're thinking it

17

was one of those idiots, they surprised him, he went nuts?'

'Anything's possible, Doyle.'

'Well, that hasn't happened for a long time,' said Bryczinski, chancing another look at the bodies. 'A homeless, I mean.'

'You've had problems with squatters?'

'Nah, not really. About a year ago — maybe longer, year and a half, I come in one morning and find dirt. Not up here, on the second floor.'

'Someone tracked in soil.'

'Person dirt. You know what I mean.'

'Someone used the place for a toilet?'

'Right in the middle of floor two, foot of the stairs. Gross. Also there was food wrappers — Taco Bell, wax cups, greasy paper. Beans and sauce stains on the floor. Someone was eating Mexican, then crapping all over.'

'What a mess,' said Milo.

'I called the company, they said clean it up. With what? There's no water, one broken hose bib out back but no pressure. I said screw that. Why bother, anyway? What's to stop the idiot from coming back the next day and doing the same thing?'

'Did he?'

'Nope. But a little later, maybe a month later, some Mexicans came in and ate again. Thank God they didn't dump.'

'How do you know they were Mexicans?'

'Taco Bell wrappers. And too much for one person.'

'All kinds of people eat at Taco Bell.'

'Yeah, well,' said Bryczinski, 'all kinds of

18

people don't leave behind Mexican money. Idiot coins, pesos, whatever. I checked them out, not worth a thing so I gave them to my niece, she's four.'

'Any other intruders?'

'Nah, that's it.'

'No evidence anyone ever came up here to fool around?'

'Nope. That second time, I figured some illegal working on one of the other rich-idiot houses around here had nowhere to go so he slept here. Big surprise to me is why more idiots don't break in. I showed you that chain. Do you want to know about animals?'

'What kind of animals?'

'Critters,' said Bryczinski, savoring the word. 'I find animal dirt all the time. Rats, mice. Coyotes, I know it's coyotes because their dirt is these little shriveled things, look like dry Vienna sausage. I seen plenty of coyote dirt back when I lived in Fallbrook.'

'Avocado country,' said Milo.

'Huh?'

'Don't they grow avocados in Fallbrook?'

'My dad was in the navy, we lived in an apartment.'

'Ah . . . any visitors during the day, Doyle?'

'Never. Place is dead.' Bryczinski flinched. 'So to speak.'

'Don't get bothered by this but like I said I need to ask routine questions of everyone associated with a homicide.'

The guard's eyes narrowed. 'What?'

'What were you doing last night?'

'You're saying I'm in some kind of suspicion because I found them?'

'Not at all, Doyle. I need to be thorough.'

Bryczinski swiped his brow with a uniform sleeve. 'Whatever. Last night, I was sleeping. I get up at four, Mom wakes me up, I hit the hay by nine.'

'You're Mom's sole caretaker.'

'Idiot cat sure can't do much.'

Milo laughed.

The guard said, 'Glad someone thinks it's funny.'

Milo watched him hobble down the stairs, wincing. 'And the diagnosis is . . . ?'

I said, 'No shortage of pent-up anger, but probably not enough physical strength and smarts to pull it off.'

'Even with a gun?'

'You find any kind of link between him and either one of your victims, I'll change my mind.'

'He claims to have only a flashlight but he could've packed. I'll have uniforms check the entire property for discarded weapons. Bryczinski's prints are on file because of the security job. Maybe they'll show up where they shouldn't be. Like on the floor, right where they're laying.'

Another glance at the bodies. 'Cute couple. Tough luck for Ken and Barbie.'

I said, 'Played with like dolls. Then discarded.'

He re-read Desmond Backer's business card. 'Up for Venice? We'll take your gondola.'

4

Gemein, Holman, and Cohen weren't advertising.

Skimpy oxidized-iron address numerals were placed low on the building's facade, barely a foot above the sidewalk. Under that: *GHC: CONCEPTS*.

This was the south end of Main Street, where calculated edgy nudges random do-your-thing and parking's a challenge. Milo said, 'Use that pay lot, on me.'

He flashed his shield to the attendant, had to shell out seven bucks anyway. The walk back took us past boutiques featuring the kind of clothes you never see anyone wearing. Sunny weekday morning in Venice, only a scatter of pedestrians, but a piercing parlor was doing brisk business. Back in his acting days, the governor had bought up chunks of Main Street, accumulating rental income that helped finance his new hobby.

Maybe he owned the architectural firm's avant-garde charmer.

A pair of isosceles triangles jousted with each other in precarious tilt, the larger one pumpkin-orange stucco, the other bluish green aluminum. A black shroud of solar panel capped the roof. A cement trough running along the base was crowded with horsetails, plant-tops lopped with neurosurgical care.

The triangles overlapped just enough to provide walk-space for the non-obese. Milo'd been working on his weight. At a relatively svelte two thirty or so, there was no need to turn sideways, but he did so anyway. Body-memory runs long.

Inside was a courtyard roofed by corrugated metal, bordered by an inch-deep, rectangular pond. Too shallow for fish; maybe microorganisms frolicked.

The front door was an oxidized-iron slab. Milo's knock produced no sound.

No bell. He said, 'Business is either real good or real bad.'

Pounding harder evoked a sorry thud. He said, 'This is gonna hurt,' and poised a foot to kick. Before he made contact, the slab swung inward silently, catching him off balance.

A gorgeous woman with a shaved head watched him stabilize. 'What is it?' All the warmth of a voice-simulator.

She was thirty-five or so, with some sort of Teutonic accent. Hemp disks the size of saucers dangled from exquisitely shaped ears. Nothing overtly medical about her hairlessness; lashes and brows were dark and luxuriant, the eyes below them a spectacular aqua. Her skull was smooth, round, and tan, stubbled white-blond, as if rubbed in salt. Like a minimal frame on a painting, the absence of coiffure emphasized everything else about her. So did a clinging, white tank top, ectodermal black tights, red spike-heeled boots.

Milo flashed the badge. 'Police, ma'am.'

She said, 'And?'

'We'd like to speak to someone about Desmond Backer.'

'Des is in trouble?'

'The worst kind of trouble, Ms . . . '

'Desmond did something illegal?'

'Desmond's dead.'

'Dead,' she said. 'And you want to come in.'

★   ★   ★

She marched back inside, left us to follow. Swinging her hips and stepping high.

The interior was one big space, unfurnished but for a black desk and a rolling chair in a corner. White walls, high windows, carpeting that matched the bald beauty's hemp earrings. Skylights in odd places, some of them partially blackened by the solar panel. Others bore the streaks and splotches of moisture damage.

The bald woman sat behind the desk, laid her palms flat. Charcoal-gray manicure, some kind of mesh effect on the nails. 'I have no chairs for you.'

'We're fine standing, ma'am.'

'Something criminal happened to Des.'

'Sorry to say, ma'am. Mr Backer was murdered.'

'That is bad.' Again, the lack of inflection.

'What can you tell us about him, Ms . . . '

'Helga Gemein.'

'You're one of the partners.'

'There are no partners. We are dissolved.'

'As of when?'

'Six weeks ago. Don't ask why.'

'Why?'

Helga Gemein was in no mood to joke. 'Who murdered Des?'

'That's what we're trying to learn,' said Milo. 'What can you tell us about him?'

'He worked here from when we started the firm.'

'Which was . . . '

'Twenty months ago. He was a good draftsman with so-so design skills. He was hired because he was green.'

'Fresh out of school?'

'Pardon?'

'Green.'

'No, no, no,' Helga Gemein scolded. 'Green, environmental. Des got his degree at Cal Poly San Luis Obispo, wrote a thesis on bio-environmental synchrony.'

I thought of the warring triangles out front, water so shallow it would evaporate within days.

'The green approach didn't work out,' said Milo.

'Of course it works, why would you say that?'

'The firm dissolved — '

'*People* don't work out,' said Helga Gemein. 'Modern humanity — post-industrial humanity is a criminal biomechanical disruption of the natural order. *That* is the point of green architecture: reshaping sustainable balance between components of the life force.'

'Of course,' said Milo. 'So what kind of projects did the firm do?'

'We planned our mission statement.'

24

'No actual buildings?'

Helga Gemein's lovely mouth screwed up tight. 'In Germany, architecture is a subset of engineering. The emphasis is upon proper theory and flawless planning. We saw ourselves as green consultants. What do these questions have to do with Des?'

'He was murdered at a construction site, ma'am. An unfinished house in Holmby Hills.'

Reciting the address on Borodi Lane.

'So?'

'I was just wondering — '

'We never intended to involve ourselves with private housing.'

'This was large-scale housing, Ms Gemein. Three-story mansion on a couple of acres. Mr Backer was found on the third floor — '

'That sounds unspeakably vulgar. Id, ego, flashing of the penis. I'd rather design a yurt.'

'When did Des Backer leave the firm?'

'When it dissolved.'

'Did he find another job?'

'I wouldn't know.'

'He never asked for a reference?'

'He packed up his desk and left.'

'Was he angry?'

'Why would he be?'

'Losing his job.'

'Jobs come and go.'

'While he was here, what was he involved with?'

'Des *wanted* to be involved with the Kraeker.'

'What's that, ma'am?'

Helga Gemein's look said if you needed to

ask, you didn't deserve to know. 'The Kraeker is a performance art gallery scheduled to be built in Basel by the year 2013. My plan is to submit a proposal for heat and light sustainability that would synchronize with the art itself. Des asked to be assigned to the preliminary drawings. Obviously, a project of that scope would help his career.'

'But it never got that far.'

'That is not clear. Once I clean up the mess my partners have left me, I may very well assemble another team. Returning to Europe will be a welcome change.'

'Had enough of LA.'

'Quite.'

'Is there anything you can tell us about Des that could be helpful?'

'His sexual appetite was conspicuous.'

Milo blinked. 'By conspicuous, you mean — '

'What I mean,' said Helga Gemein, 'is that Des was highly motivated toward maximal screwing. Was his death sexual in nature?'

'How do you know that about him, ma'am?'

'If you're asking, in that peculiarly prudish American way, if I speak from personal experience, the answer is no. My information comes from the other women who worked here. Each of them discovered that Des had requested to screw her.'

'Requested?'

'Des was polite. He always said 'please.''

'You didn't fire him?'

'Why would I?'

'That's pretty blatant workplace harassment.'

26

'Policeman,' she said, 'one can only be harassed if one contextualizes herself as helpless. Everyone said yes. Des is a handsome man. In an immature way.'

'How exactly did you learn about all this, Ms Gemein?'

'That is a voyeuristic question.'

'My job can get that way.'

She touched a hemp earring. 'There was a staff meeting. Des was away from the office on something or another and Judah Cohen was in Milan, so no men. If you knew anything about women, you'd know that, plus alcohol loosens tongues. One of them had seen another go off with Des after work and wondered out loud. It didn't take long to compare notes. Everyone agreed he was attentive and reasonably endowed, but lacking in creativity.'

I said, 'How many women are we talking about?'

'Three.'

'Four women at the meeting, but only three were propositioned.'

'If you are asking in that American way if I am homosexual, I am not. Though I am not opposed to homosexuality on moral grounds. Why did I not screw Des? He did not appeal to me.'

'He never came on to you?'

Blinking, she caressed the top of her head. 'We maintained a professional relationship.'

Milo took out his pad. 'Could I please have the other women's names?'

Helga Gemein smiled. 'I will talk slowly: Number one, Sheryl Passant, our receptionist.' Waiting until he'd copied. 'Number two, Bettina

Sanfelice, a dull girl who served as an intern. Number three, Marjorie Holman.'

'Your former partner.'

'Correct.'

'Des didn't see the need for a professional relationship with her.'

'Marjorie and I disagree on many levels.'

'Marjorie has no problem mixing business with pleasure.'

'You're being simplistic, Policeman. *Everything* is business and *everything* is pleasure. It is Marjorie who fails to integrate the two.'

'What do you mean?'

'She insists on drawing arbitrary boundaries — creates imaginary rules so that she can delight in violating them.'

'Forbidden fruit,' said Milo.

'Marjorie is quite the nibbler.'

'Is she married?'

'Yes. Now I must go.'

Milo asked her for addresses and phone numbers of the three women. Marjorie Holman's, she knew by heart. For the others, she consulted a BlackBerry.

'Now I will walk you out.'

He showed her the female victim's death shot.

Helga Gemein examined the image. 'What is this?'

'A woman who died along with Mr Backer.'

'So it was sexual.'

'Why do you say that?'

'Des with a woman. What else could it be?'

Milo smiled. 'Maybe a meaningful spiritual relationship?'

28

Helga Gemein headed for the door.

We tagged along. I said, 'How well did Des do his job?'

'Adequately. Before we dissolved, I'd contemplated letting him go.'

'Why?'

'The pathetic state of our planet demands better than adequate.'

5

Helga Gemein marched through the courtyard and continued north on Main.

'Good stamina, considering those stilettos,' said Milo. 'What a charmer.'

'Don't think of her as hostile,' I said. 'Just philosophically consistent.'

'What's the philosophy?'

'Humanity is a blot on nature.'

'That's kind of psychopathic — and she didn't react emotionally to Backer's death. Hang out with her, no need for air-conditioning.'

'Personal coolant,' I said. 'There's a green concept for you.'

'Backer jumps anything with ovaries but doesn't come on to her. Maybe the jealousy you felt at the scene was anger at being rejected.'

'Woman scorned? Those stilettos would set off clacks on plywood.'

He sighted up Main. Crossed his arms over his barrel chest. 'Asking women to screw. If Backer's libido was really that over-the-top, it expands the potential suspect base to every hetero male in LA . . . wonderful.'

He scanned the addresses Gemein had provided. 'The receptionist and the intern are both out in the Valley, but naughty Ms Holman lives right here in Venice, Linnie Canal.'

'That's about a mile in,' I said. 'We could walk.'

'Oh, sure. And I'm gonna wear spandex bicycle shorts.'

* * *

Finding the nearest entrance to the canal district, and manipulating the Byzantine network of one-ways and dead-ends by car, turned a geographic hop into a half-hour excursion. Once we got within eyeshot of Linnie Canal, the closest parking spot was two blocks east.

The canals are a century old, the product of a feverish mind devolving to yet another patch of high-priced real estate. The visionary in question, an eccentric named Abbot Kinney, had dug and dredged sinuous waterways, dreaming of replicating the original island city. A hundred years later, most of the quirky, original bungalows had been replaced by close-set McMansions high above footpaths.

A squared-off hedge echoed the curves of the canal. Nice place to stroll, but no pedestrians in sight. The water was green and opaque, flecked with hyacinth and the occasional bit of trash. Ducks floated by, pausing to bob for food. A seagull faked a dive-bomb, changed course, landed on a nearby roof and squawked a nasal, political diatribe. Maybe he felt the same as Helga Gemein about humanity.

Milo said, 'Always liked it here. To visit, not to live.'

'What's wrong with living here?'

'Too hard to escape.'

Marjorie Holman's residence was two steeply pitched stories of white-clapboard, blue-shuttered chalet, eaves bearded by jigsawed trim, a porthole window over the door suggesting the kind of seafood joint where deep-fry orders are placed at the counter.

'Not exactly postmodern,' muttered Milo. 'Whatever the hell that means.'

A wide, concrete ramp sloped up to a wooden deck. Rattan furniture was distributed randomly. Potted geraniums sat on the rail. One corner was taken up by a mammoth gas-powered barbecue with more controls than my Seville's dashboard. The goofy-looking dolphin riding the wall above the grill hadn't weathered well: aging Flipper on Quaaludes.

French doors made up the wall facing the canal. All that glass meant lots of energy loss; no solar panels in sight. A bell on a leather thong in lieu of an electric buzzer was the sole nod to conservation.

Milo tugged the thong. A deep male voice hollered, 'Hold on.'

Seconds later, a man rolled out in a motorized wheelchair. A navy T-shirt was stretched tight over rhino shoulders and abdominal bulk. Khaki trousers were barely defined by stick-legs. He looked to be sixty or so, with a full head of coarse gray hair and a bushy beard to match.

'Help you?'

'Police, sir. Is Marjorie Holman in?'

'Police? What's going on?'

'Someone who worked for Ms Holman's firm was murdered.'

'You're kidding.' Rapid eyeblink. 'Who?'

'Desmond Backer.'

'Des.'

'You knew him.'

'He came over a few times to show Marjie drawings. Murdered? That's grotesque. How did it happen?'

'He was shot, Mr Holman.'

'Ned.' A meaty hand shot forward. His lips turned down. 'Marjie's going to be extremely upset by this, I should be the one to tell her — why don't you guys come on in?'

He reversed the wheelchair into the house, motored across a big, bright room to the bottom of an ornate oak staircase. The entire ground floor was open space that maximized light. Sparse furnishings allowed easy turns of the chair.

Ned Holman cupped a hand to his mouth. 'Honey? Could you please come down?'

'What is it?'

'Please come down, Marjie.'

'Everything all right, Ned?' Footsteps thumped.

'I'm fine, just come down, hon.'

Marjorie Holman had bounced halfway down the stairs when she saw us and stopped. Tall and angular with a blue-gray pageboy, she had long limbs and a smallish face dominated by owlish, black-framed glasses. A baggy orange blouse and straight-leg jeans said little about the body beneath. Barefoot. Pink nails.

'What's going on?'

'They're the police. It's about Des Backer. He was murdered.'

A hand flew to her mouth. 'Oh, my God.'

'Sorry, hon,' said Ned Holman. 'This was starting out as a nice day.'

* * *

Marjorie Holman shook our hands limply, went into the kitchen and fortified herself with a tall pour of Sapphire gin from a frosted blue bottle. Two long swallows brought a flush to her cheeks. She stared out the window at a coral tree in flaming bloom.

Her husband rolled to her side, rubbed the small of her back.

'I'm OK, Ned.' Turning and facing us: 'Can I get you something?'

Wheeling himself to the fridge, Ned Holman grabbed a handle retrofitted low, yanked the door open, pulled out a bottle of Budweiser. A quick finger-flick popped the cap. He caught it in one hand, rolled it between sausage fingers.

Milo said, 'No, thanks.'

Both Holmans drank. He drained his beer first. She made it through half the gin before setting the glass down. 'I need some air — you'll be OK if I take a breather, Ned?'

'Of course.'

She motioned us out of the house, hurried down the ramp, turned right on the footpath. Additional gulls had assembled in the water, a grumpy quorum.

Marjorie Holman set out at a slow pace,

walked close to the hedge, brushing her hand along the top. 'I'm still in shock. My God, when did this happen?'

'Last night, ma'am. He was carrying business cards, we just talked to Ms Gemein.'

'Helga,' she said. 'That must have been interesting.'

'How so, Ms Holman?'

'Oh, come on,' she said. 'If you talked to her, you're not seriously asking that.'

'She is an interesting woman.'

'Do you suspect her?'

'Should we, Ms Holman?'

'Well,' she said, 'Helga *is* devoid of normal human emotion, but I can't say she ever displayed any hostility to Des. In particular.'

'She was hostile in general?'

'Utterly asocial. That's part of why we're no longer partners. What exactly happened to Des?'

'He was shot by an unknown assailant.'

'Good God.'

'Ma'am, if there's something to know about Helga Gemein — or anyone else — now's the time to tell us.'

'Plainly put, Helga is a weirdo, Detective, but do I have a specific reason to think she's a murderer? No, I don't. What I *can* tell you is she's a fraud, so anything she says is suspect. The firm never got off the ground because she conned me and Judah Cohen — the third partner.'

'Conned how?'

'There was no *there* there.'

'No real interest in green architecture?'

'To use your terminology, there was *alleged* interest,' said Marjorie Holman. 'In Germany, architecture is a branch of engineering, and that's what Helga is, a structural engineer. With precious few skills at that. She doesn't have to work because her father owns shipping companies, gets to play intellectual and global thinker. Judah and I met her at a conference in Prague where she claimed to have all sorts of backing for an integrated approach to numerous projects. Judah and I are veterans, we'd both made partner at decent-sized firms but felt it was time for a change. Helga claimed to already own office space, right here in Venice, all we had to do was show up and use our brains. Later we found out she'd sublet the building, had been chronically late with the rent. Everything else she told us was baloney, as well. All she wanted to do was talk about *ideas*. Judah and I had both burned bridges, we're stuck, it's a mess. In architecture, you're Gehry or Meier, or you're drafting plans for room additions in San Bernadino.'

Her nostrils flared. 'Helga tired of the game, walked in one day and announced we were *kaput*. Quote unquote.'

'Theatrical,' said Milo.

'You better believe it.'

'That explain the shaved head?'

'Probably,' said Marjorie Holman. 'When we met her in Prague, she had long blond hair, looked like Elke Summer. She comes here, she's Yul Brynner.' Head shake. 'She's one big piece of performance art. I hate her guts, wish I could tell

36

you she was murderous but I honestly can't say that.'

'Tell us about Des.'

'Nice kid, we hired him right out of school.'

'He graduated at thirty,' I said. 'Late bloomer?'

'That's this generation, adolescence lasts forever. I've got two sons around Des's age and both of them are still trying to figure it out.'

Milo said, 'The murder took place at a construction site on Borodi Lane in Holmby Hills. That ring a bell?'

'No, sorry. In Holmby it would have to be a house.'

'Your basic thirty-room McPalace.'

'Had Des found a job at another firm?'

'If he did, he wasn't carrying their card.'

'If he wasn't working there, I can't imagine what he'd be doing.'

A plastic kayak lay across the walkway. We bypassed it. Milo said, 'In terms of a personal relationship between yourself and Mr Backer . . . '

'There was none.'

'Ms Gemein claimed otherwise, ma'am.'

Marjorie Holman's hands curled but her stride didn't break.

'Ms Holman?'

'Nasty bitch.'

'Nasty *lying* bitch, ma'am?'

Sharp inhalation. 'I have nothing to apologize for.'

'We're not judging, Ms Holman — '

'Of course you are, judging's your job.'

'Only as it applies to murder, ma'am.'

Marjorie Holman's laughter was brittle,

37

unsettling. 'Well, then, we're all peachy-dandy here, because whatever I did or *didn't* do with Des has *nothing* to do with murder.'

'We're more interested in did than didn't, ma'am.'

She didn't answer. Milo let it ride and the three of us kept walking.

Five houses later, she said: 'You met my husband. He's been that way for six years. I'm not going to make tawdry excuses, but neither am I going to apologize for having needs.'

'Of course, ma'am.'

'Don't patronize me, Detective. I'm not a moron.'

Six more houses. She picked up speed. A tear track darkened her cheek. 'Once. That's all it was. Ned doesn't know and there's no reason to tell him.'

'I agree, ma'am.'

'He was tender, it was almost like being with another woman. Not that I'd know about that . . . it was a crazy thing to do, I regret it. But at the time . . . ' Drying her tears with her sleeve. 'One of my sons is the same age as Des and if you don't think that made me feel sleazy, you're wrong. It was never going to happen again and I was not going to torture myself.'

She stopped short, touched Milo's wrist. 'I want to make one thing clear, Detective: Des did not exploit me, nor am I some desperate cougar. It just happened.'

'One time,' said Milo.

'You want me to take a lie detector, fine. Just as long as Ned doesn't find out.'

38

'All we want to do is find out who killed Des.'

'I can't help you with that.'

'Did anyone at the firm have conflict with him?'

'No.'

'Not Helga?'

'I wish I could say yes but not even her.'

'She told us she was never intimate with Des.'

'Are you shocked? I doubt Helga has the capacity for intimacy.'

'She also said Des slept with every other woman at the firm.'

'I can't speak to that.'

'She said you could, Ms Holman. That she learned about all of this because you and Ms Sanfelice and Ms Passant talked about it openly. At a staff meeting.'

Marjorie Holman rocked on her heels. Walked with her head down. 'Oh, Jesus.' She let out a strange giggle and threw up her hands. 'Martinis and estrogen, what can I say?'

'Staff meeting with alcohol?'

'Staff meeting at a restaurant.'

'Without getting into details, if you could tell us where you and Des . . . trysted . . . '

'Why is that your business?'

'We're searching for patterns, Ms Holman.'

'What kind of patterns?'

'Des frequenting construction sites.'

She went pale.

'Ma'am — '

'This is humiliating.' Another brittle laugh. 'You want the dirty details, fine: One night, three, four months ago, Des and I were working late. Looking back, he probably planned it. He'd heard about the Kraeker — that's an art gallery in Switzerland we were supposedly going to be involved in. Another of Helga's fantasies, she never even filled out the preliminary forms — you don't care about that, you want sleaze. Des wanted me to put in a good word for him with Helga, I said I would. We were hungry so we went out to dinner. Des said he had a construction site he wanted me to see. Because of its design. If that makes a pattern, fine.'

Milo said, 'Where was the site?'

'Oh, Lord . . . Santa Monica, near the Water Gardens, off Twenty-sixth Street and Colorado. Des said a film studio was beginning a project that was aiming for complete sustainability, down to black-water and gray-water management. It was after dark, we drove over in separate cars, I had no reason to think it would turn out — when I got there, I was confused, it was just an open empty lot. There was a trailer set up as an office, nothing educational design-wise, and I was peeved at Des for dragging me out there. He said hold on, there's something you need to see, and took me behind the trailer.'

Her hair hadn't moved but she smoothed it. 'I suppose I was ready to be led by the nose. Des took hold of my shoulders and said, 'I know this is wrong and it may cost me my job, but I find you crushingly attractive, I've been thinking about you since I met you, and, God help me, I'd love to screw you.''

She straightened her collar, adjusted her necklace, as if primping for a portrait. 'That sounds vulgar in the retelling, but you had to be there, guys. Trust me, it was alluring.'

* * *

Ten more minutes of strolling produced an easy-to-verify alibi for the previous night. The Holmans had attended an experimental music concert at Disney Hall with another couple, followed by a late dinner at Providence on Melrose.

'Seafood orgy, guys. After we'd gorged ourselves silly, we headed clear across town to Vibrato, in Beverly Glen, thinking we'd catch some jazz, but the show was over so we went home. I went to bed and Ned stayed up reading, the way he usually does. He lives for books and language, he's an esteemed linguist, used to teach at the U. Used to do all sorts of things.' Frown. 'That was my pathetic play for sympathy. Not that I need any. It's poor Des who does.'

'What can you tell us about Des's background?' said Milo. 'Personal, not professional.'

'We never talked about things like that. Never talked much, period. He was a lovely boy, gentle, considerate. I can't see why anyone would want to kill him.'

Milo showed her the dead woman's picture.

'Who's — my God, she's . . . '

'Do you recognize her, Ms Holman?'

'Absolutely not.' Thrusting the photo back.

'The other women at the firm — Sheryl and Bettina. Single or married?'

'Single.'

'Reason I ask, ma'am, is we need to check out irate boyfriends, husbands.'

She stared at us. 'Ned? Not a chance. For a husband to be irate, he needs to be aware, and Ned isn't. Even if he did find out, he's not exactly in a position to do anything about it, is he?'

The flippant cruelty of the last sentence hung in the air.

'Speaking of which, I'd best be getting back, gentlemen. Ned might need freshening up.'

6

Marjorie Holman sprinted up the ramp to her deck.

Milo said, 'Freshening him up. Hubby as houseplant. Some nest of vipers ol' Des got himself into.'

We headed back to the car, crossed a footbridge above still, green water.

I said, 'Sounds like ol' Des dove into the nest with enthusiasm. If he took Passant and Sanfelice to construction sites, we're talking predictable, high-risk behavior.'

'Come away with me to *le beeg deeg, mon amour*. Might as well wear a *Stalk Me* sign. So maybe this *will* boil down to another jealous domestic and no matter what Holman says, we coulda just met the main players. A mister bitter over his plight. Missus thinks he's greenery but there could be plenty of animal left.'

'Charming Helga called Holman a nibbler of forbidden fruit. It's possible her flings weren't limited to Backer.'

'All the more reason for pent-up anger, but right now the only lothario I care about is Backer. Mr Smooth. Coming out and asking for it ain't exactly suave, let alone three women in the same office. But it worked, so what do I know?'

I said, 'Sounds like Backer had a nose for emotional vulnerability. Think about the Holmans' house: Ned's got no access to the second floor, where Marjie sleeps. She's an architect, if anyone could figure out a way to get him up there, it's her. They've chosen to live physically segregated lives. It's not just a matter of sex, it's intimacy. And that's what she says she got from Backer.'

'He tries a little tenderness, she falls right in.'

'My question is, if her needs were being met, why limit it to a one-night stand?'

He rolled his shoulders. 'She lied to us and she and Backer had something serious going on?'

'That would threaten Ned Holman big-time. On top of being humiliated, he's left alone physically and emotionally. We've both seen enough domestic homicides to know the pattern: The jealous spouse focuses first on eliminating the outside threat. Maybe I was wrong about Jane Doe being the target. What if the goal was to eliminate Backer, after all, and Jane was collateral damage?'

'Or,' he said, '*Jane* was more than a fling for Backer. Or both she and Marjie thought they were number one, meaning a woman scorned.' Grimacing. 'Just what I need, a bigger suspect pool . . . freshening the poor guy *up*. Why *wouldn't* she design him an elevator or something?'

'Plus,' I said, 'her alibi for last night is meaningless. She went to sleep, got up. The same goes for Ned's physical limitations because he could've paid to get the job done. Either of them could've. A pro job would also be consistent with careful planning, positioning the bodies just so.'

He worried a pendulous earlobe. 'Stunningly Shakespearean, Alex. Now all I need is

44

something remotely close to evidence, say documentation of a torrid romance between Marjie and Backer and either one of the Holmans paying a killer for hire. Hell, long as we're dreaming, I wouldn't mind a warm spot in Warren Buffett's heart. Right now, I'll settle for finding out who Jane Doe is.'

As I drove away, he phoned the crypt, learned the bodies were still in the delivery bay waiting processing. He squinted at his Timex. 'Damn numerals keep getting smaller . . . two fifteen, let's see if we can find Bettina Sanfelice and Sheryl Passant. If they're working as well as living in the Valley, there's time to make it over the hill before the rush. Also, I know an Italian place. You up for it?'

'Sure.'

As we rolled out of the canal district, he said, 'Some victim I've got. That mix of glands and charisma, he shoulda run for office.'

*   *   *

The clown-show that poses as the California legislature had finally bucked phone-company lobbyists long enough to pass a hands-free law. The system I'd installed delighted Milo, because he can sit back and smoke and grunt and stretch and scan the streets for bad guys while he chats.

As I approached Lincoln Avenue, he began punching in numbers. No one picked up at Sheryl Passant's Van Nuys apartment, but Bettina Sanfelice's North Hollywood landline

45

was answered by a slurry-voiced woman who said, 'Yeah?'

'Is this Bettina?'

'No.'

'Does Bettina live there?'

'Who's this?'

'LA police lieutenant Milo Sturgis.'

'Who?'

He repeated, taking pains to go slow.

'Police?'

'Yes, ma'am.'

'Tina's OK?'

'I need to talk to her about a case.'

'A case? What case?'

'Someone she worked with was murdered.'

'Who?'

'Desmond Backer.'

'Don't know him.'

'Ma'am — '

'I'm her mother. She's out.'

'Could you please tell me where?'

'How do I know you're not some maniac?'

'I'll give you my number at the police station and you can verify.'

'How do I know you're not giving me some phony number?'

'Feel free to look it up. West LA Division, on Butler — '

'I should do all the work?'

'Ma'am,' said Milo, 'I appreciate your caution but I need to talk to Bettina.'

Silence.

'Mrs Sanfelice — '

'She went to T.G.I. Friday's.'

'Which one?'

'All the way in Woodland Hills, I don't know the address. She likes the burgers, you'd never catch me wasting gas for that.'

'What was she wearing?'

'How would I know?'

'She doesn't live with you?'

'She sure does, 'cause she still don't have no job. That don't mean I pay attention to her clothes.'

Click.

He phoned Detective Moe Reed, asked for DMV statistics on the intern.

The young cop said, 'I was just about to call you, Loo. Prints on Backer and the female vic got run through AFIS but unfortunately nothing kicked back . . .'

'I already knew that.'

'You did?'

'It's been that kind of day.' He spelled Sanfelice's name.

Seconds later Reed said, 'Sanfelice, Bettina Morgana, thirty years old, five five, hundred and ten, brown, brown, wears corrective lenses, no wants or warrants. Here's the address.'

Living at Mom's when she'd had her license renewed three years ago.

'Anything else, Loo?'

'I'll let you know.'

Milo hung up. 'I hear intern, I figure a college kid. She's way past that, unemployed, stuck with that loving maternal entity. Like you said, emotional vulnerability. Ol' Des had a helluva nose.'

The 101 freeway was starting to clog up so I took Ventura Boulevard to Woodland Hills. The T.G.I. Friday's was like any other, which is the point.

Chain restaurants are easy targets of ridicule for expense-account gourmets, documentary filmmakers living off grant money, and trust-fund babies. For folks saddled with budgets and faced with a world that seems increasingly unpredictable, they're temples of comfort. Milo and I had grown up in the Midwest and we'd both flipped burgers in high school. The smell of the grill still evokes all sorts of memories. How I react depends on what else is going on in my life.

Today, the aroma was pretty good.

Milo inhaled deeply. 'Home sweet bacon.'

The interior was vast, chocked with corporate oak, stenciled mirrors, not-even-close-to-Tiffany lamps, red-shirted servers mostly hanging around because of the three P.M. off-hour.

A bar ample enough to intoxicate half the Valley ran the length of the room. The layout made it easy to spot every customer: a scatter of bleary-eyed truckers with no idea what time it was, a mom and a grandmom teaming up to handle a whining kid in a booster chair, two young women in a booth midway down, sipping tall pink drinks and picking at a plate of fries.

A kid in a red shirt said, 'Two for lunch?'

'We're joining friends.'

★ ★ ★

Both women were pale, thin, wore drab, short-sleeved tops, jeans, and careless ponytails. Other than platinum hair on one, they each matched Bettina Sanfelice's stats.

Milo said, 'The blonde's wearing glasses, so I'm betting that's her. Now all I need to do is separate her from her friend and get her to blab about her sex life. Any suggestions as to the proper approach?'

'There is none,' I said.

'Your optimism is a blessing.'

Neither woman noticed until we got within three feet, then both looked up. Milo smiled at the blonde. 'Bettina Sanfelice?'

The brown-haired woman said, 'That's me,' in a tiny, tentative voice. Small-boned but full-faced, she had close-set mocha eyes and puffy cheeks and looked like a child who'd just been punished. The white-sauce-slicked fry she'd been reaching for dropped back onto her plate. Not a potato — something pale green and breaded — deep-fried string bean?

Milo bent to make himself smaller, showed his card rather than the badge, recited his title as if it were no big deal.

Bettina Sanfelice was too stricken to speak, but the blonde said, 'Police?' as if he were joking. She had good features but grainy skin with some active blemish, dark circles under her eyes that heavy makeup failed to mask.

Milo kept his focus on Bettina Sanfelice. 'I'm so sorry to tell you this, ma'am, but we're investigating the death of someone you worked with.'

Sanfelice's mouth dropped open. Her hand

shot forward, rocked her drink. It would've spilled if I hadn't caught it. 'Death?'

'By homicide, I'm afraid.'

Sanfelice gasped. 'Who?'

Milo said, 'A man named Desmond — '

Before Backer's surname had been fully pronounced both women shouted, 'Des!'

The kid in the red shirt looked over. A hard look from Milo caused him to veer toward the bar.

The bespectacled blonde said, 'I have just got totally nauseous.'

Bettina Sanfelice said, 'Des? Omigod.'

The blonde removed her glasses. 'I need a bathroom.' She slid out of the booth.

'You also knew Des, ma'am?'

'Same as Tina did.' The blonde trotted toward the restrooms, moving clumsily in ultratight jeans and ratty sneakers.

The kid in the red shirt dared to come over. 'Everything OK?'

Milo expanded like a balloon. 'Everything's grand, just go about your business.'

Now was the time for the badge. Gawking, the kid turned heel.

Milo said, 'Your friend's pretty upset, Bettina.'

'Sheryl's got a iffy stomach.'

'That's Sheryl Passant?'

Nod. 'Omigod. Who hurt Des?'

'That's what we're trying to find out. Mind if we join you?'

'Um . . . ' Not budging.

Milo smiled. 'Thanks for the compliment, but I need a little more room than that, Bettina.'

'Oh . . . sorry.' Sanfelice scooted over and he wedged beside her. Milo's presence turned her tiny. An abused child.

I settled across from them.

Milo pointed at the pink drink. 'I know it's a shock, feel free.'

'Oh . . . no, thanks.' But she grabbed the glass with both hands, took a long, noisy sip.

'Frozen strawberry margarita?' said Milo.

'Frozen straw-tini . . . Des is really dead? Omigod, that's so . . . I can't believe it!'

'Tina, anything you can tell us about Des would be really helpful. You and Sheryl both worked with him, right?'

'Uh-huh. At GHC — that's a architectural firm. Sheryl got me the job.'

'You and Sheryl are old friends.'

'From junior high. We tried out for the army but we changed our mind because of Eye-rack. Instead, we enrolled in JC but we didn't like it, so we went to ITT to learn computers but we didn't like that so we switched to business technology at Briar Secretarial. Sheryl got a job right away, she can type fast, but I'm slower so I switched to computer graphics. My dream is to design furniture and draperies but there's nothing right now so when Sheryl got the job at GHC, she told me they needed a intern, maybe I could get to do design.'

'Did you?'

'Uh-uh, I mostly ran errands, answered the phone when Sheryl was tied up. Which didn't happen too much. There really wasn't nothing to do.'

51

'Was Des working at GHC when you and Sheryl got hired?'

'No, he came later. Like a week later. We said, 'Finally, a guy.'' Blushing.

'Mr Cohen's a guy.'

'He's old.'

'How old?'

'Like sixty. He's like a grandpa.'

A voice to our left said, 'He *is* a grandpa, used to bring his rug-rat grandkids in and would go off all day with them.'

Sheryl Passant looked down on us, oracle on the mount.

I got up to let her in. No more ponytail; her blond hair was long and loose and streaming and her glasses were gone.

She slid in. 'Why were you talking about Mr Cohen?'

Bettina Sanfelice said, 'We're talking about Des, Sher. To find out who killed him.'

'Us? What can *we* tell them?'

Milo said, 'For starts, what kind of guy Des was, Sheryl. Did he have enemies, who'd want to hurt him?'

Passant shifted closer. Her thigh pressed against mine. I scooted an inch away. She frowned. Flipped her hair. 'Des had no enemies.'

'None at all?'

'Des was really mellow, I can't see anyone hating him. Not even Helga the Nazi.'

'Helga the Gestapo Girl,' said Sanfelice, giggling, then turning grave. 'Sorry, we just . . . she didn't treat us good. Just getting our paychecks was a hassle. Sheryl, I mean. I was just an intern so I didn't get paid at all.'

'Which totally sucked,' said Passant. 'You did the same job as me, Teen. You should've gotten paid the same as me. Helga sucks.'

Milo said, 'Wasn't the firm a partnership?'

'Marjie and Mr Cohen didn't control the money, she did. The building was hers, the idea was hers, everything was hers. She was always talking like she was the one who'd made up Green. Like Al Gore had never existed. You think *she* killed Des?'

'You think she could've?'

The women looked at each other. Sanfelice stirred her drink. Passant said, 'I'm not saying she'd have done it. But she's not like a regular person, you know?'

'Different,' said Sanfelice. 'She's from Europe.'

The red-shirted kid reappeared, this time bearing two plates.

Bacon burgers oozing with molten white and orange cheese, salads the size of a baby's head, a hay-bale of onion rings. 'Um, do you guys still want this?'

Bettina Sanfelice said, 'I was hungry but now *I'm* also feeling nauseous.'

Sheryl Passant said, 'Yuck. Do we still have to pay?'

Milo said, 'Put the food down, son, and give me the check. Here's your tip in advance.' Forking over bills.

The kid said, 'Sweet.'

* * *

53

A few minutes of routine questions produced nothing new about Desmond Backer, whom the women described as 'Nice and totally hot.' The shock had worn off and they both seemed pleased at the attention.

Bettina Sanfelice studied her burger. 'It's probably gross but I'm going to try.'

Sheryl Passant said, 'Not me.' Moments later, a grin as she bit in, wiped her chin. 'Guess I lied.'

Milo let them eat, offered drink refills. They declined. Sanfelice wholeheartedly, Passant with some regret.

Milo stared at me.

I raised my eyebrows.

He cocked his head to the side and when I didn't respond, said, 'My partner's gonna ask you some questions now. They're a little personal, so sorry. But we really need to ask.'

Waving the red-shirted kid over, he ordered an extra-large Coke.

Both women had stopped eating.

Sheryl Passant's thigh pressed hard against mine.

7

Bettina Sanfelice said, 'Personal?'

Milo's eyebrows said *Take it from here*.

Sheryl Passant said, 'They mean sex, Teen. Because Des was a horner from day one, right? Like he was put on this earth to *do it*.' The corners of her mouth turned up as she bent over her straw. Conspicuous slurp.

I said, 'Helga and Marjorie Holman both told us about a meeting where Des was discussed by all of you.'

Passant grinned. 'Where we all admitted doing Des.'

Bettina Sanfelice's hand shot to her mouth.

'Stop being dorky, Teen. You did him, we all did him. So what?'

'Omigod.' Sanfelice hung her head.

Passant laughed. 'I have always been her bad influence, that's why her mom has always hated me. Put a horn like Des with a bunch of girls, what do you think's going to have happened?'

I said, 'Helga said it didn't happen with her.'

'That's because she's never been human — stop *spazzing*, Teen, it's *biology*.'

Sanfelice said, '*I* need to go to the bathroom.'

'In a sec, hon,' said Milo.

No argument.

Passant said, 'The moment you met Des it was pretty clear he was after one thing.'

I said, 'Marjorie said he was pretty direct, just

came out and asked.'

'At first, I thought it was gross. Like, are you kidding? But the way he did it made it not gross.'

'How so?'

'Not pushy, kind of . . . friendly. Des made it all *real* friendly.'

Her foot rested on mine. Pressure just short of pain. I slid away. She smiled.

'Was it a onetime thing, or did — '

'Seven times for me. Lucky seven.'

Bettina Sanfelice gasped.

'I know I told you three, Teen. Didn't want to freak you out but it was seven. Now you're gonna ask why wasn't it eight? I don't know, it just kind of stopped. Like he'd become my brother or something.'

I said, 'Too friendly.'

'Yup.'

'Did Des take you anywhere in particular?'

'Coffee,' she said. 'Sometimes food.' Back to caressing my shoe with her sneaker. '*Afterward*.'

'Was there a particular place for before?'

She faced me. 'You really *are* personal. No, there wasn't any one place. He took me to sites.'

'Building sites?'

'He just called them sites. Like unfinished buildings, or sometimes there was just dirt, sometimes parts of buildings. When there was just dirt, he had a blanket in his car. Basically, he got off doing it outdoors. A lot of people do.'

I said, 'Where were these sites?'

'I don't know the street, it was dark . . . they were all in the Valley — is that where he got killed? In the Valley?'

'No,' I said.

'Well, with me it was always in the Valley. He'd pick me up at my apartment, say he had a new site.'

Bettina Sanfelice mumbled unintelligibly.

Sheryl Passant said, 'Now you can tell them about Des and you.'

I said, 'I think we know enough.'

'You said it was two, Teen. Remember what I said when you told me that? Two for the road. You said he took you to sites, also.'

Sanfelice whimpered.

I said, 'We're fine, Tina — '

Passant reached across the table for her friend's hand. 'Chill, Teen, no one's going to tell your mom. They don't care about us, they care about who killed Des.'

'Any ideas about that?'

Both women shook their heads.

I said, 'Marjorie Holman told us she and Des had a one-night stand. Do you think that's true?'

Passant said, 'Could be, she's old and baggy.'

'How did you guys come to be discussing Des?'

'We all had been drinking, you drink, you talk.'

'It wasn't a business meeting?'

'That's what she called it. The Notz. Guess it was, because there wasn't any business — it wasn't like a real job, you know?'

'No assignments.'

'We just came in every day and mostly sat around except when the Nazi wanted to talk about stuff no one understood. One day, she came in and said, 'There's no coherence, we need coherence.''

Sanfelice said, 'Cohesiveness. 'There's no *cohesiveness.''*

'Means the same, Teen. Anyway, Helga-notz said we need to have something social to get cohesiveness, so we went out for drinks.'

'Just the women,' I said.

'Girls' night out. *Gerrrrls' niyett ote.* Like it had been something she'd heard in a chick movie or something, like she had been trying to be American, you know? But what the hey, she's paying, why not? She found a place near the airport, you heard planes coming in, they served these humongous margaritas. Remember those glasses, like for a plant, Teen?' Rubbing my leg for emphasis.

'How'd the topic turn to Des Backer?'

'It had just kinda happened. You remember how, Teen?'

Head shake.

Passant said, 'I guess we had been talking about stuff and that started it to talking about guys. And that started it to talking about it being a girls' night out. And that started to someone saying I wonder how Des would have liked this, being with all these girls.'

'Who said that?'

Bettina Sanfelice said, 'Sheryl.'

'I did?'

'Yes.'

Passant grinned. 'If she says I said it, then I said it. I was pretty much happy-time happy. I don't worry about what people think, anyway, always just say what's in my head.'

I said, 'So you brought up Des and — '

'And everyone piled on. Like Truth or Dare without the dare.'

'Everyone piled on except Helga.'

'Everyone with a beating *heart*.'

I said, 'What did Helga do during the discussion?'

'Sat back and listened. I started and told them about Des and me and then Tina broke in and said, 'I was with him, too.' Now, *that* had freaked me out because Tina had always been the shy one and she'd never told me nothing.' To her friend: 'Nothing like four margaritas to get truth past the dare, huh? *Go*, girl.'

Sanfelice stared at the table.

I said, 'So Marjorie Holman spoke last.'

'It was almost like she had been feeling left out, you know? Wanted to be young. Like us, younger and hotter and doing it with Des.'

'Still, she was your boss. That was pretty uninhibited.'

'She drank more than anyone and she wasn't the real boss, anyway. Helga was. And the way she said it — Marjorie — was weird. Not coming out, more like a . . . something weird.'

Bettina Sanfelice said, 'She said, 'That experience is common to yours truly, as well.' When I figured it out, it really shocked me, Ms Holman always seemed so stern.'

Passant said, 'Stern with her legs wide open. And she even got into more details.' Winking. 'She said he did her standing up behind a trailer. Facing her, it was real friendly, almost like they were having a conversation, except they weren't.'

Bettina Sanfelice said, 'She made it sound like

his being inside her was a surprise.'

The three of us stared at her.

She burst into tears. Retched and slapped her hand to her mouth and motioned frantically with the other. Milo scooted out and she ran to the bathroom.

Sheryl Passant said, 'She always had a bad stomach.'

I said, 'She said the same about you.'

'Me? No way. I've liked chili and spicy my whole life.'

'After Marjorie told you about Des, what else did she say?'

'Nothing. She just shut up and drank some more. We had to sit there a long time until she could drive. Helga left first, me and Tina and Ms Holman sat there looking at each other, like no one had anything to say anymore. There was *CSI: Miami* on a big plasma and we just watched then we all drove home.'

'What happened the next day?'

'What do you mean?'

'No mention of the discussion?'

'Nope.' Her hand dropped to fool with her napkin, again. This time she lingered at my crotch.

I shifted away. 'I'm going to make sure Bettina's OK.'

'Don't bother, she's OK — all right, fine, but she's really OK.'

★ ★ ★

It took nine minutes for Sanfelice to emerge from the ladies' room. Her steps were wobbly and her eyes were raw. When she saw me, she gasped.

'You all right?'

'I'm terrible,' she said. '*That* was terrible.'

'Sorry. I didn't intend for it to get that detailed — '

'With Sheryl it would have to. She likes to show off. Her dad's a drunk and he beat her mom all the time, Sheryl never did well in school and her mom died a few years ago. My mom says she's a slut but she's had it hard.'

Glancing toward the booth. 'You *won't* tell my mom, right?'

8

Passant and Milo weren't talking. Passant looked bored.

When Bettina Sanfelice settled back in, Milo said, 'A woman died with Des — '

'Omigod — '

' — and I've got a picture of her. It's not disgusting or bloody, but it was taken after death. Can you handle looking at it?'

Passant said, 'I just saw it, Teen, it's no big deal and you don't know her.'

Sanfelice took a deep breath. 'How can you be sure?'

'I didn't know her, so no way you did.'

'That makes no sense, Sher. Show it to me, sir.'

Milo produced the death shot. Sanfelice studied. Smiled triumphantly. 'I've seen her with Des.'

Passant said, 'Sure you have.'

Milo said, 'Where and when, Bettina?'

'Just once, sir. It was after work. Des and me were the last ones in the office. I was sweeping up and Des was drawing stuff on the computer. Our cars were parked in the lot out back and we walked out together.' Tapping the image with a finger. 'She was there, standing next to his car. Waiting for him, he wasn't surprised or anything.'

'Was he happy to see her?'

'He wasn't happy or *unhappy*. Kind of . . . in the middle.'

Passant murmured, 'Once upon a time . . . '

Sanfelice said, 'I *definitely* saw her. I can tell you what she was wearing, sir. Tight jeans and a black tank top. She had a real good body. I remember thinking Des had himself a hot one.'

Glaring at Passant. *As opposed to . . .*

Passant huffed and slurped her drink.

I said, 'Did Des address her by name?'

'Nope, they didn't talk at all. He just kind of nodded at her and she nodded back.'

'Did they leave together?'

'I can't say for sure. I drove off first and didn't see.'

Sheryl Passant picked up the photo. 'I wouldn't call her hot.'

Milo said, 'How long ago did this happen, Bettina?'

'I can't tell you exactly when but it was way before GHC closed down, I'd guess two months, maybe a little longer, like two and a half.'

'Anything else you can tell us, Bettina?'

'No, sir.'

'OK, thanks, you've been really helpful. If you think of anything else, here's my card.'

'She won't think of nothing, trust me,' said Passant. 'And give me one of those, too.'

★   ★   ★

We watched them leave, Passant yammering as Sanfelice stomped ahead of her.

Milo said, 'Blondie was nudging up against

you pretty blatantly.'

'You have no idea,' I said.

'Serious footsies?'

'Beyond.'

'Oh.'

'I'll send the department a bill for freelance decoy work. Did Passant have anything to add when you got her alone?'

'Nada, she's an airhead. Though she did try to fool with my desert boots. If only she knew, huh? What about Sanfelice over by the john?'

'Please don't tell Mom. Looks like Des was a creature of habit.'

'That *Kill Me* sign's looking bigger and brighter. OK, we're outta here.'

'Italian?'

'You're hungry?'

'I assumed you were.'

'Yeah, I could ingest, we could even stay here. Alternatively, we could go for the mixed antipasto, that headcheese with delicate but smoky overtones, the fried artichokes Roman-style, nice salad with thin-sliced Parmesan and pepperoncini and intensely cured black olives, the big, hot bowl of baked ziti with the bread-crumbs sprinkled on top. If there's still room, there's always the double-cut veal chop with the Sicilian sauce, wedge of spumoni, triple espresso, pump in the caffeine.'

Sliding his bulk out of the booth. 'Not that I've been thinking about it.'

★　★　★

Out in the parking lot, I said, 'Nice lateral pass on the interview.'

He grinned. 'Nice catch. I figured psychological sensitivity was called for.'

'Flattered.'

'It had nothing to do with the fact that I don't sleep with women.'

'That never occurred to me.'

'No?'

'Who is more aware than I of your painful shyness?'

'To be honest, Alex, if we were dealing with men, I'da come out and asked. Because men can't wait to talk about their sex lives. I figured women were different, it would be like oral surgery, but go know. Sorry for your having to deal with Blondie's lack of filter.'

'Mercy me, the trauma,' I said. 'Where's the self-help group?'

He laughed. Turned serious. 'A married woman old enough to be his mama, a wild girl, and a shy, nerdy type. Guy was all over the map.'

'What strikes me,' I said, 'is that none of them seem particularly impacted by his death. There was initial shock but once that wore off, all three discussed him objectively. Same way they did at the cocktail lounge. He meant very little to them emotionally and probably vice versa, but what if Jane Doe was different?'

'Someone Don Juan actually got involved with. Maybe. When you factor in the zip code, he did take her on a fancy date.'

★ ★ ★

Several plates full of Italian food later, I drove back to the city over Benedict Canyon while Milo phoned a judge known to skim rather than read and requested a victim search warrant for Desmond Backer's residence.

The next call was to Santa Monica PD, making nice with the day-shift homicide lieutenant by promising not to tie up her detectives and convincing her to send a locksmith to Backer's apartment as soon as possible.

We reached Santa Monica at the end of a nice beach day; tourists and wild-eyed homeless people divvied up Ocean Front Boulevard. Backer's building on California was four stories of rain-streaked white stucco pimpled by juliet balconies too small to be functional and bottomed by a subterranean lot. The view was the massive, five-story condo across the street.

Three blocks east of the beach bought you the smell of the ocean but no big blue kiss.

The building's interior was cool and gray and sterile. The locksmith was already in place at the door to Backer's second-floor flat, looking sleepy. He said, 'Murder case, huh?' and opened his bag. Milo gave him latex gloves and sheathed his own hands and mine. The locksmith said, 'Must be a biggie,' and got to work. The deadbolt yielded quickly, a receipt was signed, the locksmith tossed his gloves onto the hallway carpet and left.

I waited until Milo called out the all-clear.

Desmond Backer had been trained in structural design and aesthetics but he'd lived in a plain-wrap one-bedroom, one-bath, had made no attempt to personalize.

Brown cloth sofa and matching love seat in the living room, cheap bamboo tables, framed generic photographs of trees, lakes, foxes, owls, eagles. A cinder-block-and-glass-shelf bookcase housed architecture texts and a few large-format paperbacks. Population control, biodiversity, tropical reforestry, renewable fuels.

Plastic-wrapped six-packs of generic spring-water filled the upper shelf of the low-profile fridge. Three bottles of Corona below, along with unopened salad bags and a vacuum-wrapped package of organic trout. The fake-granite counter of the mini-kitchen held a coffeemaker, a juicer, knives in a block, yesterday's paper, still folded and rubber-banded.

No disorder, no obvious blood. No woman's presence.

Same for the puny, dim bedroom nearly filled by a king-sized bed in a black wood frame. A single high window framed the blue flank of the building next door. A birch cube nightstand hosted a gooseneck lamp, a box of tissues, two more books on forestry. No dresser, but part of the closet was sectioned into drawers. Not a lot of clothes, but what was there was high quality. Two cashmere sweaters, navy and chocolate brown, same style as the black one worn by Backer on his last breathing night. Italian loafers and a pair of New Balance running shoes.

Milo inspected the soles of the runners. 'Sand in the grooves, probably jogged on the beach.'

A you-build desk next to the closet hosted a

silver iMac and a second adjustable lamp. In a top drawer, Milo found condoms, boxes of them, in a variety of brands, styles, and colors. Below all that, several pages printed from the Internet. Straight sex, athletic positions, women in ecstasy, genuine or not, nothing cruel or outré.

I said, 'He practiced safe sex but left semen on Jane's thigh and no condoms at the scene.'

Milo scratched his nose. 'Maybe a box of rubbers was another take-home goodie for Baddie.'

'Jane's purse, whatever bedding Backer brought, the BMW,' I said. 'Interesting haul.'

He got down and peered under the bed.

I said, 'Catching Backer in the act of unpeeling a condom would be a perfect time to make your move.'

'Zoned out, off-guard, off-balance,' he said. 'Here comes the big death.'

'The alternative is, Backer didn't glove up with Jane because he did have something special with her.'

He thought about that, returned to the closet, checked a high shelf, then the floor beneath some long coats. Slid out a box. Drawing pads, pencils, erasers, pens, last year's tax return, a few credit card bills, cell phone records, loose photos.

Milo examined the receipts first. 'Not much activity last month . . . talking to someone in Washington State . . . four times — and here's our tyke, again.'

Unfolding four snaps in plastic holders.

Solo portraits of 'Samantha' except for one shot in which the child appeared on the lap of a good-looking woman in her thirties. Next to her a large-jawed, bespectacled blond man and a golden retriever. Decorated Christmas tree in the background, everyone in matching reindeer sweaters.

Dear Uncle Desi, Merry Christmas. Thanks for the play oven, I love to cook on it. Yumm numm. I wish we could hang out. Love, Samantha.

Milo said, 'Someone cared about him,' and headed for Backer's computer.

The screen opened directly to a server, preset by a 'remember me' password. Nine unread e-mails, all spam except for a missive from rickimicki08@gmail.com.

hey lil sib, how goes it? really desi you need to write more miss you, specially sam. write, call, sing a song, send an e-card use a messenger pigeon. lol. Luv xoxox ricki

Milo printed the page, slipped it into an evidence bag. Returned to the screen and checked the toolbar for Backer's recent searches.

'Nothing's been cleared for days,' he said, 'the guy definitely wasn't worried about privacy.'

I said, 'Fits with the direct approach.'

He ran his finger down the list of recently visited sites.

eBay, news outlets, ecology chat rooms, online men's clothing resellers. In a solid block at the bottom, thirty-three porn sites.

'What a shock.' He began scrolling.

Five minutes later: 'Same straight-on stuff. OK, let's see if I can ruin someone's day.'

The Washington State number connected to a message machine. Identifying himself by rank, he left his number.

'You have reached the home of Scott and Ricki and Samantha and Lionel, we're not in now but please blah blah blah. My hooh-hah detective instincts tell me Lionel's the pooch.'

Returning to the closet, yet again, he pawed through the pockets of Desmond Backer's clothing. Four crumpled Trader Joe's receipts, a half-year-old sales slip from Foot Locker for the running shoes, a cheap plastic pen, a few loose coins.

'So what's missing from this picture, Doc?'

'Anything to do with Jane Doe.'

'So — and perish the thought — you could be off about her being a significant other, she was just another booty-cutie.'

'He took Holman to Santa Monica, stayed in the Valley with Passant.'

'So maybe she lives near Holmby? But her clothes say not as a resident — an au pair or something? Time to revisit the hood. But first, this Shangri-la's parking amenities.'

The building's sub-lot was one-third full, and Backer's BMW was easy to spot. Milo gloved up again, peered through the windows, tried the doors, found them locked, ran his flashlight over the interior.

'Nothing looks off, but let's see what the techies have to say.'

I said, 'Backer and Jane got to Borodi some other way.'

'She drove? Why not, a smooth guy like Uncle Desi could probably get women to do all sorts of things. And if I had any idea who the hell she is, I could look for her goddamn car.'

'You up for another visit to the scene?'

'Why?'

'Nothing else comes to mind.'

9

Milo punched in Robin's cell as I headed to Holmby Hills. Her voice filtered through the dash-mounted speaker. 'Hi, babe. Long day?'

Milo said, 'And not over yet, Sugarplum.'

'Big Guy,' she said, laughing. 'You're his receptionist?'

I said, 'No, I'm *his* unpaid driver.'

'Or I'm *his* patient,' said Milo. 'How's it going, kid?'

'It's going well. You guys sound far away.'

'It's the hands-off,' I said, 'ergo the lack of privacy. I should be home within the hour.'

Milo said, 'Privacy? There's something to hide from Uncle M?'

Robin said, 'Never, m'dear. Not over yet as in making progress or just the opposite?'

'Nothing plus nothing, Rob. I'll get him back to you A-sap.'

'Come on over for dinner, Milo. I'll grill something.'

'I drool in anticipation, but Dr Silverman is expecting a cozy dinner.'

'Rick can come over, too.'

'Thanks, kiddo, but he's on call until late. The plan is we grab something at Cedars.'

'Cafeteria food is cozy?'

'Love hurts, darling.'

* * *

A single uniform remained at the construction site, leaning against his cruiser and talking on his cell phone. Yellow tape ran along the fence. The chain was still loose enough to allow a walk-through.

Milo sat up and shot his jaw. 'Oh, gimme a *break!*' Jabbing his finger at the parking ticket pinned under one of the unmarked's windshield wipers.

Before I cut the engine, he was out, ripping the summons free.

The patrolman lowered his phone. Milo strode over to him. 'Were you here when they papered me?'

Silence.

'You just let it happen?'

The uniform was young, smooth-faced, muscular. *A. Ramos-Martinez.* 'You know the traffic nazis, sir. They're on commission, sir, can't talk them out of nothing.'

'Did you try?'

Ramos-Martinez hesitated, decided against lying. 'No, sir. I was keeping my eye on the scene.'

'Gee, thanks, Officer.'

'Sorry, sir. I thought that's what I was supposed to do, sir.'

'That's a lot of sirs. How long you been out of the service?'

'Eight months, sir.'

'Overseas?'

'Anbar Eye-raq, sir.'

'All right, you get a pass, but next time speak up for truth and justice. Got it?'

73

'Yes, sir.'

'Anything happen while I was gone?'

'Not much, sir.'

'Not much or nothing?'

'Pretty quiet, overall, sir,' said Ramos-Martinez. 'That security guard came back, said he was still officially on the job. I told him he could stand out on the street but couldn't gain access. Or park his car anywhere on the street. He usually pulls up here on the dirt, wanted to again. I told him it was part of the scene. He decided to leave.'

'God forbid *he* should get cited.'

Silence.

'He put up any fuss?'

'No, sir.'

'You pick up any ulterior motive on his part? Like wanting to get back in there and alter evidence?'

'He didn't argue, sir. Guess guarding it now's kinda horse after the cart, sir.'

Milo stared at him.

'My dad says that all the time, sir.'

'Can I assume your fellow officers searched the entire premises — house and yard — as I instructed?'

'Yes, sir. Thoroughly. I was part of that. We found some soda cans toward the back of the property, dented and rusty, like they'd been there for a while. They were tagged and bagged appropriately and sent to the lab, sir. No weapons, or narcotics or blood or nothing like that, sir. CS techies said nothing interesting up in that room, either, sir.'

Milo turned to me. 'Where's the nearest hardware store?'

'Nothing's really close. Maybe Santa Monica near Bundy.'

Back to Ramos-Martinez. 'Officer, here's what I need you to do: Drive to the hardware store at Santa Monica near Bundy, buy a good-quality padlock and the shortest chain you can find, and bring all that back A-sap.' Fishing out his wallet, he handed bills to the young officer.

'Right now, sir?'

'*Before* now, Officer. Put a move on — pretend it's a code-two. Don't call in to report your location, either. Anyone fusses, blame it on me.'

'No sweat, sir,' said Ramos-Martinez. 'I don't mind fuss.'

'That so?'

'Yes, sir. Takes a lot to get me worried, sir.'

★   ★   ★

The day had remained warm and the turret should've reflected that. Instead, it felt chilly and dank and my nose filled with stink that didn't exist. The same stench I'd carried around for days after my first visit, years ago, to the crypt on Mission Road. Some old cluster of olfactory brain cells, activated by memory.

Milo slouched and chewed his dead cigar. 'OK, we're here. Give me some thunderous insight.'

'If the killer stalked Backer and Jane, I'm wondering why he chose to strike here. The

75

staircase is pretty well hidden and he'd have to sneak his way up in the dark, be careful not to make noise. If Backer and Jane were close to the staircase, he'd risk being seen or heard well before getting to the top. And with them higher than him, he'd be at a serious disadvantage. One good shove and our boy's tumbling.'

He said, 'So maybe our boy knew Backer and Jane came up here regularly to mess around, and had the lay of the place — pun intended. Hell, Alex, if the two of them were bumping around, heavy-breathing, that would've blocked out footsteps.'

'Familiarity with the site could also mean someone who'd worked here, a tradesmen assigned to the job. Maybe someone who knew Backer through construction. If you find a history of violence, stalking, sexual offenses, you've got something to work with.'

'Jane's jealous sig-oth just happens to be Joe Hardhat?'

'That or someone who'd seen Des with Jane and grew obsessed with her.'

'Job's been dormant for two years, we're talking a tradesman who moved on.'

'Maybe not far enough.'

He looked at his watch. 'You go on home, I'm gonna do my own walk-through of the grounds, stick around until Ramos-Martinez brings the lock and chain.'

'Keeping Doyle Bryczinski out.'

'Keeping *everyone* the hell out,' he said. 'Besides, I'm a prince among men. Why not pretend to have a castle?'

Robin was waiting for me in the living room, all sixty-three inches of her curled on the couch, listening to Stefano Grondona play Bach on old guitars. A white silk dress played off against her olive skin. Auburn curls fanned on the cushion. Blanche snuggled against Robin's chest, knobby blond head resting near Robin's left hand.

Both of them smiled. It can be jarring when a French bulldog's flat face takes on an unmistakably human expression, and some people startle when Blanche switches on the charm. I'm used to it, but it still makes me wonder about the standard evolutionary charts.

I said, 'Hey, girls,' and kissed them both. Lips for Robin, top of the head for Blanche. Unlike our previous dog, a feisty brindle male Frenchie named Spike, Blanche has no jealousy issues. I gave her bat-ears a scratch.

'You look tired, baby.'

'I'm fine.'

'Do you mind going out?'

I was still stuffed with Italian, said, 'Not at all.'

* * *

We drove to a place at the top of the Glen where good jazz was mixed with decent food and a generous bar. The band was off-set and the stand-in sound track was low-volume sax, something Brazilian-tinged, maybe Stan Getz. We drank wine, settled in.

Robin said, 'What's the case?'

I told her.

'Holmby. That's close.'

'No danger, Rob. This was personal.'

I summed up Backer's proclivities, the interviews of Holman, Sanfelice, and Passant.

She said, 'They all sound like soap opera characters.'

'Don Juan and his fan club.'

'If he was a woman, he'd be labeled a slut.'

'Or a courtesan,' I said. 'Or ambassador to a major ally. It's always a matter of pay grade.'

'Borodi Lane is serious pay grade, Alex. Maybe he took Jane there because she was a rich girl.'

'Her clothes didn't say that. I was wondering about someone who worked in the neighborhood. Anyone who spent time there knew the job was inactive and security was lax.'

The food came. The band approached the stage.

Robin took hold of my hand. 'Guess I should give you credit.'

'For what?'

'Not being a Don Juan.'

'That deserves a prize? Fine, I'll take what I can get.'

'Hey,' she said, stroking my cheek. 'Handsome dude with a fancy degree and no mortgage? Not to mention other . . . ahem . . . attributes. You could be partying like it's 1999.'

'Bring on the platform shoes.'

'That's the seventies, dear.'

'See,' I said. 'I'm out of touch, would never survive the meat market.'

'Oh, you'd thrive, sweetie. It would be one thing if you were a twerp with no libido, but I know otherwise.'

'That's me,' I said. 'Sexual Superman with the morals of a saint.'

'You laugh,' she said. 'I smile.'

10

We drove home well fed and watered. As I held the door open, Robin said, 'Nice place you've got here, Don.'

We disrobed in the dark, collapsed under the covers. Afterward, she said, 'That was great, but next time platform shoes.'

★ ★ ★

I awoke at four eighteen, was at my desk five minutes later, pupils constricting as the computer screen filled with light. Plugging in the Borodi address produced a four-year-old squib in *LA Design Quarterly*.

'Masterson and Associates, Century City, will be the architects for a mammoth project planned in Holmby Hills this fall. The 28,000-square-foot residence sits on a 2.42-acre lot on Borodi Lane and will be the LA pied-à-terre for an unnamed foreign investor.'

Marjorie Holman's dismissive comment about Helga Gemein flashed in my head. No need to work, Daddy was a German shipping tycoon.

A stretch, but you needed to be at that level for a project of that scope.

I searched some more, pairing Gemein and Borodi, found nothing.

Five hours later, I was in Milo's office and he

was shaking his head. 'Already checked the assessor, nada.'

'What about the building permit?'

'There's a perfectly legit four-year-old permit on file. And that Century City outfit — Masterson — were the architects, but the property owner of record is a corporation called DSD Incorporated, Massachusetts Avenue, Washington, DC, and for the last thirty-nine months, that address matches the headquarters of a soybean industry lobbyist who never heard of DSD. No corporate listings, anywhere. Maybe they were a sleazeball hedge fund that went poof.'

I said, 'The article said foreign investor.'

'So DSD was a holding company set up as some kind of tax dodge. Does that bother me? Not unless it relates to two bodies in a turret.'

He opened a desk drawer, slammed it shut. Wheeled his chair back the three inches allotted and knuckled his eyelids. His windowless cell was ripe with stale tobacco and fumes from the burnt coffee cooked up in the big detective room. He'd fetched two cups, had finished his. Mine cooled, untouched. Life was too short.

I said, 'Any word on the autopsy?'

'Bodies are stacked up in the fridge closet like firewood, coroner's not seeing this as high priority because cause of death is pretty obvious. I bitched, but they've got a point. The X-ray of Backer's head shows bullet frags in his brain, and Jane's a clear strangulation. What they didn't find was any sign of sexual assault. Oh, yeah, just in case I was getting the least bit cheerful, the only prints that show up in Backer's car are his

81

and Jane's but since she's not on record, big damn deal. She doesn't have a single distinguishing scar, deformity, or tattoo. Though she did get a nose job, a long time ago. I've been trolling the Doe Network and every other missing persons database, but so far nothing, even allowing for a bigger schnoz. And Backer's hard drive turned out to be more of the same: porn, ecology, architecture.'

'Sounds like a Woody Allen film,' I said.

'Sounds like a tragedy. I've already left two messages with those hooh-hah architects, still waiting to hear back. Let's go see what the neighbors have to say.'

★ ★ ★

This time he drove. 'In case the parking nazis return.'

'You've gotten yourself immunity?'

He produced the crumpled ticket. Tore it into shreds and dropped them in the trash. 'I'm a scofflaw.'

★ ★ ★

But for the crime scene, Borodi Lane was stately and sun-splotched. He stopped to check the new chain. Snug.

'I still don't get the point of a half-day patrol, nothing on the weekend.'

I said, 'People capable of building houses like this rarely deal with the day-to-day. Being across the ocean would make it even harder to stay in

82

touch. Some underling probably told a subordinate to order a plebe to maintain security but keep an eye on the budget. A peon lower down the ladder tried to earn brownie points by skimping. Besides, what was to steal? Rotten wood?'

'Unnamed foreign investor. OK, let's get to know the good folk of Borodi Lane.'

★ ★ ★

Six pushes of gate buzzers produced three no-answers and an equal number of Spanish housekeepers answering the intercom. Milo coaxed the maids outside, showed them Jane Doe's picture.

Perplexed expressions, head shakes.

The seventh house was an unfenced brick Tudor, generous but not monumental, fronted by a cobbled motor court. Bentley, Benz, Range Rover, Audi. A young brunette in lavender velour sweats answered the door. Freckles struggled through matte foundation. Long silky hair was tied up carelessly. 'Is this about the murder?'

'Yes, ma'am.'

'Ma'am? I'm twenty-five.'

Milo smiled. 'I vaguely remember being twenty-five.'

She extended a hand. 'Amy Thal. This is my parents' place. Before they left, they told me what happened. Mom didn't even want me to stay but I told her to chill. I always house-sit the cats when they go to Paris.'

'When did your parents leave?'

'Early this morning.' Widening smile. 'Don't worry, they're not fugitives from justice, the trip was planned months ago. But if you want to interrogate them, I can give you the number, even the address of their apartment. Ernest and Marcia Thal, Rue Saint-Honoré. I guess it's possible they're traveling as Bonnie and Clyde.'

She giggled.

Milo didn't.

'Sorry, I don't mean to make light of it; to be honest, it's a little scary. Though I guess it's not hugely surprising.'

'A murder?'

'Something creepy happening there.'

'There've been problems before?'

'That entire dump is a problem. Just sitting there, gathering mold, no security lights at night, the chain's wide open, anyone can walk in. Everyone hates it. My dad wanted to sue whoever owns it.'

'Who owns it?'

'I've heard some Arab,' she said. 'Or maybe a Persian. Some Mideast type, I'm not sure. No one seems to be able to find out. It's not that we're prejudiced, we're certainly not. That place — ' pointing up the block — 'that big apricot thing, is owned by the Nazarians and they're Persians and they're great people. I just don't see the point of framing up and not following through for two whole years. No one does.'

'Any neighborhood rumors about why it's just sitting there?'

'Sure. Money. Isn't it always about money? So

84

why not sell? As in to someone who'll actually build something tasteful.'

'Yeah, it is a little over-the-top,' said Milo.

'A little?' said Amy Thal. 'It's gross. I'm not talking size-wise, who're we kidding, this isn't South Central. But the style, no one can figure it out, that stupid third floor stuck up there like a wart. I'm a design student — fashion, not interior — but you don't need design training to recognize awkward and ostentatious and plain old butt-ugly.'

'I don't know design from badgers and chipmunks,' said Milo, 'and even I can tell.'

Amy Thal smiled. 'Badgers and chipmunks, that's cute — coatis and raccoons, too? Anyway, that's all I can tell you, Lieutenant. I'm just doing the parentals a favor because one of the felines is almost nineteen and we don't want her stumbling into the pool.'

'Could I show you a picture?'

'Of who?'

'One of our victims.'

'There was more than one?'

'Two,' said Milo.

'Oh . . . you're not saying it was some psycho Manson thing, are you?'

'Nothing like that.' Out came Jane Doe's photo.

Amy Thal wrinkled her nose. 'Oh, wow.'

'Ms Thal?'

'I can't be sure but I think I've seen her around. Not regularly, she doesn't live here.'

'Could she work here?'

'I doubt it, everyone knows everyone else's

staff and I've only seen her twice and she just looked like she didn't belong.' Taking another look. 'It definitely could be her.'

'When and where did you see her?'

'When would that be . . . not recently. A month ago? I really can't say. Where would be right there. Walking near that dump. That's what caught my eye. No one walks here, there are no sidewalks.' Smile. 'Which is the point, keep the riffraff out, God forbid it should be a real neighborhood. I didn't grow up here, we used to live in Encino, my brothers and I had sidewalks for lemonade stands, rode our bikes. Once the parentals had empty nest they decided fourteen thousand square feet for two people was a nifty idea.' Shrug. 'It's their money.' Dropping her eyes to the photo, once more. 'I'm really feeling it *was* her I saw. I remember thinking she was cute but her clothes weren't.'

'You saw her twice.'

'But close together — like twice in the same week.'

'Walking,' said Milo.

'Not for exercise, she wasn't dressed for that, had on heels. And a suit. Not a good one. A little tailoring would've improved it significantly.'

'What else can you remember?'

'Let me think . . . the suit was . . . gray. The way it didn't move with her said it had a lot of poly in it.'

'Walking but not for exercise.'

'Strolling past, then stopping and strolling back. Like she was waiting for someone. You have no idea at all who she is?'

'Unfortunately not.'

'Too bad,' she said. 'No ID really messes you guys up, right? I TiVo *CSI, Forensic Files, New Detectives.*'

'Was there a car nearby?'

'Not that I noticed. Hmm, guess that's another reason she stood out. What normal person doesn't drive?'

★   ★   ★

We crossed the street, tried one more house. No one home.

Talking to four more maids, one genuine liveried butler, and two personal assistants on the next block produced no further recognition of Jane Doe.

Back in the unmarked, Milo gave Masterson and Associates another try, connected. 'This is Lieutenant Sturgis, I called yesterday about a crime scene on Borodi La — a *crime* scene. A construction project and your firm is listed — Ma'am, this is a homicide case and I need to — yes, you heard me, correctly, homicide — what I need to know is — OK, I'll wait.'

A minute passed. Two, three, six. Disconnection.

Gunning the engine, he drove, looked back at rutted dirt and curling plywood, the girdle of yellow tape. 'Man's home is his castle. Until it ain't.'

11

Masterson & Associates: architecture. design. development. shared the sixth floor of a heartless tower on Century Park East with two investment firms.

The company's lobby was a duet of pale wood and stainless steel sealed by a wall of glass. Poured cement floor. The seating was black denim cushions set into C-shaped, gray-granite cradles.

Milo said, 'Kinda homey, Norman Rockwell would drool.'

A window on the other side of the glass offered a view clear to Boyle Heights and beyond. It took a while to find the call button: a tiny stainless-steel pimple blending mischievously with the surrounding segment of metallic wall.

Milo pushed. No sound.

A female voice, lightly accented, said, 'Masterson.'

'Hi, again. Lieutenant Sturgis.'

'I gave your message to Mr Kotsos.'

'Then it's Mr Kotsos I'll talk to.'

'I'm afraid — '

'You should be. If I have to come back, it'll be with a subpoena.' Hunching like an ape, he beat his chest.

'Sir — '

'And I'll be needing your name for the paperwork.'

Silence. 'One second.'

She'd underestimated, but not by much. Twelve seconds later, a pudgy little man came out, beaming.

'Gentlemen, so nice. Markos Kotsos.' Deep voice, starting somewhere in the digestive tract and emerging belch-like. Different accent from the receptionist. Thicker, Mediterranean.

Given the cold-blooded lobby and what he did for a living, I'd expected a wraith dressed in all-black, sporting Porsche-design eyeglasses and a complex wristwatch. Markos Kotsos had on an intensely wrinkled white caftan over baggy brown linen pants, sandals without socks, a steel Rolex. Middle-aged, five five, two hundred pounds, give or take, he wore his too-dark hair in a modified perm. Deep tan, too saffron around the edges not to be enhanced by bronzer.

He dropped into one of the granite chairs, folded his hands atop an ample lap. 'Sorry for any inconvenience, gentlemen. What can I do for you?'

Taking care of business in the lobby, because no visitors were expected.

Milo said, 'We're here because of a — '

'Elena told me, a murder on Borodi.' Kotsos sighed. 'That project was ill fated from the beginning. Believe me, we regret taking it on.'

'Who was the client?'

'Who was murdered?'

Milo said, 'I'd prefer to ask the questions, sir.'

'Ah, of course,' said Kotsos.

Silence.

'Sir?'

Kotsos shook his head, sadly. 'I'm afraid I cannot help you with specifics. There was a confidentiality agreement.'

'Between?'

'The client and us. Following cessation of construction.'

Milo said, 'Who sued who?'

Kotsos licked his lips. Stumpy fingers drummed a larded thigh. 'It is extremely unusual for us to take on residential projects. *Extremely.* We are as much developers and conceptualizers as we are architects, thus the projects we choose to accept are massively scaled, complex, more often international than not.'

'Middle East international?'

Kotsos crossed a leg, held on to the heel of his sandal. 'You've been to our website, yes? So you know that Dubai has been a major focus of our work because it is a fascinating locale where financial realities intersect with aesthetic adventurousness in a quite unique manner.'

'Good ideas and the bucks to make them happen.'

Kotsos smiled. 'Which is why the Al Masri Majestic Hotel will be unique and spectacular, an awe-inspiring feat of structural engineering, ten stars and beyond. We are drilling a quarter mile into the Gulf in order to support pylons the size of buildings.'

'The rendering was pretty impressive,' said Milo.

Smoooth operator.

'The reality will be groundbreaking, Lieutenant. Literally and figuratively. We have found a way to support a carrying weight of unprecedented — but you don't care about that, you're here about a murder.' Transforming the word into something trivial. 'At a project with which we haven't been involved in years.'

Milo said, 'Desmond Backer.'

Not an eyeblink. 'Who?'

'One of our victims.'

'One? There is more?'

'Two, sir.'

'So sorry. No, I don't know the name.'

'He was an architect.'

'There are many architects,' said Kotsos.

Milo said, 'This one died at your project.'

'Former project.'

'The permit was pulled by DSD, Incorporated.'

'If that's what the record says, then it is true.'

'Any reason for us to believe otherwise?'

Hesitation. 'No.'

'Sir?'

'The record speaks for itself.'

'Tell us about DSD.'

Kotsos shook his head. 'I'm sorry, as I told you, the terms of the confidentiality — '

'You can't even say who they are?'

'I'm sorry.'

Milo said, 'That was a civil agreement, this is criminal.'

'Lieutenant, I would truly love to help you, but the terms are absolute and the stakes are sizable.'

'Big money.'

Silence.

Milo said, 'You sued DSD for a substantial unpaid balance. They settled but are paying in installments, will use any excuse to stop payment.'

Kotsos sighed again. 'It is not simple.'

'Is there any reason we should suspect DSD — or anyone connected to DSD — of criminal behavior?'

Kotsos thought awhile, brightened and clapped his hands together. 'OK, I tell you this because I do not want you thinking I am hiding anything important. In terms of murder, I cannot honestly point a finger at anyone. Absolutely not, if I could, I would, no one likes murder, life is precious. If, on the other hand, you are investigating financial . . . ' Smiling and running a finger across his mouth. 'I have said enough.'

Milo produced his notepad. 'Homicide, Mr Kotsos. Financial doesn't interest me. Now, how about some names of people who worked for DSD?'

Kotsos's head shake seemed genuinely rueful.

'Here's another name for you, Mr Kotsos: Helga Gemein.'

'Who is that?'

'Desmond Backer's boss. The firm is Gemein, Holman, and Cohen.'

'Never heard of them,' said Kotsos.

'They're into green architecture.'

Kotsos snorted. 'Silly stuff.'

'Green is silly?'

'*Isolating* green as a profound concept, as if it's new, Lieutenant, is pretentious and idiotic. The Greeks and the Romans — and the

92

Hebrews and the Phoenicians and the Babylonians — every civilization of note has integrated natural elements into design, from Solomon's Temple to the Mayan pyramids. That is the natural human way. It is in our chromosomes. And shall we discuss the Renaissance? Would you consider the tri-level church in Rome anything other than deliciously synchronous and organic, despite the unexpected turns of events that led to its sequential nature?'

'You took the words out of my mouth.'

Kotsos said, 'What I am saying, Lieutenant, is that everything good about design relates to harmony. All this flabber about natural materials is . . . air.' Waving pudgy hands. 'Cement is natural, it comes from sand. Sandstone is natural. Does that mean cement and sandstone are the optimal materials for every purpose? Shall we use sandstone for our pylons in Dubai?' Throaty laugh. 'Any architect deserving of his degree considers his surroundings and attempts to integrate.' Leaning toward us. 'Do you know what 'green' has become, Lieutenant?'

'What, sir?'

'A cult of the ignorant. Using recycled cardboard as if it is platinum. Exposing ducts, planting grass on the roof, substituting raw wood for fine finishes. Reprocessing sewer water entitles one to a badge of ascetic honor? A cult, Lieutenant. Self-consciously ironic and aesthetically phony.'

'Smog doesn't bother you?'

Kotsos said, '*Ugly* will not solve *smog*. There is *nothing* new under the sun. The only meaningful question is who gets to hold the reflective lens.'

Passion had propelled him closer to the edge of the chair. Pink had spread under his tan.

Milo said, 'So you've never heard of Gemein, Holman, and Cohen.'

'I have not. Where are they located?'

'Venice.'

'I go to Venice, *Italy*. Now, if you'll excuse me — '

'You're a large firm,' said Milo. 'How many partners do you have?'

'I have never counted.'

'There are no names listed on your door.'

'This,' said Kotsos, 'is not a primary office.'

'What is it?'

'We interview clients from the West Coast here.'

'Would dozens of partners worldwide be a fair estimate?'

'Quite fair.'

'Toss in a bunch of assistants and we're talking a lot of people, Mr Kotsos. So if Desmond Backer applied for a job, you wouldn't necessarily be aware of that.'

Kotsos laced his fingers. 'If he was hired by this office, I would know.'

'What if you turned him down?'

Kotsos tugged at his caftan. 'One moment.'

★ ★ ★

Six minutes later, he was back. 'There is no record of anyone named Backer applying for

94

anything. However, in all honesty, I cannot eliminate the possibility. We don't keep paper records of rejects.' Crooked smile. 'All in the interest of saving trees, so that we may slice them up for veneer. Now if you'll — '

'Do any of your international projects include Germany, Mr Kotsos?'

'It's all on the website. I really need to go. There is a plane to Athens departing tonight and I have not yet packed.'

'Rebuilding the Acropolis?'

Kotsos guffawed. 'That would be a nice challenge, but no. I am traveling for Mama's cooking. Tomorrow is her birthday, she hates restaurants.'

'Spanakopita, keftedes, skordalia?'

Kotsos's eyelids half lowered. 'You are a gourmet, Lieutenant?'

'More like a gourmand.'

Kotsos regarded his own paunch. Two sumos, facing off. 'I agree, Lieutenant, there is no substitute for the occasional bacchanalia. Nice talking to you.'

'One more thing.' Out came the death photo.

Markos Kotsos narrowed his eyes. Placed gold-framed pince-nez on the bridge of a meaty nose. Frowning, he reached into a pant pocket, brandished a white remote the size of a matchbook.

Nothing on the face but a single red button. He jabbed. The glass door clicked open.

'You had best come in.'

★　★　★

95

We followed Kotsos's bouncy waddle up a Makassar ebony corridor lined with mural-sized photos and renderings of Masterson's projects. Resorts, office complexes, government towers in Hong Kong, Singapore, the Emirates, oil-rich sultanates like Brunei and Sranil. Despite all the talk of harmony, the buildings were an ominous collection: looming megaliths, shark-nosed sky-eaters, crenellated monsters armored with steel and gold plating, slathered with quarriesful of marble, granite, onyx. In some cases the design aesthetic began by recalling classical motifs but shifted quickly to a cold, brutal forecast of a Darwinian future.

Spoils to the victor, higher and wider is better, audacious is divine.

Against all that, for all its palatial presumptions, the house on Borodi was puny classical pretense that didn't fit. Neither did a confidentiality agreement to recover fees that would pale in comparison with Masterson's typical commissions.

Kotsos picked up his pace, Jane's photo still in hand, flapping against his hip. We hurried past a dozen unmarked office doors. Silence behind each one. Maybe good soundproofing, but it felt more like no-one-home. At the end of the hallway blocking straight access to Kotsos's corner suite sat a young, straw-haired woman wearing a formfitted, plum-colored suit from the thirties. Black desk, pink laptop. Her fingers kept moving before she deigned to look up.

'Elena,' said Kotsos, showing her the picture, 'what was this woman's name?'

Not missing a beat, Elena said, 'Brigid Ochs.'

Milo said, 'You've got a good memory.'

'I do,' said Elena. Brassy Slavic voice, edged with disdain.

Kotsos said, 'She is dead, Elena.'

'So I gather.'

Milo said, 'Tell us about her.'

'What's to tell? She was a disaster.'

'How so?'

'She was hired for backup. Nothing complicated, just relief on the phone, and all-purpose assistance when I travel with Mr Kotsos or have to be away from my desk for any reason. Her résumé was impressive. Executive sec at eBay and Microsoft and two venture capital firms in Los Gatos, and she appeared bright and eager. Later, we found out everything was forged. So much for *that* agency.'

Kotsos looked stunned. 'Elena, I never knew — '

'No need. I protect you.'

Milo said, 'Which agency — '

'Kersey and Garland. We no longer use them.'

'What was their excuse for not vetting her properly?'

'They were as much victims as we were.' Snort. 'If they'd bothered to actually check her references, a lot of trouble could've been avoided.'

'What, specifically, did Brigid do wrong, ma'am?'

Elena turned to Kotsos. 'Brace yourself: I caught her going places she shouldn't be going.' Tapping the rim of the laptop.

'Oh, no,' said Kotsos.

'Not to worry, she got nothing.'

'Cyber-snooping?' said Milo.

'There was no reason for her to be anywhere near the files. Her job was to meet my needs.'

'How'd you catch her?'

'Keystroke buddy program,' she said. 'Every move she made was traced. I do it routinely. To ensure confidentiality.' Back to Kotsos. 'You see? No worry.'

He said, 'Yes, yes, thank you.'

Milo said, 'Where'd she go other than company files?'

'Nowhere,' said Elena. 'And she got no further than addresses, which she could find anyway in public records. Because I password-protect each and every file. But that was not the point. She had no business sticking her nose in.'

'Who was hired to replace her?'

'No one. I don't want help, it's not worth the time and effort to train someone.'

Milo said, 'What else can you tell us about her?'

'Poor taste in clothes,' said Elena. Taking in his rumpled poly tie, saggy chinos and smiling. Kotsos's wrinkled outfit didn't draw a glance.

'Poor taste, how?'

'Bad fabrics, poor silhouette, careless fit. With outlets and the Internet, there's no excuse for not dressing well. I should've known her carelessness would extend to work.'

'Sounds like she was more devious than careless.'

'Yes, I suppose you're right.'

'What about Desmond Backer?'

'Who?'

'An architect who died with her.'

'An architect,' said Elena. 'Perhaps she had some sort of fixation.'

Markos Kotsos said, 'But of course. Architects are dashing fellows.'

Elena smirked. 'Your limo to LAX and your pickup in Athens are confirmed. I have ordered irises for your mother. Blue, I assume that's OK.'

'Perfect. Thank you.'

Milo said, 'Could we please have an address for that agency?'

'Not necessary,' said Elena. 'Take the elevator to the ground floor.'

★ ★ ★

As we waited by the elevator, a nervous fellow in pinstripes passed by, tugging at his hair.

Milo said, 'Know anything about Masterson?'

The banker stopped. Frowned. Muttered, 'Ghost town,' and continued.

Ding. We boarded. I said, 'Masterson's basically a West Coast clearinghouse office.'

'Just Kotsos and that little battleax. Maybe they launder money for an oil cartel or run an international human smuggling ring or lobby for some cannibalistic dictatorship. The question is, what was Brigid Ochs curious about?'

'DSD used to be headquartered in DC. The smell of international intrigue grows more intense.'

He rubbed his face. 'With friends like you.'

Kersey and Garland, Executive Search and Human Resource Consultants, was tucked into a corner past the ground-floor snack bar, not far from the public restrooms.

The weary older woman who sat at the front desk looked at Jane's photo. 'Oy, her again. *Now* what?'

Jody Millan on her desk plaque. Framed shots of face-painted, costumed grandchildren cluttered her desk.

Milo said, 'Again?'

'That's Brigid Ochs. We dropped her.'

'She's been dropped permanently, ma'am.'

'Pardon?'

'Someone murdered her.'

Jody Millan went white. 'My God . . . that's a . . . whatever you call it . . . morgue shot? I wasn't wearing my glasses.'

'You recognized her without them.'

'That much I could see, but . . . ' Out came half-specs. 'Oh, my God, I'm getting nauseous. Who did it?'

'That's what we're here to find out, ma'am.'

'Then you came to the wrong place. She hasn't been with us for months.'

'After lying about her credentials to get the job at Masterson.'

'*She* sent you here,' said the woman. 'The Russian, should've figured. I'll bet she enjoyed pointing the finger. One little slip-up, she couldn't wait to fire us.'

'Elena?'

'I got her that job and it sure as hell paid off, didn't it?'

'What do you mean?'

'She started as the boss's secretary, ended up snagging him.'

'The boss being Mr Kotsos? She's Mrs Kotsos.'

'The fourth,' said Millan. 'And no doubt determined to be the last.' Wicked smile. 'Are you checking *her* out? She was furious at Brigid.'

'Is there anything interesting in her past?'

Millan picked up a pencil. 'Honestly, no. She was crackerjack. Worked for a top exec at Kinsey and did a bang-up job. And I suppose she had a right to be upset. Still, Brigid was extremely convincing. It's not as if Elena picked anything up, herself.'

'Brigid was a good actress?'

'This town, we get plenty of that, you'd be amazed at the b.s. I get handed. But Brigid didn't come across that way, not at all.'

I said, 'She wasn't theatrical.'

'Just the opposite, quiet, well mannered, didn't play herself up at all. Such a pretty girl but she didn't make the most of it. Almost like she wanted to avoid attention. I know we should've run a background, but Elena was impatient, needed someone *now*.'

'Could we see the application?'

'Sorry, we don't keep records once they leave us.'

'Recycling?'

'There's no need to hold on to trash. I can tell you what she claimed, because I interviewed her

101

personally. Guess I shouldn't claim credit for that. But I'm not going to beat myself up, she came across bright, calm, articulate, eager to please. I don't get deeply into personal data but I do like to get a feel for the person, so I asked her about her background, the basics of her social life. She said she was single and happy to be so. I took that as maybe she was recently divorced or out of a bad relationship. She said she grew up in the Pacific Northwest, claimed to work for one of Bill Gates's top assistants, then said she moved to Los Gatos and spent some time at a tech venture capitalist, then on to eBay, where she did website organization. Her skills seemed perfect for what Elena claimed she needed.'

'Claimed?'

'Trust me, nothing will make that woman happy,' said Millan. 'Truth is, she doesn't want anyone else up there but her and Kotsos. Though, if you ask me, he's gay.'

'Odd couple,' said Milo.

'Hey,' she said. 'This is LA.'

I said, 'Masterson's office seems pretty laid-back.'

'It's a tomb,' said Jody Millan. 'Once in a blue moon, you see someone, but the only two constants are Kotsos and Elena. The only business I've seen is rich foreigners out to lunch, kissing up shamelessly.'

Milo said, 'What kind of rich people?'

'Mostly Arabs, sometimes they're wearing those robes and headdresses. Like sheikhs. Maybe they are sheikhs.'

'Have you sent Kotsos any other people?'

'Temps,' she said. 'Before Elena. Girl's got a work ethic, I'll grant you that.'

'So Brigid Ochs was the first post-Elena hire.'

'Elena said business had grown to the point where she needed backup. Because she and Kotsos were traveling more together.' Head shake. 'I pride myself on reading people well but I really got taken. Everything Brigid told me turned out to be baloney, down to her Social Security number.' Brightening. 'That I might still have. Not that it's going to help you.'

'Why not?'

'After I found out I'd been conned, I ran a trace. The number matches a poor little girl born the same year Brigid claimed, in New Jersey. A kid who died at age five. Hold on.'

She entered a back office, returned with a Post-it. 'Here you go, Sara Gonsalves.'

'Did you confront Brigid?'

'Would've liked to but the number she gave me was disconnected.'

'Where was her address?'

'Santa Monica, turned out to be a mail drop and she was long gone.'

'She died with another person. A man named Desmond Backer.'

'Don't know him. Was Brigid involved in criminal activity?'

'There's no evidence of that.'

'Well,' said Jody Millan, 'she certainly wasn't an upstanding citizen.'

We took the stairs to the sub-lot.

'Brigid Ochs,' said Milo. 'What's the chance that's her righteous name?'

I said, 'Whoever she was, she was obviously curious about the Borodi project and DSD.'

'International intrigue . . . OK, time to call in some favors.'

He flipped through his notepad, found a number, punched and left a vague message for someone named Hal.

As we got in the car, he tried Moe Reed, got voice mail, settled for his other occasional D One backup, Sean Binchy, and asked him to run Brigid Ochs through the databases, including Social Security.

Binchy phoned back in ten minutes. 'Nothing on her anywhere, Loot. There is a Brigitte Oake, spelled like the tree but with an *e* at the end, incarcerated at Sybil Brand, awaiting trial for cocaine, possession with intent. Extensive record for solicitation and drugs, but she's forty-nine. Social Security was kind of anal, said the number had been 'retired' due to misuse. I tried to get confirmation about that five-year-old Sara Gonsalves but it's like she never existed. For some reason I got the feeling they'd been told not to cooperate, but maybe I'm being paranoid.'

'Trust your instincts, Sean.'

'I'm learning to do that, Loot.'

12

A mile before the station, Milo detoured to a taco joint on Santa Monica, inhaled two burritos slathered 'Christmas style' with red sauce and *salsa verde*, gulped a mega-Coke, then a refill. 'All that green talk is making me conserve energy. Onward.'

★ ★ ★

No call-back from Hal the Fed. A note from Binchy said, 'No luck on the Internet.' Milo Googled *Brigid Ochs* anyway, did the same for *DSD Inc.*

Whole lot of zeros.

I said, 'Maybe it won't be about high intrigue and Brigid wanted Masterson's address list so she could help Backer apply for a job there.'

'Along the way, the two of them have fun-time in high-end piles of wood?'

'How do most employees abuse the office computer?'

'Porn.'

'Maybe plywood was hers.'

He sat back, twisted an ear until it turned scarlet. 'Let's try Backer's sister again.'

He dialed, hung up. 'Scott and Ricki and Samantha and bark bark bark.'

The 206 backward directory yielded a name: Flatt, Scott A.

That pulled up a one-page family website showcasing the same holiday photos we'd seen in Backer's apartment, a few more of little Samantha, now around three, and travel shots from half a dozen national parks, plus Hawaii, London, Amsterdam.

Scott and Ricki Flatt were both elementary school teachers.

I said, 'School's out of session, they get summers off, could be anywhere.'

'Gonna be a helluva welcome back.' He spun in his chair, nearly collided with the wall. Mumbled, 'There's a metaphor for you.'

'Brigid told the employment agency she'd grown up in the Pacific Northwest. Skillful liars embed truth in their stories, maybe that part was real and this is about old friends reuniting. Recalling the good old days when she and Des used to park under the stars.'

'Under the stars is one thing, Alex. Why a damn construction site?'

'Maybe the two of them were wild kids, enjoyed trespassing.'

'Nostalgia, huh?'

'Reach your thirties, nothing exciting in your life, nostalgia can take on a certain charm. Reliving the past could explain Backer going beyond the usual short-term shag.'

He phoned 206 information, probed for Backer or Ochs listings. Slammed down the receiver, shaking his head, called the Port Angeles police and talked to a friendly, basso-voiced cop named Chris Kammen. Kammen knew nothing helpful, promised to ask around.

106

'Booty-calls for nostalgia's sake.'

'Strong chemistry can linger,' I said. 'But if Brigid was involved with another man, chapter two could get complicated.'

'Alleged Brigid, who knows what her real name is? I'm thinking it's time to go public. Any reason I shouldn't?'

He was back on the phone to Parker Center before I finished saying, 'Not that I can see.'

Three underlings later, he was transferred to Deputy Chief Henry Weinberg. The DC mainlined smug. 'Sounds like you're nowhere fast.'

'It's a tough one.'

'Thought that was the kind you liked.'

'Up to a point.'

'The point where you're nowhere fast, eh? I suppose I can find it within myself to put someone on it but no station's going to flash a morgue shot on screen, too damn real for civilians. You have an artist who can make her look alive?'

'I'll find one.'

'Do your homework, first,' said Weinberg. 'Then talk to me.'

Milo's obvious first choice was Petra Connor, because she'd worked as a commercial artist before joining the department, had serious talent. A call to her office at Hollywood Division revealed she was in Cabo for R and R with her live-in, Eric Stahl. Additional poking around produced the name of Officer Henry Gallegos from Pacific Division, whose AA in art from Santa Monica College made him Rembrandt. Gallegos was off for the day at Disneyland with his wife and twin toddlers, but agreed to be in by six P.M. if traffic wasn't too crazy.

'Nothing fancy, Lieutenant, right?'

'Just make it so she doesn't scare anyone.'

'Broke my finger last week playing ball,' said Gallegos, 'but I can still do pretty good.'

* * *

That night at home, I checked the late news for the story, got a headful of politics and natural disasters, a horrific child abuse case that made me turn off the tube and hope I wouldn't be asked to get involved.

I played guitar and read psych journals and hung with Blanche and listened to a disk of Anat Cohen wailing on her clarinet and saxophones. Replaying 'Cry Me a River' a couple of times because that was a great song, period. Robin and I ate chicken and mashed potatoes, took a long bath, did lots of nothing. When she yawned at midnight, I joined her and managed to stay asleep until seven A.M.

I found her eating a bagel and drinking coffee in the kitchen. The TV was tuned to a local affiliate morning show. Pretty faces prattling about celebrities and recipes and the latest trends in downloadable music.

She said, 'You just missed that girl's face in the news.'

'Good rendition?'

'I don't know what she actually looks like but the overall draftsmanship was OK. In that sidewalk-artist way.'

I surfed channels, finally found an end-of-broadcast segment. Henry Gallegos wouldn't be giving up his day job but the resemblance was good enough.

I tried Milo's desk phone. He'd installed the recorded message that thanked tipsters in an appropriately professional tone and promised to get back as soon as possible.

The onslaught had apparently begun.

I finished a couple of reports, e-mailed invoices to attorneys, took a run, showered. Milo called just as I was getting dressed.

'Tip-storm?'

'Forty-eight helpful citizens in the first hour. Including twenty-two flagrant psychotics and five psychics posing as helpful citizens.'

'Hey,' I said, 'politicians rely on the psychotic vote.'

He laughed. 'Binchy and Reed and I have been talking to a slew of well-meaning folk absolutely convinced Brigid is someone they know. Unfortunately, none of the facts fit and they're all wrong. The only decent bit of possible is a you-guessed-it anonymous tip from a pay phone. Listen.'

A burst of static was followed by ambient hum. Rising traffic noise drowned out the first few words:

' . . . *that girl. At that unbuilt house.*' Shaky male voice. Old or trying to sound old. Ten-second gap, then: '*She been with Monte.*'

I said, 'Those hesitations sound like fear. It could be real.'

'Too scared to use his own phone and leave a

name, gee thanks. And just to keep you current, my most weak-willed judge said *nyet* to subpoenaing the Holmans' financials so it's air sandwich for brunch.'

'Could you play the message again?'

When the tape ended, I said, 'He knows this Monte well enough to use a name, has seen her with Monte but doesn't know her well enough to use her name. Maybe I've been wrong, the two of them had no relationship and this'll turn out to be one of those wrong-time, wrong-placers.'

'Bite your tongue, right now I'm going with Mr Tipster being too freaked to give me everything he knows. Damn pay phone — guy was lucky to find one that works.'

'Where is it?'

'Venice Boulevard near Centinela. Lots of apartments all around.'

I said, 'He sounded elderly. The pre-cell generation.'

'Brigid's been seen at Borodi by herself, maybe she had some connection to it — worked for one of the subs and she was the one who initiated the tryst with Backer. And maybe she knew Monte — or he knew her because your guess about a tradesman was right on. I'm going downtown, get a hands-on with all the permits for the job. Who knows, maybe it'll be constructive.'

★ ★ ★

At two P.M., he showed up at my house, lugging his scarred vinyl attache case. The customary kitchen scrounge produced last night's chicken and mash, a bottle of ketchup, stalks of celery in need of Viagra. Everything ingested at warp speed while standing at the counter then chased with a carton of orange juice. When he offered Blanche a scrap she turned away.

'Picky?'

'She doesn't want to deprive you.'

'Empathic.'

'She takes the psych boards this year. I'm predicting a pass.'

Stooping to pet, he sat at the table, unlatched the case. 'The general contractor was an outfit named Beaudry, out in La Canada, they specialize in big projects, got a website full of 'em. Not including Borodi.'

'Another confidentiality agreement?'

'I pressed a VP, couldn't pry a damn thing out, including any subs. And no knowledge of anyone named Monte. As if he'd tell me different.'

The attache case rattled, twitching atop the table like a frog in a nasty experiment.

He pulled out his cell phone. 'Sturgis . . . you're kidding . . . on my way.' Standing and brushing bits of chicken from his shirt. 'Bit of conflict at the dream palace.'

* * *

Scraps of yellow tape blew in the breeze. Two uniformed patrolmen held Doyle Bryczinski by his skinny arms. Thirty feet up, another pair of cops restrained a well-dressed, white-haired man, who wasn't going down easy. Shouting, one

111

foot stomping; the uniforms looked bored.

Bryczinski said, 'Hey, Lieutenant. Could you tell them this is my turf?'

Milo addressed a female officer tagged *Briskman*. 'What's up?'

'*This* one and *that* one took issue with each other's presence. Loud issue, a neighbor phoned 911. We got it as a 415, possible assault. When we arrived, they were just about ready to tussle.'

'No way I *tussle*,' said Bryczinski. 'Why would I *tussle*? He's an old *fart*, this is my *turf*.'

Milo placed a finger near Bryczinski's lips. 'Hold on, Doyle.'

'Can they at least let go of me? My arms hurt and I need to get off the leg.'

Milo glanced past Bryczinski, at something big and green-handled, lying just outside the fence. 'Bolt cutters, Doyle?'

'Just in case.'

'In case of what?'

'An emergency.'

'I put that chain there, Doyle.'

'I wasn't going to cut nothing. It was just in case I had to go in.'

'For what?'

'What I said, an emergency.'

'Such as?'

'I dunno, another crime? A fire?'

'Why would there be another crime or a fire, Doyle?'

'There wouldn't, I'm just saying.'

'Saying what?'

'I like to be prepared.'

'If I search your car, Doyle, am I going to find

112

anything criminally useful — or flammable?'

'No *way*.'

'Do I have permission to search your car?'

Hesitation.

'Doyle?'

'Sure, go ahead.'

'Let go of him, guys, so he can give me his car key.'

Milo rummaged in the Taurus, came back. 'Nothing iffy, Doyle, but I'm gonna have these officers bring you to my office so we can chat some more.'

'I didn't do *nothing*, Lieutenant. I can't leave, I'm on the job — '

'The job's temporarily suspended, Doyle.'

'What about my car? I leave it there, I'll get a ticket.'

'I'll put a sticker on the windshield.'

Bryczinski's eyes watered. 'If I don't work, company'll can my ass.'

'We'll talk at the station, Doyle, everything works out, you're back here today. But don't mess with neighbors.'

'He ain't a neighbor, he's a maniac. Claims he owns the place and tried to hit me upside the head when I told him to buzz off.'

★   ★   ★

'Charles *Ellston* Rutger.'

The man cleared his throat for the third time, smoothed back thin white hair, cast a derisive look.

His houndstooth sport coat was high-grade

113

cashmere with working leather buttons, suede elbow patches, and a cut that said tailor-made, but the lapels were several decades too wide. Knife-pressed cream slacks broke perfectly over spit-shined oxblood loafers. His shirt was once-blue pinpoint oxford faded to lavender-gray and frayed along the rim of the collar. A gold gizmo shaped like a safety pin held the collar in place, elevating the Windsor knot of a pine-green foulard patterned with bugles and foxhounds. More fabric erosion fuzzed the tie. Same for a canary-yellow pocket square.

Charles Rutger's driver's license made him sixty-six. Skin as cracked and dry and blotched as the seats of a convertible left open to the elements would have made me guess older. He'd lied about his height and weight, adding an inch or two, subtracting the fifteen pounds that strained the buttons of the sport coat. The white hair, slicked back, waxy and furrowed by comb marks, was topped by a yellowish sheen. Heavy eyelids were specked with tiny wens.

South Pasadena address, not the fashionable part of that city, an apartment unit. The single vehicle registered in his name was a fifteen-year-old maroon Lincoln Town Car. The very same sedan parked haphazardly near the fence.

'Bit of a drive from South Pasadena, Mr Rutger.'

'This is my homestead, I can get here in my sleep.' Plummy voice, vaguely mid-Atlantic, explicitly disapproving.

'You say you own this property?'

'I don't say it, basic *decency* says it. When I

114

heard about what happened, I rushed right over.'

'How'd you find out?'

'The news. Of course.' Charles *Ellston* Rutger tugged his lapels straight.

'The registered owner is a company named DSD.'

'Towelheads,' said Rutger. 'And I won't shrink from saying so. They bomb us and then we kowtow? Utter rubbish.'

'Arabs,' said Milo.

'Who else? Oil money, otherwise known as blood money, came into play, oh did it! In my day, they'd have been told what *for*.'

'Not allowed to buy property?'

'Covenants we called them, and a good thing they were.' Turning back toward the framework. '*Monstrosity*. This was a lovely neighborhood, put Beverly Hills and *those* people to shame.'

'Those people being . . . '

'Beverly Hills people. Hollywood. Now it's *them* with their oil.'

'Can you give us names of people associated with DS — '

'I can't give you something I never knew,' said Rutger. 'The entire transaction was manipulated by slick Jew lawyers. You'd think they'd avoid each other like the plague. Jews and towelheads. But when it comes to money, there's common ground.'

'Sir,' said Milo, 'we're investigating a murder, so if there's something you can — '

'I *know* what you're investigating, I just told you I heard it on the news.'

'And rushed right over.'

'Absolutely.'

'Why, Mr Rutger?'

'Why?'

'Yes, sir.'

'Why not? Last I heard this was still a free country.'

'Mr Rutger, this is a serious case and I don't have time — '

'Neither do I, Officer. Why did I rush over? Because I've been *violated*. Again.'

'Again?'

'This place was mine, Officer. *They* took it from me. And now blood has spilled. Barbarians.'

'Tell me how they took it from you, sir.'

'Tell?' said Rutger. 'I could write you a book. In fact, I've been thinking about doing just that. 'Pillage of the Innocent.' It could be a bestseller, given the way people feel about *them*.'

'How about a summary, Mr Rutger?'

'Why would you want that?'

'So I can understand — '

'Fine, fine, here's your summary: a tragedy that symbolizes everything vulgar this country has become. When I was a boy, a beautifully proportioned *home* sat here. A lovely Georgian Revival designed by Paul Williams. Not that you'd know who that is — '

'Top architect in the forties and fifties,' said Milo. 'Black, so he couldn't live in most of the neighborhoods where he worked.'

Rutger smoothed his tie. 'Be that as it may, he knew how to design a home. My father paid for it with honest work, not by manipulating currency or money-changing or scheming.'

'What business was your father in?'

'Honest business. My sister and I grew up in bucolic splendor. Not that she cares . . . so what do *they* do? Demolish our lineage and put up *that*.' His chin quivered. 'Visigoths.'

'You were opposed to selling DSD the property but your sister disagreed?'

Rutger glared. 'Haven't you been listening? They *stole* it from under me.'

'How?'

No answer.

'Sir?'

'No need to get into any of this, Officer.'

'I'd like to anyway.'

'Bully for you, but I do not wish to discuss personal matters.'

'Homicide makes everything public, Mr Rutger.'

'That does not concern me.' More chin calisthenics. Rutger's eyes filled with tears. Ripping the pocket square loose, he dabbed. 'Blasted dust.'

I said, 'You came here because you felt your family's memory was being sullied all over again.'

Rutger stared at me. 'You're Jewish, aren't you? My father used to play golf with Rabbi Magnin. Now, there was a shrewd man, used family money to build that temple of his. *Big* money, from San Francisco. His brothers were haberdashers, knew how to turn a nice profit.'

Milo said, 'Are you making an actual claim of ownership to this property, Mr Rutger?'

117

'I would if I could find a knight errant willing to do battle.'

'A lawyer to take your case.'

'Cowards,' said Rutger.

'OK, sir, you need to avoid any more confrontations — hold on, let me finish. Yes, it's a free country but freedom means responsibility. You're an educated man, you know that.'

Rutger humphed. 'Last I heard, this was still a free country.'

'Sir, this is a crime scene. No unauthorized entry will be tolerated.'

'That's what *he* said — that fool in a uniform. He was rude and uncouth and I was compelled to take action.' Holding up two fists. He refolded the handkerchief, repeated until he'd produced a perfect dimple. 'I'm leaving now, Officer, but I will not accept any arbitrary pronouncements banning me from my — '

'I have no objection to your driving by, Mr Rutger. But please don't stop and try to enter for any reason. And if you do observe something out of the ordinary, call me. Here's my number.'

Rutger regarded the business card as if it were tainted.

'Sir?' said Milo.

'Just like that?' Rutger snapped his fingers. 'You command and I obey?'

'Mr Rutger, I'm defining limits to avoid future misunderstanding. You may drive by to your heart's content but do not try to enter the property.'

Charles Ellston Rutger drew himself up. Jacket

buttons battled his belly. 'At this time, I see no reason to return.'

'Good choice, sir.'

'This is America. I don't need you to define my choices.'

13

Rutger's Town Car rumbled off, squeaking on bad bearings and belching exhaust.

Milo exhaled. 'Well, that was different.'

He phoned in Rutger's name. Several moving violations, nothing criminal. 'Crazy old coot but for all his attachment to this heap, I don't see him having the stamina to climb those stairs with a weapon, dominate, and double-murder.'

'Agreed,' I said. 'And despite his age, he doesn't sound like our tipster.'

We drove back to the station where he let Doyle Bryczinski simmer in an empty interview room and searched the county assessor for the Borodi property's previous owners.

Only one: the Lanyard A. Rutger Family Trust, established twenty years previously. The trust had sold the place fourteen years later, the transaction handled by Laurence Rifkin, Esq, of Rifkin, For-ward, and Levitsky, Beverly Hills. Their website pegged them as tax and estate lawyers.

Milo said, 'Start at the top,' phoned and asked for Rifkin. A mellow baritone came on the line surprisingly quickly. 'Larry Rifkin here. Police? What's going on?'

Milo summed up.

Rifkin chuckled. 'I'm not laughing about murder. I'm laughing at theater of the absurd. Good old Charlie.'

'You've got a history with him?'

'I can't believe he's still claiming he was defrauded. He was the one who pushed the sale in the first place, Lieutenant. On top of being crazy, he must be going senile.'

'So any claim of fraud is groundless.'

'Groundless? It's insane. Here's what it boils down to: Lanyard, their father — Charlie's and Leona's, that's Charlie's sister — made some money in manufacturing and investments but by the time he'd died, he'd lost quite a bit in the market and once debts were settled there wasn't much estate left. You know the rich, *my* treasures, *your* junk? Paintings Charlie thought were priceless turned out to be piddling, same for a bunch of supposedly rare books that weren't first editions. The only sizable asset was residential real estate: three houses, worth maybe five mil at the time. The place on Borodi was the biggest-ticket item. Lan built it back in the forties, got Paul Williams to design, the place was gorgeous. There's also a chalet-type weekend place with a dock on Lake Arrowhead, and a three-acre spread in Palm Springs. Lan died ten years ago, made it to ninety-one, but Barbara — his wife — died when she was much younger, so everything went to the kids. Leona's a doctor, oncologist, lovely lady. Lan was a perceptive man and named her the executor. Technically, that was logical but it accomplished the obvious.'

'Family strife.'

'Charlie strife. We — my dad was still alive, headed the firm — tried to talk Lan out of designating Leona, suggested we should execute. Or Lan could find someone at one of his banks.

121

He wouldn't hear of it.'

'And Charlie went ballistic.'

'Nuclear. Pitting one sib against the other is always a disaster and these sibs never had much in common to begin with. Not that Leona didn't try to make nice with Charlie. You won't meet a more reasonable human being. But Charlie's another matter, you don't need to be a psychologist to see why he resents Leona. She's everything he isn't: smart, accomplished, happily married, a gem.'

'Charlie never got it together.'

'Charlie has spent nearly seventy years in a dream-state.'

'Delusional?'

'That's another name for it,' said Rifkin. 'I can tell you all this because we don't represent him and nothing's confidential. In fact, he became our adversary, has threatened to sue us numerous times.'

'Over what?'

'Over he needs money and thinks Leona will give it to him if he makes enough noise.'

'Who represents him?'

'No one. He files his own paper, thinks he's smarter than everyone else. Needless to say, he gets wiped out every time.'

'Likes to think he's a lawyer.'

'And a stockbroker and a financial advisor and a freelance investor, you name it. Prior to the house being sold, he was trying to syndicate the sale of an island off Belize, lost everything he put into it. He's been married four times, no kids, is basically broke and stuck in a one-bedroom in South Pas. Sad, but it's his own doing. Leona has tried to be fair, offered to set up a trust for him managed by professionals, so he can build up a little net worth. He accuses her of trying to control him. She's never taken a cent as executor, has been scrupulous about every-thing being divvied up fifty-fifty. Which brings me back to my original point: It was Charlie who spearheaded selling the properties. That's why his bitching about it is so crazy.'

'Leona didn't want to sell?'

'Absolutely not. Her idea was to keep everything in trust for future generations. Set up a separate management account to take care of expenses.'

'But Charlie has no kids, so he figured she was bypassing him for her heirs.'

'I understand that objection,' said Rifkin. 'But it's not as if Charlie wasn't making money from Borodi. The house was renting out at twenty grand a month, and after tax and management fees, he was still netting six figures.'

'Who were the tenants?'

'Various industry people needing temporary quarters during shoots. Not stars — producers, directors. Payments came directly out of the film budgets, everything was smooth until Charlie started dropping in at the house and demanding to see if they were keeping it up to his specifications. Needless to say, no one wanted to put up with that, so bye-bye studio rental deals. Which Charlie needed a lot more than Leona. Whatever he gets hold of slips right through his fingers.'

'So he agitated to sell.'

'Not just Borodi, all three properties. One of those out-of-the-blue demands. He's impulsive, that's his basic problem. Selling directly contravened the substance and spirit of Lan's trust, Leona would've been in her rights to tell Charlie to screw off. But she didn't want to fight, so she compromised. She *was* steadfast about Palm Springs and Arrowhead — likes to use both places on weekends and so do her kids. And she felt the value of a two-plus-acre lot in Holmby would keep climbing, it paid to wait. But Charlie kept nagging, so she caved.'

'The records I've got said it sold for eight million dollars,' said Milo.

'I know what you're thinking,' said Lawrence Rifkin. 'Four mil each is nothing to sneeze at, maybe Charlie was the smart one, especially given his age. The problem is, Lieutenant, once the trust was broken, the inheritance tax kicked in. Toss in commission and other fees and Charlie and Leona ended up with closer to one and a half million each.'

Milo said, 'I'm still not sneezing.'

'No, of course not,' said Rifkin, not quite convincingly. 'But that's nothing long-term for someone like Charlie, who still thinks he's a financial genius. It didn't take long for him to plow through most of it and start howling that we sold too cheap. Unfortunately for him, he'd been involved every step of the way and we had documentation.'

'How much is most of it?'

'All but half a mil. *Then* he had the gall to ask

124

us to represent him so we could cook his books and beef up the deduction. Meanwhile, he's still threatening to sue us. Refusing him politely took some self-control.'

'So he had a half million left.'

'He goes to Europe several times a year, flies first-class, stays at the Crillon, eats at Michelin star restaurants. If he's got a hundred K left, I'd be shocked. I can't believe he's still screaming about the sale. It's been a while since I last heard from him and I figured he'd finally moved on.'

'How long?'

'I'd say . . . two years . . . hold on and I'll tell you precisely . . . here it is, twenty-eight months ago. Charlie bitching that he needed a new car and Leona was refusing to pay for one. Why should she? He's a lousy driver, no sense cracking up another one. But it wouldn't have mattered if Leona had bought him a brand-new Rolls. Every time he gets what he wants, he comes back for more. As I said, he lives in a dream-state. Hearing about that murder probably got him fantasizing about being lord of the manor. Or he just wanted to prevent himself from feeling like an ass, so he twisted reality. Because Leona was right. Eight mil was a fair prize then, but the value of the lot has skyrocketed. If they sold today, they'd probably get twenty-five mil.'

'With a nice house on it.'

'Even without a house, Lieutenant, a parcel that size is highly desirable.'

'The folks they sold it to, DSD,' said Milo. 'Tell me more about them.'

Silence.

'Mr Rifkin?'

'I'm been forthright, Lieutenant, within the limitations of my professional standards.'

'Charlie's fair game for discussion but DSD isn't?'

'There's an agreement.'

'Confidentiality.'

'Binding confidentiality.'

'Can you tell me why, Mr Rifkin?'

'Certainly not, Lieutenant. That's the point.'

'Everyone DSD has done business with seems to be held to secrecy.'

No reply.

'Mr Rifkin, are we talking some big-time political types?'

Silence.

'Foreign intrigue, Mr Rifkin?'

'I'm sorry, Lieutenant.'

'A criminal investigation trumps a civil agreement, sir.'

'You've gone to law school, Lieutenant?'

Milo wiped his face. 'Let's shift gears for a moment, sir. Is there anything you think I should know about Charlie or anyone else as it relates to murder?'

'You think Charlie could've killed someone?'

'Two people *were* murdered.'

'May I ask how they were killed?'

'Gunshot and strangulation.'

'Well,' said Rifkin, 'Charlie does own firearms but the ones I know about are antiques, inherited from Lan. Would he use them if he got angry enough? I suppose. His temper is nasty

126

and he is unstable.'

'What about strangulation?'

'Doesn't that take strength, Lieutenant?'

'Strength and persistence.'

'Then I doubt it. Charlie's health is subpar. Liver, heart, prostate, diabetes, arthritis. Leona pays his medical bills and they're extensive. And I have to be honest, he's a blowhard but I've never actually known him to follow through on anything.'

'Is there anything about the sale to DSD that could conceivably link to murder?'

Rifkin said, 'Good try, Lieutenant.'

Milo said, 'All this hush-hush is making DSD look more and more suspicious.'

'Be that as it may, Lieutenant. Good luck with your murders.'

★　★　★

Doyle Bryczinski was on his third can of 7UP.

Milo sat down close, scooted closer. 'OK, Doyle, what's the story?'

'About what?'

'Going back there with those bolt cutters.'

'Nothing, sir.'

'Bolt cutters and talk about crime and fire isn't nothing.'

'I'm sorry, sir.'

Milo's big hand landed on Bryczinski's scrawny shoulder. 'Doyle, if there's something you want to tell me, now's the time to help yourself.'

'What do I need help with?'

'Think about it, Doyle.'

'I'm thinking I don't need help.'

'Why'd you go back?'

'It's my place, that's all.'

'Your place?'

'My job. I know it better than anyone.'

'Exactly,' said Milo.

'Huh?'

'What strikes me, Doyle, is that doing a murder there would be tough for someone who wasn't familiar with the place. It gets real dark at night, that rear staircase is hidden away. You'd have to know where to find it, be super-careful walking up those wooden stairs without being heard. Though your shoes do look pretty quiet.'

'They're OK. Only I never did nothing. And no matter any shoes, I'da been heard.'

'Why?'

'My leg's fucked up, it drags.'

'Even with those quiet shoes?'

'They got soft soles,' said Bryczinski, 'but also steel arches, real heavy to lift.'

Milo eyed the soda can. 'If you're thirsty, feel free.'

'I'm OK.'

'Let's go back to the night of the murders and where you were.'

'Zactly what I told you.'

'Sleeping and taking care of your mother.'

'Buying the diapers for my mom. This time I got the receipt.' Pulling a scrap from his shirt pocket. 'Nine forty-eight, like I told you, I'm at the CVS.'

Milo examined the date. 'You found the

receipt because you've been working on an alibi, Doyle?'

'You asked me all those questions the first time,' said Bryczinski. 'So I looked for the receipt. Now you got it.'

Milo waved the paper. 'This is OK, as far as it goes, Doyle, but it really doesn't mean much. You coulda gone home, driven back.'

'Maybe coulda, but didn't.' Bryczinski's eyes remained calm.

'Monte,' said Milo.

'What?'

'Who's Monte, Doyle?'

'Ain't that a card game?'

'It's also a man's name.'

'Not any man I know.'

'Why the cutters, Doyle?'

'What I said, an emergency.'

'It's a crime scene, Doyle.'

'It's a crime scene now, but it's not gonna be a crime scene forever. You don't give me the key to that chain, I got to get in.'

'Emergency,' said Milo. 'Like the place burns down.'

'What I said was just in *case* the place burns down. I need the job, want to do it right.'

'You think of it as your place.'

'I know it better than anyone. *They* didn't.'

'Who?'

'Those two. Look what happened to them,' said Bryczinski. Reaching for the soda can, he took a long, slow sip.

'Their fault?'

'I'm not saying that, I'm saying it was stupid

129

to go in there at night.'

'What's your theory about the murders, Doyle?'

'They went up there to fool around, I dunno, maybe some psycho crashed the party. That's my point: Way the chain was before, anyone could get in.'

'So you should be happy I put on a new one.'

'Leave the key, I'll say thank you. Now I need to get back there. Can I have that ride?'

'Happy to arrange it, Doyle. If you take a polygraph before you leave.'

Bryczinski's eyes widened. 'Company gave me a poly when they hired me. I passed with honors, ask 'em for a copy.'

'So you wouldn't mind doing it again.'

Bryczinski thought. 'Hell, why not? If it don't take too long.'

★ ★ ★

Detective Three Delano Hardy was the closest to a polygraph specialist the day shift had going. He hadn't administered the test in over a year, wasn't even sure where the gear was, but he agreed to look for it.

Ninety minutes later, the procedure was over and Hardy stepped out of the room, shaking his head. 'A little jumpy on baseline, but I'm not seeing deception, not even close, sorry.'

Milo took the printout. 'Thanks for trying, amigo.'

Milo and Del had partnered a long time ago, until Del's devout wife had objected to her husband working with a homosexual.

Del said, 'No sweat, Big Guy. Good luck.'

★ ★ ★

A uniform drove Bryczinski back to Borodi. I scanned the poly results.

Milo said, 'You see something?'

'Nothing but truth,' I said. 'Especially given the anxious baseline. He's not a cold psychopath able to fake the machine.'

Milo said, 'But he is overinvolved with that site. Him and Charlie Rutger.'

'Must be the edifice complex.'

We returned to his office, where he picked up a fresh message slip. 'Well, well, well, Professor Ned Holman wants to talk.'

He returned the call. 'Professor? Lieutenant Sturgis . . . yes, sir, of course I remember . . . that so? No prob, I can be at your house in — all right, yes, I know where it is. An hour would be fine.'

Dropping the receiver in its cradle, he said, 'First time we met him, he was all mellow. Now just the opposite, definitely something on his mind. Wonder what *his* baseline is.'

14

Ned Holman had chosen to meet at a public parking lot in Playa Del Rey, the westernmost tip of the district where the neighborhood turns to a village and the ocean washes past dreamily.

Just a few miles past the Bird Marsh, where the bodies of four women had shown up last year, minus right hands, and facing east. Milo and Moe Reed had closed that case, solved two other homicides in the process.

Not a word about it as we sped past. Like a lot of driven people, he prefers the agony of living in the moment.

Holman's van was pulling into a handicapped slot just as we arrived. Other than us, no other vehicles. The van's door glided back, a ramp slid out. By the time we were out of the unmarked, Holman had rolled down in his chair and was watching the breakers.

He wore gray sweats that accentuated the heft of his upper body and tried to do the same for wasted legs. His beard was neatly trimmed, his hair plastered down hard, to resist the breeze.

We positioned ourselves between his chair and the sand.

'Thanks for coming, gentlemen. This is a place I go to relax.'

'What's on your mind, Professor?'

Holman watched a solitary beachcomber parallel the tideline, fishing through sand with a

132

metal detector. Stopping to inspect something shiny, the man tossed it back.

Holman said, 'I see them out here all the time. No one ever finds anything.' Smiling. 'Maybe everything's already been discovered.'

'Oh, I don't know, sir,' said Milo. 'My job, I'm learning new stuff all the time.'

'Good for you.' Holman licked his lips. 'This is extremely difficult, but I feel I need to.'

Thick fingers drummed the wheels of his chair. 'I want to be clear, at the outset: I love my wife. She takes good care of me.'

Tightening up on the last three words. 'Why should I complain if she has needs?' Holman's barrel chest heaved. 'Like many people in our situation, Marjie and I engage in mutual deception. She pretends not to miss what we had, I pretend not to know she's pretending.' Inhaling. 'Thirty-eight years has cemented our relationship.'

'Makes sense,' said Milo.

'So I don't blame her,' said Holman. 'I won't claim it doesn't bother me, but I'm not tormented.'

The beachcomber picked up something else. Held it to the light. Discarded it.

Holman watched with satisfaction. Grew grim. 'The ones that peeved me were so-called friends of mine, and even there, I know I'm being irrational. Two guys, in particular, part of our social group. After my accident, my relationship with them changed because it had been based on tennis, basketball, squash, all that good stuff.'

A heron soared west. Needle-nosed, blue-gray

133

pterodactyl with a six-foot wingspread. Stalking my koi pond, the bird would be the enemy. Out here, a magnificent creature.

Ned Holman said, 'I'm running on because I want you to understand Marjie. She's not some slattern, she's a fine woman.'

A button-press rotated the chair away from us. We shifted to face him. Western light limned his bulky frame with a bright silver aura.

'Sometimes, when she goes out, I follow her,' he said. 'Not every time, not even most of the time. I don't know why I do it. Perhaps its because when she leaves, the house grows silent in a rather repugnant way. Somewhat like a mortuary, I suppose, and being alone makes me feel moribund. Marjie makes it easy, she's a creature of habit, always ends up in the same place. Places.'

Milo looked at me.

I said, 'Where's that, Professor Holman?'

'In the common parlance, no-tell motels,' said Holman. 'Washington Boulevard, near the Marina, any of four classy establishments. I station myself across the street. Used to convince myself I was doing it for Marjie's sake. So she'd be safe. Of course, that's rubbish, I do it for the illusion of control, though I will say I'm tiring of it. Perhaps someday Marjie will tire, as well.'

I said, 'Four motels, but there was an exception.'

Holman's bright blue eyes fixed on mine. 'I'm rambling along and you already know the punch line. Yes, there was an exception, I'd decided not to say anything but then it bothered me and I felt

134

incumbent to tell you.'

'We appreciate that.'

'I hope so . . . I'd already known about him and Marjie. I'm referring to Backer, of course. How did I know? Because I'm not an unperceptive dolt. There was an office get-together for the firm, cheap wine and stale crackers. Marjie thought it would be good for me to get out. While nibbling, I caught her and Backer exchanging a glance. Nothing flagrant, but I've had training in picking up nuance and men who've been with Marjie get a certain look. Does that sound paranoid?'

I said, 'There's paranoia and there's reasonable anxiety.'

'Yes . . . well, I'm not anxious. Not anymore. The game's become part of our domestic routine and I find it calms me . . . comfort of the familiar. In any event, I know a meaningful glance when I see one. I won't say it didn't surprise me, Backer was younger than Marjie's usual . . . companion. That I found a bit disconcerting but as I thought about it, what difference did it make? This isn't about her feelings for me, it never is, it's about physicality and who better than a younger man? So when she told me the following week that she'd be staying late at the office, I said to myself, Aha, and followed. And sure enough, Backer's car was out back and she'd parked right next to him. The parking lot was small, I clearly couldn't stay there, and finding parking on Main Street, even with a handicapped sticker, isn't easy. Plus, my hot rod's not exactly inconspicuous — could I

135

trouble one of you to fetch water from the van? It's in a holder just right of the arm-brake.'

I went over and retrieved a black plastic squeeze bottle. The van's interior was spotless, but stale smelling. No obvious evidence of extreme cleanup. When I got back, Holman was saying, ' . . . so I decided to circle — thank you.' Swigging and licking his lips. 'It didn't take long for Backer's BMW to pull out and head north. I followed, made sure to allow several car lengths — something I've picked up from police shows. Am I right?'

Milo smiled. 'Good technique, Professor Holman.'

'Professor emeritus, Lieutenant. That's Latin for has-been. Be that as it may, when Backer reached Wilshire and kept going, I was surprised. He turned east and continued beyond West-wood, didn't turn until Comstock, then headed north, again, to Sunset. You see where I'm going with this.'

Milo said, 'Borodi Lane.'

'When I saw the news this morning, I was stunned. Mulled for a while and decided I needed to call you. Good citizen, and all that.'

'We really do appreciate it, sir.'

'Do I get extra points for humiliation? A psychic Purple Heart, perhaps?'

Neither of us replied.

Holman said, 'Back to Borodi Lane. You'll be wanting to know exactly when this occurred, correct?'

'Yes, sir.'

'And I can tell you precisely. April second.

136

Right after April Fools', at nine twenty-eight P.M. I keep a log of Marjie's adventures. But this turned out *not* to be Marjie's adventure. I should've known, she really is a creature of habit, no reason for her to break the pattern.'

She already had, behind a construction trailer in Santa Monica. No sense stomping her husband's toehold on dignity.

Milo said, 'Backer was there with another woman?'

'*That* woman,' said Holman. 'The one whose face was in the news. And yes, I'm certain, because she and Backer went out to eat afterward and I got a good look at her.'

'Not your wife, but you continued following.'

'Because in the beginning I was pretty sure but couldn't be *certain*. It was dark when they left, they hustled quickly into Backer's car. The woman appeared shorter than Marjie, different hair, different walk, but I wasn't close enough to be confident of my judgment, so I stayed on their trail.'

'Where'd they go for dinner?'

'Beverly Hills. Kate Mantilini, Doheny and Wilshire. Fortunately, they got a window seat and I was able to cruise by and felt tremendous relief. Then I realized Marjie was still out there and suddenly I *needed* to know where she was. So I called her landline at the office and she answered, said she was working on a proposal that would probably end up nowhere because Helga never followed through on anything.'

Milo said, 'Backer's car was at the office but you didn't see the woman back there.'

'But she must've been nearby, Lieutenant, because she wasn't inside the office with Backer and Marjie.'

'How do you know?'

'This morning Marjie and I were watching the news and the woman's face came on, Marjie didn't react in the least. I know my wife, gentlemen. If she'd met her, she'd have said something. And she'd also have told you when you questioned her. So my guess is the woman was either waiting outside the office, not in the lot or near it, or she was already at Borodi when Backer arrived.'

'Was another car parked nearby?'

'If there was,' said Holman, 'I didn't notice. But I wasn't paying attention to cars.'

He turned to watch the diminishing form of the beachcomber.

Milo said, 'What else can you tell us about Backer and this other woman's behavior?'

'Nothing.'

'You're sure it was the woman you saw on TV?'

'I'm absolutely certain. The image on TV was a line drawing, but to my eye, a rather good resemblance. She's — was a good-looking woman. Young — thirty, thirty-five, to me that's young. Good figure. Great figure, voluptuous but taut. As if she worked out. Not too tall, I'd say around five four, well below Marjie's five seven.'

I said, 'When you saw her and Backer in the restaurant window, what was their demeanor?'

'They didn't seem particularly enthralled. Nor were they miserable. Two people reading menus.

138

I guess I'd say bland.'

'Did you ever see the woman again?'

'Never.'

'What about Backer?'

'Him I saw a few times,' said Holman. 'At the office, coming and going.' Blinking. 'I have to say, Marjie having anything to do with him surprised me. He didn't seem her type.'

'How so?'

'Shallow.'

'How so?'

Holman's jaw set. His beard bristled. 'No doubt my opinion is informed by the fact that I'm fairly certain he boffed my wife. But I'd like to think I'm also a decent judge of character. I don't want to talk ill of the dead but to be frank, he struck me as a superficial little twit. The type who spends too much time at the mirror.'

Milo said, 'You didn't like him.'

'I didn't know him well enough not to like him.'

Milo studied him.

Holman's eyebrows rose. 'You're kidding.'

'About what, Professor?'

'You're actually wondering if *I* could've done it? Well, I'm flattered, gents. That you'd think me capable. But why would I bother? Nine men in five years have bedded my wife. What reason would I have to wreak vengeance on one particular horny little twit?'

Holman's lips clamped tight. 'No, I didn't care for Backer. He was fluff. But I don't care for most people. And whatever I felt about him did not rise to the level of violence.'

Milo said, 'Professor, we really do appreciate your coming forward, most people would have taken the easy way out. Is there anything else you'd like to tell us?'

'No, sir,' said Holman. 'Now you're going to leave and I'm going to stay here and watch the ocean.'

★　★　★

Milo gunned the unmarked past the marsh, continued east on Culver. 'What just happened? Helpful, self-demeaning citizen or smart guy playing with us?'

'Maybe neither,' I said.

'Then what?'

'Professor Holman found a way to unload a whole lot of pent-up misery while feeling momentarily heroic.'

'Free therapy? So who bills him, you or me?'

'You can have it,' I said.

'Poor bastard. But he did just admit to being a chronic stalker, which fits our jealousy scenario. A bunch of middle-aged lotharios with his wife is one thing, Backer's youth and vitality pushed him over the edge, he kept churning it, over and over, the rage didn't fade so he hired a hit man. Who he was able to tip off about Borodi being a nookie-spot for Backer.'

'Then why call for a meet where he gives himself a motive and admits he resented Backer?'

'He's an intellectual, Alex, thinks he's smarter than us. A linguist, to boot — what do those guys

140

do? Manipulate language. But maybe he just screwed himself by giving me grounds for a warrant on his financials.'

He phoned John Nguyen, asked the deputy DA what he thought. Nguyen said, 'Iffy at best but you can try. Who do you have in mind?'

Milo said, 'Judge Ferencz turned me down, any suggestions?'

'Not really.'

'What about Judge Hawkins, John?'

'Hawkins died last month.'

'Damn.'

Nguyen said, 'Your warmhearted sympathy toward his loved ones is overwhelming. If you want, I can ask around.'

'Thanks, John.'

'I'm talking a few calls, not worth a thanks.'

★ ★ ★

At Lincoln, Milo switched the police radio to felony Muzak. Too early for waves of after-dark violence but plenty of minor-league infractions to keep uniforms busy.

I said, 'If Holman's not the killer, he still gave you something useful: Backer and Brigid were at Borodi two months ago, lending support for a long-term relationship and suggesting it was a habitual spot for them. Maybe she's using a false identity out of self-defense, not criminality. As in running from a rabidly jealous ex.'

'Meaning don't lose sight of her as the prime victim, OK, time for Hal again.'

'Who exactly is he?'

'Homeland Security, owes me more than one favor.' Punch punch punch, voice mail. His second message was more detailed, click. 'Holman doesn't shake out dirty, there's still the fact that Brigid was snooping in Masterson's files and scoping out Borodi by herself.'

I said, 'The elusive DSD Inc.'

'Whom everyone seems to think are Arabs and that worries me. All I need is some jealous emir as a prime suspect.'

Two traffic lights later: 'Backing away from all that, I've got plenty of mundane local issues to deal with. Like finding out if any non-antique .22s are registered to Loony Charlie Rutger, scanning the moniker files for particularly nasty Montes, somehow getting lists of subs who worked Borodi, and checking for violent felony backgrounds.'

'Abundance of riches,' I said.

'I'd rather have cash.'

15

Reed and Binchy listened to their instructions out in the hall because four people can't fit in Milo's office.

'Sean, I need you to pay a personal visit to an outfit downtown called Beaudry Construction. The object is to get their employment list going five years back. I'm talking names of every single yahoo who worked for them, not just at the Borodi site. In a perfect world, you'll find our boy Monte. Beaudry's going to jerk you around because everyone connected to the job signed confidentiality forms, but Nguyen tells me that doesn't hold water in a criminal case.'

'So we can subpoena them,' said Binchy.

'Once we have a case, we can. Problem is, we need the list for that. But threaten them with whatever you think will work, they still don't budge, contact the state compensation board and back-reference the job for tax paper. You up for all that?'

Someone else might've taken offense.

Sean flexed a Doc Marten. 'You bet, Loot.'

'You can go now, Sean.'

'On my way, Loot.'

Reed had watched the exchange, expressionless. His blond crew cut was fresh, he had on the usual blue blazer, khakis, white shirt, and rep tie.

Milo turned to him. 'Moses, any theories about how we might break through that confidentiality bullshit and find out who these DSD yokels are? The general feeling is they're Arabs but no one can say why. I've already tried the Internet. Zippo.'

Reed said, 'I could cold-call all the Middle East consulates, ask to speak to someone associated with DSD, see if anyone reacts. If that doesn't work, I move on to the embassies in DC.'

'Why don't you start with DC, in case some consulate type sets off an alarm. See if you can find some old directories for when DSD was there, maybe the number's listing's been forwarded.'

'Will do, Loo. In terms of your Internet search, did you check oil-business sites?'

'No. Do it. Your time situation OK?'

'Got plenty of time,' said Reed. 'Only one case pending, that stupid-guy shooting on Pico.'

'Two fools in a bar? Thought you closed it.'

'So did I, Loo. Turns out, it's more complicated because they ran the thread and the bullet angles don't fit exactly. I'm not such a big thread fan, but if it looks like science, juries love it, right? I got my confession all nailed, there's no doubt whodunit, but the DA won't proceed until everything's buttoned down. I'm waiting for the autopsy to verify the flesh-troughs. My vic was supposed to be on the table last week but he's still in the fridge. I drive down there this morning, thinking I'm going to pick up the autopsy report, all I leave with is excuses.'

'DA's got you being an errand boy?'

Reed shrugged. 'Whatever gets the case moving.'

'Crypt must be crazy busy,' said Milo. 'I'm having trouble getting my female vic's autopsy done.'

'They're busy and it just got worse, Loo. One of their CI's was murdered last night, few blocks away, while I was there. Sheriff's Homicide was interviewing.'

'I know some of those guys. Who was it?'

'Someone named Bobby,' said Reed.

'Bob Norchow?'

'No, something Hispanic.'

Milo shook his head. 'What happened?'

'From what I picked up, attempted robbery gone bad. It's a tough neighborhood, guess no one's immune . . . anyway, I've got time, Loo. Anything else?'

'Matter of fact, there is. I'm trying to trace a tip that came in from a pay phone on Venice Boulevard, your old turf. Who at Pacific should I call?'

'Sergeant Sunshine's OK.'

'Sunshine,' said Milo. 'Hope he brings a glow to my damn day.'

*　*　*

Sergeant Patrick Sunshine recommended Milo talk to the car covering that sector of Venice.

A patrolman named Thorpe answered. 'That's one of the last coiners still works, mostly transient dopers use it. Once in a while, street girls when they don't want to run up their hours.'

Milo said, 'My tipster was a male. Older, or trying to sound like it. Pointed me at someone named Monte.'

'Monte,' said Thorpe. 'Nope, doesn't ring a

bell. What time did the tip come in?'

Milo checked the still-thin murder book. 'Just after six P.M.'

'Could be anyone. Want me to ask around?'

'That would be great, thanks.'

'Phone booth,' said Thorpe. 'Darn thing's on its last legs, bet the phone company kills it like all the others.'

16

I woke up at four A.M., inspired. Minutes later, I was at the computer.

Five hours later, I was headed toward Milo's office.

He was away from his desk. A report from the fingerprint lab sat next to the murder book. Desmond Backer's latents had been found on a wall of the turret, just to the right of the top step, and near the bottom frame of a window hole. Brigid Ochs, still listed as Jane Doe 014, had left palm prints on the floor.

Backer's could be explained as reaching for support while he climbed the rickety stairs, then sauntering over to enjoy the view.

The only explanation I could find for hers was a sexual position.

Milo plodded in, drinking coffee.

'Morning.'

'Zippity-do-nothing to you, as well.' He sat, drank. 'No one's budging on telling me who DSD is and I can't find a judge who disagrees. No call-back from Hal, which isn't his usual style, no weapons registered to Charles Rutger other than flintlocks and muskets classified as antiques. He might be nuts but he's never been in criminal trouble. Lab sent over prints from the scene but they don't mean much.'

'Just read the report.' I offered my interpretation.

'Sounds about right.' His phone rang. He clicked to conference. 'Sturgis.'

A woman said, 'This is Dr Jernigan from the coroner's returning your call.'

'Thanks for getting back, Doctor. I was wondering if you've had a chance to autopsy my victims.'

'The Holmby double?' she said. 'Gunshot for your male, strangulation for your female.'

'That was quick, thanks.'

'No autopsy was done,' said Jernigan. 'Not necessary. We also did a rape kit on your female. No sexual assault.'

'So the semen on her leg — '

'What semen?'

'There was a stain on her leg. I saw it at the scene.'

'Not when I inspected the body. How do you know it was semen?'

'I'm not an expert — '

'Exactly.'

'Was it something else, Doctor?'

Silence. 'There was no stain of any kind, Lieutenant. Sorry to cut this short, but I need to go.'

'No autopsy necessary,' said Milo.

'You've been doing this for a while, Lieutenant, so you know we don't cut unnecessarily. I X-rayed both of them. There's a bullet in his head that we'll pull out soon as we can, no metal in her and ruptures in all the right places. For all the talk about a crime drop, we're swamped because the powers-that-be refuse to hire any more staff and the bodies are still coming in

148

faster than we can process. Twenty minutes ago, I received four little kids from a house fire in Willowbrook and they *do* need to be opened up to check for soot in the lungs. Trust me, we're taking your case seriously, the bullet will be pulled.'

'OK, thanks. Sorry about Bobby.'

'You knew Bobby?'

'Only Bobby I know is Bobby Norchow.'

'Norchow retired last year, this is Bobby Escobar. Bright kid, spent a couple of years with us then left to get a master's in bio at Cal State.'

'I heard he got shot near the crypt.'

'Few blocks away, vacant lot that's actually county property,' said Jernigan. 'He was here working, we gave him a little space so he could have peace and quiet. He had three little kids, including a baby.'

'Oh, man.'

'Oh, man, indeed. For three years he goes through DBs' pockets, now he's one.'

'How's the investigation going?'

'Sheriff assigned a couple of rookies and they're calling it robbery gone bad — hey, how about a quid pro? You solve Bobby and we grant you autopsies on demand for the next five years, even when the body doesn't merit it?' Dropping her voice. 'Wish I wasn't kidding. Bye, Lieutenant.'

He hung up, stretched his neck, produced crackle and pop. 'Welcome to my world.'

I said, 'Maybe I can cheer you up. Sranil.'

'What's that?'

'An oil-rich island near Indonesia.'

149

'Never heard of it. And . . . '

'The government is one of Masterson's clients — major medical center still on the drawing board. Given how intimidated everyone seems by the gag agreement and the rumors of DSD being Middle Eastern, I went searching for petro-VIPs who'd lived in LA within the last ten years, co-referenced with Masterson. No Arabs came up but Asian royalty did: Prince Tariq of Sranil, aka Teddy. By *Forbes's* last count his older brother, the sultan, is worth twelve billion. The country's Muslim, so maybe that's the source of the confusion. According to the blogosphere, Teddy came here five years ago to go to law school, got called back to Sranil around two years ago. That fits the Borodi construction schedule perfectly.'

'Why was he called back?'

'The prevailing wisdom is he partied too much, spent too much of his brother's money. And guess what: The sultan's name is Daoud — he's the sixth of seven Daouds in the royal line — and his palace's official name is Dar Salaam Daoud.'

'DSD . . . got a full official name for Teddy?'

I pulled out my notes. 'Tariq Bandar Asman Ku'amah Majur.'

He swiveled, logged onto the department's database. 'Like he's gonna be in here — well looky *here*! Still on the books for . . . I'm counting twenty-six parkers and three speeders. Most are on the Strip . . . here's one in BH — North Beverly Drive . . . another on Rodeo . . . Dayton . . . the shopping district . . . five different vehicles . . . Ferrari, Lamborghini, Rolls . . . wonder why he didn't weasel out of it using diplomatic immunity.'

'Maybe he didn't want to bother. Or he got booted back home before the traffic nazis came after him.'

'Too many toys, huh? Sultan controls the purse strings?'

'Seems to, and there could be a personality conflict. The sultan's devout, shows relative restraint for someone that wealthy.'

'Only a dozen Rolls-Royces?'

'Three, according to the royal website,' I said. 'And two are classics he inherited from his grandfather. But we're not talking the simple life. The royal palace is something out of a storybook — think Taj Majal on steroids.'

'That mean a turret?'

'Whole bunch of turrets. The royal site also claims the sultan opens the place to the public several times a year. Same for his yacht — used for charitable fund-raisers. And a hefty percentage of oil profits gets reinvested in infrastructure and hospitals. I can't judge the truth of any of that, because freedom of the press is nil. But the sultan could have good reason to share the wealth. Two competing rebel groups are camped in the jungles of Indonesia, itching to get their hands on his fossil fuel. One bunch thinks he's insufficiently religious, the other's Maoist. So far, they've spent more time beheading each other, but it pays to be careful.'

'Bread and circuses,' he said. 'Brother Teddy's profligate ways would be bad PR.'

'Ergo confidentiality pledges. It's clearly in Masterson's best interest to keep the sultan happy. The Sranil project is one of their biggest: massive health-care complex, a med school, state-of-the-art research labs, luxury residential towers for imported doctors and nurses. A complete city based on health care, really. Phase One is an oncology center. I called my old department head at Western Pediatric and he's actually been to Sranil as a consultant. Described the island as a strange place — skyscrapers rising from the sand, everything spookily clean and organized, but relatively primitive tribes still living in the central jungle. He also told me the sultan has personal motivation for that cancer center: One of his children was diagnosed with neuroblastoma as an infant, sent to England for treatment but died. There's no reason to believe any of his other kids will get sick but the sultan's being careful.'

'Help your own, buy some international goodwill in the process, keep the savages from your door,' he said. 'So what's Prince Teddy doing with himself nowadays?'

'Since he returned, he's completely off the radar.'

'Anything come up about why the Borodi property hasn't been sold?'

'Maybe the sultan hasn't gotten around to it.'

'Twelve bil,' he said, 'what's twenty million, give or take?' He swung his feet off the desk. 'Interesting, Alex. Thanks, appreciated. The question is . . . '

'Does it relate to the murders.'

A knock on the doorjamb made us both turn.

Moe Reed said, 'I might've found something on DSD.'

Milo said, 'Dar Salaam Daoud.'

Reed's eyes got big. 'So you know about the murder.'

'What murder?'

'The guy who owned the property on Borodi.' Flipping pages of his pad. 'Tariq Asman allegedly killed someone. If my source is credible.'

Milo eyed the young detective. 'I'd invite you in, but you've been pumping too much iron and those biceps won't fit.'

★ ★ ★

The three of us moved to an empty interview room still reeking of intimidation. Milo made sure the taping system was off, shoved the table into the center, drew curtains across the mirror.

'Let's hear it, Moses.'

Reed said, 'I called embassies in DC, got nowhere until I reached the Israeli embassy and some guy barks, 'DSD? That's not Arab, it's Sranil.' When I asked what Sranil was, he hung up. So I went online, learned about Sranil. Including the fact that the Indonesians don't like it, worry it could be used one day as a base for insurgents. So I figured maybe I could take advantage of that and went over to the Indonesian consulate. It's a suite in an office building in Mid-Wilshire, you'd never know from the outside. The front office was full of cute girls, friendly, smiling, all of them shined me on, claimed they'd never heard of Sranil. So I leave and when I get to my car, one of the girls runs out and says, 'I'll tell you about that place but don't come back.' Real nervous and she's taken off her ID badge. Anyway, she made it clear she doesn't like the Sranil tribe, they were barbaric heathens before they became Muslims, the sultan pretends to be some righteous religious dude, meanwhile he's covering up for his brother Tariq, who's a major lowlife. She says that's what you're here about, right? Which takes me by surprise but I say sure. That's when she gets into it, telling me how there's a rumor Tariq killed some foreign party girl in LA, it got covered up, he split. I tried to get details out of her but she said she had no firsthand knowledge, it's just what she heard.'

'Heard where?'

'Around,' said Reed. 'That's all she'd say.'

'And she doesn't like Sranil.'

'So she could be badmouthing them, sure. I couldn't find anything on the Web about any murder.'

'Foreign girl as in non-Asian?' said Milo.

'As in European, she thought Swedish, but couldn't pinpoint. Think it means anything, Loo?'

Milo filled him in on my research.

'Interesting,' said Reed. 'But I'm not seeing any obvious link to the Borodi murders.'

'Me neither, Moses, but the fact that our female vic was snooping in Masterson's files and Masterson's in cahoots with the Sranilese

154

government is a start. Let's try to find out if the rumor about Prince Tariq has any substance. Look at unsolveds during the period he lived in LA. Spread a wide net but focus on foreign female vics.'

I said, 'Our female victim was a good-looking woman. She could've been a party girl, too.'

'Friend of the victim,' said Reed. 'Maybe she's foreign, herself, and that's why she faked her identity — some sort of immigration issue.'

Milo said, 'Cheap clothes says maybe the party was over, maybe she was aiming for a big score. The Borodi site definitely interested her. In addition to going there with Backer, she was spotted hanging around by herself.'

'What if the site was a previous crime scene, Loo? Tariq brought a girl up there and something went wrong — could've even been an accident, she falls down the stairs, or out of a window hole. Or he really is a scumbag. Either way, he's gone but Brigid knows what happened, decides to profit.'

'If she knew where it happened, why bother to snoop in the files?'

'OK, maybe she knew about the place in general, but needed details,' said Reed. 'Or she was searching for other real estate Tariq owned, thinking he might be back and she could get to him.'

I said, 'Blackmail could be involved but there could also be a personal component. Avenging a friend. That would explain her bringing Backer up there to have sex.'

Milo said, 'Screw you, Tariq. So to speak. But

they got spotted. Twelve bil would make it easy to hire a high-grade hit man. Sultan's already rescued Baby Bro from one murder, what's a couple more ten thousand miles away?'

Reed said, 'Plus, he's a dictator, used to having his way.'

I said, 'A dictator who opens his palace to the peasants because he knows he's on shaky sand. A fuss about Teddy murdering a girl and getting away with it could shift the sands uncomfortably.'

Milo got up, paced. 'It's a great story and I hope to hell it's wrong because how could we ever get to someone like that? There's also the same big question: If Borodi was a crime scene, why hasn't the sultan unloaded it? And why have a lame, unarmed wimp guard it part-time?'

Reed said, 'What if the body's buried there?'

'All the more so, Moses. Dig it up, dump it, move on. Why hold on to the place?'

Reed had no answer for that and neither did I.

I pulled out my cell phone. Seconds later, I was hanging up from a frosty chat with Elena Kotsos. 'She's certain Brigid wasn't European. 'Pure American.' Which she clearly considers an insult.'

Milo sat back down. 'Moses, stretch that net to the entire state. And thanks for coming up with this. You done good.'

'It's my job, Loo.'

'Hey, kid, remember what I always tell you.'

'Take all of the credit, none of the blame.'

'Better than Prozac, lad. Now be off.'

17

Milo ran image searches for the sultan and Prince Tariq.

Two smallish men who resembled each other, with boyish faces, cleft chins, thin, precise mustaches. Full regalia, both of them smiling. Determination in the sultan's eyes. Despite the show of perfect white teeth, discomfort in his brother's.

Milo printed, kept surfing. *female scandinavian murder victim u.s.*

A young woman from Göteborg missing three years seemed promising. Inge Samuelsson had worked as a bar hostess in various European and Asian cities, tried Las Vegas, vanished. But the final citation was happy news: She'd shown up in New Zealand, living on a commune, tending sheep.

'Lucky her,' said Milo. 'South Pacific, plus all that lanolin.'

The phone rang. Sean Binchy said, 'Hey, Loot, finally got employment records out of Beaudry. They really stonewalled until I threatened to go to the press, call them Constructiongate.'

'Creative, Sean.'

'I was actually joking, but they bit. A couple of suits went into an office and they must've called a lawyer because they came out announcing the gag agreement didn't apply to subcontractors, they'd give me names when they found them but

157

it would take a while, there was no central list. I said you guys do government projects, I've got friends at INS, they're pretty interested in illegals working construction. And they went back to check again and said, 'Guess what, we do have a list.' Problem is, they keep all their old records in Costa Mesa. I'm heading there right now, but with traffic, it's going to be a while.'

'Time for some ska punk, Sean.'

'Pardon?'

'Play a CD, go back to your roots. It'll lighten the journey.'

'I've got a bunch of downloads. Third Day, MercyMe, Switchfoot. That's all faith-based, Loot.'

'I could use some faith right now, Sean.'

Milo returned to the screen, broadened his search to female victims throughout Europe, had plodded through a nonproductive list when Delano Hardy stuck his head in and handed him a message slip. 'Showed up in my box.'

'Thanks, Del.'

'Why I get your stuff is beyond me, we're nowhere near each other alphabetically.'

'It's happened before?'

'Last week,' said Hardy. 'Bunch of solicitations for those fictitious charities pretend to be raising money for cops and firemen. Those, I tossed.'

'Thanks again, Del.'

'Hey, you'd do the same for me.'

Hardy left and Milo read the slip. Sat up and punched air and said, 'Welcome back, Teach. Backer's sister Ricki is home from Yosemite and wishes to talk.'

I said, 'Recess is over.'

158

***

Ricki Flatt's voice said she was expecting bad, but not that bad.

Milo tried to be gentle but there's no easy way and she wept for a long time. He stretched to turn the volume down on the conference setting, but it was already on low.

She said, 'Oh, God, Desi. I don't understand. Was it a mugging? Some random thing?'

Tensing up, I was sure, on 'random.'

Milo heard it, too; his eyebrows climbed. 'We're still trying to sort things out, Ms Flatt, so anything you can tell us would be helpful.'

'You're in LA. What could *I* tell you?'

'Did your brother have any enemies, ma'am?'

'Of course not.'

Ratcheting up her pitch on 'not.'

'Ms Flatt, your brother didn't die alone. A woman was with him and we still haven't identified her. If we knew who she was, it would speed up the investigation. I know this is a tough time for you, but if I could scan her photo and e-mail it to you, that would help.'

'Of course, do it,' said Ricki Flatt. 'I'm sitting here and not moving. Not even to unpack.'

***

Ten minutes later: 'Oh my God, that's Doreen!'

'Doreen who?'

'What was her last name . . . Doreen . . . Fredd. Two *d*'s, I think. Though how I remember that I couldn't tell you. She and Desi

159

knew each other back in high school. When we lived in Seattle, that's where Desi and I grew up. Her nose is different — smaller — but it's definitely her.'

'Anything romantic between them?'

'They were more like friends, but I really can't say. I'm three years older than Desi, didn't get into his personal business.'

'Doreen Fredd.' Milo entered the name into the databases. 'What else can you tell me about her, Ms Flatt?'

'She and Desi used to go hiking together. They all did — a group of kids, they liked the outdoors. One time, I was already in college, visiting home for midsemester break, Desi and his hiking group came in and Doreen had poison ivy, or some bad rash. Our dad tended to her, he was a firefighter with paramedic training — but you don't care about that. You're saying Desi was dating her in LA?'

'There appears to be a romantic connection.'

'Doreen,' she said. 'And she's also . . . my God.'

'Anything else you want to tell us, Ms Flatt?'

'Not really.' Tight voice, for the third time.

'Nothing at all, ma'am?'

Silence.

'Ms Flatt?'

'What happened to Desi, was it in any way political?'

Milo sat up. 'Political, how?'

'Forget that, I'm not making sense. Do you need me to identify the body, Lieutenant?'

'No, ma'am, we know it's your brother and

160

verification can be made using photos, but I would like to talk to you some more — '

'I'll come out,' she said. 'To handle . . . arrangements. I've done it before. My parents. I never thought I'd be doing it for my baby *brother* — how did you connect Desi to me?'

'Phone messages, ma'am.'

'Oh. That must've been the times Desi called to talk to Sam — my daughter. If I can catch a flight, I'll leave tonight, Lieutenant . . . I'll have to make sure Scott's OK with that . . . oh God, I'm going to have to explain to Sam. This is unreal.'

'Ms Flatt, could you please clarify that remark about it being political?'

Silence.

'Ma'am?'

'Let's talk in person, Lieutenant. I've got so many things to do.'

★   ★   ★

NCIC had nothing to say about Doreen Fredd. Neither did DMV, Social Security, any other port in cyberspace.

'Still a phantom.' Milo logged off. 'And Sister Ricki gets all squirrelly about 'something political.' This is starting to smell real bad, Alex.'

Turning to his phone, he punched numbers so hard the apparatus jumped. 'Hal, this is Milo. For the *third* time. Is it my breath or are you on some sort of overpriced taxpayer junket and can't be bothered to help the locals? I've got a name for my Jane Doe, no thanks to you. Doreen

161

Fredd.' Spelling it with exquisite, enraged enunciation. 'And guess what, Hal, even with that, she's a ghost, not even an SSN. So now I'm thinking your not calling back isn't negligence, it's proactive deception. Which is bullshit, Hal. You owe me big-time on that Aeromexico thing and I need you to come through. All in the name of God, Country, and my ready access to the chief, Hal. Who will *not* be happy to learn that no good deed has, yet again, gone unpunished.'

Slam. He slumped. 'Ready for my close-up, Mr DeMille.'

I said, 'Ready access to the chief?'

'The federal government understands entitlement. Ends justifies the means. Political . . . the obvious link is Teddy but what the hell would a newly graduated architect have to do with Sranil?'

'Maybe he had a previous life.'

'As what, a super-spy?'

'As something political,' I said. 'Or maybe, given his libido, he'd partied with Teddy's alleged victim, whom he met through Doreen. The two of them cooked up the blackmail scheme, leaned too hard and paid for it.'

'Pretty damn stupid to think they could go up against someone that powerful.'

'How much of your job revolves around smart people, Big Guy? And Backer being involved could explain how Brig — Doreen ended up at Masterson. Teddy's name doesn't appear on any of the Borodi paperwork, but that design journal listed the firm's involvement in a 'pied-à-terre' for a foreign owner. Backer was an architect, that's his type of reading material.'

'He does background, Doreen worms her way in to get the details. The two of them somehow send a message to Tariq or the sultan, one of them makes a call and a local pro is hired.'

'Or even someone flown in for the job.'

'Morons,' he said. 'Thinking they could play in that league. Then they have the nerve to go up there again for fun under the stars. Fouling the rich bastard's nest in the process. Freud's probably got a name for that, huh?'

'*Der payback*.'

Tight lips parted slightly, emitting something close to a smile. He pressed *psychic delete* and turned grim again. 'Desi and Doreen, hugging a tree. P-L-O-T-T-I-N-G.'

18

At six twenty, just as we were leaving for dinner, John Nguyen dropped in.

The deputy DA was dressed for court in a navy pinstripe, white shirt, blue tie, American flag lapel pin. Four evidence boxes were stacked on a wheeled luggage rack. Nguyen's posture was as straight as ever, but his eyes drooped.

'John, what's up?'

Nguyen unclasped the top case, pulled out a sheaf of printouts, and dropped it on Milo's desk. 'Mr and Mrs Holman's financials. You owe me.'

Milo scanned the face page. 'How'd you pull it off?'

'Been doing a robbery-gangbang trial for three days running, brand-new judge, absurdly biased toward our side so I figured she might go for your spurious logic.'

Licking a finger, Nguyen slashed air vertically. 'Score one, J. N. I got one of my eager new interns to push everything through with the banks. Which, I'd like to point out, is normally your responsibility, not mine, not to mention significantly below my pay grade. But you put in the time on the marsh murder trial, so consider it an advance Christmas gift.'

Milo flipped pages. 'Your stocking stuffer's on the way, John . . . don't see anything interesting.'

'That's 'cause there isn't any,' said Nguyen.

'He's a retired professor, she's an unfamous architect, their income, expenditures, retirement fund, et cetera, are all commensurate with a cautious, mature lifestyle. Meaning they can probably keep their house and continue to have health insurance if they don't get *really* sick or go out to eat too often.'

'This is definitely all of it, John?'

'What, some secret bank account for paying hit men? They budget tighter than my ex-wife's — never mind.' Nguyen moved toward the door. 'I can lead a judge to warrant, dude, but I can't stop the stink.'

★ ★ ★

We walked a couple of blocks to Café Moghul, the Indian place that serves as Milo's supplementary office. He tips huge, is dramatically omnivorous, and the owners are convinced his grumpy-mastiff demeanor wards off danger. The bespectacled woman who works the front always beams when he lumbers through the door, begins piling on the food before his chair warms.

Tonight was lamb, beef, turkey, lobster, three kinds of naan, a garden plot of vegetables.

He bore down, as if tackling a massive culinary puzzle.

I said, 'Hail to the sultan of West LA.'

He wiped sauce from his face. 'Keep your geography straight, *Rajah*. For one brief Cinderella moment.'

'Then the pumpkin appears?'

'Then it's back to Untouchable.'

Midway through his fourth bowl of sweet *kir* rice pudding, Sean Binchy strode in, bright-eyed and cheerful as ever.

'Give me some good news, kid, then you can eat.'

'No, thanks, Loot, Becky's cooking tonight and that's always a treat. More like good news and bad news. I got lots of names of construction workers but no Montes or anything close.'

'What's the good news?'

'I'm going to analyze it super-carefully.'

Uttered with absolute sincerity.

'That's great, Sean.'

Binchy said, 'Anything with an *M* for starts, and if that doesn't produce, I'll just check every single name for felony records. Like you always say, tortoise beats hare.'

He left.

Milo said, 'Tortoise sometimes gets squashed in the middle of the highway by an eighteen-wheeler, but sure, keep the faith, kid.'

★ ★ ★

He phoned me at eight the following morning. 'Sister Ricki's due in my office in an hour.'

'I'll be there.'

'Thought you might also want to know that Doreen Fredd is, indeed, a real person. I searched genealogy sites last night, found a distant cousin living in Nebraska, e-mailed the

166

photo. Family hasn't seen Doreen for years but verified that she got sent to Seattle when she was a teenager. Naughty girl, ended up in a group home.'

'Why Seattle?'

'The family originally hailed from Tacoma, where Doreen's daddy worked at a gas station and mommy clerked at a food store. Nice people, according to the cousin, but major alkies, no 'parental supervision.' Doreen started running away at an early age. Finally, the court declared her incorrigible. The home worked out for a while, but Doreen split from there, too. She stepped off the map, no one's heard from her in all this time, she was an only child and both parents are dead.'

'Is the group home still in business?'

'It is but there's been half a dozen changes of ownership, no staff remains from when Doreen was there, all the old records have been destroyed. Her hooking up with Des Backer makes sense, though: I back-traced his parents' residence. South Seattle, only a few blocks from the home. Cute girl, cute guy, chemistry, kaboom.'

'Chemistry reignited years later,' I said. 'The wrong kind of explosion.'

★ ★ ★

I showed up for the meet with Ricki Flatt on time, found her talking to Milo.

Des Backer's sister was faded by grief and fatigue. Long curly hair was tied back carelessly.

167

She wore a baggy gray sweater unsuitable for the weather, mommy jeans, white tennis shoes. A huge canvas purse the color of smog lowered her right shoulder. An overnight bag of matching hue sat on the floor.

Milo lifted the suitcase and escorted her to the same room we'd used to powwow with Moe Reed. He offered her coffee, something to eat.

She touched her belly. 'I couldn't hold anything down. Please tell me what happened to my brother.'

'Mr Backer and Doreen Fredd were found murdered in an unfinished house in a neighborhood called Holmby Hills. Ever hear of it?'

'I haven't.'

'Your brother never mentioned Holmby Hills?'

'Never. Where is it?'

'It's an extremely high-end area, just west of Beverly Hills. There's an indication your brother and Ms Fredd had been to that location before.'

'An unfinished house?'

'A construction project.'

'Something Desi was working on?'

Instead of answering, Milo said, 'So your brother and Ms Fredd hung out in high school?'

Nod. 'And during the plane ride, I remembered something else. One time, when she was at our house, my dad made a comment to Mom about her being troubled, it was good she was aiming for wholesome activities. You didn't say if the project was one of Desi's.'

'It doesn't appear that way, ma'am. This was what you'd call a super-mansion.'

'Then for sure it wouldn't be Desi's.'

168

'Not into that kind of thing.'

'He would've considered it grotesque. But if he wasn't working on it, why would he be there?'

'That's what we're trying to figure out, Ms Flatt. This hiking group Desi and Doreen had, how many people are we talking about?'

'Just a few other kids, I really wasn't paying attention.'

'And to your knowledge Desi and Doreen weren't romantically involved.'

'I thought about that,' said Ricki Flatt. 'Maybe, I really can't say. Desi had so many girls who liked him. They were always calling him. Dad used to joke he needed a personal secretary.'

'Do you have any knowledge of his other recent girlfriends?'

Head shake. 'Sorry, I wasn't involved in my brother's personal life back then and that didn't change after we grew up.'

'Did you know that Doreen lived in a group home not far from your house?'

'No, but you must mean Hope Lodge. That place was the talk of the neighborhood. My friends joked about it, called it 'Ho Lodge' because the girls were wild. I'm not saying they were, but you know how kids talk. That's probably why my dad said she had problems.'

'Was he worried about her being a bad influence on Desi?'

Ricki Flatt smiled. 'My parents made a big thing about Desi and me developing our own sense of right and wrong. But even if they had tried to rein Desi in, it wouldn't have worked.

169

My brother did exactly as he pleased.'

Milo said, 'Did Desi's strong will lead to any — I have to ask this — iffy behavior?'

'What do you mean?'

'Anything out of the ordinary.'

'If you consider leaving home after high school and hitting the road for ten years out of the ordinary, sure.'

'Ten years,' said Milo.

'Ten lost years,' said Ricki Flatt. 'Basically Desi disappeared. Once in a while we'd get postcards.'

'From where?'

'All over the country. National parks, that kind of thing.'

'Not overseas?'

'No.'

'What did Desi do to support himself?'

'He said odd jobs, temporary stuff that gave him time to explore nature, figure life out.'

'Postcards,' said Milo. 'No visits back home?'

'Once, twice a year he'd pop up — Christmas, Thanksgiving, birthdays. He looked great, really happy and that reassured my parents. He was reviving the whole sixties thing — long hair, beard, hemp sandals. But always clean and well groomed, Dad said he looked like Hollywood's idea of Jesus.'

'You mentioned handling your parents' affairs, so I assume — '

'Gone, Lieutenant. Four years ago. They were vacationing near Mount Olympia, decided to explore and drove onto a dirt access road that passed through a heavy logging area. A load of huge pines came loose from a truck bed and crushed their car. We wanted to sue — Scott and I and Des — but the lawyers said our case was weak because the road was chained and warning signs were all around, Dad had lifted it and driven through, anyway. In the end we settled for a hundred thousand. The lawyers took forty percent and we split sixty with Des. He'd cleaned up his act and started architecture school, said it would help with tuition and living expenses. What made it horribly ironic is we're from an old logging family, four generations. My grandfather was a master sawyer and Dad did some logging before he became a firefighter.'

'I'm sorry, ma'am.'

'It happened before Sam was born, that's what hurts the most. Mom and Dad would've loved Sam.' Tears. 'She adored Desi and now he's gone.'

'How did Desi react to losing your parents?'

'Terribly,' said Ricki Flatt. 'He got this empty look in his eyes, walked around for weeks as if he was in a trance. The walking wounded, Scott called it. I've never seen my brother like that, generally he's open and mellow and accessible.'

'He drew into himself.'

'I remember thinking this isn't healthy, he needs to deal with it, do some serious grieving or he's going to break down. I was sure he'd drop out of school but he didn't, he stuck with it and graduated with honors.'

Milo tapped his pen on a corner. 'Ms Flatt, that remark you made yesterday on the phone, about it being political. We're still curious about that.'

Ricki Flatt's eyes jumped all over the place. 'Forget that, that was silly. I shouldn't have said anything.'

'But you did, ma'am.'

She untied her hair, shook it loose, fastened it tighter.

'Ricki, we have no interest except solving your brother's murder.'

Thumping both elbows on the table, she pressed her palms to her cheeks. Her fingertips trailed above her ears, as if blocking out noise. See no, hear no.

Milo said, 'The only thing we've heard remotely political about your brother is he was into green architecture, the whole environment thing.'

Ricki Flatt's left cheek twitched.

Milo edged closer. 'Did he get radical with that? Spend those ten years doing things that might be considered illegal?'

'I don't know how he spent them.'

'But you're worried.'

'Desi . . . used to talk.'

'About what?'

'Burning down the house,' she said. 'That was the name of a song he liked. When he visited, he'd sometimes go off on speeches. About the beauty of untouched wilderness. About greedy people who raped the land and built monuments to their ego. What they needed, he said, was a good lesson.'

'Monuments,' said Milo. 'Like the one he died in. And now you're worried he put himself in a bad position.'

Ricki Flatt looked up. 'Oh, God, I should've *known* something bad was going to happen when he gave me the *money*. Desi's *never* been able to hold on to money, he's never *cared* about money.'

No need for Milo to press. He gave her a tissue, waited until she'd patted her eyes dry.

'All right,' she said. 'This is what happened: Des showed up six months ago with fifty thousand dollars in cash. Two big suitcases full. He asked me to hold it for him. I gave him a spare key to the unit.'

'We're talking last January,' said Milo.

'New Year's weekend, Scott and I were about to leave for a trip to New Mexico and Des showed up, no advance notice.'

'Did he say where he got the money?'

'I know, I should've asked. Scott was furious with me, said it had to be drug money or something else illegal and I'd gotten us in way over our heads. I said that made no sense, Desi had never used dope or alcohol, took care of his body. Scott told me I was being naïve, Desi had been on the road for years, we had no clue about what he'd done. We got into a big fight, Scott demanded I call Desi back, insist he take the suitcases.' Shrill laughter. 'It was pretty darn dramatic. Of course, I finally agreed.'

'So you called your brother.'

Ricki Flatt hung her head. 'I lied to Scott — only time I've ever done that. Why? For the life of me, I wish I could tell you. I just couldn't bring myself to confront Desi. There's something about my brother that makes you want to say yes to him. He's so sweet and direct — in high school, he was voted most popular. It wasn't just girls who loved him, everyone did.'

I said, 'Charisma.'

'Yes, but for me, it was more than that. With Mom and Dad gone, there was no one else. I guess I kept hoping we'd reconnect, be some kind of family. Sam seemed to be a vehicle for that.' Burying her face in her hands, she mumbled.

Milo said, 'You still have the money. You're worried it's political.'

Ricki Flatt looked up. 'When Desi brought it to me, he seemed nervous, made me promise not to ask questions. I keep thinking it was payment for something *wrong*.'

'Burning down the house.'

'Maybe not literally,' she said. 'But something . . . why else would he hide the money? I promise to send it back to you as soon as I get back home but *please* don't tell Scott I kept it.'

'Where is it?'

'Our storage unit. Scott and I rented one after Mom and Dad passed. For their stuff, I couldn't bear to get rid of anything. I tucked the suitcases in back, behind Mom's piano. Scott never goes in there.'

'So Desi had a key to the unit?'

'I gave him one. They were his parents, too.'

'When's the last time you actually saw the money?'

'The last time,' she said, 'had to be . . . a couple of weeks after I stored it, so five months ago, give or take. I went in there and counted it. I'd never counted it initially. Why? Once again, I don't know.'

'Fifty thousand.'

'In fifty-dollar bills, bound neatly. Do you really think it has something do with what happened to Desi?'

'Money's the most common motive we see, Ricki.'

'Oh, God, I told Scott he was being paranoid, but now I'm getting sick.' She grabbed Milo's wrist. 'Is my *family* in danger?'

'I would hope not,' said Milo. 'But we do need to get the money in a secure place.'

'I promise I'll send it straight to you. I was going to stay for a few days, to arrange for Desi to be flown back, but I'll leave today, have the suitcases shipped first thing in the morning.'

'Please don't touch them,' said Milo. 'We need to process them first.'

'Process?'

'Fingerprinting, that kind of thing. I'll arrange for everything after you sign some forms releasing the contents of the storage bin for inspection. Is there anything else in your unit that belonged to Desi?'

'No,' said Ricki Flatt. 'I'll fill out anything you need, draw you a diagram showing where I put them. I just want them out of there.'

'I'll handle it, Ricki.'

'Are Scott and Sam in danger? Please, I need an honest answer.'

'I've got no indication your family's a target.'

'Really?'

'Really.'

'Thank God.' Gazing up at the ceiling. 'What did you get me *into*, Desi?'

19

Ricki Flatt filled out the search authorization.

Milo asked her where she was staying.

'I came straight from the airport.'

'Did you rent a car?'

'I took the shuttle to Westwood, then a cab.'

'I'll get you a place. There's a victim compensation fund, but it'll mean more forms and take a while to get compensated.'

'I don't care about that.' Her hands waved restlessly.

Milo called Sean Binchy over from the big D-room. Binchy was still poring over lists of construction workers with nothing to report.

'Find Ms Flatt a clean, safe place to bunk down.'

Binchy lifted her luggage. 'The Star Inn on Sawtelle has the Triple A rating, cable, and wireless and there's an IHOP right up the block.'

'Whatever,' said Ricki Flatt.

After the two of them left, I said, 'Political, as in baby brother might be an eco-terrorist. It would take more than Backer spouting off for her to worry about that.'

'Yeah, she knows more,' said Milo, 'but pushing her right now didn't feel right. I'll have Sean keep an eye on her, make sure she sticks around.'

'Backer's lost decade preceded his parents' death, but their being crushed by logs could've kicked up his motivation.'

'Fifty grand to blow something up. Like a big house, but he never got to it. On the other hand, the money could be from dope or a blackmail payoff. Or he won big at the tables and gave it to Ricki to avoid the taxman.'

We returned to his office where Milo called Officer Chris Kammen. The Port Angeles cop agreed to watch the Flatt residence 'as much as we can' and to handle the search of the storage unit as soon as the paperwork came in. 'Two suitcases? What color?'

'Look for the ones behind the piano, stuffed with cash.'

'Fifty grand,' said Kammen. His whistle pierced the room. 'So the husband's out of the loop, huh?'

'Flatt doesn't know his wife held on to the money. She's playing nice and I want to stay on her good side.'

'Domestic issues,' said Kammen. 'Fun.'

A fourth try at Federal Hal's office left Milo red-faced. 'Disconnected number? This is starting to feel personal.'

I said, 'Sure, but maybe it's not you. It's Doreen Fredd.'

'What the hell was this girl into?'

'She knew Backer years ago. If he was into bad stuff, she'd be a good choice to gather info.'

'Problem child becomes an undercover Fed?'

'Or her problems got her into a situation where she needed to trade favors. I'd look into major eco-vandalism in the Pacific Northwest during Backer's years on the road.'

177

'She's finking on Backer and screwing him? Gives a whole new meaning to undercover.'

'That part could still be chemistry,' I said. 'Good technique on her part, too, given Backer's proclivities.'

'Guy's into blowing stuff up then becomes an architect and learns to build stuff. Don't tell me Freud didn't have a word for that.'

Moe Reed stuck his head in. 'Someone to see you, Loo.'

'Better be important.'

'FBI important?'

'Depends what they have to say,' said Milo. But he was up in a flash.

★　★　★

A short, solidly built, dark-haired woman arrived moments later. 'Lieutenant? Gayle Lindstrom. I was referred by a mutual friend.'

Gray pantsuit, black flats, molasses accent with an edge. Maybe northern Kentucky or southern Missouri. Fair skin and blue eyes were clear, her chin was prominent and square.

'Nice to meet you, Special Agent Lindstrom.'

Lindstrom grinned. 'My mom always told me I was special. Reality's a little different.' Her bag was as large as Ricki Flatt's. Black leather, authoritative straps and buckles.

'Mutual friend,' said Milo. 'Now who might that be?'

'Yesterday, he was Hal. Today?' She shrugged. 'You guys love that, don't you?'

'What?'

178

'Top-secret clandestine hooh-hah.'

'Only when it gets the job done.' She studied me. 'We need to talk in private, Lieutenant.'

'This is Dr Delaware, our psychological consultant.'

'You have your own profiler now?'

'Better,' said Milo. 'We've got someone who knows what he's doing.'

'Looks like I caught you on a bad day,' said Lindstrom.

'Not hard to do.'

She offered me a cool, firm palm. 'Nice to meet you, Doctor. No offense but I need to speak to Lieutenant Sturgis in private.'

Milo said, 'That's not how it's gonna be.'

* * *

A long, whispered phone call later, and I was authorized.

Gayle Lindstrom peered into Milo's office. 'Kind of cozy for three.'

Milo said, 'I'll find us space.'

'I like Indian food, Lieutenant.'

He glared at her.

Lindstrom said, 'Sorry, I couldn't resist.'

'Not hungry.' He marched up the corridor.

Lindstrom said, 'Oh, well,' and followed.

* * *

Back to the same interview room. I wondered if it ever got used for suspects.

Gayle Lindstrom sniffed the air.

Milo said, 'This is as fresh as it's gonna get. I'm busy. Talk.'

Lindstrom said, 'Enough icebreaking, guys. Don't coddle me 'cause I'm a girl.'

Coaxing a smile out of Milo. He hid it with the back of his hand. Yawned.

'OK, OK,' she said. 'What do you know about eco-terrorism?'

Milo said, 'Uh-uh, this isn't going to be some theoretical discussion. You want what we know, you better fill in the blanks. Desmond Backer's lost decade smells real bad. Doreen Fredd was a naughty girl who ended up as either a confederate or your informant. Go.'

Lindstrom nudged her bag with one foot. 'I'm here because the Bureau figured it was only a matter of time before you figured out some of what's going on.'

'Some? Don't swell my head.'

'If you knew all of it you wouldn't be trying to reach Hal. Who, by the way, can't help you. He's Homeland Security, so he's concentrating on people with dark skin and funny names. So is the Bureau, for that matter, which is part of the problem. Before 9/11, we were geared up to spend serious time and money on locally grown lunatics who, in my humble opinion, pose just as serious a danger to public safety as some guy named Ahmed.'

'Everything stopped to look for Ahmed.'

'We're just like you, Lieutenant. Chronically underfunded with our hands out to politicians who have the attention span of gnats on crack. The hot topic of the moment gets the appropriation and everything else gets shoved to the bottom shelf. Eco-terrorists have committed hundreds of violent acts, with plenty of fatalities. We're talking nasties who believe humanity's a plague and have no problem spiking trees to mutilate loggers. Fanatics who burn down other people's houses because they don't approve of the square footage. Nothing's happened on a grand scale yet, and they've got the secret sympathy of some mainstream environmental groups who condemn violence but continue to wink and nod. But my judgment is, it's only a matter of time before the country regrets not dealing with the problem.'

'Desmond Backer was a serious eco-terrorist?'

Lindstrom toed her bag again. 'It's a delicate situation. Not for me personally. We're talking events that precede my tenure with the Bureau.'

She unclasped the bag, pulled out lip balm, twisted her mouth into a disapproving little bud and lubricated. Basic delay tactic. I'd learned a whole bunch of them, working as a psychologist.

Milo said, 'Lost my script, what's my next line?'

'The overview I'm about to give you, Lieutenant, is based on summaries of files transferred to me by predecessors who've been transferred.'

'They get transferred to Ahmed. But you're dealing with home-grown naughties no one cares about.'

Gayle Lindstrom's half smile would have intrigued da Vinci.

Milo said, 'You don't play well with others, so

181

you're on time-out.'

She laughed. 'Let's just say I've been assigned to look into years of eco-crimes and write reports unlikely to be read. My instructions are to concentrate on the Pacific Northwest, because that's where fuzzies and trees tend to inspire the most passion. That led me to your homicide victims. Desmond Backer and Doreen Fredd met in Seattle. He grew up there, and she'd been sent to a group home for problem girls. She utilized legitimate passes from the home as well as illicit exits to associate with Backer and his friends.'

'Climbing out the window,' said Milo.

'Or just sneaking out the back door, the place wasn't exactly super-max lockdown. Like many teenagers, Fredd and Backer and their friends appear to have filled some of their free time with various vegetative hallucinogens, alternative music, video games. They also spent time engaged in apparently wholesome activities such as hiking, camping, environmental cleanups, volunteer wildlife rescue. Unfortunately, some of that may have been a cover for arson and other acts of vandalism.'

'Were they ever arrested?'

'Insufficient evidence,' said Lindstrom. 'But their proximity to several trashed homesites is revealing.'

'What exactly do you have on them?'

'What the local *police* had on them was word-of-mouth. Then, a dead boy.'

'They killed someone?'

'Not directly, but they have moral culpability.'

Out came his pad. 'Name of the victim?'

'Vincent Edward Burghout, known as Van. Seventeen when he burned to death inside an unfinished mansion in Bellevue, Washington. By now, you've probably heard of Bellevue because it's where high-tech zillionaires are building castles. Back then, that had just started and it was basically a nice, low-crime suburb of Seattle. One of the first techie-monarchs to see the potential of lakeside living bought ten acres and started building a twenty-thousand-square-foot monstrosity. It had gotten as far as the framing the night Van Burghout sneaked in and set several fires. He destroyed a good part of it but also immolated himself. We — my predecessors — found his technique especially interesting. Have you ever heard of vegan Jell-O?'

'Sounds disgustingly healthy.'

'Not if you're made of wood,' said Lindstrom. 'Or flesh and bones. It's basically homemade napalm — soap and petroleum triggered by a delayed ignition device. Any idiot can get the recipe off the Internet or in one of those treasonous loony-tracts put out by the paranoid press. Fortunately, few idiots actually go as far as to whip the stuff up, but over the years we have had incidents and the mortality rate is high, often to the perpetrators. You're talking a highly incendiary concoction and if your timer's off, you're toast. Or in Van Burghout's case, crumbs. There was nothing left of the kid, they ID'd him because he'd gotten teeth knocked out playing basketball and part of an upper bridge survived the blast.'

She fooled with the tube of lip balm. 'Mr High-Tech collected insurance, donated the land to the city for a park, moved to Oregon, and built an even bigger monstrosity on a thousand acres.'

'Everyone walks away happy,' said Milo. 'Except Van's parents.'

'Who pointed fingers at Van's friends. Maybe because they couldn't accept their son being a solo pyromaniac. But that doesn't make them wrong.'

I said, 'Van was the victim of bad influences?'

'Exactly, but like I said, there was logic to that. Van's grades were barely passing and the local law got a clear picture of him as impressionable. But they got nowhere and called the Bureau in. That's how the Bureau came to acquaint itself with Desmond Backer and Doreen Fredd and their pals.'

'How many pals?'

'The Burghouts gave the locals four names in addition to Van: Backer, Fredd, a boy named Dwayne Parris, a girl named Kathy Vanderveldt. We tried to talk to them, as well as to their teachers and friends.'

'Tried?'

'These were middle-class kids with oodles of parental and community support, so we got no direct access, everything was filtered through lawyers. We're talking upstanding folk, well respected in their community, claiming their kids were angels.'

I said, 'Doreen's parents stepped forward?'

'No, she was the exception. Her parents were

184

drunks, living out of state, seemed barely in touch with what Doreen had been doing. Also, Doreen was gone by the time we began investigating.'

'Yet another rabbit,' said Milo.

Lindstrom said, 'Sure, we got suspicious about the timing, but splitting was her habitual pattern and everyone we talked to said they couldn't imagine Doreen involved in anything violent. Just the opposite, she was passive, gentle, into poetry, blue skies, green trees, little cutie-pie mammals. The folks at Hope Lodge — the home — had nothing bad to say about her, either. Poor Doreen was a victim of family dysfunction, not a wild girl.'

I said, 'Did they change their minds when they found out she'd been sneaking out to meet up with the others?'

'Not according to what I've read, Doctor. My predecessor described the people running the place as 'idealists.' Which is Bureau code for stupid, naïve do-gooder. We were able to get a warrant for Doreen's room because a lot of Hope Lodge's funding came through government grants. Unfortunately, nothing funny showed up there. And we brought in dogs, the works.'

Milo said, 'No warrants for the others?'

'Not even close. We went judge-shopping but the one we thought might work with us said he wouldn't authorize a 'witch hunt.' We put out a nationwide alert for Doreen, placed the other kids under surveillance for a couple of months. It came to nothing, there were no more fires in

Bellevue, or anywhere else in the Greater Seattle area. We moved on.'

'But at some point you found Doreen and managed to turn her.'

Lindstrom pinched her upper lip. Balanced the lip balm tube between two index fingers. 'Is this the point where I say, 'Oh, Sherlock!' and go all wide-eyed?'

Milo said, 'Why else would you be here, Gayle?'

Lindstrom removed her gray suit jacket. Underneath was a red tank top. Square shoulders, thick but firm arms. 'It's kind of dry in here, don't you think? Must be your AC. Could I trouble you for some coffee?'

20

Detective-room brew has the refreshing tang of roofing tar and a meth-like ability to scrape the nerves raw.

Special Agent Gayle Lindstrom downed half a cup without complaint, rubbed her eyes, stretched and yawned and stretched again. Milo goes through a similar act when he's faking casual. Lindstrom needed more practice.

Taking another sip, she finally gave the expected grimace, set the cup aside.

'Yes, Doreen finally surfaced. I had nothing to do with it but it still makes me cringe.' Reaching for the cup, she deliberated another swallow, decided against it. 'Nothing the Bureau did pulled her in. Her own stupidity did.'

'She did a bad thing and got caught,' said Milo.

'She got busted for prostitution and dope five years ago. Want to take a wild guess where?'

'Seattle.'

'Heart of the city, downtown. I wouldn't be surprised if she never left. Even though she spun us all kinds of tales about hitchhiking around the country, living off the land, none of her details came together correctly and what I get from her file is the bio of a natural-born compulsive liar.'

I said, 'Des Backer traveled around the country for ten years. Did she claim to be with him?'

'As a matter of fact, she did, Doctor. Not as a constant companion, off and on. She spun weird yarns about living in forests, eating roots and shoots, foraging for wild mushrooms, whatever. But like I said, when it came to closing the deal on the finer points, as in dates, towns, cities, states, she fell apart. Bureau shrinks labeled her a histrionic personality.'

Milo said, 'They examined her?'

'I've seen no clinical report.'

I said, 'Meaning the diagnosis probably came from reviewing the file.'

'Do you disagree with the diagnosis, Doctor?'

'I don't know enough to agree, or disagree.'

Lindstrom frowned. 'No offense, but the psych stuff doesn't really matter, does it? Same for Fredd's nature-girl tales. Maybe part of it was true, maybe she was double-, triple-, quadruple-bluffing. The point is, no eco-crimes during that period can be traced to her, so either she was real good at covering her tracks or she and the other Seattle kids weren't any big deal in the first place.'

I said, 'Five years ago, Des Backer was in architecture school. Doreen's turning to prostitution around then says they'd probably parted ways well before.'

'And . . . ?'

'I'm just trying to nail down the time line.'

'I won't argue with your logic.'

Milo said, 'So she gets busted for hooking. How'd that lead to federal snitch?'

Lindstrom said, 'I haven't said anything about turning her.'

'Her identity was erased, cut the crap.'

Lindstrom played with a strap of her tank top. 'Yes, we turned her, but it wasn't the prostie part that scared her, it was the dope. We're talking kilos of weed, pills in neat little bags plus some chunks of rock. Enough to put her away for a real long time.'

'She was a major-league dealer?'

'The stuff was found in the basement of a rooming house where she habitually took johns. Downtown Seattle, not far from the Pike market.'

'She just happens to be rooming with all that?'

'Sitting on top of it,' said Lindstrom. 'Literally. One of those under-the-bed trapdoors right below her bounce-for-bucks mattress. Doreen's bad luck was popping pills in front of a john who turned out to be undercover Seattle vice. She claimed it was Advil and that was later verified. But meanwhile, the room got seriously tossed. The city had just instituted one of those temporary moral crusades — too many tourists hassled by lowlifes — so warrants were a snap. Doreen claimed she had no idea the hatch existed in the first place, had never even looked under the bed. Maybe that's even true. Lots of girls used the same room and the building was owned by a couple of Cambodian restaurateurs suspected of bringing in all sorts of bad stuff. By the time the Bureau got called in, they were gone and wrapped in layers of paper that dead-ended in Phnom Penh. Our plan was to confiscate the entire property under the RICO statutes but Seattle PD claimed the prize as theirs. There's a cute little shopping center there now. Designer coffee, sushi bar, Italian café with great pastries, yuppie gym. Tanning salon, too, which could come in handy in Drizzle City.'

'You've visited recently.'

'I was there yesterday. Trying to learn what I could about Doreen. After we found out what happened to her here.'

'What'd you learn?'

'Not a thing.' Smile. 'I did have a good panini at the Italian place.'

'How long since you had contact with Doreen?'

'I *never* had contact with her,' said Lindstrom, 'I *inherited* her. And a bunch of others like her. If that sounds defensive, it is.'

'Bunch of snitches living off tax dollars who end up burning you. Business as usual, Gayle.'

The skin above Lindstrom's neckline turned rosy. 'Like it never happens to you guys? I happen to know for a fact that six years ago, one of your best female vice D's was set up as a pimp in an apartment in Hollywood. Not some decoy thing, LAPD had a genuine D Two hiring and working real-life hookers on the street, running everything real businesslike, keeping books, recording income. All so you could pull in high-profile johns because a feminist on the city council screamed loud enough to get heard. So what happens to *your* grand plan? The street girls your D is supposed to boss slip her a roofie, strip her naked, take pictures of her being ganged by some of their thug boyfriends, put the photos online, and abscond to Mexico with the cash. *There's* police work at its best.'

Milo's expression said he'd never heard any of it before.

Gayle Lindstrom said, 'News to you, huh? Well, then thank the LAPD obstruction squad. My point is, Milo, we all win some, lose some. And we all cover our collective butts. Yes, the Bureau thought Doreen might be useful because during the same period she claimed to be nature-girling with Backer, the whole eco-crazy scene had heated up in a really nasty way. I'm talking two small children of a genetics researcher — toddlers, for God's sake — with third-degree burns after animal liberation nuts set fire to the family house because Daddy ran rats. I'm talking a bunch of loggers near the Washington — Canadian border getting blinded and losing limbs due to tree spikes. A Ronald McDonald house sprayed with threatening graffiti then overrun with live rats, with families living there. Families of kids with *cancer*, for God's sake. All because someone doesn't like Big Macs. These people are *lunatics* and they're vicious. And in addition to that, at least a dozen residential construction projects had been turned to charcoal, so why *wouldn't* we try to use Doreen? Everyone knew the dope really wasn't hers, why not deal?'

I said, 'What made you think Doreen had anything to offer?'

'She told my *predecessors* that she did. Started spilling the minute they had her in lockup, claiming all sorts of insider knowledge about the most radical fringe of the movement.

People she'd come into contact with during her years on the road. What made her credible was her insistence on getting a pass for herself on anything she talked about. Implying she had been more than a bystander.'

Milo said, 'But . . . '

Lindstrom turned to him. 'You're enjoying this way too much, but fine, I'll open a vein for you: We protected her and she screwed us over. Happy, Father O'Shaughnessy? How many Hail Marys do I need to do?'

Milo didn't answer.

She said, 'Looking back, it's easy to see the pattern, but at the time?'

'What was the pattern?'

'Once Fredd was cleared of the dope charge, she put off blabbing by claiming she was scared for her life, needed a new ID, a safe house in another city, a spending allowance. That took months. Once she was set up, she faked depression, said she had no energy to deal with life, made suicidal noises. Bureau assigned a physician to give her a full checkup, and a review by a shrink.'

I said, 'Not the one who labeled her histrionic.'

'No, a doc who thought she was a sociopath. But we needed to go along with it, not confront her. Several more months, then she brought up a new medical issue — '

'Plastic surgery,' said Milo.

Lindstrom glared. 'Don't play with me. Am I repeating stuff you already know?'

'It came up on her external exam at the

192

morgue. Why'd Doreen want her nose nubbed all of a sudden?'

'What do you think? 'I'm scared, I need to change my appearance.''

'Des Backer's sister recognized her even with the nose.'

'So why didn't she go for something that really worked? Like I said, hindsight's twenty-ten. For all I know, she just wanted to look cuter and use our tax dollars to pay for it.'

I said, 'Surgery, then recuperation. A few more months of delay.'

'By the time she got talking, over a year had passed. It started off promising, she spit out all sorts of horrendous stuff. Including nonsense about an interface between domestic eco-nuts and foreign terrorists, some major Armageddon conspiracy. But like I said, it all dead-ended.'

Milo said, 'She give you anything righteous?'

'Like most liars she spiced up her bullshit with morsels of reality. Piddling stuff, but just enough to keep us going.'

'Like what?'

'False reports of endangered species sightings in order to halt public projects — phony DNA smeared on trees, that kind of thing. Non-violent fish-huggers setting out in canoes and cutting up nets, greenies perched in old, venerable trees so they wouldn't get chopped down for shopping centers. Which — off the record — I can't say bothers me. Giant redwood gets that old, for God's sake, let it live out its golden years in peace. And when I drive through miles of clear-cut dirt where a forest used to be, it doesn't

193

make me feel patriotic. In any event, Doreen snitched minor league, nothing came of it, but it took us a while to chase down all her bum leads.'

'Did you go back and question her about the dead kid in Bellevue?'

'You bet we did,' said Lindstrom. 'She never wavered from her initial story: She was snugly bed-a-bye at Hope Lodge the night it happened, was sure none of her pals were involved, they'd never do something like that.'

'She did mention Backer being her travel companion,' I said.

'But she didn't incriminate him in anything, Doctor. In fact, each time we brought his name up, she made him out to be Johnny Appleseed, not some maniac firebomber. Still, we checked him out and like you said, he was in architecture school, channeling his green impulses in a socially acceptable manner.'

Milo said, 'How soon after you gave her deep cover did she split?'

'She's been off our screen for thirty months, two weeks, and three days,' said Lindstrom. 'You want hours and minutes, I'll go back to my federal cubicle and use a calculator. I was assigned her file — and others — a little over a year ago, have been staring at her face with nowhere to go. All of a sudden, there she is on the evening news and I just about spew my Lean Cuisine. Your artist did a pretty good job.'

'My name was on the screen, too, Gayle. So instead of picking up the phone, you tell Hal to stonewall.'

'No choice, the directive came from on up.'

When Milo didn't respond, she said, 'Like it's different with you?'

'I'm sensing a theme here, Gayle. Everyone does it as a defense.'

'What do you want from me?' said Lindstrom. 'Flash back to your Hollywood D all roofied up with her legs spread and guess what, you won't find a trace of those dirty pictures anywhere on the Web. Any written record of the operation, period. What comes from on top filters down to the peons. Our job is to clean up messes.'

'Fine,' said Milo. 'Kafka's God and we're all cockroaches. But even bugs know how to be social. Why did your bosses want to obstruct me?'

'They wanted to make sure everything was squared up before we interfaced.'

'As in cleaning Doreen's file of anything useful so as not to look stupid?'

'As in getting my own facts straight. As in a sudden trip to Seattle yesterday morning in a coach seat next to a snoring fat guy.'

'If I hadn't bugged Hal, would we be sitting here, Gayle?'

'I can't answer theoretical questions,' said Lindstrom. 'Point is, I'm here and I told you what I know about Doreen. If it helps you close her out, I'll celebrate along with you. Because one of my assignments is to get her the hell off my desk.'

'Then write a bullshit report. I'm a cockroach enabler.'

'First enable some more. As in telling me what you can about Doreen's murder.'

'Doreen and Backer were enjoying sexual congress in a big house and got surprised in the act.'

'Ouch,' said Lindstrom. 'Mode?'

'He was shot once in the head, probably a .22, she was strangled.'

'Forensics?'

'His and her prints in expected places, no one else's, nothing at Backer's crib. No crib at all for Doreen, because some unnamed government agency helped her go bye-bye and let her stay underground even after she screwed them. Why, once you realized she'd conned you, didn't you put her factoids back in place?'

'It's not done that way.'

'She was an embarrassment, so no sense calling attention to her before the next begging session at Congress.'

'Whatever,' said Lindstrom. 'I really wish you'd stop bitching, because I didn't cause any of this. All I'm after is enough data to write her damn epitaph. What else do you have?'

'Nada.'

She toed her bag closer. 'I did some checking and the owner of the property might be of interest.'

'Really,' said Milo. Grinning, his hands had curled into massive flesh-mitts, pink and glossy and twitching. Like a pair of Christmas hams revivified by some mad scientist.

Gayle Lindstrom watched them, fascinated.

Milo stood. 'Special Agent Lindstrom, I believe we're through here.'

'Oh, Jesus,' she said. 'What's *with* you?'

'First you say you've told me everything, then you toss in your own little morsel to spice up the bullshit. Unlike the Bureau, I don't have years to put up with gamers.'

Lindstrom's jaw jutted. 'I never used the word *everything*.'

'Well, that sure clarifies it,' he said, heading for the door.

Gayle Lindstrom said, 'I am *not* gaming you. I didn't say anything in the beginning because I assumed you knew about the owner. After you didn't say anything, I thought you didn't so I told you, OK?'

Silence.

'I didn't think I had to *spoon*-feed you basic — '

'Who owns the property, Gayle?'

'You really don't know?'

Milo smiled.

'C'mon,' said Lindstrom. 'Just like you, I'm a salaried employee far from the top of the food chain. You want to keep picking at me, I can't stop you, but it won't close your double homicide. You want me to go first, fine? Prince Tariq of Sranil, aka Teddy.'

Milo sat back down. 'More coffee, Gayle? We're nothing if not hospitable.'

Lindstrom gaped. 'Not that it matters, but I only learned about him right before I came over here. You don't consider him a suspect. Not directly, I mean. He's back in Sranil.'

Milo said, 'He's alleged to have killed another girl.'

Lindstrom sat up. 'Who, where, when?'

197

'Don't know, don't know, around two years ago. It's still at the rumor level, a foreign national, maybe a party girl, maybe Swedish.'

'Who's your source?'

'Someone who heard a rumor.'

'Who?'

Milo shook his head. 'We've got secrecy issues, too. For all I know, it's baloney but the timing's right: just when construction stopped on Teddy's shack. And he rabbited back home right after.'

'Then Doreen ends up there.' Lindstrom shook her head. 'I'm not seeing any obvious link.'

'Anything related to Sranil ever come up in Doreen's stories?'

'Nope. And that I can be sure of because soon as I found out about Teddy owning the property, I re-read every damn word in her file.'

'But she did talk about foreign terrorists confederating with local eco-nuts.'

'It never came to anything, plus she never mentioned anything about Asians or Swedes or Ugandans or Lithuanians.'

'Just Ahmed,' said Milo.

'Quote unquote 'al-Qaeda types.''

'Sranil's Muslim, Gayle. And the sultan's got two groups of extremists itching to cut his head off and get control of all his oil. One of them's fundamentalist.'

'Interesting,' said Lindstrom. 'You're really thinking this could be political?'

'God, I hope not. Doreen ever travel abroad?'

'Never even had a passport.'

'Same question, Gayle.'

'I just told you — oh. No, Lieutenant Sturgis, as far as my peon status can carry me, I'm unaware of the Bureau or anyone else furnishing her funny travel papers.'

Milo said, 'So someone upstairs could've granted it.'

'Sure, but why would the Bureau help her evade when we were paying her to blab and she hadn't come through? The only time she could've traveled abroad would've been between splitting on us and now.'

'Exactly,' said Milo.

Lindstrom thought about that. 'OK, I'll make some calls, promise to give you righteous info. Fair enough?'

He nodded. 'After Doreen asked to be moved away from Seattle, where'd you safe-house her?'

'Sorry, not authorized. But trust me, it wasn't anywhere outside the continental US.' Smiling. 'Think acres of plains, not a mountain in sight.'

Milo said, 'Not here in LA.'

'Not even close.'

'Seeing as you just read every damn word of the file, is there anything in there about a gal-pal who *had* traveled abroad? Or *came* from abroad?'

'Swedish party girl? Negative, yet again,' said Lindstrom. 'You'll have to believe me on this, but that file contains squat-all international intrigue associated with Doreen Fredd. And you've got no serious evidence Prince Teddy actually offed anyone. But even if he did, how would it connect to Doreen and Backer two years later? Burning down a big showy house, I

199

can believe. They probably did that back in Bellevue and God knows how many other times. But targeting Teddy, specifically? This turning into some obnoxious 007 deal? I'm not seeing it.'

Milo said, 'What if Doreen and Backer somehow found out about the alleged murder and tried to cash in? From what you know about her, would that make sense?'

'Blackmail . . . sure, why not? She wasn't a woman of high character.' She sat forward. 'She and Backer hooked up more for old times' sake, decided to do more than eat dandelions and screw? Hey, anything's possible, but there's nothing along those lines that I can help you with.'

'Does the name Monte appear anywhere in your files?'

'Nope. Who is he?'

'Maybe no one, Gayle.'

'Obviously, *you* think he's someone.'

'What happened to the other two kids Doreen and Backer hung with back in Seattle?'

'Dwayne Parris and Kathy Vanderveldt? They both went off to college and got on the straight and narrow. She was pre-med, he was pre-law. Tell me about Monte.'

'Just a name that came up in a tip.'

'As . . . '

'Someone who might've known Doreen.'

'Might? That mean you don't think the tip's solid?'

Milo gave her the details.

'Geezer without a cell,' she said. 'Monte. Nope, doesn't ring a bell, but the moment I get

200

back, I'll re-read the file, just in case it slipped by me. We're talking seven-hundred-plus pages.'

'Doreen was small-time but she merited an encyclopedia?'

'One thing we're good at is churning paper.' Lindstrom smiled. 'Poor trees.'

21

We stood in front of the station and watched Lindstrom drive away in a government-issued Chevy.

Milo said, 'How much of that was real?'

'Who knows?'

A woman exited the staff parking lot, crossed the street, and brushed by us, setting off a zephyr of Chanel No. 5. Thin, pinch-featured, with a well-styled mop of flame-colored hair sharpened by a deep green suit and a yellow scarf patterned like a rattlesnake. She carried a bag even larger than Lindstrom's, maintained a high-stepping walk as she flung the station door open.

I said, 'It probably is in Lindstrom's best interests to cooperate. You clear Doreen, she makes headway on her pile of punishment.'

The station door opened and the redhead charged toward us, bag swinging, hair bouncing. 'Lieutenant Sturgis? Clarice Jernigan, from the coroner's.'

'Doctor.'

'I was testifying around the corner, thought I might as well talk to you in person. The receptionist told me I'd walked right by you.' Khaki eyes studied me.

'This is Dr Delaware, our psych consultant.'

'We can sometimes use help on suicides. Would you mind if I talked to the lieutenant in private?'

Milo said, 'Anything I know, Dr Delaware's going to know.'

'There's nothing psychological about what I have to say, Lieutenant.'

'Sorry, Doc. It ain't done that way.'

Dr Clarice Jernigan slid her bag to the sidewalk. 'Sure, what the hey. I opened Mr Backer's head and retrieved bullet frags. Definitely .22s, lab's trying to reassemble so if you get a weapon, they can run a match.'

'Thanks — '

'I also decided to do an autopsy on your Jane Doe, after all. As I'd assumed, no big surprise in terms of COD. Manual strangulation, the finger marks are obvious, but no prints or DNA, so maybe your bad guy gloved up. This was a healthy young woman who met a rather unpleasant demise literally at the hands of another.'

'We've got a name for her, now, Doc. Doreen Fredd. Two d's.'

Jernigan whipped out a BlackBerry, entered the information. 'My report will be forthcoming. Meaning whenever I can get to it.'

Milo said, 'That's what you needed to tell me face-to-face?'

Jernigan threw back her shoulders. 'What I need to tell you is I made an error and preferred not to address that fact over the phone.' Looking at me. I settled my gaze on the parking lot and pretended to be elsewhere.

Milo waited.

'I don't see it as a major faux pas, but you might as well know, in case it impacts how

203

you direct your investigation. As I told you, the rape kit was negative and my initial evaluation was no sexual assault. But after opening her up, I did find an abrasion in the vaginal lining, just under five inches in.'

She tossed the snake scarf over her shoulder. 'So why didn't I spot it initially? Because it was on the roof of the vaginal vault, kind of tucked away. A smallish but rather nasty snag wound consistent with insertion of a hard object — no jokes, please. Something with a pointed extension on the upper surface. My guess, confirmed by my tool-mark analyst, is the barrel of a handgun with a sharp sight. Initially, I assumed a .22 because of Backer. But after checking barrel lengths, I can't see any .22 entering that deeply without inflicting serious external damage to the labia. So we're leaning toward a larger-caliber revolver with a longer barrel and a prominent sight, such as a Charter Arms Bulldog. In fact, we tried out a Bulldog and it fit quite nicely with the abrasion.'

'Two guns,' said Milo. 'Little one for shooting, big one for raping.'

'To me, Lieutenant, that smells of intimidation, rage, or maybe just plain sadism. And, of course, now you need to consider two offenders. Do you concur, Dr Delaware?'

'Makes sense.'

'Then we're all on the same page.' Jernigan checked her watch. 'Needless to say, my initial hypothesis will not appear in the report and I'd appreciate if the same goes for yours.'

'Absolutely, Doctor.'

'Just to reassure you, I took another look at Mr Backer as well. Examined his anus and his mouth for any sign of assault by firearm or anything else. Pristine on all counts, so whatever additional psychopathology was at play seems to have been reserved for Ms Fredd with two *d*'s. Have a nice day, gentlemen.'

'How's it going on Bobby Escobar?'

'So far, Lieutenant, it's going nowhere.' Angry smile. 'Are you volunteering your services? That deal still stands.'

'I don't think the Sheriff's would appreciate my meddling, Doc.'

'No doubt,' said Jernigan. 'Then again, things get bad enough, everyone wants a bailout.'

When she was gone, he said, 'When she admitted goofing, I was expecting something about the vanished sperm stain.'

I said, 'Maybe there's just so much she can own up to.'

'Gun rape,' he said. 'Two offenders or a single dominant blitz artist who managed to cow Backer and Doreen all by himself.'

'Someone with big bucks could afford to hire a team.'

'Teddy and/or the sultan dispatched a hit squad.' He pressed his palms together, looked up at the sky. 'What did I do to offend you, Herr Kafka?'

Sean Binchy showed up at Milo's office brandishing a list of felons culled from Beaudry Construction's subcontractor list.

Nine names, no Montes or close. Binchy had run down seven of the miscreants, ruled them

205

out, was headed to Lancaster to check out the last two — a pair of cement-worker brothers arrested for stealing tools from a previous job.

Milo said, 'How's Ricki Flatt doing?'

'Got her set up in the Star Inn, paid for full cable, all the movie channels.'

'That should do it, Sean.'

'One question, Loot: My dad used to be a contractor before he got into Amway, I worked summers for him. Nothing fancy, just remodels, room additions. But whenever the residents weren't living on the premises, Dad fenced the job tight, it was my job to check at the end of each day. But that place? Anyone could walk right in, it was like asking for trouble. Not that there's anything left to steal, but still.'

'I agree, kid. Any theories about why?'

'It's almost like whoever owned it had lost interest in the place,' said Binchy. 'But then, why not just sell it, make some money? Maybe they're rich enough not to care about a few million, but I just don't see the point of letting it sit there. Anyway, I'm sure I'm not telling you anything new, let me go check out those two thieves.'

When he was gone, Milo said, 'Like we never thought of it. Still, obvious doesn't mean irrelevant.'

I said, 'Maybe there's a body buried there and it has something to do with Sranil's culture.'

'As in?'

'Letting nature take its course, something akin to Zen.'

'They're Muslims, Alex.'

'There could be something like that in Islam.'

'Letting a body rot to the point where it can't be ID'd? The lot's worth eight figures. Even for a billionaire, that ain't Lehman stock.'

'The sultan's a religious man,' I said. 'Articles of faith can go a long way.'

He faced his computer, pounded keys.

Five hits later, we were both reading an essay by a Yale scholar of 'emergent and divergent cultural forces' named Keir MacElway, citing the sultanate as an example of

a postmodern society where relatively enlightened Islamic mores and laws, including a liberal and flexible interpretation of *sharia*, have supplanted a centuries-old, nature-based tribal animist religion. However, vestiges of prior beliefs and rituals remain, sometimes melding with the modern Muslim approach. Among these are sun and water rites, the worship of specified trees and shrubs, and fishing calendars based on astrologic configurations preserved as nostalgic folktales but revered, nonetheless. In some cases, such as *sutma*, contracted from the animist *sutta anka enma* — literally washing away mortal sin — ancient customs persist in Sranilese society.

The origins of *sutma* remain unclear. McGuire and Marrow (1964) hypothesize that a passive approach to the treatment of 'deserved death' arose as a reaction to cannibalism, specifically as a means of preventing the consumption of enemy flesh following battles, because illness had been observed following cannibalistic victory feasts.

Ribbenthal (1969) attempts to link *sutma* to Buddhist influence, though evidence of any extensive interface between Sranilese animism and Buddhism remains evasive. Wildebrand (1978) attributes the belief to a generalized idealization of nature and presents as proof the ascendency of *Salisthra*, the guardian spirit of the forest, to the top of the animist pantheon.

Whatever its roots, *sutma* has proved resilient, impressively so in an age where other animist elements have ceded dominance to monotheistic religions. In contrast with Western norms advocating quick burial, and the Hindu belief in purification through immolation, *sutma* insists upon unfettered exposure to the elements of any organic material construed as being linked to maliciousness, insincerity, or sinfulness, in order for the sinner to gain access to the afterlife. Though not practiced as extensively as it was by Sranilese island tribes, when the merest accusation of immorality could lead to prolonged, often demeaning public postmortem displays, *sutma* occasionally emerges when a violent crime has taken place, most commonly in remote villages, when inhabitants seek out the comfort of *maranandi muru*, The Old Way.

Milo saved, printed. Sighed. 'Teddy kills a girl in that house so the sultan sees that goddamn pile of wood as sinful organic material.'

I said, 'He's making sure his brother reaches the afterlife.'

'Teddy met up with some family justice?'

'Justice in this world, compassion for the next.'

He looked up Professor MacElway's Yale extension, talked briefly and amicably to a startled scholar of emergent and divergent cultural forces.

MacElway confirmed it: In some animist cultures, murderers' huts were left 'fallow.'

Milo said, 'Guess the sultan's a traditionalist. So where do Backer and Doreen figure in, to the tune of fifty G's?'

'What if Backer and Doreen were paid by someone to burn the place down in order to jeopardize Teddy's celestial journey? They couldn't get to him directly because he's either dead or under royal protection back home in Sranil. But knowledge of *sutma* would present a partial alternative.'

'Keep the bastard out of heaven. Someone who believes in the old ways?'

'Or doesn't, but knows the royal family does. With no ability to exact physical revenge, keeping Teddy in perpetual limbo could be a potent psychological second choice. And it would explain why Doreen hacked into Masterson's file.'

'Pinpointing Teddy's real estate so he can dangle over the pits of hell forever. That's the case, they'd have to know something about Sranilese culture.'

'Didn't take you long to get the basic facts.'

'The information age . . . OK, let's go with this for argument's sake: Someone pays Backer and Doreen fifty G's to whip up some vegan Jell-O. Then why didn't they just do the job? Why keep visiting and using it as a love-nest?'

'That could've started as scoping out the job,' I said. 'Figuring out where to stick the explosives, time their escape. But once there, they decided to mix business with pleasure. Because that was Backer's thing: love under the stars in the company of plywood and drywall and rebar. That might go back to his adolescence. If he started early as a teenage firebug, sex and kaboom could've formed an interesting mix.'

'Coupla ex-delinquents warming up the grill with a little body heat.'

'Delinquents who got away with something spectacular,' I said. 'That's a huge high, and people who go through tremendously arousing experiences young often develop intense bonds to those experiences.'

'Pheromones and accelerant,' he said. 'Then ten years of God-knows-what. What do you think of the fact that Backer turned outwardly respectable but Doreen ended up selling her body?'

'Maybe he was less burdened by guilt and she had enough conscience to want to punish herself. Or he was smarter and better educated, came from an intact, supportive home, and made smarter decisions. Whatever diverged them, they reunited here in LA.'

'Chemistry.' Smile. 'Organic chemistry.'

'For all we know, despite Backer earning a degree, he never abandoned his sideline and someone out to avenge Teddy's victim made contact. Unfortunately for him and Doreen, the sultan found out. Their bodies left in the turret could be a warning to anyone else considering messing with *sutma*.'

He stood, raised his arms, touched the low ceiling. 'Desi and Doreen play with the big boys, pay for it with a bullet and a choke-out. With time taken out to jam a bigger gun where it was never meant to go. What's that got to do with the old ways?'

'That was intimidation, just as Jernigan suggested, to control the scene — or to obtain information. What Doreen and Backer knew, who else was involved. The element of surprise was a big part of the hit: That sperm stain on Doreen's thigh suggests Backer was pulled off her just as he came. They were both overpowered, he was interrogated, shot, leaving a cowed, terrified Doreen. And just in case that didn't impress her, out came the big gun.'

'You have that way,' he said. 'Drawing ugly pictures.'

Perfectly put. Thousands of sleepless nights proved it. I smiled.

He got on the phone. 'Moses? Busy? Good, c'mere. And start working on your charisma.'

22

Moe Reed said, 'Sure.'

Accepting the assignment to revisit the Indonesian consulate without emotion.

As he headed for the door, Milo said, 'Don't you want to know why?'

'I figure something came up on that dead-girl rumor, you want me to press my source for details.'

'Nothing came up, Moses. *That's* why I need you to press.'

'Consulate closes at four, I'll be there by three. She comes out by herself, I'll try to get some face-time. She doesn't, I'll tail her till I get a clean opportunity.'

'What's your source's name?'

'She wouldn't say, Loo, and I didn't push, figured her telling me anything was more important.'

'OK, Moses, like I said, charisma. If you need to buy her a few drinks, tab's on me. If it's a dim, cozy place I promise not to tell Dr Wilkinson.'

Reed's love interest was a physical anthropologist in the bone lab. 'Liz is cool. And the girl's probably Muslim. They don't drink.'

'Good point,' said Milo. 'OK, candy's still dandy.'

'You want me to go easy or hard on her?' said Reed.

'I want you to do what it takes to squeeze out every bit of info she's got on Prince Teddy and that Swedish girl.'

'I'm thinking I'll go real slow, not threaten her unless I'm smelling bullshit, then it's full press.'

'Keep doing that, Moses.'

'Doing what?'

'Thinking,' said Milo. 'Be the guy who stands out from the crowd.'

⋆ ⋆ ⋆

I drove away from the station with Milo in the Seville's passenger seat, fidgeting, rubbing his face, growling about LA traffic, all those scofflaw morons who kept cell-phoning, look at that idiot weaving, look at that brain-dead asshole stopped at a green, what's a matter, don't we have a shade you like, loser?

The Star Motor Inn sat on a gray block of Sawtelle, between Santa Monica and Olympic. Ricki Flatt answered the door wearing the same high-waisted jeans and an oversized black *Carlsbad Caverns* T-shirt. Her hair was loose and frizzy, her mouth small. Behind her, the bed was made up to military specs. Images flashed on a TV screen not much larger than my computer monitor.

'Lieutenant.'

'May we come in?'

'Of course.'

The room smelled of Lysol and pizza. No sound from the TV. The show was a cooking demonstration, a fluorescent-eyed woman so

213

thin her clothes bagged, bouncing with joy as she stir-fried something. Carrots, celery, and a lump of what looked like yellow Play-Doh.

One of Milo's rules-to-live-by is Never Trust a Skinny Chef. Sometimes he applies that to detectives. To any profession at random, depending on how the day's going.

One time I couldn't resist and asked about personal trainers.

He said, 'I'm talking real jobs, not sadists.'

His mood during the drive had grown progressively more foul. You'd never know it from the way he handled Ricki Flatt. Sliding a chair close to hers, leaving me to perch on a corner of the bed, he unholstered his softest smile — the one he uses with little kids and old ladies. With Blanche, too, when he thinks no one's looking.

'Get any sleep, Ricki?'

'Not much.'

'Anything you need, please tell me.'

'No, thanks, Lieutenant. Did you get into the storage unit?'

'Haven't heard back from Port Angeles PD yet.'

'I just hope Scott doesn't find out I held on to the money.'

'I explained that to them.'

'It makes me nervous — having it in my possession.'

'It'll be out of your life soon.'

'Is it drug money, Lieutenant?'

'No evidence of that.'

'I really don't see it. Desi was never into drugs.'

Milo shifted closer. 'Ricki, we're working *really* hard to figure out who murdered Desi, but honestly, we're knocking our heads against the wall. If I ask you questions you may find upsetting, can you handle them?'

'Questions about what?'

'Desi's early days. When he was seventeen.'

'That far back?'

'Yes.'

Ricki Flatt's eyes tangoed. 'You're talking about the Bellevue fire.'

Milo began to blink, managed, somehow, to curtail the reflex. He moved even closer to the bed. 'We need to talk about the Bellevue fire, Ricki.'

'How'd you find out?'

'Doing our homework.'

'Someone's murdered, you go into their childhood?'

'We go as far back as we need to.'

Ricki Flatt picked at the bedcovers.

Milo said, 'The fire's been on your mind. That's what you meant by political.'

'Not really,' she said. She hugged herself. Rocked. 'I'm sorry, Lieutenant, I'm not trying to be evasive, but I just can't accept the fact that my brother was some sort of paid arsonist. But fifty thousand . . . that's why I didn't sleep last night. And the Bellevue house was huge and so was where Desi was . . . I can't bring myself to say it. Where it *happened*.'

'Two huge houses,' said Milo.

'I drove by last night in a cab. To *that* place. Even with just the framework I could tell it was massive. I kept telling myself it meant nothing,

215

what connection could there be?'

'Tell me what you know about the Bellevue fire, Ricki.'

'That boy — Vince. He wasn't murdered, he burned himself up, it was basically an accident.'

'Van Burghout.'

'Van,' she said, trying on the name.

'You didn't know him well?'

'I'm sure I saw him if he came to the house with Desi but he never registered. Desi was popular, there were always kids over. And when the fire happened, I was at college.'

'Out of town?'

'No, U of W,' she said. 'Geographically not far, but I was into my own life.'

'The arson file names Van as one of Desi's hiking companions.'

'Then I guess he was.'

'Did your family discuss the fire?'

'We probably talked about it, it was a big local story. But as I said, I wasn't living at home.'

Ricki Flatt folded her lips inward, fighting tears. Milo placed a hand atop hers. She lost the battle and burst out sobbing.

Rather than hand a tissue to her, he dabbed.

Ricki Flatt said, 'Now I'm a traitor.'

'To who, Ricki?'

'My family. I just lied, we *didn't* talk about the fire. It wasn't *supposed* to be talked about. Ever.'

'Your parents said that?'

'Unspoken rule, Lieutenant. Something I just knew not to talk about. That wasn't my parents' usual way. That's why I've always suspected Desi *was* involved.'

'Those kinds of secrets,' said Milo, 'every family has them. But being honest doesn't make you a traitor. Not now, that's for sure.'

Silence.

'You want justice for Desi, Ricki. Would your parents have had a problem with that?'

No answer.

'Would they, Ricki?'

Slow head shake.

'Tell me what you know.'

'I don't *know* anything,' she said, 'I just *feel* it. Always have.'

'Apart from your parents clamming up, what gave you the feeling?'

'For a start, Desi's books. He had these counterculture books in his room. How to build homemade weapons, how to disappear and hide your identity, techniques of revenge, *The Anarchist Cookbook*. A whole shelf of that, above his computer.'

'Your parents were OK with that.'

'What I told you was true. Mom and Dad were all about developing our own sense of morality. Though one time I did hear Dad make a comment, being a firefighter he still had that law-and-order thing going on. I overheard him telling Desi those books would've been branded as treasonous in other societies and Desi answering that those societies deserved to disappear because without free speech nothing mattered. And Dad coming back that free speech was important but it ended where someone's chin met someone's fist. And Desi ending the argument the way he usually did. By being

217

charming. 'You're absolutely right, Pops.' Dad laughed and it never came up again. That was my brother, all honey, no vinegar. Unlike me, he never wasted energy arguing with Mom and Dad. He was the easy kid.'

'No overt rebel,' said Milo. 'So he got to hold on to his treasonous books.'

'*And* his foldouts from *Hustler*, no matter how gynecologic and how much Mom considered herself a feminist. *And* his Che poster and whatever else he wanted. I'm sure Mom and Dad never imagined him doing anything more with those books than reading.'

'Until the fire.'

'The weekend after the fire, I was home for the weekend. Getting my laundry done, Ms Independence. Mom and Dad were at work but Desi was home so I knocked on his door. He took a really long time to unlock, didn't seem thrilled to see me, wasn't the least bit warm. Which was odd, generally we'd share a big hug. But this time he looked flustered, like I'd interrupted something. My first thought was something adolescent — you know what I mean.'

'Those *Hustler* foldouts.'

'He *was* seventeen.' Blushing. 'Then I saw that his room had been completely rearranged, even the bed was in a new place. Desi was always neat but now it looked downright compulsive. A lot less stuff in the room. Including the books. All gone, and in place of the Che poster he'd hung a photo of moose in the forest. I made some wisecrack about redecorating, had he turned gay or something. Instead of laughing like he normally would've, he just stood there. Then he edged me away from the door. Not by touching me, by inching forward, so I was forced to leave or bump into him. Then he closed the door behind him and we both went to the kitchen and he was the same old Desi, smiling and funny.'

I said, 'Focusing on you instead of his room.'

'Desi was great at that. He could make you feel you were the center of the universe. Then he'd ask for something and you just said yes, no hesitation.'

'Did you ever bring up the fire?'

'Not with Desi, just with Mom. She got a strange look in her eye, changed the subject. That whole weekend was strange.'

'All three of them nervous.'

'I felt like a stranger. But in the beginning, I didn't connect it to the fire. It was only after I found out that Desi and some of his friends were questioned by the police that things started to click.'

Milo said, 'Were you ever questioned?'

'No, and I wouldn't have said anything. I had nothing to offer, anyway.' She wadded a tissue, released her fingers and watched it open like a time-lapse flower.

I said, 'Did Desi keep anything suspicious in his room besides books?'

'If he did, I wouldn't know. He had a lock on his door and used it.'

'Liked his privacy.'

'Sure, but what teenager doesn't? I figured it was because of all those girls he took in there. Was Doreen one of them? Probably, but only one, he might as well have had a revolving door. And, no, my parents never objected. Desi would play music to block out the sound but sometimes you could hear the bed knocking against the wall. Mom and Dad just continued to read or watch TV, pretended not to hear.'

'So your parents were used to looking the other way.'

'You're saying that made it easier for them to cover for Desi when he did something really bad?' Long exhalation. 'Maybe.'

Milo said, 'After the FBI questioned Desi, you started to wonder.'

'The FBI? All I heard about was the police. The FBI actually came to the house?'

'They did, Ricki. Talked to your parents, as well as Desi.'

'Unbelievable . . . only reason I found out the police were involved was by reading the *Daily* — the U of W paper. Something to the effect that no progress had been made but local kids were being questioned and Desi's name was mentioned. Did I say anything? No.'

Milo said, 'What do you know about Desi's ten years on the road?'

'Just what I told you yesterday.'

'Doing the hippie thing.'

'Retro-hippie,' said Ricki Flatt. 'Original hippie was my parents' generation. Then all of a sudden, he shaves his beard, cuts his hair, buys nice clothes, enrolls in architecture school. I remember thinking, so now he wants to build, not destroy.'

'The fire stayed on your mind.'

'I'm not moral enough to be haunted by it, but every so often, it would creep into my mind. Because that boy had died and the police had suspected my brother enough to question him and my parents had acted so weird.'

'Do you have any idea how Desi reconnected to Doreen?'

'None whatsoever.'

'He never mentioned her.'

'He never brought up any woman, Lieutenant. I just assumed he was being himself.'

'Meaning?'

'Playing the field and keeping it casual.'

'Did he mention any women from his years on the road?'

'Not a one. The fifty thousand, you're pretty convinced he was into something seriously illegal?'

'That's a lot of cash, Ricki.'

She grew silent.

Milo said, 'A couple of other kids in Desi's hiking group were also questioned after the fire: Dwayne Parris and Kathy Vanderveldt. Anything you remember about them?'

'I wouldn't know them if you showed me a picture. I was three years older. To me they were all a bunch of stupid kids.'

'You mentioned before that Desi was into health. Did he ever mention vegan Jell-O?'

'Sure.'

'He did, huh?'

'Why?' said Ricki Flatt. 'What does food have to do with it?'

'Vegan Jell-O's homemade napalm, Ricki. It

might've been used in the Bellevue fire.'

She went white. 'Oh, my God.'

'What did Desi say about vegan Jell-O?'

'I . . . I don't know, it's just something I heard him mention. It's really that?'

'Yes, Ricki.'

'I honestly thought it was food, some crazy organic thing.'

'Did he talk about it before the Bellevue fire or after?'

'Let me think, let me think . . . all I can recall is Desi and some friends in the kitchen, having a snack before . . . maybe before a hike — I think they were packing trail mix, water bottles, and then someone, maybe it was Desi, maybe it was someone else, I really don't recall, said something why don't we pack vegan Jell-O. And everyone started laughing.'

'Was Doreen there?'

'Was she there . . . probably. I can't be sure, maybe not, I don't know.' Wincing. 'Vegan Jell-O . . . Now I have to think about my brother in a whole new way.'

23

Milo closed the motel door on a fetal Ricki Flatt. 'Sweet dreams? Unlikely.'

Back in the car, he said, 'Those parents had to know their boy was involved in torching that house.'

I said, 'Firefighter dad, too much to handle.'

'Backer does God-knows-what for ten years then decides to be an architect? What the hell's that, I destroy, I build, the whole God thing?'

'Or a stab at atonement.'

'Fifty grand says he felt no guilt. Wonder if anything in San Luis got the vegan Jell-O treatment while Backer attended Cal Poly.'

'It's Robin's hometown, I'll ask her.'

I instructed the voice-recognition system to 'phone cutie.'

She said, 'I've never heard of anything but I'll ask Mom.'

Robin's relationship with her mother is, to be kind, complicated. I said, 'Selfless public service.'

She laughed. 'If we keep it at serious crime, we'll be fine.'

Milo said, 'I'm in debt to you, kid.'

'Bring wine the next time I cook for you.'

'What did I give you the last time?'

'Orchid plant. Also lovely but don't you want something you can share?'

'Find me a mansion arson in San Luis two to six years ago and I'll bring you a case of the best Pinot I can find.'

'Back to you on that, Big Guy.'

She called back three minutes later: 'Mom's never heard of anything like that and neither has my friend Rosa, who's lived there her entire life and knows everything. If you'd like, I can do a newspaper search.'

'I'd have to put you on regular payroll, kiddo.'

'Like you keep threatening to do with Alex?'

'Point taken,' he said. 'Anyway, not necessary, I can push keys.'

'When's my blue-eyed boy coming home?'

'Right now, if you want him.'

'I always want him, but don't let me hinder your investigation.'

'If only there was one.'

'That bad?'

'Hey,' he said, 'we're walking, talking, breathing, I'm grateful.'

Robin said, 'I don't like that kind of talk from you.'

'I shouldn't get philosophical?'

'Not on my watch.'

Milo lapsed into that same morose silence. Back at his office, he flung his jacket atop a file cabinet and began the search for mansion arsons throughout the state. Any eco torch-jobs.

Long list. 'Quite a few big houses went up during that time frame — here's an entire luxury housing project in Colorado . . . animal research lab — that one was high school kids who got stopped early.' Wheeling away from the screen. 'It's all over the country, Alex, but if there's a pattern, I'm not seeing it. And if Backer was a pro, you'd think something remotely incendiary would show up in his apartment. But the bomb dogs found zilch. Meaning (a) Backer was an architect, nothing more; (b) He did like playing with fire but put off buying his equipment until shortly before the gig; or (c) He kept a storage locker full of combustible goodies. And please don't remind me about none of the above.'

Sean Binchy rang in from Lancaster. 'Hey, Loot, those two thieving brothers are alibied clean for Borodi. Though, if you ask me, they're still up to no good, there was a truck without tags in their driveway, they definitely didn't want me looking at it closely. What next?'

'Go home.'

'Just forget about the truck?'

'Notify the locals and call it a day. Regards to your wife.'

'Absolutely,' said Binchy. 'I'm sure she sends them back.'

★ ★ ★

Milo said, 'Can't you just see me explaining this to the brass: revenge by *sutma* interruptus. Assuming there ever was a murdered Swedish girl. Assuming someone cared enough about her to burn down the house. Assuming Backer and Fredd were involved and dallied around before trying to blow the place up and got offed before they could follow through.'

I said, 'If there was a Swedish girl and someone cared enough to avenge her, they might've also contacted the Swedish consulate about her being missing.'

225

He looked up the local number, had a civilized chat with a man named Lars Gustafson, who had no personal knowledge of any Swedish citizen in jeopardy two to three years ago but promised to check.

Milo phoned Moe Reed. 'Find that Indonesian girl?'

'Just about to call you, Loo. I was there when they closed up but she wasn't at work today. Hope talking to me didn't spook her because I didn't get a name or an address. Stupid, huh? I was trying to keep her mellow.'

'Judgment call, Moe, don't get an ulcer.'

'I'll be there tomorrow before they open up. Need anything else?'

'Go home.'

'Sure, there's nothing I can do?'

'Get some sleep in case there is, Moses.'

He hung up, sighing.

I said, 'What a good dad.'

Grumbling, he logged onto an online yellow pages, searched for storage facilities in LA County. A minority refused to divulge client information but most were surprisingly cooperative.

Call after call his torso sagged with each negative. The sum total: no units registered to Desmond Backer. Milo's eyes closed. His breathing slowed, grew shallow, his big head flopped back in the chair, and his arms dangled.

When the snoring reached nuclear-blast level, I saw myself out.

★ ★ ★

226

Robin was working her laptop on the living room couch. Blanche napped on an ottoman, her little barrel chest heaving. Not up at Milo's level, but moving some audio needles with her snuffles and snorts.

Opening one eye, she smiled, dove back into some wonderful canine dream.

The screen was full of Google hits. *Mansion arson* the keywords.

I sat down. Robin kissed me, continued scrolling. 'Playing Nancy Drew. Couldn't think what to cook. Leftovers or out?'

'Out sounds good.'

'My soul mate. Nothing turns up in San Luis, but plenty of fireworks in other cities. Someone builds a dream, someone else can't wait to take it down. How ugly.'

Years ago, a psychopath burned our first house to the ground. We rebuilt, agreed the net result was an improvement, neither of us talks about it anymore. But a fire station is perched at Mulholland, a short drive to the north, and another sits to the south, near Beverly Glen and Sunset, meaning a fair bit of nights are broken by sirens.

Generally, the banshee howls are short-lived, we touch feet in mutual reassurance, go back to sleep.

Sometimes, Robin sits up, shivering, and I wrap my arms around her and before long, morning's arrived, sour and disorienting.

She closed the laptop, stood, stroked Blanche. 'OK, I'll get dressed.'

'Chinese, Italian, Thai, Indian?'

'How about Croatian?'

'What's Croatian cuisine?'

'Let's fly to Zagreb and find out,' she said. 'Italian's fine, hon. Anything's fine, long as I get out of here. Let me freshen up.'

★ ★ ★

We ended up eating fish-and-chips at a stand on PCH in Malibu, watched the sky waver between coral and lilac, soaking in the final morph into indigo as the sun went off-shift.

When we returned home, I ran a bath. The tub's not meant for two but if someone's careful not to bump their head on the faucet, it works out. That kind of togetherness sometimes leads to more. Tonight it didn't and we read and watched TV and went to bed just before midnight.

When I woke to reverb shrieks, I thought I was dreaming, woke expecting the din to fade.

Full consciousness amplified the noise. Robin said, 'That's the fifth one. They're heading south.'

Three seventeen A.M.

Siren number six wailed. Dopplered.

'Someone's life's going to change, Alex.'

We slid under the covers, touched feet, gave it our best shot.

Moments later, I turned the TV on and we trolled for news through a swamp of infomercials and reruns of crap that shouldn't have aired in the first place. If something newsworthy was occurring on the Westside, none of the networks or the cable news outlets had picked it up.

The Internet had. LA current events blog operating in real time. Some insomniac plugged into the emergency bands.

Holmby Hills conflagration. Unfinished construction project.

Borodi Lane.

Robin's breath caught. I held her tighter, reached for the phone, punched Milo's cell number. He said, 'I'm on my way there, call you when I need you.'

When, not if. I got dressed, made coffee, told Robin she should try to get some sleep.

'Oh, sure,' she said, hanging on to my arm.

Mugs in both our hands, we plodded through the house, stepped out onto the front terrace. Frosty, dark morning. Warmish for the hour, but we shivered. Above the tree line, the southern sky was dusted with gray. The sirens had waned to distant mouse-squeaks. The air smelled scorched.

Robin said, 'Bad news travels fast.'

24

Borodi Lane was blocked by cruisers and a huffing hook-and-ladder. A uniform scowled as I rolled to the curb, barely edging past Sunset.

A skeptical call to Milo produced a reluctant nod. 'But you need to keep your car there, sir, and walk.'

I continued toward the scene, breathing heat, firewood, flame-suppressing chemicals, a hydrocarbon stench evoking the world's biggest filling station. The asphalt was slick with wash-off. Static and buzz kept up a magpie routine, red engines and hard-hatted firefighters were everywhere. Several more explanations before I was allowed to reach the property.

What was left of Prince Teddy's dream was black and stunted. Where the ground wasn't ash, it was soup. A white coroner's van was pulled up to the open gate. The chain Milo had supplied was on the ground, marked by a plastic evidence cone, and sliced through cleanly into two pieces.

As firefighters streamed in and out, a pair of morgue attendants hauled out a gurney bearing something small and lumpy and wrapped in plastic. I looked for Milo, spotted him near an LAFD ambulance, wearing a limp black raincoat, jeans, and muddy sneakers, staring at the ruins. To his right, on the ground, several objects sat on a black tarp, too dim to make out.

As I stepped next to him, he fished out a

Maglite, aimed downward.

Partially melted glass bottle. From the shape and scorched wire around the neck, probably champagne. A single intact wine goblet. A butter knife with a handle melted to a blob. A metal tin with an ornate label.

I bent to read. *Foie Gras. Imported from France.*

Milo's beam shifted to a long-barreled revolver, clearly antique, wooden grip scorched through, engraved metal blackened.

Next to the gun sat a pair of bolt cutters, seared to well done.

I said, 'Someone was having a party.'

'Probably Mr Charles *Ellston* Rutger,' he said.

'Probably?'

'Body's unrecognizable but Rutger's Lincoln is parked around the corner and there was a solid gold calling card in the ash, with his name engraved on it. Plus, some dental bridges came out half baked, same for a gold collar pin and initialed platinum cuff links.' He cursed. 'Dressing for success. Idiot cut the chain, climbed up to the turret with his Dom Whatever, goddamn goose liver, and no doubt some other comestibles that got vaporized.'

I said, 'Picnic under the stars.'

He kicked a clump of mud off a sneaker tip. 'Cretin probably convinced himself he owned the place again. Who knows how many other times he went up there, when there was no chain. I warned him but of course he can't listen 'cause I'm a dumb public servant and he's a goddamn aristokook. Talk about bad timing,

231

Charlie Three-Name.'

'Story of his life,' I said. 'Wouldn't be surprised if the arsonist saw the broken chain, took advantage. How'd the fire start?'

'What the arson guy's telling me so far is someone wadded charges of something highly combustible, probably petroleum-based, in at least eight spots distributed methodically throughout the ground floor. 'Very well thought out' was his description.'

'Petroleum-based as in vegan Jell-O?'

'Flavor of the month. The neighbors heard only one explosion, whole place went up like kindling, so it looks like a single timer. Coulda been a disaster if the winds were strong and the flames jumped to neighboring foliage. The fact that the lot had been stripped down to bare dirt actually helped.'

'Ground floor ignites, flames shoot up through all that open space, oxygen feeds it. Meanwhile Rutger's stuck on top with the stairs burned out.'

'Wouldn'ta made a difference, Alex. This was sudden, intense immolation, no chance for escape. Rutger's drinking champagne, stuffing his face, no one's the boss over *him*. So now, he's toast. Scratch that. Crumbs.'

A stocky gray-haired man wearing a yellow helmet, a blue LAPD windbreaker, and jeans approached us wiping a sooty, sweaty face.

'We're going to be here for a while, Milo. You can go unless you want to stick around.'

'Better you than me,' said Milo. 'This is Dr Delaware, our psych consultant. Doctor, Captain Boxmeister from the arson squad.'

232

'Don,' said Boxmeister. 'I'd shake your hand but mine's filthy. This was some conflagration, reminds me of you-know-which jungle, Milo, huh? Vegan Jell-O, haven't heard that in a while, yeah, it sure works like napalm. You mind continuing with the murder part of it so we can concentrate on the arson? Which isn't to say we won't be collaborating.'

Milo said, 'Sounds good, Don. That Fed I mentioned said Jell-O's an eco-terrorist fave-rave.'

'Used to be, Milo, but we don't see that kind of big-scale looniness on the Westside, except for occasional threats to animal researchers. All we had last year was a wimpy amateur fire set in one of the U's med labs and we caught the fool. Worked there, sweeping floors, no affiliation with any group — one of those guys you'd know about, Doc. Shit-for-brains thought he'd liberated all the little Mickeys but what he ended up with was rodent flambé and third-degrees on both arms. I think it stays quiet here because no one expects houses in Holmby or BH or Bel Air to be anything *but* gross. You start eliminating ostentatiousness on the Gold Coast, you get the Gobi Desert.'

'Bite your tongue, Don.'

Boxmeister grinned, pulled out a notepad and pen. 'Tell me again which oil type owned this barbecue.'

'Prince Tariq of Sranil. Not the Mideast, Asia, it's near Indonesia — '

'I'll look it up,' said Boxmeister. 'So you're thinking your original vics also planned to torch

233

the place but got interrupted by someone, they had an accomplice who finished the job and roasted whatshisname Rutger in the process.'

'That's a good summary, Don.'

'Political. That sucks. If you don't mind, I'd prefer to keep a lid on that part of it, no sense getting the neighbors thinking al-Qaeda's lurking near their tennis courts.'

'Good idea,' said Milo. 'Especially because all I've got are guesses.'

I said, 'How was the body positioned?'

'There was no body, Doc. Just bones and ashes and some dental plates.'

'Did the fire move it?'

Boxmeister thought. 'That high up, probably not.'

'Where in the turret was it found?'

'Right in the middle.'

'Not near the stairs?'

'Was he trying to escape? Doesn't look like it.'

'Quiet killer,' I said. 'Rutger had no idea.'

'Or he knew but couldn't do a damn thing about it. No traces of a cell phone were found.'

Milo said, 'Phone would've survived the blast?'

'Some part of it probably would,' said Boxmeister. 'Tell you one thing, I'm going to look into the composition of that liver can. Anything that can survive something like this, I'm stockpiling.'

A woman's voice, argumentative, caused the three of us to turn.

A young brunette in the grip of a female officer pointed at Milo. Slim, long-haired, the house-sitting daughter who'd spotted Doreen Fredd on Borodi.

Amy . . . Thal. She wore a red silk robe over pajamas and fuzzy pink slippers. Protested as the cop held her back.

Milo jogged over, excused the officer, returned with Thal. High-intensity lights turned her freckles to Braille dots.

'Don, this is Ms Thal, a cooperative neighbor. Amy, Captain Boxmeister from the arson squad.'

Boxmeister said, 'I'd shake your hand but mine's filthy.'

Amy Thal rubbed the arm the cop had held. 'I tried to explain to her that I knew you, had something to say. It's not like I'm some looky-loo, this is my frickin' neighborhood.'

'Sorry,' said Milo. 'What's up, Amy?'

'I saw another woman I didn't recognize. Yesterday, jogging past this place at least three times.' Sniffing burnt air. 'This is crazy, what's going on, Lieutenant?'

'Tell me about the woman.'

'Blond, long hair, tight bod. She looked like a runner, at the time I didn't think much of it but now I'm wondering. Because she kept running back and forth and why do that when there are all sorts of interesting runs you can take? I mean, cross the street and go by the Playboy Mansion, or Spelling's old place, go down to Comstock and run around the park. Why keep passing back and forth? I mean it's suspicious, right?'

'Three times,' said Milo.

'Three times I saw, Lieutenant, could've been more. I was in the living room, stretched out on the couch, reading. Generally, it's real quiet, so anything that moves you notice. Yesterday, I saw a huge coyote, just ambling past, like he owned the street.'

'Was there anything strange about her?'

'She seemed kind of intense. But that's runners, right? I wouldn't have given it a second thought. But now? What do you guys think?'

'We think we appreciate your coming forth, Amy.'

Boxmeister nodded. 'Anything more you can say about what she looked like, ma'am?'

'Black tights, bare tummy, sports bra. Decent face, at least from a distance. Maybe real boobs but with a sports bra, I can't be sure.'

Milo said, 'What kind of blond?'

'Ultra,' said Amy Thal.

'Platinum?'

She nodded. 'Long and shiny — and no ponytail like most girls do when they run. She just let that sucker flap in the breeze. Like 'Look at me, I am *soooo* silky.' She reminded me of that comedy thing a while back, my dad used to love to watch them, my mom always got pissed off because she thought it wasn't humor that got his interest. The Swedish Bikini Team. I think they sold beer or something.'

Don Boxmeister said, 'Old Milwaukee.'

Amy Thal said, 'It was years ago, I was a kid. Dad loved them. This girl was like that. OK, I'd better get on the horn, tell Mom and Dad to keep enjoying Paris.'

Milo thanked her. She gave his wrist a sudden squeeze, turned and left.

Boxmeister said, 'Nice ass, like to do a hand-count of those freckles. Too bad her info's useless. Hottie jogging in Holmby, big shock.'

'Don, the girl this prince is reputed to have offed was Swedish.'

'Oh . . . ' Boxmeister's smile was sheepish. 'Back up the tape, erase. Our firebug's a lady out for personal revenge? Then how do your first two vics figure in?'

'Like you said, they could've been in it together. Or she was a family member of the Swedish vic, hired them, they got killed, she decided to finish the job.'

'You're seeing *her* as why they got killed? That's kinda thin.'

Milo didn't answer.

Boxmeister slapped his back. 'Look on the bright side, be nice to have a good-looking suspect in the box, for a change. Just in case Blondie has nothing to do with it, though, I'll be doing it old-school, combing the files for any serious pro torches recently paroled or released. Let you know if I come up with something, and you find anything pointing to Anita Ekberg, you call me pronto.'

We watched him leave.

Milo said, 'How early do you think diplomat types get to work?'

25

The Swedish consulate rents space on the seventh floor of a high-rise at Wilshire near Westwood. Consular assistant Lars Gustafson was at his desk at eight thirty, took Milo's call with puzzlement but agreed to meet in an hour.

'Out in front, please, Lieutenant.' The faintest trace of accent.

'Any reason we can't come up?'

'Let's enjoy the nice weather. I'll be there promptly.'

'How will I know you?'

'I'll do my best to look Swedish.'

Milo hung up. 'Aw shucks, thought I'd get a look at the furniture. Bet it ain't IKEA.'

★　★　★

We were in place by nine twenty-five, watching the revolving door accept people dressed for business.

At nine twenty-nine A.M., a throng emerged and dispersed. The man who stayed behind was around thirty, tall, athletically built, wearing a fitted brown suit, yellow shirt, butterscotch shoes.

Blond and blue-eyed, but his hair was kinky, his skin milk-chocolate, his features those of a Masai warrior.

'Mr Gustafson?'

'Lars.' Energetic pump, flash of diplomatic teeth custom-made for news conferences and lunch with genteel old ladies. 'I have researched your issue, Lieutenant. There have been no complaints by any Swedish citizen — at home, or here — regarding missing persons or homicides. I did find a case involving a Danish citizen who was thought to have disappeared in San Diego. However, she showed up and the matter was resolved. A love triangle, no royalty involved, Muslim or otherwise, thank heavens.'

'The Muslim thing bothers you.'

Gustafson smiled. 'Nothing bothers us, we are neutral. The Danes, on the other hand . . . remember those Mohammed cartoons?'

'That why you didn't want us up in your office?'

'No, no, heaven forbid, gentlemen — please forgive me if I seemed unwelcoming, but the consul general felt police officers could serve as a distraction.'

'From the daily challenge of stamping visas.'

Gustafson kept smiling but the wattage went out of it. 'We do attempt to be useful, Lieutenant. Next week, we're hosting a dinner for over two dozen Nobel laureates. In any event, I have nothing to tell you. Good luck.'

Milo took out his pad. 'How about some details on the Danish case.'

'A woman named Palma Mogensen was working as an au pair for a family in La Jolla when she met an American marine in Oceanside. Unfortunately, she was already married to a Danish man and after she stopped returning her

239

husband's e-mails, he showed up.'

'Things get nasty?'

'Oh, no,' said Gustafson. 'Everyone talked it out and the couple returned to Copenhagen.'

'Civilized,' said Milo.

'We try to be good influences, Lieutenant.'

'You and the Danes.'

'All of us who must contend with endless night. It breeds a certain patience.'

★ ★ ★

Gustafson headed back toward the revolving door, managed to sidle in as the mechanism remained in motion.

Milo said, 'Swedish, Danish — time for a pastry.'

We found a coffee shop in the Village. Two bear claws and a crème-filled chocolate eclair for him, a coffee for me. Later, we were back in the station parking lot.

'Jogging,' he said. 'Sports bra. This is gonna be another washout day.'

He was wrong.

★ ★ ★

One message slip atop his computer. Barely legible scrawl. He squinted, put on reading glasses. Frowned. 'Now it's *Mrs* Holman wanting a meeting.' Punching numbers. 'Ms Holman, Lieutenant Sturgis, I got your — about *that*? Really. Why don't you tell me what it is you . . . Sure, we can meet but if you could just fill

me in before — you sound upset, Ms Holman
. . . Yes, of course we appreciate leads, I can be
there in thirty, forty minutes, that work for you?
. . . Fine, then. You're sure there's nothing you
can — all right, then, Ms Holman, I'm on my
way.'

He placed the phone in its cradle as if it were
breakable. 'That's one very uptight architect and
her voice says she's been working on the gin.'

'She knows something about the fire?'

'Claims to but wouldn't say what. I guess I
should call Boxmeister. I guess I won't.'

★ ★ ★

Another pretty day at the canals.

Marjorie Holman was out on her front porch,
wearing a black sweater and slacks and looking
like a model for a high-end retirement
community.

Next to her stood a tall, white-haired, goateed
man close to seventy. His gaunt frame was a wire
hanger for a black suit and turtleneck.

Milo muttered, 'Looks like a funeral.'

No sign of Professor Ned Holman.

His wife waved us up impatiently. The man
in the black suit didn't budge, even when we
were two feet away. His eyes were blue and
world-weary. Stick limbs, a long neck, and a beak
nose evoked an egret. Mournful bird on a bad
fishing day.

'This is Judah Cohen,' said Holman. 'My
former partner.' Husky voice; the slight slurring
Milo had picked up over the phone.

241

'Mr Cohen.'

'Lieutenant.' Cohen studied the floorboards.

'What's on your mind, Ms Holman?'

She hooked a thumb. 'Inside.'

No trace of her husband or his chair on the ground floor. Milo said, 'Professor Holman OK?'

'Ned? He's at the doctor, one of his checkups. I use a special-needs van service because I never know how long it's going to take.'

Marching to the sink, she poured Sapphire and ice cubes into a glass. 'Anyone joining me — Judah, how about you? Glenlivet?'

'Not today, thanks,' said Cohen. He sat on the edge of an overstuffed sofa. Shifted position, cupped his hands over a bony knee. From the look in his eyes, nothing would make him comfortable.

Holman returned with her drink, perched next to Cohen. 'Judah and I have some serious suspicions Helga had something to do with that fire.'

Cohen winced.

It didn't get past Holman. 'Would you care to take over, Judah?'

'You're doing fine, Marjie.'

'So we're together on this.'

'We are.'

'Well, then, onward. As I told you the first time, Helga boondoggled us — got us to leave some very nice professional situations under pretense of establishing a groundbreaking green-architecture firm. She claimed that her father was a wealthy industrialist, owned a shipping company, money was *not* going to be a problem.

However, money turned out to be a *serious* problem. As in, Helga did nothing but talk, failed to follow through on financing the firm. At the time, Judah and I were puzzled. Now it becomes clear: Helga never had any sort of serious intention. Judah and I were part of a cover-up.'

Milo said, 'Of what?'

'I'll get to that.' Holman sipped an inch of gin. 'I need to do this in an organized manner, Lieutenant . . . where was I? The ruse . . . one day, Helga announced that funding hadn't developed, she was disbanding the firm, returning to Germany, have a nice day.' Turning to Cohen.

He said, 'Bit of a shock.'

'You always were the master of understatement, dear. Basically, Helga played us for the fools we apparently were.'

Cohen said, 'No sense beating ourselves up. Helga had valid credentials and her technical knowledge was solid.'

'She was an engineer, Judah, not a spark of creativity.'

'Be that as it may,' said Cohen, 'the manner in which she described the initial project was valid, conceptually as well as structurally.'

Milo said, 'The Kraeker Gallery.'

Both architects stared at him.

Holman said, 'How do you know about that?'

'Helga told us.'

'Did she? Then you were played, as well. Yes, it's an actual place and yes they are taking bids on a major expansion. But Helga never applied

243

to be part of the bidding process. And *they* have never heard of her.'

'When did you find out?'

'A few days ago, Lieutenant, when it became clear that Helga had no intention of compensating us for our time and loss of prior employment.'

'We can't find her,' said Cohen. 'Or rather, our attorney can't.'

Holman said, 'Don't ask why we didn't check her out more thoroughly. A partnership, like a marriage, is based on trust.'

Milo didn't blink. I was willing to bet on his internal dialogue. *Motels on Washington Boulevard.*

Holman said, 'While she was truthful about her educational credentials, she lied completely about other things.'

'Such as?'

'First off, she's not German, she's Austrian. And her father's not a shipping tycoon, he's a banker.'

'Is Gemein her real name?'

Reluctant nod. 'What should have tipped us off was her take on green: hatred for humanity rather than feed and save the planet. The woman's a *total* misanthrope and as time went on, she felt freer to share her opinions on how the evolutionary process had failed when it produced human beings. How *Homo sapiens* disrupted the crucial balance, what the world really needed was a good plague or a world war. Which coming from a Teutonic type is pretty damn breathtaking.'

244

She turned to Cohen.

He said, 'Rather impolitic.'

Milo said, 'Could we talk about the fire?'

'I'm *coming* to that,' said Holman. 'This needs to be logical, so that you'll understand we're not just a couple of disgruntled malcontents. Where was I — Helga's lies. The home address she gave us here in LA was phony, as we learned when we tried to serve her with papers.'

'You're suing her.'

'Damn right we are. Professional alienation, breach of contract, anything else our lawyer can come up with.'

'Where was the phony address?'

'Brentwood. As to why we didn't find it odd that Helga never had us over, we believed she was all business and that was fine. We were motivated to create something *important*. Correct?'

Cohen nodded.

Finishing her drink, she returned to the kitchen, poured a refill. Cohen watched her with sadness, turned to us. 'It might be helpful for you to know that Helga hired Des Backer before she talked to us. She presented him as a rising star whom she'd met looking for young architects with green credentials. We did check those credentials. Top of the class, his professors had nothing but praise for him. However, when our attorney recontacted them, none had ever spoken to Helga, nor had Des asked them for letters of recommendation. So she found him some other way.'

Holman said, 'Given the advantage of

245

hindsight, it's clear Des's work product was nil.' Smirking. 'In terms of architecture.'

Cohen said, 'Our attorneys had someone go through the office computers. Des did a lot of gazing at pornography as well as surfing through some disturbing websites. Which brings us to the fire.'

Milo said, 'Arson websites?'

'Eco-terrorist websites. Congratulatory photographs of vandalized luxury housing and animal research labs, chat strings of people who believe the ends justifies the means.'

'We'll need those office computers.'

'Sorry, *we* need them,' said Marjorie Holman. 'Our attorney has instructed us to place all the furniture and equipment in storage, so we can show that Helga clearly abandoned the office.'

Criminal trumps civil, but Milo didn't push it. 'Those websites — '

'Were sent to Helga. We had no idea the two of them had any relationship beyond the firm. On the contrary, Helga claimed not to even like Des.'

'Even though she hired him?'

Cohen said, 'Helga was good at putting things — and people — in boxes.'

'Acceptable professionally,' said Milo. 'Unacceptable personally.'

Holman said, 'There *was* no 'personally.' The woman is cold-blooded. As was her version of green.'

Cohen said, 'The unfortunate truth is, a strong misanthropic streak exists within the green community. But it's a minority view and

Helga seemed to take it to the extreme.'

'Plagues and wars.'

Holman said, 'Des sent her j-pegs of burned-out buildings and she sent him LOLs and happy faces. Singing the praises of 'selective pyrotechnics' as a tool of 'biological cleansing.' '

Milo had her repeat that, scribbled in his pad.

Cohen said, 'What was surprising was Des mirroring Helga's point of view. *He* had seemed so sociable and humanistic. Talked about his niece, wanting to build a better world for her.'

Holman said, 'She's capable of anything, probably killed Des simply because she felt like it. Or maybe he was supposed to burn down that house, chickened out, and she executed him for disloyalty to the fatherland, whatever.'

Milo said, 'Who's your attorney?'

Holman said, 'Manny — Emmanuel Forbush.'

Cohen said, 'Forbush, Ziskin and Shapiro. Here's their number.'

'Thank you, sir. What else?'

Holman said, 'That's not enough?'

'It's a good start, Ms Holman — '

'Then get *going* with it. Run that bitch into the ground and do the world a favor.' Making progress on the booze slur. She drank, spilled gin on her lap. Cohen handed her a tissue. She ignored him, drank some more.

Milo said, 'Any idea where Helga is, ma'am?'

'For all I know, she's back in Shwitzerland.'

'Why Switzerland?'

'Because that's where she's from.'

'Thought she was Austrian.'

'She was *born* in Austria but the family *moved*

to Spritz-Shwitzlerland, her father owns a bank there. Manny found that out easily enough.'

'Do you have the bank's name?'

'Why would I?'

Judah Cohen said, 'GGI-Alter Privatbank, Zurich. The address is a *postfach* — a post office box.'

Holman stared at him. 'You should go on Jee-epardy.'

Milo said, 'A bank with no office?'

'I'm sure there's an office,' said Cohen, 'but perhaps they're all about investing, have no interest in walk-ins. Apparently, it's not unusual in Zurich, according to Emmanuel Forbush. He's sent several certified letters but no answer so far, feels a civil suit will take years to unravel, we need to be patient. If we choose to persist.'

Holman said, 'Oh, we *choose*, all right.'

Cohen didn't answer.

Milo said, 'Years to unravel unless Helga can be tied in to a criminal case.'

Holman said, 'She *is* a criminal, catch the bitch before she braids her hair and puts on lederhosen and disappears into the land of cuckoos and chocolate.'

Milo stood.

Marjorie Holman said, 'Exactly. Time to get a move on.'

Judah Cohen said, 'Good luck.'

26

Emanuel Forbush, Esq's, baritone boomed through the car speakers.

'I've been expecting your call. Guess you want the computers.'

'That would be helpful, sir.'

'No problem, Lieutenant, pick them up at your convenience. Of course, we will be keeping copies of every single word of data. Don't imagine you'll mind, without our coming forward you'd be in the dark.'

'Sitting on evidence in a criminal case could have caused problems, Mr Forbush.'

'If you ever found out.'

'Thanks for the vote of confidence, Mr Forbush.'

'No, no, I'm not — I just want to make sure our civil case is preserved.'

'You really think a civil suit's worth the effort, sir?'

'Why wouldn't it be?'

'It just doesn't sound as if the stakes are that high for all the trouble.'

'Well, I suppose I'll have to be the judge of that.'

'I suppose you will, sir.'

'Lieutenant,' said Forbush, 'I don't want to get off on a bad foot with you. Sorry if I came on too strong.'

'No problem, Mr Forbush. I'll send a detective for those computers today.'

'Great. So how's Marjie doing?'

'I just watched her down two stiff drinks and my guess is they weren't her first this morning.'

Forbush tsk-tsked. 'That's always been an issue for Marjie, poor kid.'

'You're friends?'

'Ned and I go way back, we used to play squash. Hell of an athlete, damn tragedy. Marjie's had a lot to deal with, a victory would be good for her. *That's* why I took on the case.'

'Friend in need,' said Milo.

'The only kind that counts,' said Forbush.

Milo hung up. Laughed. 'One of Ned's old squash buddies. Should've asked him about the current décor of Washington Boulevard no-tells. He took on the case to keep the sheets hot, Cohen's along for the ride, they squeeze out a settlement, it's found money for him. So now I've got dead ends in Sranil *and* in Zurich.'

I said, 'Maybe you're in luck and Helga's still in LA. Or was, this morning.'

'What do you mean?'

'She's a good-looking, well-built woman in her thirties with Nordic features. Cover that bald dome with a platinum wig — something that flaps in the breeze — and all a witness would focus on would be blond, blond, blond.'

'Amy Thal's jogger,' he said. 'Yeah, she does have that Valkyrie thing going on.'

'Not Swedish,' I said. 'Swiss. What if Reed's source was almost there?'

'Seen one European, seen 'em all. Including the girl Teddy supposedly offed.' He rubbed his face. 'His vic was Helga's sister, or a close friend.

She comes to LA to get revenge, starts a shell firm for cover, looks for Teddy. Tries to find his local address by having Doreen — who she met through Backer, maybe on some anarchist chat line — comb through Masterson's files.'

'Her primary goal was to kill Teddy, but she found out he was out of her reach in Sranil, either hiding in the palace or dead. So she settles for burning down his house. Pays Backer and Fredd fifty thousand to do the job.'

'Not much bang for all that buck, Alex.'

'If she banked on Teddy being dead, messing with his *sutma* would've been emotionally appealing. The sultan's religious, so the thought of his brother dangling in perpetual purgatory would be unsettling.'

'You fuck with my family, I fuck with yours? With Backer and Fredd gone, Helga cases out the place herself, decides on a do-it-yourself?'

'Maybe she arrived this morning with her own bolt cutters, saw the gate open, and walked right through.'

'Meanwhile, Rutger's snarfing bubbly and liver, making himself easier to ignite . . . so who killed Backer and Doreen? The sultan's hit squad or Helga herself because she learned how to go kaboom from hanging with them, decided they were expendable?'

'If Helga is involved, I don't see her acting alone. Overpowering two people by herself, even with two guns, would be tough for a woman, even a strong one. And using a gun to rape Doreen doesn't fit.'

'Everyone says she hates people, Alex.'

'Even so,' I said. 'That scene reeked of *male*.'

'Helga's more social than she lets on, has a pal? Or this whole damn theory's one big house — mansion of cards.'

He phoned Captain Don Boxmeister at the arson squad, left a message. Followed up with a call to Special Agent Gayle Lindstrom, connected, gave her a recap, asked her to research Helga Gemein.

She said, 'Is she a Swiss citizen or Austrian? It makes a difference, tactically.'

'They both extradite, Gayle.'

'They do, but the Swiss make it a lot more difficult. Prying out a Swiss citizen is going to be hell.'

'I don't know where her passport's from.'

'Either way,' said Lindstrom, 'she could be already gone.'

'Sitting in the International Terminal as we speak, Gayle. So how about dispensing some of your guys in dark glasses and walkie-talkies?'

'I'll get an airport check going soon as I hang up. Including private charters, seeing as Daddy's a money-mover. Give me the name of his bank.'

He flipped through his pad. 'GGI-Alter Privatbank.'

Lindstrom said, 'Sounds fancy. Soon as you snag those computers, make sure I get a full copy of the hard drives.'

'Done and you're welcome, Gayle. Once you get hold of her passport info or anything else, get on the horn A-sap.'

'Done and *you're* welcome. I'll give your regards to Hal.'

'He takes your calls, does he?'

'Must be my feminine mystique.'

★ ★ ★

Sean Binchy was dispatched to pick up the computers.

Moe Reed answered his page, alert and focused. 'I'm right across the street, my source came to work this morning but she was with a bunch of other girls and I couldn't isolate her. She's due out soon for lunch.'

Milo said, 'Don't waste time on subtle, Moses, just pull her aside. What I *need* to know is how sure she is about the Swedish thing. Even if she says she is, ask her could it be 'Swiss.''

He explained why.

Reed said, 'Blond is blond, huh? I'll nab her as soon as I see her, Loo.'

★ ★ ★

A search using *ggi alter privatbank zurich gemein helga*, and *family* as keywords, paid off.

Embedded among German-, French-, and Italian-language business sites was a single photo, dated six years ago. One of many snapped at a fund-raiser for the Kraeker Gallery's exhibit of outsider art, featuring well-fed, well-groomed people in black tie and gowns.

One thumbnail off to the right. Milo enlarged it two inches square: Banker George Gemein, his wife, Ilse, daughters Helga and Dahlia.

Both parents, bespectacled, ramrod-straight,

253

unsmiling. Helga matched their stance, the obedient child. Even with a honey-colored schoolgirl bob and a baby-blue gown trimmed in lace, she came across grim, disapproving.

Dahlia Gemein appeared several years younger than her sister. Shorter and curvier than Helga, she sported a conspicuous tan, a headful of ash-blond waves, a saucy grin. Defying the family commitment to good posture, she cocked a hip and slouched forward, threatening to spill ample bosoms out of her blood-red, skintight sheath. Bejeweled fingers held the stem of a cobalt-blue cocktail.

The only Gemein caught drinking, she'd separated herself physically, standing half a foot apart.

The clan. The mutation.

Milo switched to NCIC, ran a search on *dahlia gemein*, pulled up nothing there or on the Doe Network, any MP or crime file. But the Web spat back another photo dated the same year as the Kraeker gala, snapped at the record launch party of a rapper named ReePel. Malibu party house, Broad Beach. I'd heard about the place. Closed down after a torrent of neighbor complaints.

In that one, Dahlia Gemein wore a pink string bikini and stood flanked by two men in flowered bathing shorts: the guest of honor, obese and cornrowed, and a baby-faced, muscular Asian man identified as Teddy K-M.

Milo shot a fist into the air. Flipped through his pad and shouted, punched the air harder. 'Dig this, Alex: K-M as in Tariq Ku'amah Majur. Something *real*.'

254

He studied the shot. 'Girl like this isn't going to be a throwaway, someone's bound to report her missing. So why isn't she in the database?'

'Maybe someone forgot to enter it.'

'Human error? Oh, come now.'

A call to Missing Persons revealed that Dahlia Gemein's disappearance had never been reported. Follow-ups everywhere else confirmed the same.

Milo slumped. 'For all we know, she's not missing. She and Teddy fell in love, she went back to Sranil with him, is living the life of a princess, and there goes Helga's motive.'

He checked with Moe Reed. 'Your source out yet?'

'Out and right here, Loo. See you in about twenty.'

27

Ati Meneng was tiny, gorgeous, terrified.

She looked ten years younger than the twenty-nine listed on her driver's license, took up so little space that Milo put her in his office and had room to spare.

Standard California license, no special consulate perks. She typed documents in the secretarial pool.

She had on a cinnamon-colored pantsuit that covered everything but hands and face. The office was warm but that didn't stop her from shivering. Tilting her head, she created a glossy sheet of blue-black hair that masked her face. 'I still don't know why I'm here.'

Milo said, 'Just what I told you, Ati. You're helping us and we really appreciate it.'

'There's nothing I can help you with.'

Milo wheeled his chair closer. 'This doesn't need to be stressful, Ati.'

I sat just inside the open door. Moe Reed stood behind me. Young guy with a fondness for Aqua Velva. My father had slapped it on religiously, cursing as the alcohol ignited booze-inspired shaving nicks.

If Reed was breathing, I couldn't hear it.

Milo said, 'Is it OK if I call you Ati?'

Murmurs from behind the hair curtain.

'What's that?'

'Call me what you want.'

'Thanks, Ati. First off, we're sorry we had to take you away in the middle of work but this is a murder investigation. If you have problems with your boss, I can talk to him.'

'No, don't. I don't know about murder.' Crystalline voice, no accent.

Milo said, 'How long have you been living in LA, Ati?'

Hair slithered away like glycerine on glass, revealing a flawless oval face, pouty-lipped, ruled by enormous black eyes. 'All my life.'

'Where'd you grow up?'

'Downey.'

'How'd you come to work at the Indonesian consulate?'

'They advertised in an Indonesian paper. Needed someone who knew Dutch, my parents speak Dutch in the house.'

'How long have you been working there?'

'Like nine months.'

'And before that?'

'A bunch of places.'

'Such as?'

'Why is that important?'

'Just trying to get to know you, Ati.'

'Why?'

Milo rolled back a few inches. 'Can I get you something to drink?'

'No, thanks.'

'Tell me about some of your previous jobs.'

'Mostly temps.'

'Don't like to be tied down to anything long-term?'

'Temps are what I could get while I auditioned.'

'You're an actress?'

'I thought I was.'

'No luck, huh?'

Black hair swung. 'I did some commercials for Asian cable. I thought I could model downtown for petites, but they said I was too small for even that.'

'Tough gig, the audition circuit,' said Milo.

'Every stupid girl thinks she can do it.'

'That include Dahlia?'

Pouty lips separated on white teeth slick with saliva. Brown hands the size of a ten year old's met each other and clenched hard.

Ati Meneng said, 'You found her?'

'Would that surprise you?'

'I just didn't think it would ever happen.'

'Why's that?'

'People like that,' said Ati Meneng. 'They get away with things.'

'People like who?'

Silence.

Milo said, 'People like Prince Teddy?'

Long, slow nod. 'I didn't know who he was. Later, I found out.'

'How did Dahlia meet him?'

'I don't know.'

Milo said, 'Dahlia was your friend but you don't know?'

'I don't know exactly. That's why I talked to you — to him — in the first place. Because I *do* care, she *was* my friend.'

'Tell me what you do know, Ati.'

'My parents can't find out,' she said. 'They think all my temp jobs were secretarial.'

'They won't, I promise.'

Silence.

Milo said, 'You did some other things besides secretarial.'

'I wasn't getting any secretarial jobs so I registered at a website, OK? Asian Dolls. It's not what it sounds, they just linked visiting businessmen with presentable young ladies suitable to be taken to social events.'

That sounded like a direct quote.

Milo said, 'Helping them feel at home.'

'Mostly it was Japanese guys,' said Ati Meneng. 'When Japanese girls were available, they got first dibs, but when they weren't it opened up to all the girls. They were mostly nice. The guys, I mean. Older.'

'Mostly.'

'I never had problems, it was totally a positive experience for me. It was an honest business, the woman who ran it, Mae Fukuda, died a few years ago, her kids didn't want to keep it going. Some of those other businesses are sleazy. That's why I'm at the consulate, totally bored.'

'Asian Dolls,' said Milo. 'That wouldn't seem to include Dahlia.'

'Dahlia didn't need to work, she had tons of money.' Gazing at the floor. 'OK, I know how I met her. A party. After that, we started to hang out. She got me into some cool places.'

'What kind of cool places?'

'VIP rooms at clubs, private parties — like at the Playboy Mansion, we went to three separate parties at the Playboy Mansion, it was incredible. Hef wasn't there, he let them use his house to raise money for charity. We got to swim in the Grotto.'

'Where'd you meet Dahlia?'

'A club in Chinatown.'

'Which one?'

'Madame Chiang's.'

Milo said, 'Hill Street, in the big mall, right? Big restaurant downstairs, upstairs banquet room.'

'Uh-huh.'

'Great dim sum at lunch, it closed down a few years ago.'

'If you say so.'

'So how'd you come to be there, Ati?'

'It was a business party, jewelry. I went with a businessman from Cambodia. He gave me a gold chain to keep. Mostly he talked to other jewelers and I could do what I wanted.'

'Who else was at the party?'

'Jewelry guys. Armenians, Israelis, Chinese, Persians. Some white guys. The speaker was a white guy. From the mayor's office, or something like that, welcoming the jewelry business to LA.'

'What brought Dahlia there?'

'She was with one of the white guys. He sold watches.'

'Remember his name?'

'Never knew it,' said Ati Meneng. 'Older, white hair, fat. Swedish, like her.'

'Dahlia told you she was Swedish?'

'Uh-huh.'

'Actually, she was Swiss.'

Huge black eyes expanded to cartoon proportions. 'Yeah, *that's* what it was. You probably think I'm stupid.'

'It's an easy mistake to make,' said Milo.

'Dahlia didn't like to talk about it. Being Swiss.'

'Why not?'

'She said it was a boring place to live, that's why she sometimes said she was from other places.'

'Such as?'

'I don't remember. Maybe Sweden — maybe that's where I got it. She only told me about being Swiss after we hung out for a while. The guy she was with that night, she said she knew him from back home, he was a big watch dealer, knew her father because her father collected watches, had hundreds of them in little boxes that kept moving to keep them winded. She was at the party to do him a favor. The watch guy.'

'Being his arm candy.'

'We all were. The men were really into business, the girls were mostly left alone and a whole bunch of us ended up at the bar. That's where I met Dahlia. We were both getting drinks and hers was weird, bright blue. I said something about it looking like dishwashing liquid. She laughed. We started talking, before she left, she said, 'It's been fun, let's hang,' and she gave me her number.'

'You guys hit it off,' said Milo.

'Easy with Dahlia,' said Ati Meneng. 'She was pure sunshine. Even though she was rich she was cool about it, I didn't even know until we'd hung out awhile.'

'How'd you find out?'

'I mean I kind of suspected it because she didn't have a job and she drove a Porsche Boxster, really cool little red one. When I found out for sure was when she took me to her house. Real nice and all done up. She said her parents bought it for her 'cause they hated her.'

'Interesting way to show hatred,' said Milo.

'I'm sure they didn't really hate her, she just meant they needed space from each other.'

'She had problems with them.'

'She didn't like to talk about it, just said they were all religious and stuff. They sent her to Catholic schools, she kept running away, taking trains to Germany and France, going to clubs, meeting guys. She never went to college, like her sister did, and that made them mad. She just liked to ski and swim and travel on trains and hang out. When she told them she wanted to see Hollywood, they were happy to see her go, bought her a house. To her that meant *Stay away as long as you want.*'

'How'd she feel about that?'

'She laughed about it. That was Dahlia. She used to say maturity was highly overrated.'

'How long were you guys friends?'

'Half a year? Maybe a little longer? We actually didn't hang out that much because I had to work. Sometimes Dahlia would call, mostly she'd wait until I called and if she was free, we'd hang out. She had platinum cards, was real generous, but I didn't take advantage. Being with her gave me a chance to dress up. Be my best, you know?' Her eyes welled.

'What else did she tell you about her family?'

'That's it.'

'Did she say what her father did to make all that money?'

'Oh, yeah. He owned a bank. It was like in the family for generations.'

'How many siblings did she have?'

'Just her sister, Dahlia was the younger one. She said her sister was the smart, serious one. Studied to be an architect, or something.'

'The two of them get along?'

'She never said they didn't. She didn't talk much about her sister.'

'So her parents bought her a house and she took that as their wanting her to stay away.'

'I used to say maybe you should call them, try to reconnect. 'Cause I did that with my father. He's real old-school, wanted me to marry an Indonesian guy, stay at home and raise kids. When I got those commercials he refused to watch. But now we get along.'

'Did Dahlia take your advice?'

'If she did, she never said.'

'How'd she meet Prince Teddy?'

'At first she didn't know he was a prince.'

'She found out after they'd been dating.'

'Uh-huh. Guess she liked him for himself.'

'How they meet?'

'At the Le Beverly — it's a hotel in Beverly Hills, small, from the outside you can't tell, it looks like an apartment building. Dahlia had a pass to get into the private bar, it's up at the third floor. I was supposed to go to a party but my date canceled and I was bummed and bored and I called Dahlia and she said, 'Let's go to

BH, we'll have some fun.' She'd been there before. I could tell 'cause the bartender knew her drink — Blue Lagoon, they mix it with a special orange liqueur that's colored blue. Dahlia said she liked the taste but mostly used it like an accessory.'

'Fashion accessory?'

'She had these incredible blue eyes, liked to wear colors that brought them out, mostly red and yellow. But also a bit of blue, here and there. Like jewelry, you know? She said the Blue Lagoon worked like jewelry, helped bring people's attention up to her eyes. She was like that. Artistic. Her house was full of her paintings. All blue, these wavy designs. Like the ocean, you know?'

'So,' said Milo, 'you and Dahlia were in the private room of the Le Beverly.'

'I was drinking my Mojito and Dahlia was drinking her Blue Lagoon and the only other people were some Asian guys across the room, playing backgammon. Dahlia made a joke about their being Asian. 'I take you to this great place to get away from work and it ends up looking just like work.' I laughed and she laughed and then one of them came over and for a second I thought they heard us and were ticked off. But the guy was smiling, saying, 'Women are beautiful when they're happy. If you'd agree to join us, we'd be highly proud.' Something like that, kind of lame. He had an accent but you could understand him. We figured he was the assistant because he was the smallest of them and not the most handsome and the worst dressed. The other two guys were younger, taller, real handsome, in Zegna suits. Later I found out *they* were the bodyguards and he had come over himself.'

'Prince Teddy.'

'He just called himself Ted. You'd never know he was anything important, he just had on a sweater and jeans. And he looked real young. Shorter than Dahlia, but she said, 'Sure,' and we got up and joined them. Without asking me, but that was OK, mostly I let Dahlia make the decisions. It was her got me in there in the first place.'

'So you joined Ted and his bodyguards.'

'We didn't know they were bodyguards, we just thought they were three guys. They ordered some bar food and more drinks, put their backgammon away. No one was nasty or gross, it was nice and polite. The bodyguards, you'd never know they were bodyguards.'

'They didn't act tough.'

'They acted like his friends. Just guys hanging out.'

'Rich guys.'

She blinked. 'Yeah, I guess so, being in the private lounge. But that's not what got Dahlia to join them, money didn't impress her, she had her own. She told me afterward she thought he was cute and sweet and real smart. I guess he was smart, he could talk about all sorts of things.'

'Like what?'

'Nature, travel? I really wasn't listening.'

'Dahlia reported to you afterward,' he said.

'The next morning,' said Ati Meneng,

265

coloring. 'Yeah, OK, she went home with him. But it wasn't like she ditched me. When we were in the ladies' room, she told me she'd decided to do it, but only if I was OK with it. He seemed like fun, she wanted some fun. She insisted on giving me cab money. I had an early audition, anyway.'

'Was that pretty typical for Dahlia? Going with guys she just met?'

Black eyes sparked. 'She was *not* a slut.'

'Of course not,' said Milo. 'I'm just asking if she made quick decisions.'

'No,' said Ati Meneng. 'She'd dance with guys, kiss them on the dance floor, even . . . sometimes she'd go off to a private VIP room. But I never saw her leaving for a whole evening with a guy. Never.'

'She must've really liked Teddy.'

'Once they started dating, I hardly ever saw her. But I was cool with that, everyone has their own life.'

'Eventually, she told you who he was.'

'That was maybe . . . weeks after, I can't remember. We hadn't seen each other and all of a sudden Dahlia called to catch up. Said he was out of town, let's go to Spago. She thought it was funny.'

'What was?'

'How we thought he was the assistant and he turned out to be from one of the richest families in the world. She said he still didn't like to dress up. Sometimes he rented a cheap car and drove to McDonald's and ate cheeseburgers. Next day he'd be in his Gulfstream, that's a jet, flying anywhere he wanted. She flew in it, too, said it was all pimped up, black wood, black everything inside.'

'Where'd he fly Dahlia?'

'Mostly Vegas, but one time Hawaii. He liked to gamble. Dahlia's only thing was when she was with him she didn't drink, 'cause he was Muslim.'

'He wasn't drinking that night at the Le Beverly?'

'Diet Coke,' she said. 'His thing was Diet Coke. But he wasn't whack about it, you know? Religion, I mean. Basically, she thought he was a cool little guy. That's what she called him. My cool little guy.'

'She ever talk about problems in the relationship?'

'He could get grumpy, had a temper, but not to worry, he was already a member of the . . . ' Blushing, she drew hair across her face.

Milo said, 'Member of what?'

'It was just a joke.'

'A joke about what?'

No answer.

Milo said, 'What club was Teddy a member of?'

The hair fell away. 'Not a real club, just a joke. The Three F Club. She said it was the only way to a man's heart. Three F's — feed 'em, flatter 'em, fuck 'em. Don't write that down, I don't want my parents to see it.'

'You see paper and pencil anywhere, Ati?'

'I'm just saying.'

'So Dahlia never complained about Teddy

267

being aggressive or violent with her?'

'Never.'

'Just grumpy with a temper.'

'Nothing whack, like any guy.'

'But you told Detective Reed he hurt her.'

'Because I believe he did.'

'You believe?'

'I can't prove it, but . . . '

'You suspect.'

Nod.

'Why, Ati? This is important.'

'Did he?'

'We don't know, Ati. Help us.'

She breathed in. Exhaled slowly. 'The last time I heard from her she was going traveling with him, she said she'd be back in a few days, we'd hang out. But she never called and I never heard from her again and when I called her phone, it was disconnected and when I went to her house, no one was there.'

'Where'd she say she was traveling with Teddy?'

'Back home,' she said. 'His home.'

'Sranil.'

She frowned. 'My parents told me about it. It's a weird place, full of like old-fashioned peasants. Indonesia's modern. Sranil's just an island that never became part of Indonesia. Teddy didn't like it himself, was going over there to get a bunch of his money and come back here and live with Dahlia. He was already building a house. He wanted to be modern and be with any woman he wanted even if she was white, not be under his brother's thumb.'

'Dahlia told you all that.'

'Yes.'

'Maybe she went there with Teddy and decided to stay.'

'No way,' said Ati Meneng. 'That's why I know something happened to her. She totally planned to come back. Promised me we'd hang out when she got back. But she never got back.'

'Did you report her missing?'

'She wasn't missing, she was with *him*.'

'You suspected he'd hurt her.'

'I didn't think so at the beginning. I just . . . I don't know, maybe it was his brother but I was too afraid to say that. His being a sultan, who'd believe me?' Looking at Reed. 'I didn't think you'd believe any of it, period. Mostly I forgot about it, then you showed up and it was like something clicked inside my head, you know?'

Milo said, 'You told Detective Reed about a Swedish girl but you didn't use Dahlia's name.'

'I didn't — I wasn't sure. It's not like I was still thinking about it. I *used* to think about it. Then it stopped. Then he showed up . . . I shouldn't have said anything.'

'No, no, you did great, Ati. We really appreciate it. Now tell us everything you know.'

'That is everything.'

'Dahlia definitely planned to return to LA.'

'We had plans,' said Ati Meneng. 'A whole day, soon as she got back. First we were going to the Barney's warehouse sale and have lunch at this café at the Santa Monica Airport — that's where the sale is. Then we were having dinner at the Ivy — not the beach, the one on Robertson.

269

Then we were going dancing. But she never came back. And she left her car at her house and when I looked in through the window, all her stuff was still in there.'

'You went over because you were worried.'

Tears turned the black eyes to pond-stones. 'I kept calling. Her cell was disconnected, she had no more Internet for IM'ing, her house was dark. My mind started running. I mean I liked him the couple of times I met him, but I didn't really know him. And what my parents said, that started to bother me.'

'About people from Sranil.'

'Superstitious peasants. Cannibals, rituals. You know?'

'Scary,' said Milo.

'Really scary, so I stopped thinking about it. I would've called her family but I didn't know how to reach them. I figured if she stayed away long enough, they'd do something.'

'Even though her parents wanted her gone.'

'She just said that,' said Ati Meneng. 'It probably wasn't even true. Families love each other. Like her sister, Dahlia said they were different but they still loved each other.'

'The serious sister.'

'Dahlia said she even thought about becoming a nun then she became an architect, built houses.'

'Speaking of houses,' said Milo. 'Do you remember the address of Dahlia's?'

'Never knew the address, Dahlia always drove me there and took me home. She liked to drive real fast, said in Germany there were roads with no speed limits, she used to go a hundred miles an hour.'

'What neighborhood was the house in?'

'Brentwood.'

'Could you find it?'

'For sure.'

Milo stood. 'Let's do it.'

'Right now?'

'Can't think of a better time, Ati.'

28

The house that evoked Ati Meneng's 'That's it!' was a mini-colonial wedged between two much larger Mediterraneans. Twenty-minute drive from the station, nice section of Brentwood, a short walk to the Country Mart.

One symmetrical story was faced with white clapboard. Lead-pane windows were grayed by curtains and sideburned by black shutters. A red door was topped by a fanlight. The lawn was compact and trimmed, the empty driveway spotless.

Two blocks away was the vacant lot Helga Gemein had given her partners for her nonexistent residence.

Milo said, 'You're sure, Ati?'

'Totally. I remember the door. I told Dahlia a red door could mean good luck in Asia. Dahlia laughed and said, 'I don't need luck, I'm adorable.''

'OK, thanks for all your help. Detective Reed will take you back.'

She turned to Reed. 'You can just take me to my car. Or we could have lunch, I could call in sick.'

Reed's voice was flat. 'Whatever you want.'

Ati Meneng said, 'I guess I'm hungry, they'll probably yell at me, anyway.'

★ ★ ★

Milo ran the address. Taxes were paid by Oasis Finance Associates, an investment firm in Provo, Utah. A call there elicited the guarded admission from the controller that the owners were 'non-US citizens who wish to retain their privacy.'

'Swiss or Asian?' said Milo.

'Pardon?'

'Swiss or Asian, which is it?'

'This is important?'

'It's a murder investigation, Mr Babcock. The victim's a woman named Dahlia Gemein.'

'Gemein,' said the controller. 'Then you already know.'

'I'll take that to mean Swiss.'

'You never heard it from me.'

Milo clicked off.

I said, 'Daddy Gemein's held on to the house two years after Dahlia disappeared. Maybe it's the family's West Coast getaway, as in sister gets to live here, too.'

Milo said, 'Kinda cute and traditional for Helga, but with Daddy paying the bills, she's flexible.' Gloving up, he loped up the driveway, paused to peer through windows, continued to the garage, tried the door. Locked, but he managed to budge it an inch from the ground, squint through the crack.

Standing, he dusted himself off. 'Little red Boxster, red motorcycle, looks like a Kawasaki. Be interesting if either was spotted on or near Borodi.'

He called Don Boxmeister, gave him the info. Perfect timing; the arson squad's canvass was

273

in full swing and a red bike had been spotted the day before the fire. Three blocks west of Borodi, parked illegally on a particularly dark section of street. The neighbor who'd seen it hadn't bothered to call it in. Boxmeister's other nugget was forensic: Initial analysis of residue found at the scene was consistent with vegan Jell-O, and scorched wires suggested electronic timing devices.

Milo gave Boxmeister Ati Meneng's story, then hung up and searched the inside cover of a notepad where he keeps a list he doesn't want on his computer: phone numbers of cooperative judges. Each time he begins a new pad, he recopies meticulously.

Running his finger down the small-print, back-slanted columns, he said, 'This is your lucky day, Judge LaVigne.'

LaVigne was available in chambers and Milo went full-bore, making more of the blonde jogger than was justified by the facts, labeling the red Kawasaki as 'rock-solid physical evidence.' Emphasizing Helga Gemein's virulent hatred for humanity and evasive behavior when initially questioned, he tossed in speculation about international terrorist links, maybe even neo-Nazi connections.

'Exactly, Your Honor, like Baader-Meinhof, all over again. Meaning the house — and I'm looking at it right now — could be a source of weapons, explosives, bomb timers, all of which has been implicated in the arson as well as the multiple murders. Top of that, the suspect may already be gone, we really need this warrant now.'

It was as good a performance as I've seen and within seconds, he was winking and giving the thumbs-up. 'Love that guy, he'll draft it himself, all I need to do is get it picked up and filed.'

A call to Sean Binchy took care of the trip to the criminal courts building. Binchy was still at Manny Forbush's law office, soon as he had the dupes of GHC's hard drives he'd head downtown.

We waited for the locksmith and the bomb squad and the explosives dogs. Milo's cell battery was depleted and he switched to my car phone to get his messages. Lots of bureaucratic trash and one that mattered: Officer Chris Kammen of the Port Angeles, Washington, police department.

Kammen's basso rattled the hands-off speaker. 'Hey, how's it going? We went over to that storage unit at four A.M. These people are neat-freaks, just about the most organized junk pile I've ever seen. Which is why I'm confident telling you there are no suitcases full of money. Not behind the piano or anywhere else.'

'You're kidding.'

'Wish I was,' said Kammen. 'Fortunately for you, the facility's got after-hours video that actually works. Unfortunately for you, it doesn't tell much. At eleven forty-three P.M. a male Caucasian in a dark hoodie used a key to gain entry and came out ten minutes later carrying what my grandma would call two stout valises. I'm getting a copy of the tape to send you, but trust me, it's not going to accomplish diddly. All you got is shadows and blur, the hood covers his face completely.'

'How do you know he's Caucasian?'

'White hands.'

'He didn't bother gloving,' said Milo.

'Apparently not.'

'Maybe that's because finding his prints in the bin wouldn't be suspicious. *Mrs* Flatt was really nervous about *Mr* Flatt finding out she held on to them. Maybe he did.'

Kammen said, 'I wondered the same thing so first thing I did was look Flatt up, and trust me, it's not him. He's a *big* boy, six six, used to play basketball for PA. High, power forward, good outside shot, I remember the name now. We used the gate as a frame of reference to get a measure on Hoodie and he's closer to five ten.'

'Definitely a male?'

'Why? You got a bad girl in your sights?'

'Square in our sights. Looks like she burned down the big house early this morning.'

'The same one?' said Kammen. 'Where the bodies were?'

'Yup.'

'Whoa, it's complicated out in LA. What time did the house fry?'

'Three A.M.'

'Then Hoodie's not your torch, no way he could be here close to midnight and get back in time. You can't get a direct flight out of here that late and even if you made it to Seattle, what with drive time and airport time and two-plus hours of fly time? I'll send you the tape so you can judge for yourself, but this is a guy. Unless your bad girl has broad shoulders and humongous hands and walks like a guy.' Chuckle. 'Then

276

again, you're in LA.'

Milo said, 'I'm sure you're right, but our girl does have theoretical access to a private jet.'

'Oh,' said Kammen. 'Yeah, you're *LA*. But even so, it would be a hell of a squeeze. Tell you what, though, I'll call general aviation at our airport, see who flew in and out and from where.'

'Thanks.'

'Hell of a thing, someone beating us to the storage bin. We would've gone in at a normal time but we didn't want the husband to show up. Can't help it if the gods weren't smiling. Bye.'

The car grew silent.

I said, 'Two people do the murder, two people manage the arson and recover the money. Maybe Helga's not as antisocial as she claims.'

'Dick and Jane murder duet?'

'Down from a quartet. Helga paid Backer and Doreen to torch Teddy's real estate. Gave them a cash deposit, meaning the total payment might have been more.'

'Six-figure job, no shortage of motivation,' said Milo. 'Helga hires them but in the process learns enough about arson to make the two of them unnecessary and gets rid of them. Then she sends her buddy to get the dough back. How would she know where Backer stashed it?'

'That's the kind of info a fellow might divulge when bargaining for his life. Or watching his girlfriend get raped by a gun. Same for the location of the storage locker key. If Backer was carrying it on his person, that made it even easier.'

'Helluva lot of effort to burn down a heap of

277

wood.' Reaching back, he retrieved his attaché case, found the Gemein family photo.

I said, 'Helga lied to everyone about applying for the Kraeker expansion contract. The place means something to her, maybe because that party was the last time the family was together. As cold as she is, she loved her sister. Dahlia may have been the only person she ever loved. Take that away, you focus your anger, destroy what you can.'

'*Sutma*. For all we know, Helga's got a secret religious side, gets off on visions of Teddy never entering heaven.' He studied the shot some more. 'Look at how they're positioned: Dahlia's standing away from the rest of them.'

'But she's also standing closer to Helga than to Mom.'

'Maybe that's 'cause Mom looks like she's got all the charm of frozen halibut. Dad, on the other hand, is more . . . cod. And Helga's our shark.' Grinning. 'How's that for dime-store psychoanalysis? What I'm wondering is whether the revenge plot is Helga's thing or a family affair.'

'We can't eliminate Mom and Dad's involvement, and one way or the other it's family money that funds Helga's lifestyle. Dahlia's, too, including this house, which is immaculately maintained. Be interesting if the neighbors remember any of the Gemeins living here.'

'We'll start canvassing soon as the house is cleared.' Another glance at the little colonial. 'Only thing missing is the picket fence.'

Checking his watch, he followed up with the bomb squad. They were a couple of minutes away, arriving with high-tech toys and three of their best canines.

A couple of minutes turned into fifteen. Then, twenty-five. Milo fidgeted, smoked, made another call. One of the high-tech toys needed last-ditch tinkering. Milo spat out an expletive, bounded out of the car, and began knocking on doors. I caught up.

Ten minutes later, three neighbors had confirmed that Helga Gemein lived in the house, but they'd seen no sign of any other occupants.

A rangy woman sucking on a pink Nat Sherman said, 'She changes her looks. One day it's blonde, the other day it's brunette, next time it's red. I figured her for an actress, or trying to be.'

Back at the car, Milo said, 'Whole collection of wigs. So why the hell would she shave her head in the first place?'

'Maybe a rite of self-denial,' I said.

'Giving up hair for Lent?'

'Or until she got the job done.'

★ ★ ★

The bomb squad arrived, checked out the perimeter, returned to the front. The red door was unlocked and pushed open with a long pole, everyone standing back.

No explosion.

A lieutenant stuck his head in, ventured inside, came out giving the thumbs-up.

The dogs ambled in.

The dogs were interested.

29

Dahlia Gemein was gone but the house remained hers in spirit.

Lacy linens, pastel walls, a cheerful country kitchen that looked as if it had never been used. Cute little wicker tables were crowded with cute little glass figurines; clear preference for dolphins and monkeys. Half a dozen amateurishly daubed, pale blue abstractions bore a *Dahlia* signature. A tiny golden sun dotted the *i*.

Drawers and closets were filled with expensive clothing, much of it bearing German or French labels. No family photos, but two nail holes in the center hallway said something had been removed.

Despite the girlie décor, the house felt hollow, temporary.

The dogs had sat down in nearly every room, prompting a five-hour search that unearthed nothing in the furnished spaces. But a vacuum of an empty bedroom produced coppery lint among the meager dust. Barely visible to the eye, the snippets of metal had been sucked up from the crack between the floor and the shoe molding. The bomb tech's best guess was granulated waste from clipped wires and when the dogs really took a liking to the adjoining bathroom, a forensic plumber was summoned.

It didn't take long for him to find remnants of a petroleum-based gelatinous substance: rubbery remnants scraped from the drainpipe of the sink.

'Like someone washed their hands of the stuff,' opined a bomb-squad cop. 'Like that gal in the play, Lady Macbeth.'

Milo said, 'That assumes *our* gal feels guilty. More likely, she just wanted to be squeaky-clean after a hard day's work.'

The bomb guy said, 'You're figuring this was her chem lab?'

'You're not?'

'I'd expect more trace, no matter how well she scrubbed up.'

'The dogs like it here.'

'The dogs can sniff half an atom divided by a zillion. She tracks in a molecule, they'll react. To me this feels more like the place she came home to after the chem lab. If I were you, I'd keep looking. Maybe tube your suspect on the six o'clock and see if anyone recognizes her.'

Milo phoned Public Affairs. A lieutenant there said, 'This is something I'm going to have to check out with the bosses.'

'Why?'

'Foreigner? Big money? You really need to ask?'

★   ★   ★

Ambitious fingerprinting and DNA swabbing by the crime lab techies continued into the evening. Plenty of hits in all the expected places, at least six different print patterns but a predominance of two. If Dahlia and Helga Gemein were ever found, chemistry would confirm what was already known.

The VINs of the Boxster and the bike in the garage matched vehicles Dahlia Gemein had registered three years ago. The paper on both had lapsed. DMV had sent a couple of reminders before consigning the matter to the black hole of government records.

Nothing but oil stains in the otherwise spotless garage. The dogs walked through the space nonchalantly.

The bomb guy said, 'She wanted to set up shop, this would be a perfect place. I'd *definitely* be looking elsewhere.'

★ ★ ★

Milo gave a courtesy call to Gayle Lindstrom, was pleased to get voice mail. He tried Reed. 'Finished with Meneng?'

'Long finished and back at the station, Loo.'

'How'd lunch go?'

'I suggested a coffee shop, she pushed for the Pacific Dining Car on Sixth, ran up an eighty-dollar bill. Surf and turf, plus all the trimmings but no new info.'

'Big appetite for a small girl.'

'She doggie-bagged nearly all of it, talked the whole time about wanting to be an actress,' said Reed. 'I think she gave it all up to you.'

Milo said, 'The good news is one way or the other, you'll get reimbursed for the grub. The bad news is 'the other' might mean Uncle Milo shelling out.'

'No way, Loo. It was my decision.'

'You *bet* way, Moses, Uncle Milo takes care of

his troops. The *other* good news is I won't snitch to Dr Wilkinson about you chomping steak with a hottie.'

'I had soda water,' said Reed. 'The eighty was all her. She'll probably get a week of calories out of that doggie bag. So what do you want me to do next?'

'Start a real estate search for any properties owned by the sultan of Sranil, we already know Teddy has nothing obvious on file.'

'Local or national?'

'Start local, work your way out. I'm sure His Imperial Poobah is layered up thicker than a Sherpa in winter, but we need to try. Start with Masterson, tell the battleax who works the phones that someone's on the rampage against their star client, but don't say who. Also, have Sean do a few drive-bys on Borodi and the surrounding streets, just in case La Balda returns to the scene.'

'You figure she might've gotten a sexual thrill from the torch?'

'This was personal, Moses, there's all kinds of thrills.'

★　★　★

He got out to check on the crime scene techs. An hour or so more. As he returned to the car, Officer Chris Kammen rang in.

No planes from Southern California had flown in last night to the general aviation section of the Port Angeles airport. Kammen had taken the extra step and checked with SeaTac: Not a single flight to LA, Burbank, or Ontario departed late enough to accommodate the luggage thief's near-midnight departure from the storage unit, let alone the drive to Seattle.

'So you're definitely dealing with two separate suspects, Hood-boy could've blown into our town at any time. We're no LA but we don't have the available manpower to search every dark corner. Specially without what the city council calls a compelling reason.'

'Fair enough,' said Milo. 'Once I get a suspect, we can cross-reference.'

'Hey,' said Kammen. 'Optimism. I once read about that.'

★ ★ ★

Milo's second try at Public Affairs was met with a secretary's curt 'We're working on your request.'

'Working, how?'

'You'll be notified in due time, Lieutenant.'

Clicking off, he muttered, 'Time to pole-vault over their little pea-heads,' and dialed Deputy Chief Weinberg to press for a news feed featuring Helga Gemein's photo. Toning down the spiel he'd given Judge LaVigne, he made it through one sentence before Weinberg broke in.

'PA already called me. Don't play games.'

'No one's told me anything, sir.'

'Guess there's nothing to tell,' said Weinberg.

'The answer's no?'

'You can't be serious, Sturgis.'

'Given what we found at the house, it seems

284

the next logical step — '

'A foreign national? From a prominent family? You're asking me to create an international terrorist scare on the basis of *copper* dust?'

'It's more than a scare, sir. My suspect's already killed three people.'

'I haven't heard *evidence* linking her to *any* murders. Even on your arson, it's all air. A woman jogging? Pardon me if I'm not awestruck. And even if she *did* do the torch, what does that come down to? Getting rid of an eyesore the neighbors are happy to see gone. Wire dust and something goopy in a pipe? For all we know, it's rubber cement, she liked putting together model airplanes.'

'The dogs reacted, sir.'

'I love dogs,' said Weinberg. 'But they're not infallible. What if she spilled kerosene trying to clean off beach tar? Believe me, that would make them sit on their little canine rumps.'

'But in this case — '

'You can't seriously expect me to have this woman's face plastered all over the evening news based on what you've given me. You have nothing concrete against her and we are *not* talking suicide belts at Disneyland.'

'OK, let's forget the terrorism angle, even the murders, and just describe her as an arson suspect.'

'You don't have enough, Sturgis. Besides, if the arson's the big deal, I need to be talking to the arson squad.'

'I can have Captain Boxmeister make the — '

'If he asks the same question, I'll give him the

same answer. A few bubbles in a pipe and some wire shavings add up to crap. Bring me finger-prints, body fluids, something *serious* before I have embassies driving me nuts.'

'FBI and Homeland Security think she's serious enough to look for.'

'*They're* involved?'

'FBI came to me.'

'Just like that? All of a sudden those morons have ESP?'

'I called Homeland for info and they called the Feds — '

'And you didn't think to let me know.'

'Sir, I wanted to wait until I had something substantive to tell you.'

'Then why the hell are we talking *now*?'

'The sum total seems substantive to me,' said Milo.

'Then you need to back away and get some perspective.'

Clenching his jaws, Milo middle-fingered air. 'OK, sir, I'll keep digging.'

'I know you're going to be bad-mouthing me the minute this conversation terminates, brass is always the big bad enemy,' said Weinberg. 'But try — I know it's hard, but try anyway — to pull yourself away from the moment and see the bigger picture. By your own account, this woman comes from megabucks, is a respected profes-sional, and has no criminal record. What you have on her is hearsay twice removed. On a good day.'

'Her sister — '

'Could very well be alive. What's your

evidence any kind of crime was perpetrated against the sister? By some oil sheikh, no less. This is the stuff of migraines, Sturgis. Cut the fantasy and get back to shoe leather. I'm sure you've worn out your share of desert boots.'

Milo's gaze dropped to today's footwear. Crepe-soled, brown sailcloth oxfords, long in need of resoling. 'Anything you say, sir.'

'Don't patronize me, Sturgis.'

'Wasn't trying to, sir. May I call you should what you deem substantive come up?'

'Have I ever been unresponsive to your needs, Detective?'

'No, sir. I'll start eroding my shoes and let's hope nothing gets blown up in the interim.'

Silence.

'Sir?'

'Let me make something clear,' said Weinberg. 'I find no merit in your request but in the name of *esprit de corps*, I'm going to talk to the chief about a news feed. Just in case.'

'In case what, sir?'

'Porkers are spotted soaring in the western sky.'

'Thank you, sir.'

'Think nothing of it,' said Weinberg. 'Because that's what it's going to amount to.'

★　★　★

I hadn't heard from Milo by ten the following morning, figured the night hadn't gone well.

Robin said, 'We've got steaks, let's feed him.'

I tried all his numbers, got no answer until

nearly six P.M. He was curt, subdued. All business, none of it encouraging.

Gayle Lindstrom had followed through, with disappointing results: no sign of Helga Gemein at any airport, commercial or private, nor was she listed on any passenger manifests.

Moe Reed's calls to Masterson had remained unanswered and he'd followed up with a visit. The firm's glass doors were locked. If Elena Kotsos or her husband was on site, they weren't letting on.

Real estate searches throughout California had produced nothing. Reed was working on Nevada, but as the day progressed and government offices closed down, options were fading.

No better luck on the lush streets of Holmby Hills, where Sean Binchy had prowled wearing skater duds. Starting at the wheel of his private drive, an '84 Camaro inherited from his father, then repeating the circuit twice on in-line skates.

I'd done a drive-by myself, on the way to the station. Huge houses, towering trees, no people. As if Helga Gemein's dream of a human-free world had come to pass.

Milo's expanded door-to-door had boiled down to reassuring the neighbors they were safe. A few additional residents had seen Helga entering or exiting the little white house but no one had exchanged a single word of conversation with the blonde/brunette/redheaded women they described as 'kind of cold,' 'frosty,' 'distant,' 'off in her own world.'

One man was sure Helga drove a midsized American sedan, make unknown. *Black, dark blue, dark gray, I don't really remember.*

No one had ever seen Des Backer or Doreen Fredd near the house, ditto Prince Teddy. Dahlia Gemein's picture evoked vague recollections of blonde and pretty and cheerful. One neighbor thought she'd favored the red motorcycle.

They're sisters? Pretty different.

Milo said, 'One shred of theoretical hope: Computer lab's sending over the transcripts of GHC's hard drives. Pages of printout, I could use some help going through it. I figured you and I could grab some dinner at Moghul, go back to the office and analyze. Unless you've got plans.'

'Robin and I were talking barbecue, I called to invite you.'

'Oh. Haven't checked messages. Thanks, but gotta pass.'

'Take a break for a steak,' I said. 'Or two.'

'Appreciate the offer but I won't be my usual fun self and I need to watch my cholesterol.'

'All of a sudden?'

'Better late than never.'

'Well,' I said, 'Moghul's good with veggies.'

'I was thinking tandoori lamb, spinach with cheese, maybe some lobster.'

'Someone's bred low-cholesterol sheep and crustaceans?'

'So I lied. Sup with your true love.'

I hung up, talked to Robin.

She said, 'Like there's a choice? Grill's still cold, anyway. Go.'

★ ★ ★

By six forty, Milo and I were sifting through GHC's download history and every bit of e-mail generated during the architectural firm's brief life.

Bettina Sanfelice and Sheryl Passant had spent most of their screen time searching eBay and discount fashion sites and gossip blogs. Both of them loved Johnny Depp.

Judah Cohen hadn't logged on once.

Marjorie Holman had used her keyboard sparingly: researching green architecture sites, news outlets, checking her finances, which were as conservative and modest as John Nguyen had reported.

Using a separate screen name, she'd arranged regular trysts with six different men, among them 'mannyforbush' at forbushziskinshapiro.net.

Helga Gemein and Desmond Backer conducted infrequent but telling exchanges. Cyber pen pals during working hours, they typed away as they sat in the communal office.

The correspondence was focused: coolly exchanged information about explosives, incendiary devices, the goals and techniques of eco-terrorism, nostalgic reflections about ugly days gone by.

Milo had cited the Baader-Meinhof gang while spinning for Judge LaVigne, but the reference was prophetic: One week prior to the killings of Desmond Backer and Doreen Fredd, Helga Gemein had invoked the murderous German band eight times. Describing them, without a trace of irony, as 'refreshingly nihilistic and efficient.'

Helga: the wonder years. my regret is having been born too late.

Backer: for me it was the weathermen. if only, huh?

Helga: knowing which way the wind blows.

Backer: bill and bernadette and now they're mainstream sellouts.

Helga: inevitable. blood thins.

Backer: good old days blood was thick and hot the wind was gonna blow hard and hot. emphasis on blow. lol.

Helga: again, that? with you, it's always carnality.

Backer: got something better lol too bad it's not with u.

Helga: from what I see you've got your hands full.

Backer: hands and other body parts. lol.

Helga: enough i don't lol about stupidity.

Backer: meant to talk to you about that.

Helga: about what?

Backer: ur state of mind.

Helga: my mind is fine.

Backer: ur never ☺

Helga: what's to ☺ about?

Backer: hmmmm . . . how about big go-boom?

Helga: that? one small step.

Backer: for the elimination of mankind?

Helga: wish I believed in god.

Backer: why?

Helga: i could say god-willing.

Milo put the pile aside, squared the corners. 'Creepy.'

I said, 'There's a flirtatious quality to it. Initiated by Backer, but she went along with it.'

'Guy never stopped trying. Guess his batting average proved it was a good strategy.'

'Except with Helga.'

'The one who got away,' he said. 'She's a cold one, Alex.'

'She'd contemplated becoming a nun. Maybe she's one of those people with a low libido. Or she decided to suppress her urges.'

'Or she's doing it with another guy and decided to be loyal.'

'Helga and Hoodie?' I said. 'It's possible, but I'll bet sex is low priority for her.'

He smiled. 'I could tell you about nuns.'

'The joys of parochial school?'

'Some of them were angels, greatest women I ever met. A few were monsters, about as warm and cuddly as Helga. Can you imagine her with a metal-edged ruler? Guess she found her own religion. First commandment: Lose the hair.'

'In a lot of cultures, hair's a symbol of sensuality. Fundamentalists tend to cover their women and keep their own hair short. Buddhist monks shave their heads. It's all about pruning vanity and focusing on nirvana.'

'Sista Skinhead aiming for a no-people nirvana. She finds common ground with Mr Happy-face horndog. Poor fool had no idea Helga was using him.'

He flicked the transcripts. 'I think I finally get Backer doing Doreen at Borodi. There never was any distinction between business and pleasure, for ol' Des it was all about fun.' Shaking his head. 'In flagrante destructo.'

★ ★ ★

He locked up, we took the stairs down, passed the clerk out front, and were at the door when a shout brought us to a halt.

The clerk stood and brandished the phone. 'Call for you, Lieutenant Sturgis.'

'Who?'

A hand clamped over the receiver. Near-whispered reply: 'God, delivering the tablets from Mount Sinai.'

'That was Moses.'

'Whatever, here, take it.'

Milo accepted the phone. 'Sturgis — evening, sir . . . Yes I did . . . Yes, he did . . . I see . . . Thank you, sir . . . I hope so, too, sir.'

He hung up. The clerk said, 'Is he mad? He sounded mad when I told him you weren't in your office.'

'He's peachy.'

'Good, good, I'm hearing bad talk about budget cuts. I'm new and I really need this job.'

'I'll put in a good word for you.'

The clerk brightened. 'You could do that?'

'If the topic comes up.'

Leaving the man to puzzle that out, we left the station and stepped out into warm night air. Cruisers pulled in and out of the staff lot. A uniform stood near the fence, smoking and texting on his iPhone. A shabby-looking man stepped out of the bail-bond office half a block up and slouched toward Santa Monica. A woman walking her dog saw him and crossed the street. When she spied the badge clipped to

Milo's jacket pocket, she relaxed.

Traffic hummed. The air smelled like hot tar.

Milo breathed in deeply, spread his arms wide. 'I *love* when something finally happens.'

'Weinberg changed his mind?'

'Screw Weinberg, that was no chief with a small *c*.'

'His Holiness?'

'In all his celestial glory. Turns out *he* thinks putting Helga's face on the news is a *capital* idea. As long as it 'leads somewhere and you don't end up making me look like a histrionically overreacting conspiracy-nut paranoid schizo loony-tune.''

'Congratulations,' I said. 'Now all you have to do is get that passport photo.'

'Already delivered to the networks,' he said.

'Palace guards move fast.'

'You bet,' he said, lighting up a cigar. 'Miss Skinhead debuts at ten. Sports and weather to follow.'

30

Robin and I watched the news in bed, Blanche wedged between us, dozing and alternating between snorts and squeaks, flicks of her left bat-ear.

The story was the final segment of a slow news day. Someone not looking for it might've missed it.

Twelve seconds total, half of that featuring a cloudy passport shot of a barely recognizable Helga Gemein with blunt-bangs black hair. No mention of nationality, terrorism, murder. Just a woman considered a 'person of interest' in an arson case, anyone with information was requested to call Lieutenant Miller Sturgis at . . .

'Now on to tonight's caught-in-the-act feature, with celebrity heiress Roma Sheraton found shopping for jeans on Robertson with no makeup and looking as if she just woke up on the wrong side of the bed! For more on that, here's entertainment reporter Mara Stargood.'

I clicked off.

Robin said, 'Miller Sturgis?'

'Even the chief has limitations.'

The phone rang.

I said, 'She looked like Bettie Page.'

Milo said, 'How'd you know it was me?'

'The ring tone was kind of weepy and the receiver sagged.'

'Ghost of Salvador Dalí. Yeah, it'll probably come to nothing.'

But he was wrong.

By ten o'clock the following morning, fifty tips had come in. Only one was good, but who needed quantity when you had quality?

★　★　★

Hiram Kwok operated a secondhand furniture store on Western Avenue between Olympic and Pico. The hipper-than-thou, vintage-craving renaissance that had sparked La Brea's discount case-goods emporiums had eluded Western. Half the block's storefronts were dark, shuttered, or blocked by accordion gates.

Kwok's space was a pack rat's paradise crammed with velveteen and carelessly gilded almost-wood, chipped crockery, limp lamp shades, ratty furs, fake Tiffany glass that didn't even come close. A barely negotiable aisle had been cleared through ceiling-high stacks of treasure.

Kwok was fiftyish, thin and hollow-cheeked, with sparse gray hair and nicotine teeth. A photo of a handsome Asian kid in full-dress Marine Corps regalia hung above the Formica folding table Kwok used as a desk.

Milo said, 'Your boy?'

Kwok said, 'Over in Iraq right now, they say he's coming home next month, then heading to Dubai. Guess we got to protect them Arabs.'

'You must be proud of him.'

'He has a head for business, knows computers.

I wanted him to take over so I can retire but he said it put him in a bad mood.'

'Business?'

'Being around too much junk. So you're here about her, huh? What a bitch, no big shock she did bad things. Come on, I'll show you her place.'

Leading us through the shop, he encountered the sides of a disassembled crib, shoved them aside, continued to the back door.

We exited into a pitted alley that looked out to block walls of neighboring properties. A Toyota Camry took up one slot of Kwok's three-space lot. *HIRAM* on the license plate. Multiple alarm warnings on the side windows, heavy-duty crook-lock on the steering wheel.

More security than the mansion on Borodi.

Kwok continued walking south, stopped at the rear of the adjoining shop.

No cars, no painted slots; weeds poked through the pavement. Most of the back wall was a corrugated aluminum garage door. Manual, a pull handle, bolted by a serious combination lock.

Hiram Kwok said, 'She keeps no regular hours but is in and out all the time. I always knew when she was here because she was an inconsiderate pain in the butt, leaving her car parked so it stuck out into my area. Look at the layout, she had tons of her own space, why the hell did she have to invade mine? And when her buddies were around, it became a worse problem. I asked her nice at first, she looked at me like I was retarded, finally moved the car. But the next time, same damn thing. Over and over, like she was trying to annoy me.'

'What kind of car did she drive?'

'Buick LeSabre, 2002, I know the license plate by heart.' Kwok rattled off numbers. Milo copied.

'I know it by heart because I called it in to you guys, had to be twenty times. Know what they told me? Disputes between private property owners needed to be settled privately. And now she burned something down. You guys need to change procedures.'

Milo nodded. 'Tell me about her buddies.'

'Two of 'em, yuppies,' said Kwok. 'Mr Pretty Boy and Miss Pretty Girl in the BMW. What they were *doing* with her I could never figure out, I even wondered about a porno shoot, something like that.'

'Why?'

'Because it's a hidden place, having to go in through the back. And those two looked like actors.'

'Good looking.'

'*Too* good looking,' said Kwok. 'Like they spent a lot of time in front of the mirror. Especially him. Also, the two of them didn't fit with *her*. She was like one of those Goths, you know what I'm talking about?'

'All-black clothes, the wigs,' said Milo.

'That Bettie Page wig they showed on TV was a favorite. You know who Bettie was, right? Hottest pinup in the history of the world. Once in a while I find her memorabilia, sells immediately. The Goth thing, one of my daughters went through that, a phase, so I know all about it. She was too old — the German — to be acting like that, but she did.'

'Unlike the other two.'

'The other two were preppies — Ken and Barbie, you know? It just didn't fit. So I figured porno. Turns out it was even worse, huh?'

A six-pack photo lineup would've been optimal procedure but all Milo had were photos of Des Backer and Doreen Fredd, hers postmortem.

Kwok nodded. 'Yup, that's them. So they're all in it together?'

'Right now, we're unraveling their relationship.'

'Bunch of firebugs planning who-knows-what, right next door, that's just great,' said Kwok. 'You noticed when you got here that the whole front of her window is blacked over, from the street it looks closed. We've got lots of back-door tenants here — musicians use the place five to the north for rehearsals, there's a girl, they say her brother's a movie star, I forgot his name, uses hers for a photography lab. But none of them causes problems. I tried to tell the traffic cops something was off about her, they couldn't care less.'

I said, 'Off how?'

'Way she walked, talked, when I tried to tell her about the parking situation, she just looked through me. Like I didn't exist. Like I was nothing to her.'

'When's the last time you saw her here?'

'Not for a while, I'd have to say . . . a month.

What exactly did she burn down?'

'We're still working on that,' said Milo.

'Meaning none of my business? Fine, just as long as she doesn't come back and blow me up.'

'If you do see her again, here's my card, Mr Kwok.'

'You're not going to keep an eye out for her — surveillance?'

'We'll be doing everything to catch her, sir.'

Kwok hadn't taken the card. Milo held it there.

'You'll take me more seriously than those traffic cops?'

'I already have, sir. Your help is deeply appreciated.'

Kwok pocketed the card.

Milo said, 'Next time you speak to your son, tell him Dad's a hero, too.'

Kwok winced. 'I don't know about that, I'm just being logical. Yeah, I'll call you. Who the hell wants her coming back and burning the whole neighborhood down?'

★ ★ ★

No sign of Helga Gemein. By the next day, the tips had ebbed to a handful of useless leads.

Milo traced ownership of the rented storefront to an elderly couple named Hawes living in Rancho Mirage. The lease had been negotiated through a commercial brokerage and the listing broker had since moved to New Jersey.

'Nothing iffy about the move,' he said. 'Broker had just gotten married and hubbie was

300

transferred to Trenton. Maybe that's why she got careless. Helga used her own name but all the backup information she gave was bogus and no one checked. Also, a full year's rent in cash, up front, tends to ease the process. I got permission to search from Ma and Pa Hawes, nice folks, about as radical as Norman Rockwell, and plenty scared their place was used as a kaboom factory.'

'That's confirmed?'

'Bomb squad found Jell-O ingredients, cookbooks like the one Ricki Flatt saw in Desi's room, Swiss and German newspaper articles on eco-sabotage, computer searches on Sranil, copper wire, switches, timers with remote triggers, tools and workbenches to put it all together. Also, a collection of women's wigs triple-wrapped in plastic. Fortunately, no booby traps, so we left everything in place in case Helga comes back, have a twenty-four-hour watch going on the house and the alley, divided into three-hour shifts. Sean, Moses, me, Del Hardy because he's ex-Special Services, *really* has a thing for terrorists, and eight plainclothes officers.'

'Milo's army, courtesy His Munificence.'

'He loves being divinely right. There's no reasonable place to park a vehicle in the alley itself but the Haweses own a whole bunch of other storefronts up and down the block and some are vacant so we're stationed on both sides of Helga's little lair, she shows up she's Chopped Misanthrope. The hitch, of course, is she may already be road-tripping in that Buick, which has been BOLO'd. The tag numbers Kwok memorized trace back to a stolen truck. Some guy with a car-washing business, got ripped off eleven months ago when he was in — guess where — Holmby Hills.'

'She scouted the neighborhood for a long time,' I said. 'She and Hoodie. Her intention right from the beginning was to be actively involved, not just a financier. Backer and Fredd were expendable the moment they signed on.'

'Yeah, she's a sweetheart. I'll be in that alley at seven, right now I'm headed over to Ricki Flatt's motel because she's finished all the paperwork on Desi's body and I'm driving her to the airport.'

'Beyond the call,' I said. 'Meanwhile, you probe for what she hasn't told you.'

'You,' he said, 'are immovably skeptical, that's why we're pals. Want to come? It could conceivably get psychological.'

31

Ricki Flatt was waiting outside her room, jacket zipped, luggage on the ground.

Milo jumped out, beat her to the rear car door.

'You really didn't need to do this, Lieutenant.'

'We'll take streets, freeway's a bad idea at this hour.'

Moments later: 'How'd it go with the coroner, Ricki?'

'It took a while, but we're finally settled. I'll be able to ship . . . to have Desi sent back in two days, spoke to the cemetery in Seattle, where my parents are buried and they've got a plot available. They referred me to a mortician here who's handling the logistics as well as the cosmetics. He said there wouldn't be that much to do, Desi still looked handsome. Any progress, Lieutenant?'

'We're chipping away, Ricki. Oh, by the way, those suitcases are out of your storage bin.'

'Great,' she said. 'I spoke to Scott this morning and he didn't mention anything, so we're fine.'

'Yes, you are, Ricki.' A beat. 'Unfortunately, we're not.'

'What do you mean?'

'Port Angeles police didn't remove the suitcases. This guy beat them to it.'

Hooking his arm, he dangled the copy of the

surveillance photo sent by Chris Kammen. As Kammen had predicted, too blurry to be useful.

'Who is this?'

'We were hoping you might know.'

'Me? Why would I?'

'Could be someone local.'

'Well I don't know,' she said. 'I have absolutely no idea.' Squinting. 'He took everything?'

'Sure did.'

'How'd he get in?'

'With a key,' said Milo. 'Who besides you and Desi had one?'

'No one — does Scott know about this?'

'No reason for him to know. How about Scott? Does he have a key?'

'No, we rented it to store my parents' stuff, Scott was always bothering me to get rid of everything. Someone stole all that money? The same person who murdered Desi?'

'We don't know yet.'

Ricki Flatt returned the photo. 'That's why you offered to drive me. You think I've held back on you and want to ask more questions.'

'I'm just informing you of the situation as it stands, Ricki. Only you and Desi had keys and the guy in the photo obtained one. Do you happen to have yours right now?'

'I'm a — of course I do.' Opening her purse, she fumbled, produced a ring, shuffled. 'This one. This is mine. Meaning that person used Desi's. Meaning he *did* murder Desi. For the money, it's always about the damn money!'

Burying her face in her hands, she rocked.

Milo drove another half a mile. 'Ricki, what

304

did Desi tell you about his boss, Helga Gemein?'

'Her? This is related to Desi's job?'

'At this point it's all questions, not answers, Ricki. Did Desi talk about Helga? About work, in general?'

'He liked the job, said it was fun, kind of easy. Said he met her at a convention and she offered him a job.'

'What kind of convention?'

'He didn't say. Why? Was she involved — oh my God. The time Desi brought the money, he was traveling with a woman. I didn't tell you because it slipped my mind — it's not like he brought her with him; what happened was after Desi and I took the suitcases to storage, I asked him to stay for dinner. He said he'd love to but he needed to get back to his hotel, someone was waiting. The obvious assumption was a woman because with Desi there was always a woman. I made a crack, you're in town for a day, already have a hot date? Normally, he'd give that cute smile of his. This time, he frowned, said, 'A hot date would be the ideal, but don't lay odds on it.' Which was unusual for Desi, he was always so upbeat.'

She choked back tears. 'I remember I actually kind of gloated to myself. Finally, Don Juan has failed. How petty of me, all those stupid childhood feelings.'

I said, 'What else did he say about this woman?'

'The only other thing was that the car he was driving was hers, he needed to get it back to her. Almost as if he was . . . intimidated by her.'

'The way you would be by a boss.'

'That's what made me think of it right now. Why else would Desi be intimidated by anyone, let alone a woman, unless she had some kind of power over him?'

That hadn't stopped him from propping Marjorie Holman up against a sheet of plywood.

Milo said, 'What kind of car was it?'

'American, dark, I don't remember. I really wasn't paying attention.'

Milo nudged the file over to me. I thumbed through, found the Internet photos he'd printed of 2002 Buick LeSabres.

Ricki Flatt said, 'Cars aren't my thing, but sure, that could be it. This is Helga's car?'

Milo said, 'It's similar to hers — hey, look at this, free sailing, it's good we avoided the freeway.'

★ ★ ★

Moments after he'd carried her bag into the terminal, he was back on the phone with Chris Kammen.

'I can narrow the time frame for Backer's trip, friend. All I need is verification that either Backer or Helga Gemein registered at one of your hotels.'

Kammen said, 'Friend, huh? Every time I talk to you, my life gets complicated.'

'Thanks, Chris, I appreciate it.'

Kammen laughed. 'Like I said before, we ain't Gotham but we also ain't Mayberry, it'll take a while. Who's this Helga?'

Milo filled him in.

Kammen said, 'International terrorism. Now I can brag to my kids about something. Not that it's going to help with teenagers.'

★ ★ ★

His return call came in before we'd returned to the station. Bass tones vibrated with triumph.

'I used logic, figured people from LA might want some creature comforts, but since they were involved in something illegal they might want to stay off the main drag. We've got a place that fits the bill, twenty miles out, set on the water, real woodsy, they got a spa, honeymoon couples like it. The Myrtlewood Inn, I'm fixing to take my wife there for our anniversary if she behaves herself. Anyway, sure enough, Ms Helga Gemein used her platinum Amex during that exact time. One-night stay. Or stand, depending on your perspective.'

'Excellent,' said Milo. 'Give me the card number.'

Kammen read it off. 'If your boy Backer was there with her, it was a stay, not a stand, 'cause she rented two rooms. Paid for both, there's no record of who stayed in the other. But whoever it was racked up hours of rent-a-porn. Unlike Ms Helga, who didn't watch a second of pay-per-view, probably drank tap water because there were no room service charges, not even peanuts from the mini-bar.'

'Living like a nun,' said Milo.

Kammen said, 'Your boy Backer, though, he

watched four dirty movies, ordered steak and shrimp cocktail, and raided the bar for all kinds of goodies. Not exactly two peas in a pod.'

'They had enough rapport to do bad stuff, Chris.'

'Sounds like your typical marriage.'

I said, 'How many rental car companies do you have in Port Angeles?'

'All the majors and a couple of minors. Why?'

'Be good to know if either Backer or Helga used a hired vehicle.'

'The sister said Backer was driving her car.'

'She wasn't with him when he gave his sister the suitcases. They could've gone their separate ways.'

'Ah,' said Kammen. 'OK, I'll check that out — stay on the line, maybe I can do it fast.'

Four minutes later: 'Call me Speedy Gonzales, Myrtlewood Inn's got Avis on the premises. Ms Helga rented a Chevy Cobalt during her one day stay. It's going to take a while to find out how much mileage she put on but I can do it, if you want.'

Milo said, 'Much appreciated, Chris. I'll keep you informed.'

'This is starting to be fun.'

★ ★ ★

I said, 'Separate cars means Helga could've followed Backer to the storage bin. Once she got hold of the key, getting the money was a breeze. She didn't even need to bully him to get it: They worked in the same office, Backer, ever sociable, goes off to lunch with his female friends. Helga, ever the loner, stays behind and goes through his desk or a coat pocket, makes a mold.'

'Then why the gun rape?'

'Everyone's got their own notion of fun.'

Milo said, 'Lord, I want a date with this girl in a small, bright room.'

★ ★ ★

A warrant for Helga's financial transactions revealed little. She'd canceled the Amex account within days of the Port Angeles trip, no others had shown up under her name.

I said, 'Daddy keeps vaults full of crisp bills. Maybe the department will fly you to Zurich.'

He phoned Gayle Lindstrom, asked for a probe of GGI-Alter Privatbank.

She said, 'I'll try but good luck, those places are tighter than missile silos.'

'Still nothing at the airport?'

'I'm not into secrets, Milo. If there was, I'd tell you.'

He hadn't told her about the storefront on Western. When I asked why, he said, 'At this point, all she can do is complicate matters. Any suggestions on tracing Ms Hellish?'

'I'm wondering if she'd chance a road trip. She wouldn't exactly blend into middle America.'

'Helga in the heartland — sounds like a movie.'

'The exception,' I said, 'being Vegas.'

'Yeah, a three-headed albino monkey would blend in there, it's Fugitive Central. OK, I know a US marshal, maybe Helga will materialize at the craps table at Caesars. If not, you're probably right, she's still in town. Hopefully sooner or later she'll return to her bomb shop.'

'My vote's for sooner.'

'Because you're my pal?'

'Because it's her house of worship.'

★ ★ ★

Gayle Lindstrom phoned to say she'd talked to her bosses about probing the bank. Given past dealings with the Swiss government over Nazi gold and looted wartime accounts, the best guess was years of wrangling.

Milo said, 'Nothing like neutrality.'

'What we were able to do,' she said, 'is institute passport scans of the entire Gemein family, to build a conspiracy case should you ever find Helga. This whole thing is making the Bureau nervous.'

'The fact that Doreen was your paid stooge and she used you?'

'Used my predecessors,' said Lindstrom. 'My goal on this one is being seen as outside the loop.'

★ ★ ★

At five forty-three P.M., Milo ate junk food at his desk, preparing for the beginning of his alley shift.

He had a mouth full of packaged burrito when Sean Binchy called.

'Got her, Loot! Cuffed and in the back of my car, she went down real easy!'

310

32

Helga Gemein, in all-black and her Bettie Page wig, parked her Buick carelessly, barely clearing Hiram Kwok's area. She had her key in the lock of the bomb factory when Sean Binchy took her from behind.

Shouting 'Police' and drawing her arms back, Binchy used long-fingered bass-player's hands to secure her wrists, had the cuffs on within seconds.

Helga said, 'All for twigs?'

Binchy patted her down lightly and spun her around. 'Twigs?'

Helga's look said he was beyond help.

By the time Moe Reed arrived from the opposite end of the alley, Sean had her in the rear seat of his unmarked, belted in. She glared through the window.

Reed said, 'Excellent, bro.' Opened the door to get a better look.

Helga said, '*You* look like a storm trooper.'

Reed said, 'And you're an expert on that. You didn't think to change your appearance?'

'Why would I?'

'You look just like on the news.'

'What news?'

'The TV broadcast.'

'TV,' said Helga, 'is garbage. I don't waste my time.'

Two hours later, she sat in a West LA interrogation room, as bored as she'd been when Milo spieled off Miranda. A group watched from next door: Binchy, Reed, Don Boxmeister.

The guest of honor: Captain Maria Thomas, a tweed-suited, blond-coiffed, well-spoken aide to the chief.

The last few minutes had been spent discussing the Western Avenue rental, which Helga dismissed as '*my studio.*'

'*For what?*'

'*Conceptual art.*'

'*Those fuses —* '

'*For a collage.*'

'*What kind of collage?*'

'*You couldn't hope to understand.*'

Milo hadn't bothered to ask her where she was living. A rental-agency key was traced to a house in Marina del Rey. Del Hardy had gone there with a crew of cops. Five flat-screens but no cable or satellite hookup in place. No computer, either, but drawers full of paper included a trove of e-mails. Everything in German, which Hardy sent for translation to Hollenbeck Division Detective Two Manfred Obermann.

Hardy said, 'Guess who she's renting the place from, Alonzo Jacquard.'

Milo said, 'Doctor Dunkshot? He have any idea who his tenant is?'

'He's coaching in Italy, everything went through an agency. Ms Friendly paid up front in cash, just like with the storefront. Funny choice for her, the place is tricked out way past vulgar, pure Alonzo — trophy room, six fully stocked wet bars, disco room, stripper's pole, home theater, racks of the kind of DVDs I wouldn't keep out in the open. Great view of the water, though. But she had the drapes drawn, is sleeping in a small guest room near the service porch, might as well be in a convent. Except for the toys.'

'What kind of toys?'

'I'm a churchgoing man, Milo, don't make me go into detail.' Chuckle. 'Let's just say the latex lobby likes her.'

Milo said, 'You're sure they're not Alonzo's toys?'

'No, these were definitely hers, all girlie stuff.' Hardy sighed. 'Alonzo, man he was talented. Too bad he wasn't around to sign an autograph for my kid.'

★   ★   ★

Milo asked a few more questions about art.

Helga answered each with 'Don't waste my time, you are ignorant.'

Captain Maria Thomas said, 'She's breath-takingly arrogant.'

Boxmeister said, 'That could work for us, no? She thinks she's in charge, doesn't lawyer up.'

Thomas checked her BlackBerry. 'So far so good, but he hasn't gotten into serious stuff.'

Milo made a show of putting on reading glasses, dropping papers, retrieving them. 'Um . . . OK . . . so . . . how about we talk about the house on Borodi — '

Helga cut him off: 'Blah blah blah.'

'The house on Borodi Lane, where — '

'Blah blah *blah* blah *blah*.'

Milo grinned.

'Something is funny, Policeman?'

'Blah blah blah is one of *my* favorite phrases.'

Helga rotated a finger in the air. 'Is that supposed to give us commonality?'

'I don't imagine commonality would be possible between us.'

'Oh?'

'You despise people,' said Milo. 'Most of the time I consider myself part of the human race.'

'I despise people?' said Helga.

'So you said the first time we met.'

'You, Policeman, need to stop decoding literally.'

Milo snapped his fingers. 'I *knew* I should've paid attention in metaphor class.'

Helga ran a manicured finger under chopped black bangs. 'A policeman who has studied the dictionary.'

'Started with *A* and working all the way to *B*. Unfortunately, I kinda got hung up on *boom*.'

Helga didn't answer.

Milo said, 'The house on Borodi — '

'I burned some twigs. So what?'

'Twigs.'

'A heap of rotting wood, a monstrosity. I did the world a favor.'

'By burning down the house — '

'Not a house,' Helga corrected. 'Ruins. Twigs. Garbage. Monstrosity. Shit. I cleansed in the

314

name of aesthetic righteousness, structural integrity, epistemological consistency, and meta-ecology.'

'Meta-ecology. Didn't get even *close* to that in the dictionary.'

'It won't be in there. I constructed it.'

'Ah.'

Helga Gemein held up the rotating finger. 'It means stepping back from trivial components of the gestalt that endow the system with no functional autonomy.'

Milo said, 'Looking at the big cosmic machine, not the cogs.'

Helga studied him. 'You can't hope to understand because you are American and Americans are all religious.'

'We've got a few atheists.'

'In name only, Policeman. Even your atheists are religious because American faith is infinite. The suckling pig that never stops offering its flesh.'

'I'm not sure I'm — '

'You people have convinced yourself possibilities are endless, endings are happy, puzzles are to solved, the future is an advertising jingle, your way of life is sacred, might makes right. If Americans would tear themselves away from their twigs and their shit and use their eyes and ears and noses to *dissect* reality, they would alter their cognitive structure.'

Maria Thomas muttered, 'And become clinically depressed like Europe.'

Helga said, 'Americans are the domesticated pets of the world. Submissive and eating their own shit. Until they turn vicious and then we have war.'

Boxmeister said, 'Talk about a cuckoo clock.'

Thomas said, 'I've been to Interpol conferences. She's just another spoiled Euro-trash brat.'

'But maybe a little whack, too?' Boxmeister nudged me. 'What do you think, Doc?'

Thomas said, 'Bite your tongue, Detective, and don't answer, Dr Delaware. It's going to be pain enough dealing with a foreign national, last thing we need is diminished capacity.'

Milo was saying, 'So burning the twigs was an act of cleansing.'

'Refuse removal.'

'Taking out the garbage.'

Helga's blue eyes narrowed.

Milo said, 'Wouldn't *altruism* be a better word?'

Two sleek, black-nailed hands clenched. 'It would be a *stupid* word.'

'Why's that?'

'Altruism is nothing more than a mutation of selfishness.'

Milo crossed his legs. 'Sorry, I'm not decoding.'

'I do what society *says* is nice so I can *feel* nice. What is more narcissistic than that?'

Milo pretended to contemplate. 'OK, so, if it wasn't altruism, it was — '

'What I told you.'

'An act of meta-ecological cleansing. Hmm.'

'Don't play stupid, Policeman. You have enough natural defects, there is no need to supplement.'

316

Boxmeister said, 'Ouch. Heil, Helga.'

Milo uncrossed, scanned his notes again, edged his chair back a few inches. Removing a handkerchief from a trouser pocket, he wiped his brow. 'Getting hot in here, no?'

Helga Gemein tugged at her wig. 'I am comfortable.'

'To me it feels hot. I'd think that thing would make it worse for you.'

'What thing?'

'The hairpiece. Dynel doesn't breathe.'

'This,' she said, 'is genuine hair. From India.'

He smiled. 'So you're not a hothead.'

Helga snorted and turned away.

Milo said, 'No, I mean that seriously. It's clear to me that you rely on reason, not impulse.'

Maria Thomas leaned forward. 'Yes, yes, go for it.'

Helga Gemein said, 'Should I not rely on reason?'

'Of course you should,' said Milo. 'We all should. But sometimes being spontaneous — '

'Spontaneity is an excuse for poor planning.'

'You're into planning.'

No answer.

Maria Thomas was at the edge of her chair. 'Easy, now.'

Milo said, 'Being an architect, I imagine you'd favor blueprints.'

Helga turned to face him. 'Without blueprints, Policeman, even chaos doesn't work.'

'Even chaos?'

Up came the pedantic finger. 'There is chaos that emanates from stupidity. Think of flatfooted

317

policemen in brass-buttoned tunics and tall hats tripping over themselves. Then, there is corrective chaos. And *that* must be planned.'

'Burning those twigs didn't result from stupidity,' said Milo. 'You considered every detail.'

'I always do,' said Helga.

'Always?'

'*Always.*'

Maria Thomas punched her fist. 'Yes!'

Helga Gemein sniffed. 'This room smells like a toilet.'

'It does get a little stale,' said Milo.

'How often do you bring prostitutes here?'

'Pardon?'

'For your policeman after-hour parties.'

'Must've missed those.'

'Oh, please,' said Helga. 'It is common knowledge what policemen do with women they've dominated. Down on the knees, the man feels so *big.*'

Boxmeister said, 'I must work in the wrong division.'

Maria Thomas shot him a sharp look. He shrugged.

Milo said, 'The cops do that in Switzerland?'

Helga said, 'If you are interested in Switzerland, buy a plane ticket. Good-bye, Policeman. You have bored me enough, I am going.'

But she made no attempt to stand.

Milo said, 'Going?'

'Twigs? Brush clearing? What is that, a penalty? I will pay you.'

'Out of that cash in your purse?'

'Since when is it a crime to have money? America worships money.'

'No crime at all. But six thousand's a lot of cash to be carrying around.'

Helga smirked.

Thomas said, 'That was pure rich kid. This one's never been told no.'

Helga said, 'What is the amount of my fine?'

Milo said, 'I'm not sure of the penal code on twigs yet. We're still checking.'

'Well, do it quickly.'

'Soon as the district attorney lets me know, I'll get the paperwork going. Meanwhile, let's go over this act of cleansing.'

'Not again, no, I will not.'

'I just want to make sure I understand.'

'If you do not understand by this time, you are hopelessly defective.'

'Anything's possible,' said Milo. He shuffled papers, knitted his brows, stuck out a tongue, hummed a low tune. 'You're sure you don't want more water?'

'I still have.' Eyeing the cup he'd brought her five minutes in.

Boxmeister said, 'Garsh, Gomer, when you gonna call for a hayseed and a spittoon?'

Milo said, 'OK, you can drink that.'

Helga Gemein picked up the cup, sipped it empty. Power of suggestion.

Turning point in the interview.

She put the cup down. Eyes still on his notes, he said, 'So . . . you planned and burned the twigs all by yourself. Tell me how you did it.'

'The fine is insufficient penance?' said Helga,

319

smirking again. 'In America, money fixes everything.'

'Even so, ma'am. We like to have all the facts.'

'The facts are: As an architect with a strong background in structural engineering, I have a thorough understanding of structural vulnerability. I located the inherent structural defects of that garbage heap, set devices precisely, operated a remote timer, and watched as everything turned to dust.'

'So you were right there.'

'Close enough to bathe in heat and light.'

'A few houses down?'

'I didn't count.'

'But you parked the motorcycle three blocks away.'

Blue eyes sparked. 'How do you know I drive a motorcycle?'

'It was spotted and reported.'

'So you know the answer to your question. So do not waste my time.'

'Like I said, we need to verify,' said Milo. 'For our report, so we can let you go and be done with all this.'

'Proper procedure,' said Helga. 'Enabling you to pretend competence.'

'You know about procedure.'

Helga arched an eyebrow.

Milo said, 'That old joke? Hell is the place where the Italians establish procedure and the Swiss are in charge of design?'

'Hell, Policeman, is the place Americans gorge themselves to unconsciousness and delude themselves to mindless optimism.'

'Never heard that version,' said Milo. 'But you have to admit, the Swiss are darn good at design — who makes the best watches? Speaking of which, let's talk about those timers. Where'd you get them?'

'From Des.'

The quick reply caught him off-guard. He covered with a prolonged nod. 'Des Backer.'

'No, Des Hitler — yes, Des *Backer*. I want to go and pay my fine and be gone.'

'Soon,' said Milo. 'What else did Des supply you with?'

'Everything.'

'Meaning — '

'You have invaded my studio, you know what is there.'

'The fuses, the wiring, the vegan Jell-O. Des knew about all that because he was . . . '

'He claimed to be an anarchist.'

'Claimed? You think he was faking?'

'Des indulged himself.'

'Des and women.'

'He was not a serious person.'

Milo said, 'Where'd you two meet? An anarchist convention — guess that's kind of an oxymoron, huh?'

Helga said, 'In a chat room.'

'Which one?'

'Shards.net.'

'As in broken glass?'

'As in broken *universe*,' she said. 'It has closed down. Anarchists are not good at self-perpetuation.'

'Poor organizational skills,' said Milo.

Silence.

'So you met online . . . Des being an architect must've made it seem perfect. Though the combination is kind of odd. Building up and destroying.'

'There is no contradiction.'

'Why's that?'

'As I told you, everything depends on context. But anyway, I am not an anarchist, I do not join movements.'

'So you're a . . . '

'I am,' said Helga Gemein, with the first smile I'd seen her offer, 'myself.'

Milo fiddled with his papers some more, feigned confusion. 'Kind of a one-woman truth squad . . . So you met Des online and the two of you decided to burn some twigs.'

'*I* decided.'

'He was your supplier,' said Milo. 'Knew where to get equipment. That was the real reason you hired him. The real reason you established your firm.'

Silence.

'Nice shell,' he went on, 'for explaining your presence in LA, giving you a reason to be hanging with Des. Covering expenses — fifty thousand in cash? Who's the real source of all that money, your father?'

No response.

'The road trip to Port Angeles, Helga. Nice, crisp bills in two suitcases. The kind you get fresh from a bank. The kind that gets released when one bank talks to another.'

Helga Gemein poked a finger under her wig. 'I

would like some water.'

Milo collected his papers and left. Alone, Helga fooled with the hairpiece some more, massaging the top of the glossy black strands, working a finger joint under the hem and poking around.

Don Boxmeister said, 'What, she's got cooties? Maybe we should've strip-searched her.'

Maria Thomas said, 'What I said still stands, Don: No sense alienating her right off, he needs something to work with. And it's paying off, she admitted premeditation.' Several pokes at the BlackBerry. 'I'm needed back in an hour, hope he can nail the bitch soon.'

Helga straightened the wig, turned, leaned on the table. Sat and planted her boots on the floor. Her eyes closed. Her head swayed.

'What the hell's she doing?' said Boxmeister. 'Some kind of meditation?'

I said, 'Probably dissociation. Putting herself somewhere else is her default strategy.'

Milo returned with a small cup of water. Helga didn't acknowledge him, but her eyes opened when he said, 'Here you go,' and placed it in front of her.

He put on reading glasses, reviewed his notes. She eyed him, finally sipped.

'OK, tell me about the trip to Port Angeles.'

She touched a fringe of wig. 'I engaged in tourism. The great lifeblood of American pseudo-culture.'

'A pleasure trip.'

'I have been to Disneyland, as well.'

'Guess I don't need to ask if you liked it.'

'Actually,' she said, 'it was quite pleasing in its own repugnant way. Consistent.'

'With vulgar American culture?'

'With a world devoid of reason.'

He harrumphed. Slid a couple of sheets toward her. 'This is your registration form from the Myrtlewood Inn in Port Angeles. And this is your car rental receipt.'

'I stayed at a nice hotel,' she said. 'So?'

'You and Des Backer both stayed there. You took separate rooms, the staff remembers you paying for both. They also recall seeing you and Des at breakfast together.'

Guesses. Good ones. Helga Gemein frowned. 'So what? I already told you I got my equipment from him.'

'It was a purchasing trip.'

'Sightseeing, then some purchasing.'

'Why'd you give Des your car and rent another vehicle for yourself?'

'Because we were not together.'

'As . . . '

'As being together.'

'Did you drive up together?'

'I drove, he flew.'

'So no one at the office would suspect anything.'

'I wanted to drive,' said Helga. 'He wanted to fly. He wanted to visit his family.'

'What did you do when he was visiting?'

'I shopped.'

'For timers and fuses?'

'Among other things,' said Helga.

'What things?'

'Clothing.'

'Find some bargains?'

'Jeans,' she said, stroking one shapely thigh. 'Black jeans on sale.'

'You drove because you couldn't risk an airport security check with fifty thousand dollars in two suitcases.'

Helga took several seconds to respond. 'If you know so much, why are you wasting my time?'

'That darn old procedure thing. I need to hear it from you.'

'All because of twigs?'

'Afraid so. They were big twigs. Owned by an important person.'

'No one is important.'

'Obviously someone was to you, Helga.' He moved in closer, like I'd seen him do so many times. Spreading his shoulders and hardening his voice.

She flinched reflexively. Forced a smile.

He asserted his big face inches from hers. 'Helga, someone was important enough for you to pay fifty thousand dollars to burn down twigs. Important enough for you to set up a shell company. Important enough for you to plan precisely.'

Helga Gemein's chest heaved. She looked away. Beginning of the end.

'Helga, you'd like me to think you believe in nothing, but the way I see it, *everything* you did was an act of pure faith. Because that's what vengeance is, right? Pure faith in the power of correction. That wrong can be made right.'

Pretty lips quivered. She stilled them with

another smirk. 'Ridiculous.'

'Faith motivated by love, Helga.'

Silence.

Milo said, 'You loved Dahlia, nothing to be ashamed of, on the contrary. But it is downright fundamentalist, taking faith that far. You may not *be* religious, Helga, but you have no trouble *drawing* upon religion when it works for you.'

Helga Gemein rolled her eyes. Let loose with a ragged, too-loud laugh.

The sudden rise of her shoulders, the rippling along her jawline gave her away.

Milo said, '*Sutma.*'

No answer.

'You've heard of *sutma*, Helga.'

'Primitive nonsense.'

'Maybe so, Helga, but the point was Prince Teddy and his family don't agree.'

Waiting for a reaction to the name.

A single blink. Then nothing.

Milo said, 'Or maybe it's not just them. Maybe you really *do* believe in heaven and hell and all that good stuff. But that doesn't really matter, Helga. The point is the sultan and the rest of the family believes and after what was done to Dahlia, you needed to grab hold of any shred of revenge you could find. Because Teddy's out of your reach, geographically, financially, you can't touch him. But cosmically? You burned those twigs in order to leave Teddy dangling in cosmic limbo. Downright terrifying for someone who believes in *sutma*.'

Silence.

He said, 'It is a funny concept, though. If *I* was

326

a religious person, I'd want to believe just the opposite — destroying material remains speeds *up* entry to the next world.'

He laughed, clapped his hands hard, sprang up, paced the room twice.

Helga watched, alarmed. Forced herself to stop following his circuit. Sat still as he came to a halt behind her.

She stared straight ahead, pretending not to care about the massive figure shadowing her.

Her jawline was an information highway.

'Reason I just laughed, Helga, is I had a sudden insight — an epiphany, I guess you'd call it. You're *totally* into ritual. Like shaving your head. Since the first time I met you I've been trying to figure it out, why would you do something like that. But now I *get* it. It's a ritual of self-abasement you took on until you achieved your goal. Like fasting on Lent — wouldn't surprise me if you've done your share of that, too. Other kinds of fasting. Maybe even a vow of celibacy.'

Her jaw clenched.

'How long ago, Helga, did you start eating meat during Lent? If you ever did. Do you eat your Lent veggies and explain it as meta-ecology?'

Helga Gemein shut her eyes.

'Even so, it's religion, Helga. Are you a strict vegetarian? Or do you sneak meat when no one's looking?'

Silence.

'Once a Catholic, always a Catholic, Helga. Believe me, I know.'

She folded her arms. Let them drop. Began deep-breathing.

'Oh, come on,' said Milo. 'Let's be just a little bit honest and 'fess up like they taught you in convent school: At the core, you're devout, believe sin must be punished. And there's no greater sin than murder. Especially the murder of an innocent like Dahlia.'

Helga Gemein's eyelids scrunched tighter. Tears trickled out.

'You *loved* Dahlia, that's not a bad thing, that's a good thing, she loved you, too. *Believing* is a good thing, Helga. It helps me understand what you did. Everything you've done since you arrived in this country has been aimed at getting justice for Dahlia. You're powerless to go to Sranil and do what you dream about — though I'm sure you haven't given up on that. And maybe Daddy hasn't, either. But meanwhile . . . '

She let out a cry. Clamped a hand over her mouth.

Milo bent close, spoke softly, inches from her ear. 'You're a survivor aiming for justice. That's *human*, Helga, and no matter what you say, you're a member of the species.'

The entire lower half of Helga's face began to tremble. She pressed one palm to her cheek, failed to still waves of twitches.

Milo pulled his chair so their knees were just short of contact.

'Let the bastard dangle,' he said tenderly. 'He deserves it.'

Moving in closer. 'What I *don't* understand is why you had to kill Des and Doreen?'

328

Helga opened her eyes. 'What are you talking about?'

'I think we've moved past self-delusion, Helga.'

'You are ridiculous.'

He handed her a tissue. She swatted it away.

Milo watched it flutter to the floor. 'Why'd you have to kill them, Helga? Did they get greedy and ask for more money?'

Helga Gemein shook her head. 'Fool.'

Milo said, 'Or were they just a nuisance and expendable? Time to cover your tracks.'

She tried to scoot her chair back. The legs stuck. He pressed closer. She cleared her throat. Drew back her head.

Boxmeister said, 'Uh-oh — '

Milo jerked away just in time to avoid the missile of spit.

A wet gob landed on the floor.

Her hands were balled. Flush-faced, she panted.

Milo shook his head, ever the patient schoolmaster. 'Looks like I touched a nerve, Helga.'

'You have touched *stupidity*,' she said. 'I have never killed *anyone. Never.*'

'What's the big deal? You claim to hate humanity — '

'Humanity is *shit*. I don't put *shit* on my hands.'

'Except when it suits your purposes.'

She shook her head. 'Idiot.'

Reaching for his papers, he pulled out another sheet. The picture of the man in the hoodie.

329

Adroitly, no more fumbling. 'You killed Desi and Doreen with this guy's help.'

Helga Gemein's jaw turned smooth. A smile spread slowly. That serene smile tightened my gut.

'I have never seen this person.'

Maria Thomas said, 'Uh-oh.'

'What?' said Boxmeister.

Thomas said, 'That look like a tell to you? That picture *mellowed* her. Damn.' She turned to me: 'Either she is nuts or she really doesn't know what he's talking about, right, Doc? Either way, it's *mucho problemo*.'

Milo continued to display the photo.

Helga said, 'You can wave that around forever, your little policeman flag.'

'This guy's your partner, Helga. The person who helped you murder Des and Doreen. Did you drive up to Port Angeles with him?'

Helga shook her head. 'You are an utter fool.'

'This photo was taken in Port Angeles a couple of days ago. This man was there to retrieve the money. Talk about good planning. You never had any intention of letting Des keep a penny. Because you never had any intention of letting him live. The real reason you rented him a car was so you could follow him and find out where he stashed the money. After you returned to LA, you got hold of his storage key — plucked it out of a pocket or found it in his desk drawer, made a mold. Maybe you did it when he was off having fun with the ladies and you were in the office all by your bald-headed, self-abasing, not-so-lapsed Catholic *fundamentalist* self.'

330

Helga Gemein giggled. 'You truly believe this *scheiss*.'

'The evidence makes me believe, Helga.'

'Then the evidence is *scheiss*.' Clucking her tongue. 'I have burned twigs, that is all. Now I wish to leave and pay my fine and not hear any more of this crazy nonsense.'

'Twigs,' said Milo. 'We call it arson and it's a felony.'

Helga shrugged. 'I will hire a lawyer. He will make it into a prank that got too big and I will be free and you will remain stupid.'

'Damn,' said Boxmeister.

Thomas said, 'She hasn't actually *asked*, she's only *threatened*.' Shifting close to the mirror. 'Change the *subject*, dude.'

Milo said, 'More water?'

'Yes!' said Thomas.

Helga said, 'No, thank you.' Sweet smile. Unsettling. Wrong.

'Desi and Doreen were murdered in that turret. You went back to the house anyway.'

'I had business to do.'

'The murder didn't bother you?'

'Not my concern, Policeman.'

Milo slid another piece of paper toward her.

'What is this, Policeman?'

'This is what's left of a gentleman named Charles Ellston Rutger. He grew up in a house that once sat on the Borodi property. Had one of those stupid sentimental attachments to the land, which is why he liked to sneak up there, sit in that same turret, reminisce about the good old days. See that shiny thing?' Pointing. 'That's

331

what was left of his wineglass. And that, over there? That used to be a tin of foie gras. Mr Rutger was enjoying a snack, washing it down with a nice Bordeaux the night you reduced *him* to dust.'

Helga Gemein grabbed the paper.

'That's a crime scene photo, Helga. Check the date. He doesn't look like much, does he? You killed him.'

Helga gaped. Whispered, 'No.'

'On the contrary, Helga. *Yes.* A big *fat* yes. Mr Rutger had the misfortune to be enjoying a quiet moment in the turret of that monstrosity when you came in and set your fuses and your timers and your plugs of Jell-O. He didn't hear you because you were careful and quiet and he was an old man and being all the way up there on the third floor muted the sound. He was sipping wine as you stood on the sidewalk and enjoyed your act of cleansing, but maybe you already know that.'

'*No!*'

'He didn't hear *you*, Helga, but you're young, your ears work just fine, so my bet is you heard *him*. But you didn't care, what's another piece of human *scheiss?*'

Helga let go of the photo as if it were toxic. It slid to the floor. She stared at it, eyes wide with horror.

First time she'd shown anything close to appropriate emotion. I liked her better for it. But not much.

'Oh, God,' she said.

No atheists on the hot seat.

'Your twigs became a pyre for a human being, Helga. *That* we call felony homicide. Loss of a life during the commission of any major crime, even without prior intention. That's *not* a fine, Helga.'

'I never knew,' she said, in a small, thin voice. 'You must believe me.'

'I must?'

'It is *true*! I did not *know*!'

'You haven't been listening, Helga. Whether or not you knew, it's still felony homicide.'

'But that . . . makes no sense.'

'I don't write the rules, Helga.'

She studied him. 'You are lying. That is special effects. Anyone can stamp a date. You try to confuse me so I will confess to Des and Doreen but I *will* not because I *did* not.'

'You did a whole lot, Helga. Trust me, Mr Rutger's real. Was. Want me to show you his autopsy report? You fried him to a crisp.'

'I do not kill.'

Milo shook his head. 'Unfortunately, you do. You've already admitted the arson, admitted planning it. A man died in the process, you're facing a long prison sentence. The only way I can see you extricating yourself from this mess is by explaining yourself. Tell me why you decided to eliminate Des and Doreen. I can see a motive right off the bat: They were trying to blackmail you. If they were, that's a good explanation, people can understand that, it's kind of self-defense.'

She shook her head.

He said, 'And if this guy in the hood did the

actual killing and you didn't really know what was going to happen and you tell me who he is, that will also help you.'

'That,' said Helga Gemein, wringing her hands, 'would be all idiocy. I killed *nobody*.'

'Truth is, Helga, I'm leaning toward your partner as the major bad guy for Des and Doreen because there was a certain masculine stupidity to the murders and I don't see stupid as part of your makeup. So let's start with who he is.'

'The Dalai Lama.'

'Pardon?'

'Today he is the Dalai Lama. Tomorrow? Emperor Franz Josef, Nikola Tesla, Walter Gropius. Take your pick.'

'You're not helping yourself, Helga.'

'You think I care to help you?' she said.

'I understand, maybe you didn't actually pull the trigger so you think — '

'You understand *nothing*!' she shrieked. 'I did not *kill* anyone!'

'Charles Rutger would debate that if he could.'

'An accident,' she said. 'Had I known, I would have waited.'

'Even though you don't care about people.'

'I avoid complications.'

'Well,' said Milo, 'you've ended up with a whole bunch of complications.'

'You are stubborn beyond rationality.'

'Like someone else you know?'

'Who?'

Milo smiled. 'I had a dad like that.'

Helga shuddered. Her turn to cover the stab of

emotion with an even bigger smile. 'Pity for you, Policeman.'

'Let's get back to basics, Helga: You're not leaving here. But you do have a chance to help yourself by telling me — '

'Policeman,' she said, 'at this time, I need to . . .'

'Oh, shit,' said Maria Thomas.

' . . . have time to think. Alone. Please.'

Soft voice, almost gentle.

'You have surprised me,' she said. 'I need to think. Please, some time.'

Milo said, 'Take all the time you need.'

33

The door to the observation room swung open. Milo stepped in, wiping sweat from his face.

He'd remained cool in Helga's presence: Zen and the art of detection.

Maria Thomas said, 'I have to say she didn't look the least bit hinky on those two murders.'

Don Boxmeister said, 'Even with that, we get her on Rutger, she's away for a long time.'

'Don't get overconfident about Rutger,' said Thomas. 'She has family money. Want to take bets the first thing any decent lawyer does is move to throw out the last two hours because she was under emotional duress?'

'Milo didn't persecute her, Maria.'

'Who's talking reality, Don? It's a game and rich people have a better win-loss record.' She turned to Milo. 'You're lucky she's arrogant. Only reason she hasn't lawyered up is she thinks she's smarter than you. But now that she's faced with Rutger, don't count on that lasting. What's your next step?'

Milo sat down heavily. Watched Helga through the glass.

She'd remained in her chair.

Black-wigged statue.

Thomas said, 'Milo, you with us?'

'I don't know.'

Thomas's BlackBerry sent her a message. She checked the screen, poked with a stylus, scrolled.

'Detective Obermann has your German trans-
lations all done, he'll e-mail them to you but is
happy to talk to you over the phone. And
... looks like he identified some of those
numbers you found on Gemein's papers. GPS
coordinates, matching a private hangar at Van
Nuys Airport. Registered to ... DSD, Inc. That
ring any bells?'

Milo sat up. 'Loud ones. The sultan's holding
company.'

'So our Swiss Miss had more arson in mind.
I'll talk to the Sranilese consulate, ask for
consent to enter the hangar.'

'There is no consulate.'

'The embassy in DC, then.'

'They'll say no and clean the place out.'

'Of what?'

'Their royal family's involved in murder,
they're gonna be in total ass-covering mode.'

Thomas thought. 'Guess we have a problem.'

Helga Gemein closed her eyes.

Boxmeister said, 'How about this: We apply for
warrant under exigent danger. Likely presence of
volatile chemicals, imminent risk of ignition.'

'The hangar's ready to blow?' said Thomas.
'What evidence do we have of that?'

'We've got prior bad acts by Helga and her
looking for GPS coordinates. To me that's clear
intent.'

'She can look to her heart's content, Don.
How's she going to gain access to the hangar?'

Milo said, 'She's got money to charter a
private jet. Maybe once she's in there she could
find it.'

'Exactly,' said Boxmeister. 'Like one of those private clubs. Getting past the rope's a bitch, but once you're in, anything goes.'

Thomas said, 'No judge is going to buy it and we're talking royalty, to boot.'

Milo said, 'But what if she's already gotten in there and set her Jell-O? All those aircraft nearby? All that jet fuel?'

Boxmeister said, 'Shit, I don't want to even imagine. Sure hate to be the one who failed to take precautions.'

Thomas said, 'Subtle, guys. You want me to ask the boss.'

Milo glanced toward the one-way mirror. Helga remained frozen. 'Up to you but I used all my charm up with her.'

Thomas drummed her BlackBerry. Began texting.

Helga Gemein stood up, walked to the mirror, turned her back on us.

One hand reached up. Fooled with the wig.

'That's her anxiety tell, messing with the rug,' said Boxmeister. 'She's gonna cave, I can feel it.'

If that comforted Milo, he didn't show it.

Thomas kept texting.

Helga Gemein turned again, faced us.

Looking but not seeing.

Blank eyes; she'd arrived at a solitary place.

Snatching off her wig with one deft movement, she exposed a beautifully shaped head shaved white and glossy. Holding the hairpiece in front of her, bowl up, like a chalice, she smiled.

Sad smile. Second time I'd seen it. I liked her no better.

Reaching into the wig, she pulled something out. Small and white and capsule-shaped, pincer-grasped between thumb and forefinger.

Still smiling, she opened her mouth, popped the white thing. Swallowed.

Her smile spread. Her breathing quickened.

Boxmeister said, 'Oh, shit.'

Milo was already up, rushing for the door.

Maria Thomas looked up from her Black-Berry. 'What's going on?'

Milo ran past her, let the door slam shut.

Inches away, blocked by glass, Helga Gemein wobbled. Clutching her abdomen, she let out a gasp.

Retched.

Something green and slimy trickled out of her mouth.

Slack mouth, the smile was gone.

Thomas said, 'Omigod,' and ran out of the room. Boxmeister hustled after her.

I stayed in my chair. No reason to crowd the space.

Helga began convulsing. Her breath grew labored. Staggering closer to the one-way, she panted raggedly. Filmed the glass. Flecked it with glassy spit, then pinpoints of pink.

The massive convulsion began at her eyes, raced downward as her entire body was seized.

Rag doll, shaken by an unseen god.

Foam began pouring out of her mouth, a Niagara of bile. Chunks of slime coated the glass, clouded my view. But I managed to make out Milo rushing in, catching her as she fell.

Laying her down gently, he began chest

compressions. Thomas and Boxmeister stood by, transfixed.

Milo's technique was perfect. Rick insists he recertify every couple of years. He gripes about the colossal waste of time, homicide is brain-work, when would he ever have the opportunity to get heroic.

Today, he did.

Today, it didn't matter.

34

The police chief's face is pocked more severely than Milo's. A lush white mustache does a pretty good job of camouflaging a harelip.

He's a lean man with no discernible body fat. The lack of spare flesh stretches the skin that sheaths his skull, highlighting pit and crater, glossing lump and scar. The skull is an oddly shaped triangle, broad and unnaturally flat on top, coated with silky, blond-white hair, and tapering to a knife-point chin. His eyes are small and dark and they alternate between manic bounces and long stretches of unblinking immobility. When he turns his head a certain way, patches of taut, tortured dermis give him the look of a burn victim.

He turns that way a lot and I wonder if it's intentional.

Take me on my terms.

Everything in his history supports a *Screw-you* approach to life: the up-from-nothing ascent, the graduate degree at an Ivy League university he disparages as 'an asylum for rich brats.' War heroism followed by clawing up the ranks of a notoriously corrupt East Coast police force, the combative years spent kicking bureaucratic ass and clearing out departmental deadweight. Defying the brass and the police union with equal-opportunity contempt, he arm-twisted his way to dramatically lowered felony rates in a city considered 'ungovernable' by pundits he dismissed as 'fat-assed brats with mental constipation and verbal diarrhea.' Stunning success was exploited to demand and receive the highest law enforcement salary in US history.

A month later, he quit unceremoniously, when LA upped the ante.

Everyone said LA would be his fatal challenge.

Within a year of arriving, he'd divorced his third wife ten years his junior, married a fourth twenty years his junior, attended a lot of Hollywood parties and premieres, and lowered felony rates by twenty-eight percent.

When he'd taken the job, departmental wienies had bad-mouthed Milo as 'a notorious troublemaker and a deviant,' and urged demotion or worse.

The chief checked the solve-stats, most of the wienies ended up taking early retirement, Milo got the freedom to do his job with relative flexibility. As long as he produced.

I'd met the chief once before, when he'd invited me to his office, showed off his collection of psych texts, expounded on the finer points of cognitive behavior therapy, then made me an offer: full-time job heading the department's department of behavioral sciences. Even with his promise to raise the pay scale by forty percent, the salary didn't come close to what I earned working privately. Even if he'd tripled the money, it would never be an option. I know how to play well with others, but prefer my own rulebook.

During that meeting, he was dressed exactly as

he was today: slimcut black silk suit, aqua-blue spread-collar shirt, five-hundred-dollar red Stefano Ricci tie embedded with tiny crystals. On a lesser man it would've screamed *Trying too hard*. On him, all that polish emphasized the roughness of his complexion.

My terms.

He faced Milo and me across a booth at a steak house downtown on Seventh Street. A pair of massive plainclothes cops watched the front door; three more had staked out positions inside the restaurant. A velvet rope blocked other diners in this remote, dim section. The waiter assigned to us was attentive, vaguely frightened.

The chief's lunch was a chicken breast sandwich, seven-grain bread, side salad, no dressing. He'd ordered a thirty-ounce T-bone, medium-rare, all the fixings, for Milo; a more moderate rib eye for me. The food arrived just as we did.

Milo said, 'Good guess, sir.'

The chief's smile was crooked. 'In the gulag, we keep files on dissidents.'

His sandwich was divided into two triangles. He picked up a knife and bisected each half. Got five bites out of each quarter, chewing daintily and slowly. Sharp white teeth, somewhere between fox and wolf.

He wiped his lips with a starched linen napkin. 'I bought you an insurance policy on Gemein, Sturgis. Know what I mean?'

'Captain Thomas.'

A gun-finger aimed across the table. 'Lucky for you Maria was there when that crazy bitch

343

cyanided, because, like all hot air, blame floats to the top. *Extra*-lucky for you, Maria was the one who didn't want to strip-search. She's smart and industrious but she does tend to overthink.'

Milo said, 'Even without her directive, I wouldn't have strip-searched, sir.'

'What's that, Sturgis? Penance?'

'Telling it like it is, sir.'

'Why no strip?'

'At that point, my emphasis was on getting rapport with Gemein.'

'Plus,' said the chief, 'even a super-sleuth like you couldn't conceive the bitch would hide anything under her wig. Talk about an overblown sense of drama. Lucky for all of you, I managed to block the pressscum when they started up the trash-vacuum. They live to tear us down, Sturgis, because they're useless pieces of crap. They've also got the attention spans of decorticate garden slugs. I recently devised what I think is a tasteful and adroit method of handling press cretins.'

Out of a jacket pocket came a sterling-silver card case, conspicuously monogrammed with his initials. A single, deft button-push sprang the lid. Inside were pale blue business cards. He removed one, passed it across the table.

Heavy-stock paper, elegant engraving. Three lines of type.

Your Opinion Has Been Duly Received
With Great Enthusiasm.
Fuck You, Very Much.

'Excellent, sir.'

'Let's have that back, Sturgis. I'm still not sure if the wording's right.'

The chief resumed eating. The side salad was half a head of iceburg lettuce. Thin, pallid lips curled as his knife reduced it to coarse-cut coleslaw. Spearing a few green shreds, he masticated with relish, as if undressed greens were a sinful indulgence.

'In any event, Ms Gemein's ludicrous act of self-destruction appears to be receding from the public's attention span, ergo, no need to throw anyone under the bus.'

'Thank you, sir.'

'So tell me, Dr Delaware, why'd the bitch snuff herself?'

'Hard to say.'

'If it was easy, I wouldn't be asking you. Theorize like you're getting paid for it, I won't hold you to your answer.'

I said, 'She may have been living with a serious underlying depression for a long time.'

'Poor little rich girl? From what I hear she wasn't the sniffly, breast-beating sort.'

'Not a passive depression. She reacted like some men do, with hostility and isolation.'

'Men with borderline personality disorder?'

'That's one possible diagnosis.'

'Depressed.' He put down his fork. 'What kind of family has a suicide, doesn't give a fuck? Not a squawk from Zurich. Which is good for us, these are über-rich people, all we need is a lawsuit. I had DC Weinberg call them personally in Switzerland, do his Colin Powell bit — august authority plus diplomacy. The mother thanked him for letting her know, like he was informing her about the weather, then she handed the phone off to the old man who did the same damn thing. Polite, unemotional, no questions, send the body when we're finished with it. What a bunch of coldhearted fucks, guess that could depress you. You think that's why she didn't have sex, Doctor? Shaved her damn hair off — that was a good phrase, by the way, Sturgis. Self-abasement. I'm going to work that into a speech one day. You're saying this mess was all the result of not enough Prozac, Doctor?'

'I'm saying depression could've been her base state and she tried to give her life meaning by taking on a mission.'

'Burning down that ridiculous heap of wood to avenge her sister, that whole tribal thing whatchamacallit . . . '

Milo said, '*Sutma.*'

'Sounds like kama sutra,' said the chief. 'Something out of a National Geographic special. Then again, we live in *multicultural* times, so far be it from me to disparage stupid primitive customs. OK, she went on a mission, fucked up, offed herself out of shame. I'll go with that. You see her for the turret murders?'

'Can't say for sure, sir, but my gut says no.'

The chief ate more lettuce. 'Anyone have a feel for whether Prince Teddy's dead or alive?'

Milo said, 'No, sir.'

'What's your *plan* on the turret murders?'

'No plan yet, sir.'

'Then develop one and do it quickly. I've got a

case I want you to deal with. Gang scum in Southwest Division sucking the federal tit — gang prevention grant. Which is like pedophiles getting paid to run a preschool. I've got reason to believe the money's being used to buy heavy artillery.'

'Southwest Division needs my help?'

'I determine who needs what. You've got two weeks to close the turret murders before it goes in the fridge.' Manicured fingers lifted a quarter of sandwich. 'Don't like your steak?'

'It's great, sir.'

'Then wolf it down the way you usually do. Couple of refreshing burps and you're on your way to Van Nuys to check out that hangar.'

'The Sranilese embassy granted permission?'

'Forty-eight hours of ignoring our reasonable request, plus exigent danger? Fuck them, Sturgis. *I* grant permission.'

35

Beautiful afternoon at Van Nuys Airport.

No security lines, no delays or other indignities. This was the Mont Blanc of travel, all private, every happy sojourner owning or leasing one of the spotless white jets luxuriating on the tarmac.

Quiet afternoon, a single craft ran its engines. Citation X as sleek as an Indy car. Porters hurried to fill the hold with a dolly-ful of Vuitton luggage as a well-fed, sunglassed family of four boarded. Thirtyish mother, fiftyish father, two kids under ten. Everyone in suede.

The luxury terminal backing the runways was nestled in greenery. So were the three other luxury depots we'd passed. The hangars sat at the north end of the airport, monumental toy chests.

The bomb squad was waiting at Hangar 13A when Milo and I arrived. Familiar faces from the search at Helga's house and her workshop, all the tech toys in place, ready for a replay.

New dog today, a beautifully groomed flat-coated retriever named Sinead who stood patiently at her handler's side, emitting the confidence that comes from good looks and serious talent.

Milo said, 'OK to pet her, Mitch?'

The handler said, 'Sure.'

A big hand stroked the dog's head. Sinead

purred like a cat. 'She's a solo act?'

Mitch said, 'She's the only one we can trust because she won't get distracted by jet fuel and such.'

'Good nose, huh?'

'The best,' said Mitch. 'We already did the outside perimeter. Clean. Let's go inside.'

★ ★ ★

Sinead was in and out within seconds. The bomb squad followed up with a detailed search, declared the hangar safe, motioned us in.

The interior was smaller than the house on Borodi, but not by much, with twenty-foot ceilings, a carpeted floor, and cedar paneling. At the center sat a navy-blue Gulfstream 5. Numbers on the tail conformed to Sranil's international designation. One of three planes registered to the island, all belonging to the royal family. A gold-painted crest on the door showcased the Sranilese flag: palm fronds, a crown, three stars in a single horizontal row.

Behind the jet were stacks of wooden crates piled ten feet high. Milo had officers lower a few to the ground, began prying them open.

Mikimoto pearls in the first. Thousands of them in velvet-lined boxes. The next three contained plastic-wrapped fur coats with an emphasis on sable. Crate number four was devoted to a four-foot-wide Tiffany chandelier: hollyhocks in a riot of color and luminosity.

Five and six: gold ingots. Onward to platinum jewelry. Tapestries. Paintings, mostly of the sweet-domestic-scene variety. Old Master etchings, more gold, bags of loose-cut diamonds.

One of the cops said, 'We get a finder's fee?'

Milo put down his crowbar, walked to the opposite end of the hangar where, blocked by the jet's mammoth body, a fleet of cars sat under navy-blue covers. Same royal insignia on each.

Removing the cloths revealed a red Ferrari Enzo, a black Bugatti Veyron, a lime-green Lamborghini convertible, a silver Rolls-Royce Phantom limousine. Behind the limo, a white Prius.

'Oh, man,' said the same cop. 'I shoulda been born in Saudi Arabia.'

'Sranil,' said another.

'Whatever, dude. This level of bling, call me Hussein and circumcise me with a dull knife and no anesthesia.'

'The first time didn't hurt enough?' said his buddy.

Another officer said, 'Heard they didn't leave much to work with.'

'You heard wrong, dude. Ask your wife.'

Laughter.

The first cop said, 'What's with the hybrid, looks like a zit on the Roller's butt.'

'Probably got a solid-gold engine block, dude. Or maybe some serious tuning — can I pop the hood, Loo?'

Milo held up a restraining palm. Circled the cars, gloved up. Smoked windows on each vehicle, but unlocked doors. He opened the Prius's driver's door and stopped.

We rushed over.

A cop said, 'Oh, Jesus, that's rank.'

Two skeletons took up the rear of the hybrid, huddled, embracing, a duet of interlocking bones. To my eyes, not a staged pose; the natural instinct to draw together when faced with the worst news of all.

Milo aimed his flashlight on the bones and I peered around his bulk. Cottony blond tufts fuzzed the smaller skull, darker strands greased the other.

Femurs and tibias pressed together, fingers entwined.

Eternal lovers.

Milo said, 'Two bullet holes in each skull, forehead and under the nose.'

'Execution,' said the cop who'd asked for a look under the hood. 'And they made 'em watch.'

Milo continued to work his flashlight. 'There's some skin, mostly at the lower extremities, looks leathery.'

'Mummification,' said another cop. 'This place is humidity — and temperature-controlled, probably slowed the decomp but didn't block it.'

'Whoa, dude, someone's been watching *Forensic Files*.'

'Loo, how long do you think they've been there?'

Milo said, 'We'll wait for the coroner on that but my guess is a couple of years.'

'Makes sense, Loo. Security guy didn't remember seeing anyone here and he's been on the job eighteen months. As opposed to the next one over, that's Larry Stonefield's little Porsche garage, Larry likes to drive a different car every

351

day, his crew's in and out all the time.'

'Fifteen? Gimme one, dude, I'm happy.'

'Gimme one of those *boxes*, my girlfriend would kill for a millionth of what's inside.'

'Good choice of words, dude.'

Milo aimed his flashlight at the skeleton's feet, poked his head in deeper, emerged. 'All sorts of crust and stains on the carpet. If they weren't done in the car, they were done nearby. OK, let's get this place roped off.'

★ ★ ★

Mitochondrial DNA comparison of bone marrow from the blond skeleton and Helga Gemein's corpse confirmed that Dahlia Gemein had never made it to Sranil.

Identification of the second victim wasn't established, might never be, as if anyone wondered. The government of Sranil had lodged a formal complaint regarding unauthorized entry to the hangar, demanded immediate return of the plane, the crates, the dark-haired skeleton. Invoking diplomatic privilege and bringing in a supporting army of faceless men and women from the State Department.

'Must be my lucky week, Sturgis,' said the chief. 'I get to see you twice.'

'I'm the lucky one, sir.'

The chief touched his rear. 'Feels nice to be licked. So in come the ill-fitting suits with their small-print weapons. We get the female skeleton, the rest goes back to *sutma*-land. Do I look upset, Sturgis?'

352

'No, sir.'

'Diplomats are amoral, rim-jobbing worms, not worth my time. If the president called, I'd tell him the same thing.'

'I'm sure you would, sir.'

'Think about elections, Sturgis: Some sociopath spends hundreds of millions of dollars for a six-figure job. That's some serious psychopathology, right, Doctor?'

I smiled.

The chief said, 'He thinks I'm kidding. Anyway, to hell with the Feds, to hell with the sultan, to hell with that filthy lucre Teddy was stockpiling. Lot of good it did him. Though I guess I can't blame the sultan for not wanting to be bankrupted by all that spending.'

Milo said, 'And Dahlia?'

'Wrong place, wrong time. Or maybe they don't like blondes in Sranil.'

'So we're finished.'

'With international affairs, we are, and the clock's still ticking on the turret murders. Twelve more days, then off you go to Southwest.'

'Thank you, sir.'

'Don't thank me, just row like a galley slave.'

36

Days passed. A week. Milo resigned himself to Southwest Division.

'Used to be a rib joint there. Meanwhile, I'm eating healthy.'

Today, that translated to triple portions of lamb and unlimited vegetables from his personal buffet at Moghul.

The woman in the sari refilled iced tea as if she were paid by the pitcher.

'Guess what,' he said. 'One of the prime gunrunner suspects is the nephew of Councilman Ortiz and Ortiz is the oily sludge in His Munificence's tap water.'

'Politics,' I said.

'Whatever he claims, he's one of them.'

The door to the street opened. A midsized, bespectacled man in a dark green hoodie, jeans, and sneakers stepped in, walked straight toward us without hesitation.

Late twenties, shaved head, sharp cheekbones, rapid, purposeful stride.

Telltale bulge under the sweatshirt.

Milo's Glock was out before the guy got ten feet away.

The woman in the sari screamed and dropped to the floor.

The man's eyes saucered behind thick lenses. 'What the — Oh, shit — sorry.'

'Hands on head, don't move.'

'Lieutenant, I'm Thorpe. Pacific Division?'

'Hands on *head*. *Now!*'

'Sure, sure.' The man complied. 'Lieutenant, I had to pack, doing a GTA sting, decoy car's not far from here, I figured I'd — I called your office first, sir, they said you were here, I figured I'd just . . . '

Milo reached under the sweatshirt, took the man's gun. Another Glock. Did a pat-down, found the badge in a jeans pocket.

Officer Randolph E. Thorpe, Pacific Division.

Wallet photos advertised a pretty young wife and three toddlers, Thorpe perched proudly on a Harley-Davidson, a house with a gravel roof in the background. Two credit cards and a certificate of membership in a Baptist church out in Simi Valley.

Milo said, 'OK, relax.'

Thorpe exhaled. 'I'm lucky I didn't soil myself, sir.'

'You sure are. What can I do for you?'

'We talked a while back, sir. About a pay phone on Venice Boulevard? You were looking for a tipster, a suspect named Monte? I think I might've found him for you. Not Monte, your tipster.'

Milo returned the gun. 'Sit down, Officer Thorpe, and have some lunch. On me.'

'Um, no, thanks, Lieutenant. Even if I hadn't already eaten, my guts are kind of knotted up.' Thorpe rubbed the offending area.

'How about tea to settle them down?'

'I'm OK.' Thorpe looked around. 'Is this place dangerous or something?'

'Someone comes toward me, no introduction,

355

obviously armed, I get a little self-protective. You looked pretty intense, friend.'

'The job does that to me,' said Thorpe. 'I concentrate hard on whatever I'm doing. My wife says I turn into a robot even when I'm watching TV. Sorry if I — '

'Let's chalk it up to a misunderstanding. How about some tea for Officer Thorpe, here?'

The woman in the sari said, 'Yes, sir.' Back on her feet and looking none the worse. Downright happy, actually. Her faith in Milo's protective powers validated, yet again.

'Who's the tipster, Officer Thorpe?'

'Randy's fine, sir. I can't be sure, but there's this old guy, I thought of him a few days after we spoke, he's a local. I didn't call you right away because I had nothing to back it up, then yesterday I spotted him approaching that same phone booth, my last day in uniform before the GTA thing. I was on Code Seven, having coffee across the street, he walks right up to the booth, makes like he's going to call, changes his mind, leaves. Returns a few minutes later, gets as far as picking up the receiver, changes his mind again, leaves. I stuck around but he didn't come back. It could be nothing, but I figured.'

'Appreciate it, Randy. Got a name?'

'All I know is George. But he lives in one of those old-age homes nearby. Here's the address.'

'Excellent,' said Milo. 'Keep those eyes sharp, Randy. This works out, I'll put in a good word with the chief.'

'You can do that?'

'Anytime.'

Two Georges in residence at the mint-green apartment complex recast as Peace Gardens Retirement Center. George Bannahyde was wheelchair-bound and never left the building. George Kaplan, 'one of our healthier ones,' resided in a second-story room.

Too many old-age homes are hovels designed to stuff owners' pockets with taxpayer largesse. This one was clean, fresh smelling, softly lit, with snacks in abundance and well-fed, nicely groomed residents playing board games, exercising on mats, watching movies on wide-screen TVs. A posted schedule listed activities every daylight hour, mealtimes excepted.

Milo assured the desk clerk that Mr Kaplan wasn't in trouble; just the opposite, he was important to LAPD.

She said, 'George?'

'Is he in?'

'Up in his room. I can call him down if you'd like.'

'No, that's fine, we'll just drop in.'

Lots of head-turns as Milo and I walked past the activity. We climbed the stairs to a freshly vacuumed corridor. Bouncy brown carpeting, mock-adobe walls, burnt-orange doors equipped with name slots.

G. Kaplan's door was open. A small, round-backed, light-skinned black man sat on a neatly tucked bed, wearing a white shirt buttoned to the neck, knife-pressed maroon slacks, spit-polished black-and-white wingtips.

Skimpy silver hair was pomaded to iridescence. Gray-blue eyes, not that different in hue from mine, studied us with amusement. A box of Tam Tam crackers, a bottle of dry-roasted peanuts, and a setup for instant coffee sat on a nightstand. The wall above the headboard bore portraits of Martin Luther King and Lyndon Johnson, the latter signed.

Two chairs faced the bed. George Kaplan said, 'Sit, Gemma called from downstairs, officers, all ready for you.'

Singsong cadence, velvety intonation; maybe one of New Orleans's many variants. His eyes were serene but both hands trembled and his head rocked at irregular intervals. Parkinson's disease or something like it.

'Thanks for meeting with us, Mr Kaplan.'

'Nothing else to do.' Kaplan's lips parted. Too-white dentures clacked. 'What does law enforcement have in mind with relation to George S. Kaplan?'

Milo studied the photos before settling. 'LBJ? Usually it's JFK.'

'George S. Kaplan isn't usual. Those Kennedys were fine, if you like pretty faces. President Johnson didn't look like a movie star — Lord, those ears, he got no respect. But it was him pushed through legislation to smooth out the races.'

'The Great Society.'

'He was a dreamer, same as Dr King. I did the man's shoes, Ambassador Hotel. The president, not Dr King, unfortunately. Had a stand there for forty-eight and a half years. Was there the night RFK got shot, tried to tell the cops I'd seen that Jordanian lunatic skulking around the hotel for days, muttering to himself. No one cares what I have to say.'

'We care.'

Kaplan massaged a pearl shirt button, fought to still his hands. 'Know how old I am?'

'You look good, sir.'

'Take a guess, Officer — 'scuse me, Detective. You're a detective, right?'

'Yes, sir.'

'What's your guess? Don't worry, I won't be insulted.'

'Normally, I'd say seventies, Mr Kaplan, but if you worked at the Ambassador for forty-eight years and it closed around — '

'It closed in 1989. Place gave sixty-eight years of service and they let it go stone-cold. Architectural masterpiece, designed by Mr Myron Hunt. Know who he was?'

'No, sir.'

'Famous architect. Designed the Rose Bowl. Ambassador was a palace, drew in all the finest people. You should've seen the weddings, the black-tie galas, I did my share of last-minute patent-leather touchup and that's a lost art. City bought the property, says it's going to be a school. Just what we need, teenagers making a mess. So how old am I?'

'Eighty . . . '

'Ninety-three.'

'You look great, Mr Kaplan.'

'Then appearances are deceiving. I'm missing a whole bunch of internal organs, doctors keep taking things out of me. Apparently, God gives us extra organs that can be removed without serious consequence. As to why, you'd have to ask Him. Which I'm figuring I'll get a chance to do, soon. Care for crackers?'

'No, thanks, sir.'

'Peanuts?'

'We're fine, sir.'

'So what about George S. Kaplan is of interest to the Los Angeles police?'

'Monte.'

Kaplan looked at his knees. 'I got a Jewish name, in case you didn't notice. Kaplan comes from Hebraic. Means chaplain. I still haven't figured it out. Someone said my family might've worked for Jewish slave owners but that's wrong, we've been freemen since the beginning. Came over *after* emancipation, from Curacao, that's an island in the Caribbean, lots of Jews used to live there so who knows? What do you think, Detective? Can the mystery be solved?'

'The Internet has lots of genealogy web-sites — '

'Tried all that. My great-grandson Michael, he's a computer geek — that's what he calls himself. That's how I learned about the Hebraic origin of my name. But it led nowhere. Guess some mysteries don't like being solved.'

'Some do, sir. Monte?'

'How'd you locate me?'

'We traced your tip-call to the pay phone.'

'Lots of people use that pay phone.'

'Not as many as you'd think, Mr Kaplan.'

'Cell phones. Don't want one. Have no need for one.'

'An officer watching the booth saw you approaching it yesterday. It appeared to him as if you were ready to make another call, changed your mind.'

Kaplan laughed. 'And here I was, being careful.'

'You wanted to help but didn't want to get overly involved.'

'He's a frightening person, Monte. I lived ninety-three years, would like a few more.'

'There's no need for him to know, Mr Kaplan.'

'You arrest him based on my word, how's he not going to know?'

'You'll be listed in my notes as an 'anonymous source.''

'Until some lawyer pokes around and you feel the pressure.'

'I don't respond well to pressure,' said Milo. 'And I never break my word. I promise your name will never appear in any case file.'

Kaplan kept his eyes down. 'Sure you don't want a cracker?'

'It's not food I need right now, sir.'

'You think Monte killed that girl.'

'I think I need to hear what bothers you about him.'

'Huh,' said the old man. 'George S. Kaplan does his civic duty like his mother taught him and look where it gets him.'

'If Monte's dangerous, sir, all the more reason to get him off the street.'

'I've never seen him do anything dangerous.'

'But he's a scary guy.'

361

'I've lived long enough to know a frightening person when I see one. No respect for his elders.'

'He was discourteous to you?'

Kaplan's head shifted from side to side. When it stopped moving, he said, 'That girl on the TV, the pretty one who was killed in that big house near Bel Air. She lived with him. Him and his other girlfriend, the three of them going in and out of that house. Normally, you'd think they were up for hanky-panky but all the times I saw them, they didn't look like they were having recreation.'

'Serious?'

'More than serious, I'd called it purposeful. Sneaky eyes, like they were up to something. I walk around the neighborhood a lot, good for the joints and the muscles, I notice things other people don't. There's a woman right down the block, been cheating on her husband with the gardener for near on six years, kisses her husband when he comes home like she's madly in love with the poor fool, when he's gone she's with the gardener. People do crazy things, I could tell you all sorts of stories.'

'Tell us about Monte and the girl on TV.'

'The last time I saw her with him was maybe a week before she got killed. Monte's other girlfriend wasn't there, just that girl and Monte, and they were going into that house and I started thinking maybe Monte's cheating on one girlfriend with the other girlfriend, she's certainly a better looker. But they didn't look up for fooling around — grim, that's the word. Real grim. After Monte let the girl in, he turned

362

around, gave me the dirtiest look you've ever seen. Said, 'Got a problem, old man?' I just kept on going, could feel him watching me, made the small hairs stand up. Never walked near there again. A week or so later, I'm watching the fifty-inch downstairs and the news comes on, there *she* is. A drawing, but it's her. So I do my civic duty. What I didn't figure on was having to do more.'

'Any idea what Monte's last name is?'

'I just heard his girlfriends calling him Monte.'

'Where's the house?'

'Two blocks east, one block north. He drives a black pickup truck. She drives a Honda. Gray, the other girlfriend. Never saw the pretty one with a motor vehicle, always riding with one of the other two.'

'You wouldn't have the address by any chance, would you?'

'You swear on a stack my name won't appear anywhere?'

'Scout's honor, sir.'

'You were a scout?'

'Actually, I was.'

'I would've liked to be a scout,' said George S. Kaplan. 'No colored scouts in Baton Rouge back then. I learned to be prepared, anyway.' Denture grin. He reached for a bureau drawer. 'Let me find that address and copy it for you. Do it in block lettering so no one can trace my handwriting.'

37

The house was a flat-face stucco bungalow the color of curdled oatmeal, narrow and tar-roofed and shuttered tight. Cement square instead of lawn, no vehicles parked there, no mail pileup.

Milo and I did a quick drive-by, parked half a mile up. He celled Moe Reed, asked for an assessor's check.

Owned and managed by a Covina real estate firm, rented to a tenant named M. Carlo Scoppio.

'Looked him up, Loo. Male white, thirty-two years old, no wants or warrants, no NCIC. Owners can't evict him but they'd like to.'

'What's the problem?'

'He always pays his rent but does it chronically late,' said Reed. 'Like he's trying to irritate them by squeezing out every bit of delay. They say getting rid of a tenant is a hassle even when you're faced with a total deadbeat and Scoppio makes sure not to give them grounds. Top of that, he's a lawyer, they don't want the aggravation.'

'What are his physical stats?'

'Five nine, one seventy-eight, brown and green. The picture makes him a guy you'd never notice. You anywhere near a fax?'

'Nope, but the stats are consistent with Hood-boy. Where does Scoppio practice law?'

'Haven't checked yet, but I will.'

'Don't bother, I can do it. Thanks, Moses, you can climb back up Olympus, now.'

★ ★ ★

I said, '*Monte Carlo?*'

Milo said, 'Smells right but ol' George really *is* ol' George. More like ancient. Scoppio gives him attitude, Kaplan builds up resentment, a few days later he sees a drawing on TV, convinces himself he just got dissed by a murderer.'

'Ol' George seemed pretty lucid to me. More important, you've got nothing else and who knows if that rib joint is still in business.'

'Desperation time . . . always been a favorite season of mine.'

★ ★ ★

A search for the working address of M. Carlo Scoppio, attorney at law, pulled up nothing. Same for an inquiry at the bar association.

Milo said, 'He lied, excellent start.'

I said, 'Lawyers can work in other capacities.'

'Hush your mouth, whippersnapper. Let's go back to the office, return close to five. If the timing's right, I'll have a little chat with this charmer.'

★ ★ ★

Googling *m. carlo scoppio* pulled up the website of Baird, Garroway and Habib, an East LA law firm specializing in personal injury civil suits. Scoppio's name appeared near the bottom of the staff roster. Paralegal.

'He didn't just lie, he puffed himself up,' said Milo. 'We're a little closer to sociopath.' He scanned. 'Hablo Español . . . and five other languages. Could be one of those slip-and-fall deals, poor stooges get the whiplash, lawyers get the dough. Maybe paralegal means Scoppio ropes them in.'

Probing for articles on the law firm produced several news pieces about an investigation by the city attorney. All three partners were suspected of setting up phony traffic accidents, working in concert with corrupt physicians, physical therapists, and chiropractors. No indictments had been brought.

No mention of Carlo Scoppio.

Milo tried a contact at the city attorney's office. The woman had no personal knowledge of the case but looked up the current status.

'Appears to be pending, Lieutenant.'

'Meaning?'

'My guess would be insufficient evidence to file. Looks like they used illegals as their stooges, try finding witnesses willing to testify.'

'Does the name M. Carlo Scoppio appear any-where?'

'Scoppio . . . no, doesn't look like — oh, here it is, he's a para . . . suspected of being a recruiter. He killed someone? We might be able to use that.'

* * *

By four forty-eight we were back on Scoppio's block, cruising past the bungalow.

366

Still no sign of the black pickup George Kaplan had described but a gray Honda sat on the concrete pad.

Milo said, 'Girlfriend's here, maybe boyfriend will show up soon.'

Too few cars on the street made getting close risky. I parked four houses up, switched off the engine. Milo positioned a pair of binoculars in his lap, chewed a panatela, paused from time to time to spit shreds of tobacco out the passenger window.

'We could be here for a while, you want to put on music, it's fine with me.'

'What are you in the mood for?'

'Anything that doesn't make my ears bleed — well, looky here.'

A black Ford half-ton approached from the south and pulled up next to the Honda.

Milo snatched up the binocs, was focused on the driver's door as a man exited the truck.

'That's him — guess what he's wearing? Gray hoodie.'

Carlo Scoppio walked around to the truck's passenger side, retrieved something.

Plastic bags. Five of them. Scoppio laid them on the concrete.

Milo said, 'Albertsons, ol' Monte C. does the shopping, how touchingly domestic.'

Scoppio returned to the driver's side, reached in, honked the horn.

The bungalow's front door opened and a woman stepped out. Tallish, dressed in a white top and jeans.

Scoppio pointed to the bags. The woman

walked toward them.

Milo's shoulders tightened. 'You are not going to believe this. Here, take a look.'

'At what?'

'Her.'

38

Dual lenses highlighted a pleasant face framed by long rust-brown hair. Late twenties to early thirties, rosy-cheeked, clear blue eyes.

Milo said, 'Our rookie CI, Lara whatshername.'

I said, 'Helpful Ms Rieffen.'

Carlo Scoppio lifted three bags, left Lara Rieffen to carry two. No pleasantries exchanged between the two. No talk, at all.

They entered the house. The door closed.

Milo said, 'This changes everything.'

* * *

During the drive back to the station, he reached Dave McClellan, the head coroner's investigator, asked if Lara Rieffen's assignment to the turret murders had been scheduled routine.

McClellan said, 'She screwed up?'

'No, I just need to know, Dave.'

'Don't have the schedule in front of me, I'm at City Hall trying to impress city council members. Why do you need to know?'

'Who do I talk to about the schedule, Dave?'

'Now you're scaring me — tell me the truth, did Rieffen screw up in some major way?'

'Is she a screwup?'

'She's new, tends to be a little lazy.'

'She gave the opposite impression at Borodi,

369

Dave. Made herself out to be Eager Annie.'

'Maybe she likes you.'

'The burden of charm, story of my life. Where can I get hold of the schedule?'

'You're not going to tell me why? All of a sudden, my gut's churning.'

'It could be nothing, Dave.'

'Now my bowels are loosening,' said McClellan. 'Call Irma, my administrative aide. She knows everything. Wish I did, too.'

★ ★ ★

Irma Melendez took thirty seconds to come up with the answer: A CI named Daniel Paillard had been next up for the Borodi call.

'He didn't take it, Lieutenant Sturgis? My record says he did.'

'Lara Rieffen did.'

'Her?' said Melendez. 'How come?'

'I thought you might know.'

'I have no idea, Lieutenant. The two of them must've worked something out — maybe Dan had an emergency. She doesn't volunteer for anything.'

'Not a workaholic?'

'That's putting it mildly.'

'Where can I find Paillard?'

'He's off today.'

'Give me his cell and his home landline, please.'

'Dan did something wrong?'

'Not at all.'

'Good,' said Melendez. 'Him, I like.'

★ ★ ★

Daniel Paillard was at Universal Studios with his girlfriend.

'This is a big deal?'

'Probably not,' said Milo, 'but tell me about it.'

'Nothing to tell,' said Paillard. 'She came to me the day before, said she needed time off next week, was I willing to swap. I said sure, why not.'

'What day did she need time off?'

'She never said.'

'She never collected on the trade?'

Silence.

'Dan?'

'I guess she didn't,' said Paillard. 'I guess I forgot — looking a gift horse, you know? Am I in trouble? I mean it was between the two of us.'

'You're not in trouble.'

'I mean, I'd been working my ass off for weeks, all those gang shootings,' said Paillard. 'When she came to me, I didn't see any problem long as the job got done — did she screw up?'

'Is she a screwup?'

'She's green,' said Paillard.

'Do me a favor, Dan. Don't tell her about this conversation.'

'She's in some other kind of trouble?'

'Not yet,' said Milo. 'Be discreet, Dan, and I will be, too.'

'Yeah, yeah, sure,' said Paillard. 'She's green, maybe a little lazy, that's really all I can say about her.'

Milo swung his desk chair around, faced me. 'Lazy rookie but she makes herself out as gung-ho. A faker like Scoppio. She processed the bodies, made comments about Doreen's clothes being cheap. That takes on a whole new flavor now.'

I said, 'Rieffen trading shifts the day before the murder says she knew Backer and Doreen would be up in that turret. Doreen lived with her and Scoppio, so that's no mystery. If Scoppio's our Port Angeles hoodie, we've got fifty grand of motive. But the scene's always reeked of personal to me, so it could've gone beyond the money. Kaplan said the three of them looked grim when they were together. Maybe the gloss was off the relationship.'

'Threesome gone bad.'

'Possibly because threesome had turned to twosome.'

'Doreen threw her roommies over for Backer,' he said. 'Old flame reignited. So to speak.'

'Backer and Doreen were paid by Helga to blow up Teddy's palace, scoped the scene and found the turret a fun place. Ned Holman saw them use it two months before the murders, they could very well have turned it into their private party spot, could've even taken Rieffen and Monte up there. Either way they'd be easy to track. The scene's always pointed to two killers. Now we've got a new pair.'

'Rieffen's involved in the murder, makes sure she's assigned to the scene. Cute. The obvious reason is monkeying with evidence, as in concealing any record of her presence and Scoppio's. She was up there before I arrived, Lord knows what she did during that time.'

I said, 'One thing she *didn't* conceal was the semen stain on Doreen's leg. On the contrary, she called it to your attention and that makes me wonder if she was playing head games. Backer always used condoms, we've assumed he made an exception for Doreen. What if he didn't and the semen came from someone else?'

'Monte chokes out Doreen then abuses her corpse? Why would Rieffen point out the stain? And why not wipe it off right at the murder?'

'Maybe Monte didn't want her to. Proud of himself, playing his own head game. On her own, Rieffen might've been more cautious. Or she thought it was fun, too. In either case, she knew the stain would be gone by the time the body got to Jernigan. That's exactly the kind of highrisk adrenaline rush psychopaths crave. Rieffen takes control of the evidence, making herself look sharp-eyed in the process. Then she finds a quiet moment at the crypt and destroys the evidence, making the rest of the coroner's staff look incompetent.'

'It's not enough that I succeed,' he said. 'You have to fail.'

'Antisocial, self-aggrandizing puffery at its finest, Big Guy.'

'One speck of DNA could've screwed the deal — if anyone would bother to analyze the stain. But she's a goddamn CI, would know how to do it right.'

'No reason to analyze DNA,' I said. 'The way the bodies were posed, the obvious donor was Backer.'

'Speaking of Backer, maybe we're talking foursome down to twosome. They all knew each other. One shot to the head, Desi's out of the picture, they get the storage key. Leaving Doreen to deal with two armed baddies, piece of cake subduing her. Rieffen trains the little gun on her while Monte jams the big one. Then he strangles her, delivering an incredibly demeaning *coup de grâce*. Then they reposition the bodies.'

'They left Backer's ID in place, but took Doreen's because she'd lived with them, could be traced to them.'

'Rieffen and Monte living with a pyro, and Monte's copping the fifty G's says they knew about the plot. What if the foursome was a business arrangement, Alex?'

'They were all involved in the fire,' I said.

'Eliminate Backer and Doreen and the share doubles.'

'Foursome,' I said. 'Two other kids were suspects in the Bellevue fire. Kathy Something, I forget the boy's name.'

He snatched up his pad. 'Kathy Vanderveldt, Dwayne Parris. Lindstrom said they turned out fine, she went to med school, he went to law school.'

'Lindstrom never actually met them, she's relying on the previous agent's notes. What if Kathy and Dwayne *planned* careers in medicine and law, but fell short? A CI deals with the human body but works under a physician's supervision. A paralegal — who tells people he's a lawyer — has to answer to an attorney.'

'Wannabes, they change their names . . . the Feds being their usual thorough selves miss it.' He faced his computer. 'OK, let's see what we locals can come up with.'

He called up a series of high school reunion sites, found one that offered yearbook photos for a fee, zeroed in on Seattle. Plugging in *kathy vanderveldt* struck gold at Center High. After confirming that Dwayne Parris had been a member of the same class, he used his own credit card to pay for the shots and printed.

Black-and-white shots, but clear enough.

Younger versions of the two faces we'd just seen carrying groceries.

Kathy Lara Vanderveldt had smiled warmly for the camera. Member of the science club, the nature club, Future Physicians of America.

Dwayne Charles Parris had maintained a narrow-mouthed stoicism. An average-looking kid, in every way, with bushy dark hair worn low over his forehead. Varsity hockey, Model UN, accounting club.

I said, 'She's using her middle name as her first, he's Carlo as in Italian for Charles. Wonder where he got Scoppio.'

'Maybe it means something in Italian.'

It did.

Explosion.

Milo said, 'Monte go boom.'

★ ★ ★

He kept searching, starting with *kathy vanderveldt*. No criminal record on file, same for

375

Dwayne Parris, but a five-year-old account of the Vanderveldt — Rieffen family reunion was featured in *The Seattle Times*. Serious human interest, because a hundred fifty-three people had participated. Page-wide group photo, Kathy nowhere to be seen but a small child with the same name sat in the front row, beaming.

Milo said, 'Little cousin makes it to the party but Big Kathy doesn't, because she's using an aka. She's running from something bad, but no record?'

I said, 'It's possible that whatever she's running from never made the files. As in her own lost years.'

'Another teen eco-terrorist who kept it going?'

'And whose career somehow got derailed. Doreen conned the FBI, but Lindstrom did say she'd tossed them a few bones. Minor stuff, but everything's relative, to the Bureau minor could mean big buildings aren't blowing up. What if Doreen's info implicated Kathy and Dwayne seriously enough to screw up their educational goals and force them underground? Kathy and Dwayne figured out who'd betrayed them, but Doreen and Backer didn't realize that. Years later, the four of them reconnect in LA, agree to collaborate on a torch job. Shades of the Bellevue fire that killed Van Burghout, but now they're getting paid serious money. Kathy and Dwayne go along with it until they figure out how to get hold of the money. After that, Backer and Doreen are history.'

'Reunion of the nature-hiking eco-pyros,' he said. 'OK, it's time to have a go at Gayle's ego.'

39

Special Agent Gayle Lindstrom met us at a pizza joint in Westwood Village, not far from the Federal Building. College student clientele meant oceans of cheap beer on tap, not much in the way of décor.

Milo talked, Lindstrom listened, growing steadily more tense with each revelation. When he finished, she said, 'Those two. Oh, crap.'

'Kathy and Carlo are your buddies.'

'They're names in a file.'

'You made it like they turned out sterling. She's a doctor, he's a lawyer, all that's missing is an Indian chief.'

'I said that because that's what's in the *file*. There's absolutely nothing pointing to them being criminal, let alone homicidal.'

'All you know is what you read.'

'Cut it out,' she snapped. 'You don't have to make me feel stupider than I already do.'

'If you had nothing to do with working Vanderveldt and Parris, there's no reason for you to feel stupid — '

'You just don't *get* it, do you? The first time we met, you figured out I've got my issues. As in having trouble ignoring obviously brain-dead decisions being made with more concern for butt-covering than the public's welfare. I like to tell myself if I'd been in charge, 9/11 never would've happened. Maybe that's self-delusional

377

crap, maybe I need to stroke myself because the job's turned out to be not what I had in mind. However you want to see it, I'm an *outlier* and what I need — what I need*ed* — was a reprieve. When I learned you nailed the Swiss witch, I was ready to buy you dinner at Spago. *Then* I find out the Swiss witch had nothing to do with killing Doreen and the State Department's on our butts because you went into that hangar without authorization. Not only haven't you helped me, you've made my life more difficult.'

'Gee,' said Milo. 'Here I was thinking solving murders was my job, when all along it was being your life coach.'

Lindstrom's hands clenched.

Milo plucked pepperoni.

'Milo, we're the good guys, why are we going at each other?'

'Help me out, Gayle, and we'll be sandbox buddies again.'

'What makes you think I can help you? I'm an unpopular girl with a cubicle full of old cold files and a directive to clear them or else. Which is like asking me to teach Britney nuclear physics.'

'Forget physics,' said Milo. 'Let's talk medicine. And law.'

'You want me to find out if Kathy ever enrolled, fine, I can do that. Same for Parris and law school, but what's that going to tell you? You need physical evidence.'

'Whatever builds the case is worthwhile, Gayle. Now tell me exactly what Doreen gave the Bureau before she split.'

'Dinky stuff.'

'I like dinky, Gayle.'

'This was real minor-league, it stayed with the Forest Service. There was a chunk of disputed federal land in northern Washington State. The usual logging/farming/dune-buggying/tourism side fighting the totally leave-it-for-the-mosquitoes side. Doreen had volunteered as a tree-hugger a few months before she got nabbed hooking in Seattle. Doing field tests, whatever. What she gave up when we pressed her were two schemes. The first was her fellow volunteers tilting the odds by planting Canadian lynx hairs near tree trunks — smearing the DNA then 'discovering' it. Apparently, the lynx is mucho endangered, so that would've meant big-time land restriction. The second con involved poisoning wild horses and leaving carcasses in spots grizzly bears didn't frequent to draw grizzlies and enlarge estimates of *their* habitat. See what I mean? Low-rent, the Forest Service gave even less of a crap than the Bureau took no action. Then a senator who got tons of logging money found out and he raised a stink and an investigation ensued. No one went to jail but people lost their jobs.'

'Names,' said Milo.

'I don't have any, the guy from whom I inherited the files wasn't into extraneous detail.'

'Maybe not so extraneous, Gayle, if Kathy Vanderveldt and Dwayne Parris were among those volunteers. Some people lost their jobs, others might've lost their careers.'

'Expelled from med school and law school due to moral turpitude?' she said. 'Yeah, I guess that could happen.'

She stood, tried to put money on the table. Milo's big hand closed around hers. 'My treat, Gayle.'

'Why?'

'You deserve it.'

'Yeah, sure,' said Lindstrom. 'When I got a bad grade, my dad lied to me the same way.'

★ ★ ★

I said, 'Manipulating physical evidence.'

He said, 'Kathy Lara can't be a doctor, but gets herself a gig where she can still have fun with biology. Same old story, with twisted types it's all about control.'

'With everyone it's about control,' I said. 'The key is how you go about it.'

★ ★ ★

Lindstrom's call came as we drove back to the station.

'That was quick, Gayle.'

'Wish I could say I pulled strings, all I had to do was pull our copy of the Forest Service file. Vanderveldt and Parris are named as a participants in both cons. In fact, they're the only participants named. And Vanderveldt was, indeed, booted out of U of Idaho med school — where she'd been at the bottom of her class. Parris's standing at U Wash law school was actually pretty good but he also got tossed. Both of them appealed twice. Denied. You really see that as motive?'

'That and fifty G's, Gayle.'

'Yeah, I guess that covers a lot of bases,' said Lindstrom. 'So what now?'

'So now I talk to them.'

'I'd like to be involved.'

'When the time's right.'

'Hope *that's* not a lie. With my dad I could tell. With you, not so easy.'

40

Deputy DA John Nguyen confirmed what Milo already knew: insufficient grounds to arrest Rieffen and Scoppio for anything, all interviews would have to be voluntary.

'You are cordially invited to chat?'

'Unless you witness them committing some kind of naughty and bust them for that.'

'Bad lane change do the trick?'

Nguyen laughed. 'I was thinking something involving blood.'

'How about smearing lynx DNA on something?'

'What the hell's a lynx, anyway?' said Nguyen. 'Something you make a coat out of, right?'

'Bite your tongue, John.'

'I'm talking theoretical, Milo. My pay grade, the wife's lucky to get wool.'

* * *

A review of the little we knew about the suspects suggested Rieffen would be less violence-prone, more likely to turn. Maybe.

Reed and Binchy took separate cars and began subtle surveillance on the man calling himself M. Carlo Scoppio. He'd left for work at nine A.M., drove to the East LA law firm, was still there by eleven thirty.

'Loo, one thing occurred to me,' said Reed.

'The office is awfully close to where that CI, Escobar, got shot.'

'How close, Moses?'

'Like three blocks. It's county land, owned by the med center but undeveloped.'

'You scoped it out?'

'It was close, I started wondering. There's an intersection nearby. Not much traffic but a long red light. If Escobar was a law-abiding type, it would've been easy enough to catch him when he was stopped, commandeer the car.'

'Go back and take photos,' said Milo. 'After Sean takes over the watch.'

'I'll buy a camera,' said Reed.

'A cheap one's good enough for making memories, Moses. One day, we'll scrapbook.'

★　★　★

Lara Rieffen was on shift at the crypt, processing a shooting in Pacoima. The plan was to 'find' her in the parking lot when she returned to file paper, Milo coming on friendly, pretending to be there on business. Then walking her in and finding a space in the building for a 'follow-up' interview. Keeping it low-key, so she wouldn't be threatened and the coroner's staff wouldn't be aware of any disruption.

But the boss had to know so Milo phoned Dave McClellan, gave him the bad news.

He said, 'I've been grinding my teeth since we spoke. She's really that evil, huh? *That* makes us look great.'

'No way you could know, Dave.'

383

'Whatever it takes to nail the bitch, Milo. I'll make sure there's an open room on the bottom floor.'

'Thanks. I'll keep it as quiet as possible.'

'Way I'm feeling about her, you can hog-tie her in full sight,' said McClellan. 'And don't worry about quiet, we're already crawling with cops, anyway.'

'Why?'

'Bobby Escobar. All of a sudden, Sheriff's Homicide decided they need to inspect his office, sent their own techies over, but they won't say why. They've been all over us since six A.M.'

'Who's the lead detective?'

'New replacement, Irvin Wimmers.'

'I know Irv. Good man.'

'I think they're here just to cover their asses. Anyway, want me to reel Rieffen in at any particular time? Or whatever the hell her name really is.'

'When's she expected back?'

'Four, five, depending on particulars and drive-time.'

'Let's aim for five.'

'You got it,' said McClellan. 'Good riddance to bad rubbish.'

★ ★ ★

Milo phoned Sheriff's Homicide Detective Irvin Wimmers and asked for a meet when Wimmers had time.

Wimmers said, 'I'll make time, Milo. How about now?'

'You don't even know what it's about, Irv.'

'You're calling me is what I know. How many of the same conferences we been to? Denver, DC, Philadelphia — that fun one in Nashville, all those slides on decomp. When we see each other, we generally sit down for coffee. We get back to LA, how many times do we call each other?'

'I don't know.'

'I'll tell you how many,' said Wimmers. 'Once. That Compton hatchet case, you clued me in on that old file one of your retired guys worked, we ended up nailing the bitch for turning two husbands to hamburger, not just one. So I'm figuring you've got something else useful to tell me. Maybe about Escobar? Say yes, it would make my day.'

'It is about Escobar, Irv, but it could turn out to be nothing. Did he have a predictable schedule at the crypt?'

'He had no schedule at all,' said Wimmers. 'Going to school, not working there anymore, but they let him keep his key, gave him a little closet office for working on his master's thesis.'

'What was he researching?'

'The technology of negligent evidence transfer — people screwing up with fingerprint brushes, careless fiber collection, that kind of thing. What's on your mind, Milo?'

Wimmers listened to the bare-bones recap, said, 'That's pretty freaky — OK, this is something I need to sit down and think about. My partner's due in soon and I been up since five, need to eat or I'm gonna pass out. Where you calling from?'

385

'The office.'

'You got the time for meeting about halfway? I know a place, you'll like it.'

★   ★   ★

Ruby's Theatre of Turkey operated from a storefront on Eighth Street just west of Wilton.

Monumental birds dunked into deep-fryers, carved to order, served up glistening.

Irvin Wimmers was a black man taller and wider than Milo, with a pencil mustache and a soul patch and a gleaming shaved head furrowed longitudinally. He wore a double-breasted cinnamon-brown suit, a long-collared maroon shirt, a narrow olive tie patterned with orange battleships.

The platter in front of him held a crisp, brown turkey quarter, chunky cranberry sauce, okra, collard greens, a sweating heap of macaroni and cheese. A side plate hosted biscuits the size of baseballs, sodden with what looked like redeye gravy. Leave your Louisville Slugger at home, the turkey leg would be a fine substitute.

Milo said, 'Thanksgiving came early, Irv.'

Wimmers said, 'My philosophy, celebrate anytime you get the chance. So how's it going, City Boy?'

'It's going.' Quick handclasps. Milo introduced me.

Wimmers said, 'I heard about you, Doc. Ever think of coming over to the county side? We're the one's really out for truth, justice, and the American way.'

I smiled.

'Unspoken like a true shrink — sit down, guys. Want me to order you half a bird?'

'Quarter'll do fine, Irv.'

'Each?'

'Both.'

'On a diet, Milo?'

'God forbid.'

Wimmers rumbled amusement. 'What're you drinking? The iced tea's good, they throw in some pomegranate juice, supposed to be healthy, slow us down from rusting.'

'They're outta that,' said Milo, 'I'll take WD-40.'

★   ★   ★

Wimmers lumbered to the counter, returned with a pair of twenty-four-ounce glasses of red-brown tea. 'So you're thinking this crooked CI had something to do with Bobby Escobar?'

'I can't prove it, Irv, but I'm certain she wiped away a semen stain because it belonged to her boyfriend. And Bobby's specialty was monkeying with evidence, meaning he coulda been sharp-eyed, seen something.'

'From what I hear, Milo, he was definitely sharp-eyed. Back when he worked as a CI, he used to get on people's nerves for being a little too gung-ho, you know? The kid in class who points out the teacher forgot about the test?'

Milo said, 'How far was his office from that fridge-closet where they stack up the tagged bodies?'

'Right across the hall,' said Wimmers. 'Hmm,

ain't *that* cute? So let's frame this: I told you Bobby didn't have a set schedule but before I drove here I called his wife and she said between school and a part-time job at a medical lab, it wasn't unusual for him to come in at midnight, stay for a while. Which is exactly what he was doing the morning he got killed. Same for the two days preceding, which was the period when Rieffen would've done her tampering. So maybe she sneaks in late to do her mischief, figures no one's there. But Bobby's in his office, behind a closed door, typing on his laptop. She goes into the fridge, does her bad thing, just happens to encounter Bobby as he pops out.'

Milo said, 'She was official, had a badge, someone else might've ignored her. But Bobby got curious.'

'Only problem, Milo, from what I've learned about Bobby, he sees something hinky, he reports it. There's no record he ever did.'

Milo said, 'Maybe he left a note on someone's desk, Rieffen saw it, snatched it.'

'Guess so,' said Wimmers. 'But try proving that.'

I said, 'Even if Bobby suspected something and checked in the fridge, how would he have found her out? We're talking evidence removal, how do you confirm the absence of something?'

'Then why bother killing him?'

'Maybe he gave her a look that unsettled her. Or made a comment. Not enough for him to report, but more than enough to get Rieffen worried. She told Monte, he decided to fix the problem.'

'Homicidal boyfriend,' said Wimmers. 'Can't believe she actually finagled herself to process a murder she'd done. That's gotta be a first.'

'Didn't take much finagling,' said Milo. 'She offered a trade to another CI. The tipoff is she never bothered to claim her share.'

'Too good to be true,' said Wimmers. 'Man, this girl's a piece of work. Now all we have to do is prove it.'

'What brought you back to Escobar's office today?'

Wimmer pushed cranberry sauce around his plate. 'What brought me back was my perception of the case. It wasn't mine, initially. Two rookies caught the call, got pulled off to do gang stuff and wrote up the prelim as a robbery gone bad. Given the neighborhood and Escobar's wallet being gone, that made superficial sense. But when I looked closer, it started to fall apart. Escobar's cell phone was right there, on the passenger seat. So was a bunch of bling on his person, all inherited from his dad, who was a pawnbroker. I'm talking a big gold ring with a diamond, a gold ID bracelet, a gold-and-diamond earring. Stuff that would've been easy to fence. Plus, Escobar was sitting behind the wheel of his car when we found him but most of the blood was outside and when I revisited the scene, I found what looked to be drag marks.'

'He got shot outside and put back in?'

'How many armed robbers you know gonna take the time to do that? To me it smelled staged.'

'Rieffen and Monte are veterans at that.' Milo

389

described the turret murders in greater detail.

Wimmers said, 'Please tell me your guy was shot with a .22 revolver or maybe an automatic and the shells were collected.'

Milo nodded.

'Your bullet clean enough for analysis?'

'Coroner says frags but they can be put back together, so maybe.'

'Who's making the call to the gun lab, you or me?'

'Be my guest, Irv.'

Wimmers phoned Ballistics, arranged for the comparison asap. 'They said forty-eight hours, I got 'em down to twenty-four.' Two giant hands rubbed together. 'This is starting to taste even better than my bird.'

41

There's a sixth sense, a high-definition sensitivity to threat, experienced by soldiers in combat, veteran cops, and a certain class of cold-blooded psychopath.

Milo's approach to Lara Rieffen was subtle, faking good cheer as she exited her county car in the crypt lot. She went along with the chitchat, synched with his loose, slow gait, but I was reading her eyes, bet she had a different rhythm in mind.

Milo probably figured it out, but he kept up the performance as the three of us entered the northern half of the coroner's complex. Where the wet-work gets done.

Once inside, he used the barest touch of thumb on arm to direct Rieffen toward the empty room Dave McClellan had provided. The trajectory took her toward her cubicle, no reason for her to resist or suspect but her mouth tightened and she pushed ahead of Milo. He caught up and when they reached the open door, took hold of her elbow and stopped the parade.

'I could use a few minutes of your time, Lara.'

Stiff smile. 'For what, Lieutenant?'

'Go over the Borodi scene a bit. I need to nail down a few details before I finish my report.'

'You've closed the case?'

'I wish, just the opposite. It's actually looking real bad for a close, but I've got a new assignment from the brass, need to move on.'

Blue eyes blinked. 'Oh. That must be frustrating.'

'Part of the job. So just a few secs, OK?' Propelling her inside before she could answer.

Two chairs facing one, a table to the side where Milo's jacket was bunched up. Kathy Vanderveldt aka Lara Rieffen sat where she was supposed to.

No one-way for observation, no space or practical way to work Gayle Lindstrom in and Milo had informed the SA.

Appetizer goes down smooth, you can share the entrée, Gayle.

I sat down next to Milo. Lara Rieffen watched me. More concerned with my presence than Milo's.

He said, 'Doc's along for the ride.' Snapping his attaché case open, he spent some time behind the lid, fumbling, like an inept magician scrounging for a prop.

Lara Rieffen wanted to look bored, but her body wouldn't go along. She tried to will herself loose, ended up with something contrived and edgy, what a yoga novice might achieve the first few times on the mat.

Milo kept shuffling papers. Rieffen checked her watch. I said, 'Busy day?'

'Always. Before I took the job, I had no idea.'

'Where'd you work before here?'

'Labs,' she said. 'Nothing forensic, medical settings.'

'Always been into science, huh?'

'Always.'

Milo said, 'Sorry, it's a mess in here, bear with me.' He clicked his tongue. Lara Rieffen started to relax — the real deal. Put at ease by his incompetence.

'Take your time, Lieutenant. I want to be part of the solution, not the problem.'

'Thanks, Lara. I wish everyone felt that way.'

'OK, here we go.' Instead of drawing out papers, he snapped the case shut, placed it on the floor. Smiled at Rieffen and kept observing her with that lazy, hooded look he produces when the mood's right.

Her lips turned up. More sickly confusion than anything related to glee.

'What do you need to know, Lieutenant?'

'Well, for starts, let's talk about Monte.'

Lara Rieffen's head retracted. Pretty blue eyes shot to the door.

Milo crossed his legs and put his hands behind his head. *Try to bolt, go ahead, you're mine, I'm not worried.*

Lara Rieffen said, 'Monte?' as if trying out a foreign word.

'As in Carlo. As in Scoppio.'

No answer.

'As in Dwayne Parris.'

Rieffen shook her head.

'As in *boom*, Lara.'

Rieffen crossed her own legs. Smiled weakly and exhaled. 'Thank God.'

'For what, Lara?'

'He *terrifies* me, says if I ever think about leaving him he'll cut me up, dump the pieces where they'll never be found.'

393

Milo winced. 'That's heavy-duty.'

'Super-heavy-duty, Lieutenant, but if you're asking about him, you probably know that.'

Angling for info. When that didn't work, she scrunched her eyes, worked at pushing out tears. Produced a couple of sorry-looking droplets.

Milo's big, thick fingers rested atop hers.

'Finally,' she said. 'Someone who can help me.'

'Protect and serve, Lara. OK, let's get the details so we can nail this bastard good.'

★ ★ ★

Lara Rieffen's technique was classic con: a mix of understatement, distraction, and outright lies. Painting Dwayne Parris/Monte Scoppio as ultimate evil, herself as submissive victim, all the while trying to pry out what Milo knew.

He fly-fished her, dangling error as bait then withdrawing, puncturing minor falsehoods with good nature while ignoring the whoppers.

Setting the hook.

★ ★ ★

'So . . . when exactly did you meet Monte?'

'Couple of years ago.'

'Really? Hmm.' Another mumbling foray into the attaché case. 'Um, I could be wrong here, but I think I had a notation here . . . unfortunately, I can't seem to find it . . . never mind.'

'What kind of notation, Lieutenant?'

'We've been talking to people about Monte. Doing background, you know? Someone claimed you and he knew each other way back — in high school.'

'Not really.'

'It's not true?' More rummaging. 'Ah, here it is Center High, class of — '

'Oh, that. Technically it's true, but Center was huge, we hung in different crowds.'

'So you knew who he was — '

'Barely. We met up years later and even that was nothing intense.'

'Couple of years ago.'

'Yes.'

'Where?'

'I was backpacking with some friends in Oregon. He was at the same campsite. I didn't recognize him but he recognized me. He can be charming, I'd just broken up with a boyfriend, guess I was vulnerable.'

'Ah.' Scrawl. 'Well that clears that up . . . Would you like something to drink, Lara?'

★ ★ ★

'So . . . it was Monte who ran into Des Backer and Doreen in Venice — I'm guessing a Sunday.'

'Definitely a Sunday, Lieutenant. Monte went to skate. He's into that.'

'You're not.'

'I bike. That's what I was doing when he was skating the path and saw them.'

'What were Des and Doreen doing?'

'Monte never mentioned. He just came back and told me he'd met up with someone else from Center.'

'By that time, did you know he was violent?'

'Not really. I mean I knew he had a bad temper but he hadn't touched me, not yet.'

'Later, that changed.'

'Oh, yeah.'

'Want another tissue, Lara?'

'I'm fine.'

'OK . . . so Monte told you he'd run into Des and Doreen. How did he feel about that?'

'What do you mean?'

'Was he happy? Surprised? Upset?'

'Definitely upset. He blamed them for something but wouldn't say what, I still don't know. Something from his past, when he talked about it he'd get furious.'

'But he wouldn't say why.'

'Monte's an extremely closed person.'

'Something from his past . . . maybe something to do with messing up his law career?'

'He never got into it.'

'But does that make sense to you — law school?'

'I suppose.'

'We know he went to law school but was asked to leave. He ever explain that to you?'

'No and I knew better than to ask.'

'Well, here's what folks have told us: Des and Doreen mighta done something that got Monte kicked out of law school. That would be something you'd carry a grudge on, don't you think? He tells people he's a lawyer when he's not.'

'Makes sense.'

'By the way, when did he start calling himself Monte?'

'Back then.'

'Back when?'

'High school. That's what I heard. He liked to gamble.'

'Monte Carlo.'

'He used fake ID's to gamble at Indian casinos. At least that's what people said.'

'OK . . . one more thing, Lara. Folks have also said Des and Doreen mighta messed you up, too. Something about med school?'

Silence.

'Lara?'

'You must be mistaken.'

'You never attended med school? University of Idaho, class of — '

'I started there but changed my mind.'

'Because . . . '

'My primary interest isn't making money, I prefer pure science.'

'Being in the lab.'

'Exactly.'

'So it had nothing to do with lynx hairs?'

Silence.

'Lara?'

Prolonged sigh. Sick smile. 'OK, I guess I'm going to have to get into that. I didn't want to because, frankly, Lieutenant, it's too painful and I just didn't see the point.'

'I understand, Lara, but the point is I need you giving me anything I can use against Monte. So if Des and Doreen did do something underhanded to you, that makes it more likely they did something to him and I'd like to know about it. And from what the Forest Service told us, they were blatant snitches.'

'Lieutenant, it was a big misunderstanding. Obviously I don't talk about it because jobs are hard to come by and I love mine. Also, afterward, I realized I was lucky.'

'Lucky about what?'

'Leaving medicine, it worked out for the best. Medicine's become nothing but a big business, my orientation's research.'

'Working here you get to do research?'

'I hope to eventually. Meanwhile, I'm constantly learning and that satisfies the curious part of me. Eventually, I hope to go back to school, get a PhD.'

'Makes sense . . . so the lynx hair business . . .'

'Big misunderstanding, Lieutenant. Another of Monte's brilliant ideas. But I admit, I was stupid to go along with it.'

'OK . . . I appreciate your being straight with us, Lara. Even though we had a few false starts.'

'I'm sorry for those, Lieutenant. You caught me off-guard, I'm not always the greatest at multitasking. When I have to, I can do more than one thing at a time but it's hard not to get sidetracked. It's some sort of learning disability, my parents had me tested when I was a kid. The psychologist said I was gifted but had organizational and memory issues. So if I forget something, please don't hold it against me.'

'Deal . . . OK, let's talk about Monte's weapons.'

'That I can tell you about. He's got tons of them. Rifles, shotguns.'

'We're primarily interested in handguns.'

'Those, too.'

'Which one did he use to shoot Des Backer?'

'I have no idea.'

'We recovered a .22-caliber slug from Des's head. Does Monte have a .22?'

'That would be a smaller gun?'

'For the most part.'

'He has an entire box of small guns, Lieutenant. Keeps them all loaded, keeps the box on the floor of our bedroom closet. Right next to my shoes, I've had nightmares.'

'About . . . ?'

'His temper, what if he goes crazy, it would be so easy for him to just — he also keeps one loaded in his nightstand. Sometimes I have literal nightmares — crazy dreams but they seem so real.'

'Tell me about them.'

'It's the same dream, over and over. There's a fire in the house and it spreads to the closet, the guns get ignited by the heat and start going crazy, shooting off randomly, there's no escape. I wake up sweating, my heart's pounding. One time I woke him up, wanting some comfort. He told me to shut the fuck up, go back to sleep.'

'Prince Charming.'

'I've gotten in so deep, Lieutenant. It's like finding yourself in a hole with no way to climb out.'

'We'll get you out — so Monte keeps a whole box of small loaded guns.'

'Yes, sir.'

'What about larger-caliber guns?'

'I'm sure. I've never taken a close look, don't like firearms.'

'Don't go to the range with Monte?'

'No, he goes by himself.'

'Reason I'm asking about a large-caliber gun is one was inserted in Doreen's vagina. Before he strangled her.'

'Omigod, even for Monte that's brutal.'

'Want another tissue, Lara?'

'Yes, please.'

'So . . . Monte never talked about what he did to Doreen. The big gun.'

'No, no, never.'

'What did he say about what happened up in that turret?'

'Nothing . . . he just came back home and told me he'd done it.'

'Done what?'

'Taken care of Des and Doreen — his words. 'I took care of them.' I was too terrified to talk about it.'

'You must've wondered why he'd do some-thing like that.'

'Of course.'

'Did you come up with any theories?'

'There are no logical theories, Lieutenant. Nothing justifies murder.'

'Well, that's true . . . what I'm getting at is, did you think about that old grudge? Lynx hairs? Could revenge have been Monte's motive?'

'Doesn't that seem out of proportion?'

'Like you said, murder always is. But did it occur to you?'

'Not really.'

'Not really . . . OK, so we're making good progress here, painting a picture. So to speak . . . there is a small problem, though, Lara. Nothing serious but you deserve to know.'

'Know what?'

'We've got Monte in custody and he tells a different story.'

'What does he claim?'

'That you planned the whole thing. That it was your grudge — Doreen and Des ratting you out on the lynx hairs and screwing up your medical career. That Doreen and Des split after they sold you out but you put it together because they were the only ones other than you and Monte who knew.'

'No, no way, it's Monte's grudge. I'd already changed my mind about medicine.'

'I'm just passing along what Monte's saying, so you can give me something to work with . . . for example, he claims it wasn't some chance meeting that got you together with Des and Doreen. They tracked you down, learned you were in LA from someone in Seattle, couldn't find you under your own name but figured out you might be using your mom's maiden name 'cause you'd done that before. You do have a Facebook page and Monte doesn't.'

'I don't know how they did it but it was Monte they contacted.'

'That Sunday in Venice.'

'Yes.'

'But maybe it wasn't an accidental thing — Monte running into them.'

'Guess not.'

'Well, at least that matches with Monte's story. Except he's claiming you were there, arranged for him to meet up with them. Because you had experience with explosives as much as he did — all of you did — and Des and Doreen were trying to get hold of some help on a job.'

'I don't know anything about any of that.'

'Monte also says the deal was for the four of you to split a hundred thousand.'

'No way.'

'You know about the fifty thousand Desi got paid. The half he was supposed to share but didn't.'

'No, I don't.'

'But you can figure out what I'm talking about.'

'Some kind of payoff?'

'For expertise and equipment — vegan Jell-O, for example.'

Silence.

'You do know what that is?'

'I've heard of it. A long time ago.'

'Never used it.'

'No way!'

'Makes sense, why would you . . . I just need to sort out Monte's story from yours, he's the one with the violent streak, he'd obviously say anything to save his own skin.'

'The guns are his, I've never owned a gun.'

'I'm sure that's true — '

'I can't stand firearms. That's why I'm Cl'ing, not working in the ballistics lab.'

'Makes sense . . . let me check something . . . OK, here it is. Speaking of ballistics, here's a report. We found Monte's box exactly where you said it was, so I know you've been truthful about that and I appreciate it. Unlike Monte, who's spinning a yarn about having no clue. Like we're not going to find it.'

'He can be that way.'

'What way?'

'Mindless. Denying.'

'I'll bet . . . anyway, we found the box and recovered the .22 that was used to shoot Des Backer. Unfortunately it's your fingerprints that are on it, not Monte's.'

Silence.

'Lara?'

'That makes absolutely no sense.'

'That's what I told the lab, so they ran the prints again — yours are on file because when you got the job they printed you and we obtained Monte's when we arrested him. His are all over the box. And some of the other guns. But not that one.'

'Oh, wow — I just figured if out. After Monte came back he gave me the gun to put away. I didn't want to be an accessory, even after the fact, but you don't defy him. He'd just murdered two people, for God's sake.'

'So you stashed the gun.'

'Right back in the box. I'm sure you found it on top.'

'That's exactly where we found it.'

'I wanted it to be obvious. So if someone ever searched, they'd see it.'

'You figured we'd search.'

'I was hoping. Unfortunately, I wasn't thinking

403

straight, didn't glove up. Not that I could've gotten away with it, Monte was right there.'

'Monte stood there and ordered you to stash the gun.'

'He could've done it himself but he was into domination.'

'Ordering you around.'

'Constantly.'

'Must've been hard, Lara.'

'It was soul-eroding.'

'Same for carrying around the knowledge of what Monte did and not being able to tell anyone.'

'Everything I've done since the night he told me has been a form of self-defense, Lieutenant. When I met you, at the scene, I thought you might be someone who could help me but ... taking that step ... I should've done it sooner, I'm sorry. Thank God I finally did.'

'Let's talk about that first time, Lara. How'd you come to work the Borodi scene?'

'I was up next. I've never been a big believer in coincidences but I'm starting to change my mind because lately my life's full of them.'

'Like meeting up with Monte at the campsite.'

'Exactly. Like Monte bringing Des and Doreen into our lives. He must've been plotting revenge for years.'

'So you got called to the scene not knowing.'

'It was just another call, Lieutenant.'

'When Monte told you he murdered Des and Doreen, did he say where it happened?'

'I didn't ask. Next morning, I take a call and it's them. You can imagine. I nearly fainted.'

404

'When I met you, you seemed to be holding it together pretty well, Lara.'

'It took every ounce of energy to not start screaming, Lieutenant. The moment I was out of there I just fell apart.'

'Too scared to tell me what you knew.'

'I'm sorry, it's obvious I should have, I was so freaked out, and then, later, when I thought about it, I figured I'd get in trouble for not coming forward right away, I was . . . I felt totally stuck.'

'I can understand that.'

'It's obstruction, isn't it?'

'Frankly, it could be, Lara. Whether or not John Nguyen — he's the deputy DA in charge — decides to pursue that is up to him. If you continue to help, I have no trouble talking to John on your behalf.'

'I'd appreciate that.'

'Sure . . . coincidences — yeah, I've seen that in my own life. What some folks might call fate, karma, or just plain luck. What do psychologists call it, Dr Delaware?'

'Yet another mystery of life.'

'Heh heh — OK, let's move on. You show up at the scene, find out who the vics are, try to maintain.'

'My insides were churning.'

'Freaky coincidence . . . there is one sticking point. You made a special effort to take that call. We found out because we weren't thinking in terms of coincidence and wondered how you came to work a scene with vics you knew. So we checked the work schedules here at the crypt.

Confirmed it with Dave McClellan. You asked to switch with another CI, Dan Paillard. Dan verifies it.'

Silence.

'Lara?'

'I know what it looks like but that had nothing to do with what happened. Absolutely nothing, I was eager for more experience. This is an intense place, being new, I felt I needed to catch up.'

'You traded with Dan but never collected on your half of the bargain.'

'What do you mean?'

'You never asked him to cover for you in return.'

'Guess I didn't . . . I forgot he owed me anything, like I told you, Lieutenant, I've got memory issues.'

'I guess that could also explain forgetting you traded with Dan in the first place.'

'Sometimes I forget where I put my shoes.'

'That I can tell you, Lara. They were right where you said, near the box of guns.'

'I . . . I was speaking rhetorically. But . . . sure.'

'So you traded with Dan to get experience.'

'Exactly.'

'OK . . . looks like you've explained away each of the question marks I had when I came in. The problem is, each one makes sense but when you put them all together, John Nguyen doesn't like what he sees. I know because he told me. John's basically a good guy, but he's also a highly suspicious guy. I had a case I didn't want to file because I felt the evidence didn't justify it but

406

John bulldozed ahead anyway. And got a conviction. He's aggressive, smart, and really good at convincing juries.'

Silence.

'Lara?'

'So what do we do, Lieutenant?'

'What we do is maybe you can explain something away as more than coincidence or memory lapse. Anything that breaks up this . . . big database of coincidence.'

'I already admitted I knew Carlo back in high school. I just didn't know you meant Knew with a capital K.'

'Understood. But I can tell you for a fact that John is not going to buy the part about switching with Dan Paillard as self-education. He's convinced you were part of the murder and were aiming to control the situation. That means premeditation and that's like a big martini for a guy like John.'

'But — '

'Hear me out, Lara — you OK? Here's another tissue. It's important that you see it from a prosecutor's perspective: What you're asking John to believe is that you had no idea what Monte was up to when he left the house, that he came home and told you he'd murdered someone, that you stashed the murder weapon for him and didn't report anything because you were scared. John's seen plenty of women in domestic situations, that much he can probably buy. But then you want him to believe that you just happened to work the scene for self-education. John is not going to accept that. And, to be honest, in my opinion neither is a jury. They watch too much TV, want everything to make sense by the third commercial. Combine that with your prints on the murder weapon and you can — '

'I did have an idea.'

'About what?'

'About the call. I guess you'd call it a premonition. But I didn't know for sure. I wasn't even certain he'd actually killed them, he's been talking about it for so long I kind of brushed the whole issue off. Then, when I got to the crypt and a Westside call came in, I got a really sick feeling and asked to trade with Dan.'

'Because . . . '

'Just what you said, I was feeling out of control, just wanted to get a handle on it. I guess part of me was hoping it wouldn't turn out to be them. That Monte really had lied and the nightmare would end. I'd decided to leave him, anyway.'

'So you intentionally traded to work the scene.'

'I know it was wrong — not saying anything to you. If they want to charge me with obstruction, I can't stop them. But given what Monte's done compared with what I've done, I don't think there's any question who you'll want to believe.'

'We sure do, Lara.'

'Pardon?'

'Want to believe you.' He opened the case; closed it. 'Um, I just glanced at my notes and there's another problem, let's resolve that, too. I'm talking the date.'

'Of what?'

'When you asked Dan to trade. It wasn't the morning of the murder, it was the day before. So if you traded specifically to get control . . . you can see what I'm getting at.'

'Who told you that date?'

'Dan did.'

'Then he'd have to be wrong.'

'Normally I'd say that's possible, no one's memory is perfect, especially for small stuff like that. But Dan changed the log right after, dated, signed his name to the change. He may be wrong but to John Nguyen — and a jury — that's evidence.'

Silence.

'Lara?'

'I don't know what to say, Lieutenant.'

'Let's put it aside for the moment, maybe you'll figure out a solution — '

'Wow. My brain feels kind of scrambled. The psychologist who tested me said it happens under stress. I'm sure you've seen that, Dr Delaware?'

'Of course.'

'What are you scrambled about, Lara?'

'The sequence. The reason I traded Dan — the first reason, wanting more experience — was the right one.'

'Not the part about psychological control?'

'That's also true but it came later — an afterthought, you know? When the call came in, I couldn't be sure it was going to be them but I was scared. Because they lived on the Westside — both of them, in Santa Monica — '

'Des on California. Where did Doreen live? We still haven't found out.'

'Somewhere on the Westside, she never said. So it made sense the Westside was where they'd — where Monte would do it.'

'Close to home.'

'Don't geographical profilers say that? Crimes occur in comfort zones?'

'That refers to the killer's comfort zone.'

'Monte lives on the Westside, too, it made total sense. I just had to see for myself. So there's really no contradiction. I wanted more experience plus I wanted psychological control.'

'Did you learn anything at the scene to help you up your control level?'

'I learned Monte was even worse than I imagined. He claimed he was just getting even, but then I saw that she'd been strangled, up close and personal. Saw that semen stain and knew he'd done something twisted.'

'You suspected the stain was Monte's.'

'Des uses condoms and that kind of thing fits Monte — dominant, cruel. That's why I pointed it out to you, Lieutenant. I was too scared to come out and tell you but I hoped you'd follow the trail.'

'Aiding and abetting me, huh?'

'Right from the beginning.'

'So you figured out the semen was Monte's, not Des's? OK . . . um, how do you know Des used condoms, Lara?'

Silence.

'Lara?'

'Must be something I heard. Back in high

school. Des was a huge player, everyone talked about it, how he'd jump anything with a pulse. How he carried condoms in his wallet.'

'We didn't find any condoms at the scene.'

'I figured Monte took them.'

'Why would he do that?'

'He's evil — maybe for a trophy, some kind of sick male dominance. Just like ejaculating on Doreen's leg.'

'You're sure it wasn't Des's semen?'

'I can't be sure of anything. I just figured Monte was capable of something twisted like that. Killing Doreen, then demeaning her. When I pointed it out, I was hoping you'd analyze it, find out it was Monte's, and that would tell you you had something more than a simple murder.'

'One thing this case hasn't been, Lara, is simple. Something John Nguyen reminds me every day. Now it looks like it's not gonna close anytime in the future. Especially with that semen stain gone. What do you think caused that?'

'Someone here screwed up. It happens more often than you think.'

'A screwup as opposed to something deliberate.'

'Who would do that deliberately?'

'That's what Bobby Escobar wanted to know.'

'Who?'

'Bobby Escobar, CI, used to work here — the position you filled — before he went back to school to get a master's. Well liked, so they let him come in after hours, work on his data.'

'He told you about the stain?'

'Basically.'

'OK . . . good, so someone will look into it and hopefully they'll tighten up procedures. For the chain of evidence, I mean.'

'That would be useful . . . but here we go again, Lara, with another annoying problem. Bobby reported to Dave McClellan that a couple of days after Des and Doreen's bodies came in, he was here working late, happened to step out of his office, which is right across from the fridge-closet, at the exact same time you walked out of the fridge. That ring a bell?'

'Short Latin guy? Big mustache?'

'That's Bobby. He went into the fridge, found one of the bodies looked like the plastic wrap had been messed with. Doreen's. Dave didn't think much of it, you were staff, maybe you were clearing a serial number for your paperwork. But now that we know about the stain, you can see what it looks like.'

'That's all it was, I was checking numbers.'

'But someone else got in there and removed the stain?'

'Or it got washed away by accident, Lieutenant. That kind of thing happens around here, believe me.'

'I can hear John Nguyen groaning.'

'What do you mean?'

'See it from John's perspective, Lara. You're seen entering the fridge, the plastic's disturbed, a piece of evidence is missing.'

'Maybe he did it.'

'Who?'

'That guy Bobby, maybe he wanted his job back, so he tried to cast suspicion on me.'

'Bobby's busy with school and a part-time job.'

'He might've changed his mind.'

'Anything's possible, Lara, but I wouldn't even try to offer that to John Nguyen — hold on, let me shoot another one at you. A problem, I mean: Bobby was murdered.'

Silence.

'Lara?'

'Oh, that.'

'That?'

'I heard a CI was shot off the premises. I didn't know it was him.'

'It was, Lara. He was shot in the head, same as Des Backer. With a .22, same as Des, no shell casings left behind, same as Des. Which makes sense, because the gun — the one with your prints on it — is a revolver, that little Smith and Wesson 650 we found in the box in the closet. So obviously we ran comparisons and unfortunately, the striations from the bullet in Bobby's head match those from the bullet in Des's head. I say unfortunately, because now we've got your prints on a weapon of multiple destruction. So to speak. Monte has an explanation for that — one that doesn't depend on coincidence. Want to guess what he says?'

'Something that incriminates me. But he's a sociopath and a liar.'

'Be that as it may, Lara, John Nguyen likes what Monte has to say. Which is that you were the one who ambushed Bobby. Monte admits to following Bobby when he left the crypt and to waiting until Bobby caught a red light then jacking him, pulling him out of his car, and dragging him over to where he says you shot Bobby. He even admits to putting Bobby back in the car. All you did, according to his version, is pull the trigger. John likes that story because it doesn't depend on coincidence.'

Silence.

'This is ridiculous, Lieutenant.'

'So is sticking lynx hair on trees where it doesn't belong. Which, when you think about it, isn't that different from wiping away a stain. A stain Monte was too macho to get rid of at the scene — like you said, he's a gambler, likes to take risks. Probably told you no way would they even analyze the stain. Two people are found in a sexual pose, there's semen, why even suspect someone else contributed? I'm willing to believe he intimidated you that night, Lara, that's why you couldn't get rid of the stain right then and there. You both had guns but Monte's was bigger. Size mattering and all that. You were training your little gun on Doreen while Monte did his big-gun thing, weren't you? Then he strangled her, came on her leg.'

Silence.

'Lara?'

Silence.

'Lynx hairs, stains, it's always about playing with evidence, Lara.'

Silence.

'Now you're getting kind of closed up, Lara, the way you say Monte tends to be. That is not in your best interest, John Nguyen will not appreciate that.'

Silence.

'Lara, I've been open to your explanations, will continue to be open. But you've got to meet me halfway. Like that trip to Port Angeles to get the money. We've got Monte on video taking those suitcases, but both your names on the passenger list to Seattle. On a day you were off-shift.'

Silence.

'Tell me what really happened, Lara. Start at the beginning, it's in your best interest.'

'We're over.'

'Pardon?'

'Over. Finished. I need to have an attorney.'

'You're saying you absolutely want an attorney.'

'Finished.'

'Suit yourself, Lara. You always do.'

42

Knock on the door.

Milo said, '*Entrez-vous.*'

A Mutt-and-Jeff duo of female sheriffs stood over Lara Rieffen.

'Thank you, ladies, give this one the full strip — use that room across the hall.'

The shorter cop said, 'Will do, Loo.'

He turned to Rieffen. 'See you around, Lara? Or should we start using Kathy? For old times' sake.'

Her reply was scalding eyes and a toss of strawberry blond.

The taller cop said, 'I like your highlights. What do you use, L'Oréal?'

★　★　★

Stepping back inside, Milo removed his coat from the table, checked the mini-video-recorder he'd secreted under the garment. High-tech loan from Reed's half brother Aaron Fox, formerly an LAPD homicide D, now a Beverly Hills private eye with a penchant for toys.

A partial replay revealed clear images and sound. 'Perfect. Except for those extra ten pounds, can't they invent a camera won't do that?'

Gloving up, he searched Rieffen's bag.

Inside were coroner's credentials, five photos

of her and M. Carlo Scoppio wearing hiking clothes, backdropped by forest.

'She look intimidated to you?'

'Not in the least.'

A wallet held a hundred twenty-three dollars in cash and some change, ID's and credit cards under Lara Rieffen, Kathy Lara Vanderveldt, Laura Vander, Kathleen Rieffenstahl, Laura Rice, Cathy Rice, Lara Van Vliet.

A push-button stiletto and a pepper-spray dispenser shared a zipped compartment with two tampons.

Milo said, 'That cries out for wit, but I lack the energy.'

A second pouch held a pair of opal earrings. He inspected the backs.

One was engraved.

DF

'Trophy of the kill, poor Doreen.'

Another pouch, deeper and secured by a snap, contained lip balm, breath mints, a single sheet of white paper, letter-sized, folded twice.

Four-month-old e-mail from montecarlo@bghlaw.net to KLV@pkmail.com.

hey baby someone at the office put up one of those stupid posters today, that affirmation for inner peace and I thought of you and made this up:

KATHY AND MONTE C.'S SUPREME NEGATION (FOR OUTER CHAOS)

417

> I tell the truth. They lie.
> I'm strong. They're weak.
> I'm good.
> They're bad.

that about sums it up, hey, babe? you want it you name it you the bomb LOL love you forever continue to light my fuse

Irvin Wimmers showed up with two more tan uniforms. After a brief, happy chat with Milo, Wimmers and his team took Rieffen away, marching her through the crypt, cuffed, head-down, past stunned co-workers and Dave McClellan's look of utter contempt. When she passed close to McClellan he made a point of directing a thumbs-up at Milo.

Rieffen looked up at him. Cobra disturbed from its nap.

I said, 'Master manipulator.'

'Lotta good it did her,' said Milo.

'I was referring to you.'

'Moi? I'm crushed.' Grinning. 'So how'd I do, Cecil B?'

'You deserve a percentage of the adjusted gross and a big chunk of the marketing revenue.'

'Hooray for Hollyweird — not that I really fibby-fooed.'

'Perish the thought.'

'Think about it: Monte will soon be in custody, I just got there a little early.'

'I'll jump-start your election committee soon as we're back in the office.'

'Once we get him, is there any doubt he'll turn

on her? And Bobby *did* kind of talk to me. From the grave. *That's* a form of talking, right? And look, he was right, Bobby, I mean. I guess fibby-fooing about the gun was a little naughty, but I *had* to, I was *so* scared I'd *never* close the case, my boss can be so *mean*, when he yells at me it makes me feel *bad*. And hey, *that* worked, too, and now I can get hold of that nasty old *gun* and it won't be used to make anyone else *dead*, please tell me I'm a good *person*, Dr Delaware.'

I was still laughing when we reached the car.

He wasn't.

I said, 'What's the matter?'

'Nothing's the matter, life is grand. I'm just focused on playing onecard Monte.'

43

Baird, Garroway and Habib, Attorneys at Law, occupied a triple-wide storefront on Soto, window glass painted black, promises of quick settlements in five languages emblazoned in bright yellow paint. As Reed had pointed out, walkable from the County Hospital complex.

SA Gayle Lindstrom said, 'No need to chase ambulances very far.'

She sat at the wheel of a Chevy sedan financed by federal income tax, wore a white tank top, tight jeans, wedge sandals. Hoop earrings sparkled. More makeup than her usual quick morning dab, including too much frosted pink lipstick.

Milo said, 'New side of you, Gayle.'

'I love being a girl.'

He slouched in the front passenger seat. I had the rear to myself. The car was impeccable but it smelled of vanilla, as if someone had partied with cookie dough.

The man his employers knew as M. Carlo Scoppio had remained inside the law firm since arriving, save for a ten-minute smoke break out in the rear parking lot. No chance to take him as he puffed away; three other nicotine freaks indulged themselves close by.

Several times Scoppio had walked people on crutches to the firm's front door. A couple of the limpers actually seemed to be disabled.

At three P.M., when the roach coach honked 'La Cucaracha,' Scoppio wasn't part of the small crowd surging for snacks.

'Maybe he's brown-bagging,' said Lindstrom. 'Saving his hard-earned blood money for a rainy day.'

Seven cops from the fugitive apprehension squad were positioned at various spots in the neighborhood. The location wasn't ideal for stakeout: Heavy traffic on Soto would make a quick dash across the street hazardous, and light pedestrian traffic killed the chance of sidewalk surveillance. The lot where Scoppio had smoked was blocked to the north by deeper buildings, one way in and out, a cracked driveway. To the east coiled a warren of residential side streets, to the west was the thoroughfare, freeway-close, the on-ramp in sight, raising the risk for a high-speed chase. Though at four thirty P.M., any lam artist would encounter bumper-to-bumper.

While Scoppio worked the wonderful world of personal injury, the house he'd shared with Lara Rieffen and Doreen Fredd got tossed by Moe Reed, Sean Binchy, and a Sheriff's crime scene tech.

No remnant of Fredd's residence, no blood beyond a few pinpoints under the bathroom mirror, probably shaving-nick spritz. No indication anything violent had ever taken place in the bungalow. The tech swabbed and pulled up prints and left.

Binchy and Reed found the gun box right where Rieffen had said it would be. Resting on top was a black plastic case housing the .22

S&W, serial numbers filed off but probably accessible chemically.

Binchy drove the gun to the ballistics lab. The final report would take time, but the analyst saw enough to opine that the bullets from Backer and Escobar came from the same weapon.

Reed's meticulous room-by-room produced an arsenal under the bed: three rifles, a shotgun, boxes of ammunition. Maybe Rieffen had been telling the truth about bad dreams.

Both her prints and Monte's showed up on the murder weapon. The longer-barreled gun inserted in Doreen Fredd's vagina could be any of several in the collection but a Charter Arms Bulldog did show up, fitting Dr Jernigan's guess.

The top drawer of a desk in a spare bedroom held newspaper accounts of the lynx hair episode, along with Rieffen's med school acceptance letter, well thumbed. Baggies of prescription tranquilizers and crystals of what looked like methamphetamine showed up in a bottom drawer.

A pantry cupboard was filled with heavy-duty muslin bags crammed with packets of bills.

Reed calculated the total three times. $46,850.

'Checked both credit cards for expenditures since they got back from Washington, Loo. They've been to dinner three times, he's a bad tipper, total charges were $146.79. Nothing else substantial pops out on the cards, just a hundred or so in piddly charges. But I did find some matchbooks from three Indian casinos in his nightstand, so that could account for the rest.'

'You're slipping, Moses.'

'Sir?'

'Those dinners, what'd they eat for dessert?'

'Hopefully humble pie, Loo.'

*   *   *

At four fifty-six P.M. two middle-aged Hispanic women in casual clothes rode away from the law firm in a battered Nissan, followed by a younger blonde, identified as Kelly Baird Englund, daughter of the senior partner and a lawyer herself, in a powder-blue Jaguar convertible. Seconds later, Daddy Bryan Baird, corpulent in a bad blue suit, waddled to his black Mercedes. Ed Habib, in no better haberdashery, steered his black Lexus LX haphazardly while talking on the phone, followed by Owen Garroway, patrician in pinstripes, handling his black Porsche Cayman with aplomb.

'Black's the new black,' said Gayle Lindstrom.

No sign of Carlo Scoppio and that hadn't changed by five fifteen.

Lindstrom fidgeted. 'Maybe he tried to contact Rieffen, couldn't reach her, somehow found out she was in lockup.'

Milo said, 'She was brought straight to High-Power. Wimmers handled it himself.'

'I'm just saying.'

'Keep doing that, Gayle.'

'What?'

'Being a little bundle of human Prozac — OK, here we go.'

Scoppio hadn't appeared but a gaunt, furtive, sandy-haired man wearing a backpack walked around to the back, checked out Scoppio's pickup truck, jogged to the door. Binocs revealed a face ravaged by pustulant eruptions. Constant, jerky movement was the dance of the hour.

'Your friendly neighborhood meth man,' said Lindstrom. 'Speedy delivery.'

The door cracked. The dealer was inside for ninety seconds, hurried off.

Milo picked up the radio. 'For those who can't see, our subject just bought dope, probably meth, could be tweaking right now. So factor that into the danger level.'

Multiple assents from the field.

Four minutes later, Carlo Scoppio walked out.

He'd changed from business casual to jeans, running shoes, a baggy gray hooded sweatshirt that lent his medium-sized frame the illusion of bulk. A small white rip on the left sleeve matched the hyper-enlarged security photo from the storage bin.

In his hands, a gym bag.

Unremarkable man with sloping shoulders, a soft, square face, dark curly hair. Roller-coaster eyes.

He shook himself off like a wet dog. Ran in place. Bobbed his head. Headed for his truck.

Lindstrom said, 'To me that's definite tweaking. Hopefully there's nothing nasty in that bag.'

'Maybe he's gonna exercise,' said Milo.

'Mr Literal.'

'I'm getting too old for symbolism.'

Scoppio's truck rolled out of the lot.

Lindstrom said, 'Ready?'

'Hold on, Gayle.'

'You're calling it.' Her hands bounced on the wheel. 'Though I should point out that if he does get too far ahead — '

'Yes, dear, whatever you say, dear, I'll wash the dishes, dear.'

'You and me in domestic bliss,' said Lindstrom. 'I'm sure my partner would find it as humorous as yours would.'

Milo laughed. 'Now we go.'

★ ★ ★

Carlo Scoppio passed the freeway on-ramp, continued south to Washington, headed west. Just past Vermont, he pulled into a shabby strip mall. Plenty of vacant spaces, but a donut shop and a coin laundry were doing OK. So was *Dynamite Action Gym*, the name co-written in Thai lettering, the wide-open door showcasing bright light.

The truck parked in front. Scoppio got out, entered.

Lindstrom said, 'Guess literal takes it.'

Milo picked up his radio. 'Anyone look like a gym rat?'

The head fugitive cop said, 'Gotta be Lopez.'

'Where is he?'

Another voice said, 'I'm here, Loo, a block south.'

'What're you wearing?'

The head cop said, 'What he always does, the sleeveless sweat, showing off those guns of his.'

Snickers from the field.

Lopez said, 'You got it, flaunt it.'

Milo said, 'How about going inside and flaunting. If it's safe, scope out the subject.'

'If it's an open situation should be easy, sir. If it's one of those membership things, a front-desk block, it could be tough.'

'Only one way to find out, Officer Lopez.'

★   ★   ★

At six eleven P.M., Jarrel Lopez's nineteen-inch neck, twenty-inch biceps, and beef-slab thighs made their way inside the gym.

He was out moments later. Trotted to the Fed car. 'Nice open setup, mostly martial arts but some regular boxing. Subject's working the speed bag.'

'A pugilist.'

'He hits like a girl. You want me to buy a one-day trial membership, go in and keep an eye?'

'Rather have you back with your buddies, armed and dangerous.'

'That's what I told myself this morning, Loo. Nice blue sky, I could use some armed and dangerous.'

★   ★   ★

By six forty-eight P.M. Gayle Lindstrom was out of the car and Milo had taken the wheel. Checking her makeup, she fluffed her hair, sashayed to the donut shop, emerged with a steaming cup. Her own hoodie, slim-cut and peach velour, did a good job of concealing the wire tucked into the rear of her jeans.

No loan from Aaron Fox, the Bureau had its own toy chest.

Lindstrom said, 'This one we call the electric thong.'

'Ouch,' said Milo.

'Not necessarily.'

★　★　★

At seven fourteen, Carlo Scoppio left the gym looking tired, slightly flushed.

Before he reached his truck, a young woman in a peach hoodie walked up to him, smiling but conspicuously nervous.

'*Excuse me?*'

'*Uh-huh.*'

'*I think I'm lost. Is this a bad neighborhood?*'

'*It can be. Where are you from?*'

'*Tempe. That's Arizona. I was supposed to meet someone at Hollywood and Vine. Is that close to here?*'

Derisive laughter. '*Not exactly.*'

'*You're kidding.*'

'*You're pretty far from there — do you have a car?*'

'*I took the bus. From Union Station. They said get off at Jefferson then transfer to the . . . I forget. So it's nasty around here?*'

'*I wouldn't be out here alone after dark.*'

'*Oh, man . . . can you point me toward Hollywood?*'

Laughter. '*I can point — it's that way. North.*'

427

But you can't walk it.'

'*Is there a bus?'*

'*No idea — what the —* '

Carlo Scoppio stiffened as Milo and six other large men ran toward him shouting. Gayle Lindstrom had her cuffs out, told him he was under arrest. Scoppio swatted the cuffs, made contact with Lindstrom's forearm, threw her off-balance.

A bass chorus of commands filled the strip mall as Scoppio dropped his gym bag, assumed a pugilist stance. Fists up, ridiculously quaint.

'*Policepolicepolice putyour hands where they can be seen hands up yourhands hands up!'*

Scoppio blinked.

Raised one hand.

Dropped the other to the waistband of his hoodie, reached in, brought out something long-barreled and shiny.

The choir switched hymns: '*Gungungungun-gun!'*

Scoppio straight-armed his weapon.

Milo aimed his Glock.

Same instincts as a few days ago at Moghul, where'd he'd taken years off Officer Randy Thorpe's life expectancy.

Thorpe had been smart.

Scoppio squinted. His finger whitened.

Milo fired.

So did everyone else.

44

Dr Clarice Jernigan said, 'This autopsy was fun.'

'Real hoot,' said Milo.

The pathologist's office at the crypt could have been anywhere.

No specimens swimming in formaldehyde, no morbid humor. Potted Peruvian lilies and cactus sat atop a low, white bookshelf, along with cheerful family photos. Jernigan and five healthy-looking kids and a husband who looked like a banker.

She said, 'I mean fun from an intellectual puzzle perspective. Your Mr Scoppio had twenty-eight bullets in him from five different firearms, with at least four wounds theoretically fatal. I don't need to pinpoint which one did him in, because frankly, who gives a damn, he's a sieve. But if I was writing this up for *Journal of Forensic Science*, I'd tag the frontal head wound. Big-caliber bullet, went straight through the cortex and dipped down into the brain stem.'

'Three five-seven?'

Nod. 'Yours?'

'Mine's nine-millimeter.'

'Like two other shooters. No rifle fire. How come? Fugitive guys always bring assault rifles.'

'The officer didn't have a clear shot.'

'Shootout at the OK Mall . . . well, if your nine-millimeter impacted anywhere above the rib cage, you can award yourself honorable mention.

If you got him in the legs?' Shrug.

Milo didn't fill in the blank.

Jernigan said, 'In terms of why he faced off against such heavy firepower, that's Dr Delaware's bailiwick.' To me: 'I'm comfortable with suicide by cop. How about you?'

I said, 'Works for me.'

'I'm going to write that his inherent psychiatric issues were helped along by amphetamine intoxication, 'cause we want to lay everything at this bastard's feet, make sure no ACLU types start bitching and moaning.'

Milo said, 'He was tweaking big-time?'

'I'm surprised he didn't jump out of his skin, Lieutenant. Anyway, I don't see a problem, hopefully the pencil-pushers won't, either.'

'I'll find out soon enough. Meeting with the chief in an hour.'

'That should be fun.' She walked us to the door.

Milo said, 'Thanks, Doc.'

'Thank you. For what you did on Bobby. Bobby was a great kid. I know I'm supposed to be objective but when I found out the bastard ambushed him, I allowed myself a little pleasure when I peeled his damn face off his damn skull. And by the way, I remember my pledge about autopsies. Long as you don't push it.'

45

Milo drove to the chief's office and I returned home.

Detouring, I drove past the lot on Borodi. All the embers gone, bulldozed clean and level, surrounded by a new, substantial fence. Doyle Bryczinski sat in his car by the curb. He seemed to be snoozing, but as I drove by, he waved.

I backed up. 'Back on the job, huh?'

'Company finally got their act together,' he said. 'Realized they better have me every day, all day. Sometimes they give me a double. When Mom doesn't need me, I'm here.'

'Keep up the good work.'

He saluted. 'Only way I know how.'

★ ★ ★

Milo didn't phone after the meeting with the chief and I wondered if it had gone badly.

Probably on his way to Southwest Division. Maybe that rib joint was still operative and he'd dive into seven courses of trans-fat bliss.

He dropped in the following morning, wearing a puce aloha shirt, baggy brown pants, desert boots. I'd been working on custody reports, Blanche curled on my lap.

She bounced off, smiled up at him.

He said, 'I gotta bend? Next time get a Great Dane,' but patted her head far longer than mere courtesy called for.

I said, 'Vacation or wishful thinking?'

'Two weeks of sun and fun, Rick managed to finagle some time, we're headed for the Big Island tomorrow morning.'

'Think of me at the luau.'

'What I think of at a luau is more luau.'

He walked to the kitchen, took a half pint of orange juice out of the fridge, put on glasses and read the expiration date. 'A week past, I'm doing you a favor.' He upended the carton, guzzled.

Blanche watched, fascinated. His eating habits have never stopped puzzling her.

I said, 'Two weeks. No Southwest gig?'

Crushing and tossing the empty carton, he took out a plate of cold roast beef, brought it to the table. 'Change of plans.'

'Gunrunners off the radar?'

'Still on the radar but I won't be watching the screen.'

'Chief's happy.'

'Not a relevent concept for him. What I did was bring up the fact that I'd closed Backer and Doreen well before his deadline, in addition to preventing a potential arson disaster by nabbing Helga. But that I wasn't happy, because of two skeletons in a Prius. Yeah, it was Van Nuys' case but I'd checked and Van Nuys wasn't working it, no one was, and I thought that was a crying shame. I also informed him that when I drove out to Van Nuys Airport a few nights ago, Hangar 13A was totally cleared. No jet, no cars, no gazillion dollars' worth of gold and furs and diamonds and art. No accounting of the skeletons ever being taken to the crypt and the FAA had no record of the jet ever taking off. Not to mention the absence of a single letter of press ink. His Exaltedness's response was his brand of empathy.'

'I know what you're going through?'

''Don't bitch, Sturgis, we're both victims of the politicians and the diplomats, they're all Ivy League faggots compensating for short dicks — and don't get touchy about 'faggot,' I'm talking generically.' Then he ushers me out of his office, informs me I need to concentrate on West LA, not stick my nose in any other sectors' cases. I say, 'Can I take that to mean Southwest as well as Van Nuys, sir?' He says, 'Don't make me explicate, Sturgis. It saps my prostate.''

46

During his interview of Lara Rieffen, Milo had used John Nguyen's relentless approach to prosecution as a scare tactic.

A bit of performance art, but part documentary, as well.

Rieffen's defense lawyers filed motions to dismiss; Nguyen countered each with growing ferocity, won every time.

Their next step was to attack the admissibility of various pieces of evidence. As part of that, I was deposed to testify about Rieffen's mental state during 'Detective Sturgis's clearly intimidating and abusive interrogation.'

Nguyen said, 'Don't respond, I'll handle it,' and when the defense team tried plea-bargaining down to a series of lesser charges, Nguyen threatened to go for the death penalty, pointing out that Rieffen's prints on the murder weapon made it a no-brainer, special circumstances due to multiple victims, lying in wait, extreme cruelty and depravity, murder for profit.

Rieffen pled guilty to one count of second-degree murder in exchange for the theoretical possibility of parole.

Nguyen said, 'I'm happy with it, anyone else isn't, that's their problem.'

★ ★ ★

I kept checking the Internet for some mention of Dahlia Gemein or Prince Teddy.

Her name never came up, but four months after the turret murders, an Asian news service reported the 'tragic death of Prince Tariq Bandar Asman Ku'amah Majur in a diving accident off the coast of Sranil.' The sultan, 'grief-stricken and dismayed,' had declared a week of national mourning and announced that the pediatric cancer center crowning the world-class medical center planned for Sranil would be named after the prince.

'My brother was a selfless man with a special place in his heart for children.'

One week later, insurgents attempted to storm the island's southern beaches. The sultan's troops turned them away but several commentators believed this was only the beginning.

Logging off, I got into running clothes, jogged south on the Glen, made a few well-practiced turns, ended up on Borodi Lane.

Doyle Bryczinski was gone. Men in hard hats were busy nailing up the framework of an enormous house. Three stories, subterranean parking lot, multiple gables, and adventurous windows. A style that couldn't be pinned down beyond *Look At Me!*

Where a sidewalk would be, if this was that kind of neighborhood, a couple stood, pointing and talking.

Stunning blonde, mid to late thirties, well-toned body, sculpted face. She wore pink cashmere, a pale blue silk scarf, brown croc pumps, big diamonds. The man with his arm around her was closer to sixty, a little thick around the middle, with wavy silver hair of a tint that required effort. Soft blue blazer, white linen pants, a red pocket handkerchief that tumbled from his breast pocket like blood from a gunshot wound.

Designer sunglasses on both of them.

As I ran past them, the woman said, 'Oh, it's going to be gorgeous, honey.'

We do hope that you have enjoyed reading
this large print book.

Did you know that all of our titles
are available for purchase?

We publish a wide range of high quality
large print books including:
Romances, Mysteries, Classics
General Fiction
Non Fiction and Westerns

Special interest titles available in
large print are:
The Little Oxford Dictionary
Music Book
Song Book
Hymn Book
Service Book

Also available from us courtesy of
Oxford University Press:
Young Readers' Dictionary
(large print edition)
Young Readers' Thesaurus
(large print edition)

For further information or a free
brochure, please contact us at:
Ulverscroft Large Print Books Ltd.,
The Green, Bradgate Road, Anstey,
Leicester, LE7 7FU, England.
Tel: (00 44) 0116 236 4325
Fax: (00 44) 0116 234 0205

Other titles published by
The House of Ulverscroft:

GONE

Jonathan Kellerman

Called in to evaluate an aspiring actress accused — along with her boyfriend — of staging her own abduction, Alex is indifferent when the case seems to go nowhere. But then the girl is savagely murdered, and suddenly a straightforward script takes a decidedly unexpected turn. Dylan Meserve, the victim's boyfriend, has also disappeared, and the caretaker at the couple's acting school has a disturbing history. Is Dylan a deranged killer, or another victim? Alex and homicide detective Milo Sturges begin auditioning suspects and trawling the depths of LA's seedy underbelly. Then more dead wannabes start turning up . . .

RAGE

Jonathan Kellerman

Eight years ago, psychologist Alex Delaware
was appointed to evaluate two teenage boys
charged with the brutal murder of young
Kristal Malley. Now Rand Duchay, one of the
teenage murderers, phones Delaware and it
seems that the case is not over yet . . . Fresh
out of prison, Rand asks Alex for a meeting.
But the killer doesn't show up; then he's
found next morning with a bullet-hole
through his head. Is there more than meets
the eye to his murder — and the death of
Kristal Malley? . . . Alex and Detective Milo
Sturgis look for answers but find themselves
following a trail of blood that will lead them
into the depths of cruelty — and straight to
the heart of murderous betrayal.

TWISTED

Jonathan Kellerman

A year after the Cold Heart murders and Detective Petra Connor is working Holly-wood Homicide solo. She's struggling with a drive-past murder when Isaac Gomez, assigned to Petra's care, suggests that there's a connection between six unsolved murders in the LAPD area over the past six years, all at around midnight on June 28. Then the links become more and more clear. A series of killings so meticulously constructed that the mind behind them would have remained invisible without Isaac's sharp probing. And June 28 is just one month away — will Petra be able to stop the murderer from striking again?